Free Falling

JILL SHALVIS

sourcebooks
casablanca

FOR EVERYONE WHO HAS EVER FALLEN
FOR THE ONE PERSON THEY ABSOLUTELY,
DEFINITELY, 100 PERCENT SHOULD NOT HAVE…
THIS ONE'S FOR YOU.

Published by Sourcebooks Casablanca, an imprint of Sourcebooks
1935 Brookdale RD, Naperville, IL 60563-2773
(630) 961-3900
sourcebooks.com

Cataloging-in-Publication Data is on file with the Library of Congress.

Printed and bound in the United States of America.
PAH 10 9 8 7 6 5 4 3 2 1

PROLOGUE

Caleb

DUFFEL BAG THUMPING AGAINST my hip, I marched down the hallway toward the living room, a gauntlet of chipped paint and forgotten laundry. All I had to do, *somehow*, was say goodbye to Tucker and Kiera—a.k.a. the human equivalent of a sugar-fueled tornado and a glitter bomb, respectively. Easy enough.

And when I'd started lying to myself, I had no idea.

In the La-Z-Boy sat Hank. A.k.a. former Marine Henry Colburn. A.k.a. Dad. He had a remote in one hand, a beer in the other. Eyes closed.

I wasn't buying it. "Hey."

Nothing.

I nudged the base of his chair with my foot. Okay, maybe I kicked it.

His eyes opened, already angry. "Thought you were getting the fuck out, boy."

"Oh, I am," I said conversationally, even though we hadn't

had a civil chat in years, if ever. From a sheer protect-my-own-ass standpoint, I rarely looked him in the eye, much less instigated a one-on-one. I did both now.

Deliberately, he stood. "Good riddance, you piece of shit."

"Don't call him that." Tucker, who usually had the longest fuse of all of us Colburns, got between me and Hank, trying to protect me.

But that was my job. I shoved Tucker aside just as Hank swung. One second, I was in the old man's face, and in the next, I lay flat on the floor, taking stock: face on fire. Pain in my chest, which had nothing to do with any physical injury. Gingerly, I lifted a hand to my aching eye. Damn, he'd gotten me good.

The blare of a horn echoed from the driveway. Ryder, the eldest Colburn sibling, had zero patience when he was on a mission, and this was a biggie—Mission Get Caleb the Hell Outta Dodge.

I sat up slowly, and then Tucker was there, hauling me to my feet, his barely sixteen-year-old face tight with worry as he carefully probed the swelling around my eye. With a hiss, I pushed him away. "I'm fine."

I went to the kitchen just as Ryder barged through the back door. "Clock's ticking." He stopped short when he saw my face and swore viciously while Kiera handed me a bag of frozen peas.

I brought the bag to my burning eye, then slid my arm around a trembling Kiera. "I'm okay, kiddo, I promise."

She nodded tightly.

Ryder looked to be grinding his back teeth to powder as he took in my face. *"Where is he?"*

"No time." Tucker shoved me at Ryder. "Get him out of here."

"No." I planted my feet. I couldn't go. I wouldn't. Not when Tucker and Kiera would be stuck here, with...*him*.

Ryder, who'd come home from college just to deliver me to mine, grabbed my arm and my duffel bag, hauling me toward the door. Quite the feat, given I had two inches and twenty pounds on him. "I'm not leaving them."

"We'll be all right," Tucker said.

I looked back. Tucker nodded. Kiera offered me a small encouraging smile, the two of them trying to be happy for me. I shook my head. "No."

"You can and you will," Ryder said. "You've got a part-time job at your college gym. You're going to try out for a walk-on spot on the hockey team, and believe me, they'll want you." His voice was gruff, thick with emotion. "If you're lucky, you'll never look back."

Kiera's eyes shimmered with unshed tears. Tucker's too. But neither let them fall. They wouldn't. Like me, like Ryder, they'd long ago become pros at burying emotions deep. We'd never been apart. Even Ryder had stuck to a college close to home to keep an eye on us. But I was going to San José State, three hours south of our small Sonoma County town of Star Falls, and I'd be working on campus, without a vehicle, studying architectural history, and hopefully playing Division One hockey, complete with travel. My time wouldn't be my own.

I'd have no way to get home to check on Tucker and Kiera.

From the living room came a grunt and the metallic sigh of our recliner chair moving to an upright position.

"*Now*," Ryder said firmly.

I nodded, wincing at the pain that caused in my eye. "One sec." I strode out of the kitchen and down the short, narrow hall.

"Lay a hand on either of them after I've left," I said, "and I'll end you."

He took in my throbbing eye and slid his gaze back to the TV without a word.

I'd been dismissed. But there was a reason I'd taken to working out and beefing up in high school, a very purposeful reason. That it had only made me better on the ice didn't matter to me at all. "Try me," I warned, then left him in my dust.

CHAPTER 1

Emma

Present day

MY CAR, BLESS ITS rusty heart, sputtered as I stopped in front of a sprawling 1886 American colonial. The house—manor, more like it—gave off some serious *Clue* vibes. I half expected to find Professor Plum in the library with a candlestick.

Staring in wonder at the architectural beauty, I was sucked in by the early morning sun's long shadows playing hide-and-seek across the weathered stone. Knowing I couldn't stall forever, I started to get out, stopping when my phone buzzed a call from RIDE OR DIE. "Hey, can't talk. I'm about to walk onto the jobsite—"

"I know." Suzie, my longtime best friend, was a professional in worrying about her people. "Just wanted to make sure you're okay."

"Why wouldn't I be?" I asked.

"Oh, gee, I don't know, maybe because a few weeks ago, your apartment building burned down, and since you were in a sublease and didn't have rental insurance, you lost everything. And then your asshole ex was—shock—an ass and wouldn't let you stay with him—"

"What a fun recap, but I've *really* gotta go."

"Fine, but starting a new job is stressful. So repeat after me: *I've got this.*"

"*Suze.*"

"Say it."

I had no idea where her optimism came from. We'd both grown up in Santa Rosa, about forty-five minutes from here. My life hadn't been easy, but hers had been far harder.

"Remember when we lived in that tiny hovel above that dive bar in college?" Suzie asked. "Remember that massive spider who lived in our bathroom? You totally almost killed it before our screaming brought over the cute guy from across the hall. So don't you let anyone tell you that you can't. You're an Ameri-CAN."

"You've been reading *The Art of Being Kind* again, haven't you."

"Well, the first time didn't take, so yeah."

"I promise I've got this," I said on an affectionate laugh. "But I really gotta go. Love you."

"Love you more."

I slid my phone away, and juggling a hot tea and a cross-body bag filled with my work essentials, I headed up the cracked stone pavers to the time-worn wraparound porch. The surrounding acreage was dotted with gnarled oak trees, long bent to the wind's whim, along with a big old barn and several other structures. Just past the property line ran the lazy waters of the Russian River, and beyond that, the rocky California Coast.

Drawing a deep breath against the butterflies taking flight

in my belly, I stepped past two fluted white columns to the front door, which was painted a deep, inviting shade of blue and looked like a portal to another time.

Before I could knock, a massive wasp with long, dangling legs and bad vision darted right for me. I gasped and ducked.

The wasp weaved and bobbed.

With a startled scream, I went into automatic wasp-dance mode, which was also spider mode. It involved a lot of hopping, spinning around, swearing, and slapping at my clothes.

When the wasp finally got the hint and left me alone, I surveilled the damage. I'd lost my tea, my bag, *and* my dignity. I picked up the first two, accepted the loss of the third, and furtively looked around to make sure no one had seen.

The coast was clear.

Pretending I didn't now have a tea stain seeping across my chest, I quickened my steps. *House* was definitely the wrong word for this place with its ten thousand square feet of homestead that had been infamous during the Prohibition era for bootlegging. It was the biggest historical landmark in the small, quirky town of Star Falls, possibly the biggest in all of Sonoma County.

"What could possibly go wrong?" I whispered to the butterflies in my belly.

Keep your chin up.

My mom had always said that, but only because the Legend of Star Falls claimed that if you caught sight of the rare phenomenon of three falling stars arching together across the sky, then your soulmate would enter your life. Had to have your chin up to watch for it, which we'd done anytime we'd come through Star Falls.

Personally, I wasn't sure I believed in soulmates, but a warmth

7

settled in my chest from thinking about my mom. Pasting on a smile, I lifted a hand to knock, but before I could, the front door opened. The guy who opened the door wore a suit so perfect it had to be illegal and a smile that managed to be both charming and suspiciously polite—like he knew he had the power to ruin your day and might be considering it. "Can I help you?"

I wasn't great at polite smiles, so I abstained. "I'm Emma Sumner, the architect from Henderson and Hall Architects." Darren Henderson, my boss's boss, had inherited this beloved Star Falls historical landmark, which once upon a time had been the mayor's mansion and was soon to be an exclusive corporate retreat.

As Henderson and Hall's newest architect specializing in CDM—Construction Design Management—I was the liaison between the firm and Colburn Restorations, the high-end construction company Henderson had hired to handle the renovations. At least I was for the next three months anyway, and at the reminder, my stress crept back in like a mischievous goblin lurking in the shadows. "I'm here to meet with Ryder Colburn."

He frowned. "You're not Ruth."

"She's on maternity leave." I felt thrown that he hadn't been told. "I'm her temporary replacement, here to review some requested change orders."

He offered a hand. "Ryder Colburn." He turned as someone appeared at his back. A slightly younger version of Ryder, with the same strong jaw and wind-tousled dark hair, though he was a few inches taller and broader. Unlike Ryder, this guy wore cargos and a Colburn Restorations T-shirt that didn't cover the interesting tats on his arms. His aviator glasses slipped a little on his nose because his face was practically buried in a set of blueprints. "Ry, setbacks are wrong—"

I had no idea what else he said because that voice...I knew that deep, husky voice. How did I know that voice?

Then he looked up, and even as the lenses on his glasses darkened to adjust for the sun, I caught sight of vibrant hazel eyes behind the glasses and froze in shock and disbelief.

He did not freeze, though I caught the quick flash of surprise before he schooled his features into a neutral calm and said nothing. Like I was nothing and nobody.

Which, to him, I absolutely was.

Colburn... How didn't I put it together and see this coming?

"Caleb," Ryder said. "This is Emma—"

"Exacting Emma," Caleb Colburn said with zero inflection.

Ryder's brows rose at the nickname.

An antacid would be good about now. In college, Caleb had taken great pleasure in using a nickname when speaking to me, always a different adjective before my name, always starting with an *E* to match. My blood pressure had risen then, and it did so now.

"And Emma Sumner," Ryder said to me, "this is—"

"*Colburn.*" I last named him because, no, this couldn't be happening. And how dare he look as sexy as ever, a fact that sent odious little sparks skating through my belly. Where was a hole to fall into when I needed one, maybe even a new time continuum so I could avoid this reunion I'd never seen coming?

"Caleb's the project manager," Ryder said. "And since there's no problem he can't solve, we call him *The Fixer*. You two know each other?"

I shook my head and said, "Nope."

At the same time, Caleb said, "Yes."

"Well, that clears that up." Ryder turned to his brother,

something in his gaze I couldn't begin to understand since my brain had gone offline at the first sight of Caleb. The two men exchanged a look as Ryder's phone rang. Gesturing to it, he walked away to take the call.

Caleb leaned his big self against the doorway, casual as you please. "Never expected to see you again," he said.

I could only stare at the one man on the planet who could throw me off course, the man who, once upon a time, had destroyed my world without a thought. "Same. Is it *Mr. Fixer* then? Or do you still go by *Cheater*?"

He cocked his head. "You're still mad my senior project beat yours. Interesting."

No, that was most definitely not it, and he knew it, knew he'd been the golden boy who got everything he wanted in spite of the work other people put in. I'd hoped to never see him again. So then why did his deep, rich voice bring back all the memories: him, the country's favorite college hockey player, and me, a nobody. We'd been academic rivals and nemeses. No matter how hard I worked, he was always one step ahead of me in our architectural program. No surprise since he had tutors and overseers at his disposal. He never had to sweat a single thing. Teachers loved him, favored him, and there was no fighting against that, or the scholarship and summer internship in Europe that he stole from beneath my nose.

And it wasn't just teachers. He was surrounded by fellow students, most of them women, all wanting time with him—which he happily gave in exchange for lab and study assistance. He'd rarely had to do his own work, and it had driven me crazy.

Caleb took in my black trousers, black flats, unbuttoned blazer, and…the tea-stained white shirt beneath.

"Wasp incident," I said, nose high enough that I risked a nosebleed.

He rubbed a hand over his stubbled jaw, and I refused to acknowledge the little quiver that went through me at the rasping sound. "Didn't see this coming," he finally said, then shrugged those broad shoulders. "But Ruth was a hard-ass, so this probably works in my favor."

Of course that's how he'd see it. "Maybe I'm harder to please than Ruth."

He finally smiled, and damn, it was the hockey-superstar smile. I refused to melt even a tiny little bit, but I did have to lock my knees, which I'd admit only upon threat of death.

"You don't think I can be a hard-ass?"

Those eyes of his, with that unique swirl of green and gold, danced. "I probably shouldn't answer that for the sake of our new relationship."

"We don't have a relationship."

His smile faded. "We do now. This project is everything to me. So we both need to leave all the personal shit at the door."

Both? What did that mean? "I've never done anything to you."

He leaned casually against the doorway, hands in his pockets like he didn't have a care in the world. "Rewriting history, Emma Sumner?" His voice rumbled in the back of his throat, a velvety rumble that curved around my spine.

Just like that, all those long-ago feelings of inadequacy, and impostor syndrome, and a whole bunch of other things churned in my gut as I tossed up my hands. "Why can't you be like all the other men on this planet and either ignore or run from conflict?"

He snorted. "Trust me, that's my usual MO."

"Great, go with your instincts." I drew a breath. "Look, let's just get this over with, okay? We need to go over those change orders."

"Yes, but not with that," he said of my laptop. "Flipping back and forth on a screen gives me a migraine." He gestured to the site plans tucked under his arm and walked away.

"Oh sure, I'll just follow you then," I muttered, annoyed by his easy, confident gait. "What's wrong with right here?" I asked, stopping in the middle of the massive open living room, which was clearly being used as the restoration staging area, with more tools and equipment than I could name.

"Still always on a fast break, rushing the puck." He glanced over his shoulder at me, his eyes shining with Trouble—with a capital *T*. "You really should see the whole place firsthand, especially if you're going to give me shit on the change orders."

Two minutes in, and he had me on the defensive already. "I'm only going to argue the changes that affect structure or your historical-landmark status."

He made one of those very masculine sounds that could mean just about anything sarcastic.

"What?" I demanded.

"Nothing."

"It's something," I said.

"Fine. Just admit you're going to bust my balls every chance you get because you always have to win."

I choked on a mirthless laugh. "No, that's you."

"Keep telling yourself that," he said, and I realized he was limping slightly as he moved across the floor, clearly favoring his right leg.

"You hurt?" I asked.

"Nope."

"All right, so maybe I do always have to win," I admitted, "but at least I know my limitations."

He had the nerve to laugh, and I rolled my eyes at his broad back as he opened the sliding glass door. Out back lay an abandoned pasture, a glorious old red barn that had seen better days, and several smaller wooden structures. A single-track trail ran through the property, sloped down to the river, winding around aged oak trees and empty pens, all of it an overgrown sea of wild grass surrounded by green rolling hills. We were on the far outskirts of Star Falls out here, nestled between wineries and ranches.

I concentrated on not tripping on the rough terrain as Caleb expertly maneuvered the tight trail, his posture relaxed, his broad shoulders angling away from branches whenever he passed too close.

I hated how he made it seem so easy—made *everything* seem so easy—and that old bubble of resentment got stuck in my throat. At the river's edge, Caleb pointed to a downed tree, which had been chopped into four rounds and arranged in a circle. "Our outside office slash lunch area slash secret talk space."

"Secret talk space?"

"Yep." He peered at me from behind those sexy glasses that seemed to make the gold flecks in his eyes glow. "Any secrets you wanna get off your chest?"

"Not a single one."

He actually let loose a real smile. "Liar."

I shrugged. Sharing secrets was not my thing. I liked them locked up deep inside my chest, thank you very much.

"You live in Star Falls now?" he asked.

Speaking of secrets… I tried not to tense up. Tried to ignore the way my heart beat faster with embarrassment and shame. "Yeah, near downtown." And then I started walking, leading the way this time, not stopping until we stood in front of a gloriously time-worn, faded-red barn. Our first problematic change order. "In the progress reports, it says you're tackling the roof first—for obvious safety reasons," I said. "And then the foundation, framing, windows, siding, and flooring, in that order."

He crossed his arms. "Why do I hear a *but* on the end of that sentence?"

"But…the plans call for electrical before the flooring."

Surprise flared in his eyes, like he might be impressed, which irritated me more than flattered. "Usually, yes," he said. "But the owner's toying with making the barn a different sort of retreat experience, an off-the-grid one—no electricity or running water, etc. He asked us to hold off until he makes up his mind."

"If he goes that route, you'll need to get the permits adjusted."

He dipped his head in agreement.

"And schedule an inspection."

He grimaced, which I got. No one enjoyed inspections, but they were a necessary evil to get a final permit.

"A problem for another day," he said.

I wondered what that was like, to be able to shove your day-to-day worries aside. Back inside, we walked the manor. Even with its pants down, so to speak, the place was incredible: Simple elegance and natural lighting, high, slanted ceilings, and large windows all gave off a warm, cozy vibe that thrilled my inner architecture geek. I'd always had a thing for old manors just like this. On the third floor, I nodded to the attic access at the end of a long hallway. "What's up there?"

Instead of answering, he steadied a ladder at the base of the access door, which creaked loudly as he muscled it open. I climbed in ahead of him, entering the attic, only to stop short in shocked delight. "It's furnished."

Caleb nodded when he climbed in behind me, sliding his big self through the small access door with athletic grace, nudging me over with a hand to my lower back to make enough space. "Henderson's great-grandmother lived up here." He looked around. "His directive was to leave it as is. So we have, other than one of the guys occasionally crawling up here to nap. Yesterday, Miguel came to work after being up all night with his newborn niece, so we sent him up here to grab some Z's before he cut off a finger."

Turning in a slow circle, I took in the antique furnishings: a four-poster bed devoid of bedding, a tall ornate armoire, a full-length bronze-framed mirror, and a gorgeous wood bench at the end of the bed. Dust motes floated through the air, visible in the muted light slanting in from two high windows. In spite of the neglect, there was a warmth here, a sense that this had been a room where a happy person had lived. "It's homey."

"Feels like good memories were made here," he agreed, and I stared at him, unable to hide my surprise at the genuine insight.

"What, you think you're the only one here who loves this old shit?"

I didn't know what I'd thought or expected, but it hadn't been him, that's for sure. "There's one more place I really want to see before we get to it," I said.

He let out a genuine grin that unexpectedly disarmed me. "You want to see what we discovered in demo."

I found myself smiling helplessly back because he

understood; I could feel it: He really did love this stuff as much as I did. "Yes."

We headed down the stairs, and if I hadn't been watching so closely—so I didn't trip and absolutely not because he had a great ass—I'd have missed the way he favored his leg. "Should you be doing physical labor with…?" I gestured to his leg.

"I'm good."

Of course he was. That leg could be literally falling off his body, and he'd have said the same thing.

We moved through the gutted kitchen to the laundry room, where the basement access had been discovered. No one had known about it, not even Henderson himself, until Colburn Restorations had discovered the secret opening under the old water heater of all places.

Caleb squatted low to open the heavy door. Absently rubbing his left thigh, he gestured me in. "Ladies first."

I stared at the steps that vanished into inky nothingness. "Is this a test?"

"It's my good manners."

I rolled my eyes, pulled a small penlight from the bag still slung over my shoulder, and aimed it into the opening. The penlight barely touched the first few steps, and I gulped. But hell if I'd give unfairly gorgeous Caleb Colburn the satisfaction of thinking I couldn't handle this. So I straightened my shoulders, sucked in a breath, and took the first step.

Big-girl panties on. All systems go.

CHAPTER 2

Caleb

FOLLOWED EMMA DOWN the noisy old stairs, each rickety step sounding like a ghost with a grudge. And since Emma's ineffective flashlight was the same as trying to put out a fire with a drop of water, I held my Maglite above her, aiming it downward so she didn't take a header.

"Thanks," she said grudgingly, the hand at her side fisted, probably to hide the fact she was shaking.

On brand. Emma Sumner didn't do vulnerable. At least not with the likes of me, someone she'd long ago decided was nothing more than a meathead jock. "Golden rule," I said.

She glanced back with those dragon-slaying emerald eyes dialed to suspicion and mistrust. With her hand now on her hip, sass spilled from her every pore; she looked like the best thing that had never happened to me as eight years of my life vanished on a phantom wind.

She stood there, petite as hell, with her *non*-petite attitude and scrunched-up brow—no doubt caused by my presence. If I weren't also feeling the same bad attitude about this blast from my past, I'd admit she was still smoking hot.

"Golden rule?" she queried, tapping an impatient foot.

"*Always* back your teammate, even if you hate them."

"This isn't hockey, and I'm not your teammate."

Of course she didn't dispute the hating-me thing. Whatever. I spread my hands. "Look, like it or not, we've once again been paired together. So I'm going to have your back, and in good faith, I assume you'll do the same."

"If you're referring to our college co-projects, you didn't have anyone's back but your own."

"Your hindsight needs a prescription." Her presence was making me feel like I'd been shot out of a cannon—I knew a hard landing was coming. Her and that laptop and those smarty-pants eyes and wildly wavy chestnut hair that made a man's fingers itch to touch it. Fuck. Why her? With her every impertinent, irreverent word, those old feelings of being known as nothing more than a puck chaser hit me all over again.

The old stairs creaked under our combined weight, and Emma gripped the banister like her life depended on it. "If you turn out to be a serial killer and I've just let you lure me down here to my dramatic death, I'm going to be really pissed off."

"If I were going to kill you, I'd have done so on the ground level so I wouldn't have to carry your body up these stairs."

She snorted and nearly tripped. I didn't dare say *watch your step* or anything else that might suggest she wasn't up to the challenge, but these stairs were rickety as fuck. If she fell, she'd probably accuse me of pushing her.

Her phone buzzed in the silence, lighting up her back pocket before she pulled it out to look at the screen. I inadvertently caught sight of her home screen, with text previews. One from Verizon that said, **Bill Overdue**, and the other from Henderson and Hall. She ignored the bill text and quickly thumbed a response to work, her face lit up in the ambient cell light.

She'd both changed a lot and not at all. At age eighteen, she'd known a hundred times more about architecture than I ever could.

In contrast, I'd been good on skates and could sink a puck into a net, and as a result, most people treated me like the crown prince of the campus.

Except Emma.

In the years since, she'd grown into herself, sharpened her edges even more, and I liked it. Liked, too, the way her body had filled out, all warm, sexy curves, but what I liked the most was the newfound confidence radiating from her. It looked good on her.

She slid her phone away. "Just the office, checking in."

I *wasn't* new to my job, but I understood the pressure more than she knew. "We've got this, you know."

She craned her neck to look at me. *"We?"*

I flashed my most charming smile. "Sure. The Fixer and Exceptional Emma."

Her expression said I'd lost my marbles, and I had to laugh. Charming people was my superpower, except with Emma. But this wasn't college. This was real life, *my* life, and this project was critical to proving to Ryder that I had a place in Colburn Restoration at the very top. Right next to him—as partner.

I'd made mistakes in my stupid, wild, feral youth, way too many, and didn't have the best track record. I'd disappointed him in the past, but I intended to remedy that. I needed to be of value, to lift some of the heavy weight off the brother who'd sacrificed so much for me.

All I had to do was make this project, Colburn Restoration's biggest project ever, the sweetheart of our portfolio, and I'd have my life where I wanted it. But to do that, I needed a cohesive, strong team. Emma was now a part of that team, which meant I had to find a way in with her.

At the bottom of the stairs, Emma took in what she could, and her jaw dropped.

"Looks like it has a story to tell, doesn't it?" I said quietly.

A huff of air escaped her as she turned in a slow circle. "Wow. It's amazing."

I agreed. A bar stretched out along one wall, dark oak now dulled with age; dust clung to beaten-up barstools, and various alcohol bottles lined up like silent sentries, some still holding murky liquids that looked like they'd bite if anyone dared take a sip.

Behind the bar, the shelves held chipped and broken shot glasses, tarnished brass drink shakers, and an old-timey cash register whose keys probably clicked to the beat of 1920s jazz.

The room had been set up for intimacy, a scattering of low tables and red velvet booths half-dissolved by years of neglect. Faded posters adorned the walls, their edges curling with age.

This wasn't just a basement. It was a gateway to a time when people risked everything for a taste of the forbidden.

"This was a secret speakeasy," Emma whispered, face in bold relief from the flashlight's glow.

I nodded. "Even Henderson had no idea."

She shook her head, awed. "I can almost still smell the tobacco and spilled whiskey, and hear all the secrets this room's held for all these years. What's that?" Without waiting for a response, she crossed the room, taking her beam of light with her. On the far side of the bar, she stopped in front of shelves built into the wall. She blew away a bunch of dust, waved it out of her face, and then ran her fingers down the side of the time-swollen built-in. "I've seen this before," she said, and without concern for the dirt and dust, she got down on her hands and knees to eyeball the bottom part of the shelving unit up close with her pathetic penlight.

"What are you—"

"Shh a sec," she said, then stunned me into amused silence as she knocked on the side panel. "Hear that?"

"Oh, am I allowed to talk now?"

She was tugging now, fingers gripping the side panel with a grunt of effort. "You gonna help me, or is that muscled bod just for show these days?"

With a snort, I dropped to my knees beside her, knowing she'd never once been impressed by me, muscled bod or no. "What are we doing?"

She knocked on the wood again, then turned her head and beamed at me. "It's hollow. The secret speakeasy has a secret panel!"

I knew her bright smile wasn't for me, but it was still a showstopper. "Wait here a second," I said, then jogged back up the stairs. In the kitchen, I grabbed a portable construction light, plugged it into a long extension cord, and took it back down to the basement. I flicked a switch and lit us up in a halogen glow.

Emma laughed in delight and gave the wood another tug. The shelving unit budged a fraction of an inch. Reaching in, my hands joined hers. "Ready?" I asked.

"Yes," she breathed, the back of her head so close to my face that strands of her hair caught on my stubble. I gave a single tug, and the shelving unit pivoted 180 degrees, revealing a secret entrance.

We shined our lights in. The space was the size of a large walk-in safe. Two walls were all shelves, bare with the exception of one tattered canvas bag. On the other wall hung a very old-looking dartboard, all of it covered in layers and layers of dust and spiderwebs.

Emma, apparently not bothered by either, crawled in, waving a hand to clear a web near her face as I reached for the canvas bag.

"Wait," she said.

I crawled in next to her, ignoring the bolt of fire that went through my leg. I eyed the dust smudged along one of Emma's cheeks and in her hair, loving that she didn't seem to give a shit about that or the state of her work clothes. "What?"

"Well, what if I want to be the one to look in the bag?"

We stared at each other. "Darts," we said at the same time. My brothers and I had played darts our entire childhood. In college, my every spare second had been spent at the local bar hustling my friends. I wasn't about to hustle poor Emma. She wanted this so badly, and I'd let her have it.

"First to hit the bull's-eye," I said.

"Too chicken to play Three-Oh-One?"

I laughed low in my throat at her taunt. "I was trying to be nice, but you're on."

The object of 301 was to land on the highest numbers, being the first player to bring their starting score of 301 down to zero. I could do this in a few moves—in my sleep.

"Ladies first," I said, picking up one of the darts in the gutter beneath the board and handing it to her.

She concentrated on her stance, gripping the dart, brow furrowing in concentration as she threw the dart.

And hit the bull's-eye. "That's fifty points off for me."

I looked into her smug face and shook my head. "You hustled me."

"Who, me?" she asked innocently.

Ten minutes later, she'd wiped the floor with me. I was still standing there, staring at the dartboard, wondering what the fuck had just happened, when she carefully pulled the canvas bag off the shelf and opened it.

With a gasp, she pulled out a wad of hundred-dollar bills. "Oh my God."

"Henderson is going to be pleased," I said, thinking about how good she smelled in spite of the dust, the look of sheer joy on her face when she'd kicked my ass without remorse, the excitement this hidden room had brought her.

"We should frame one of the bills for the entranceway." She stared down at the money. "A pretty cool item to show off."

And she was thinking about work... Well, that tracked.

"We're not demoing this room," she said.

"I'm insulted you think I would." I ran a hand along a shelf. "This room has a history, and we won't lose it."

"Really?"

Her suspicion of me burned. "I'm a lot of things, Emma." For instance, I was a total asshole who'd enjoyed the sight of her on her hands and knees, glaring at me. "But a liar isn't one of them." I rose with more difficulty than I'd ever admit and offered a hand, pulling her up. "We'll talk to Henderson, see what he wants to do, but I suspect that, like the attic, he'll want this left as is."

Eyes still on mine, she nodded. "Sometimes the past is best left alone."

And how well we both knew it.

In silence, we made our way back to the living room. If it hadn't been drizzling outside, the front windows would have revealed a distant view of the rocky California shoreline where, once upon a time, my siblings and I had run wild and feral, completely unsupervised.

"Back to the change orders," she said, all business now, as she pulled out her laptop. "First, the barn. You've pointed out a structural issue with how Henderson wants to change up the windows. Is it because you'd have to deal with the weight-bearing beams?"

"It'll be time-consuming and expensive, and tricky to get past the Historical Board." Ryder had put it on me to somehow talk sense into the man—or, as it turned out, his dusty proxy at my side.

"So change his mind," she said.

"That seems like a you problem."

She snorted. Her ponytail had given up the fight, strands loose around her face, somehow still scented like coconut and vanilla. Shit. I was a dead man walking.

"This place is going to be incredible," she said. "I still can't quite believe I get to be a part of it."

"So you at least trust me enough to know that it's going to turn out well."

"Actually, I don't trust you as far as I can throw you. And given you're the size of a mountain and I'm only five foot four..." She shrugged. "What I trust in is the architectural and engineering plans. I'll see if I can design a work-around."

"If you're five foot four, I'm Santa Claus."

"Hey, I'm *totally* five foot four." She paused. "Okay, fine. Five foot three *and* a half."

I stepped into her personal space and looked down at her. She barely hit my shoulder. "Five foot two, *tops*. I could get out my measuring tape and prove it to you if you'd like."

She snorted. "I bet you also use it to measure your—"

I laughed. I wanted to resent the hell out of her for some of the things she'd pulled on me in our architectural program, but I'd never been able to hold a grudge, and certainly not against those eyes and spirited attitude. "Are you going to be this annoying the whole job?"

"Pot. Kettle," she said. "You're even more guarded than I am, and that's saying something."

I shrugged. "It's not necessarily a bad thing, you know."

She processed this as if searching my words for a speed trap before shrugging—the closest she'd get to admitting I might be right. I opened my mouth to bait her again, just for the pleasure of seeing those eyes flare, but stopped, remembering that, for this job to go smoothly, I needed her on my side.

An hour later, we'd gotten through ten of the eleven items on the list, and we'd each gotten our way on five of them.

"Tied," she said. We'd ended up in the kitchen around a large worktable, going back and forth between the plans and the list.

"Didn't realize we were keeping track."

She smirked. "Another lie."

I smiled. True. "Last change order will be the tiebreaker. The wall between the pantry and back mudroom your boss wants removed—it's another load-bearing wall."

"And?"

"And it'll eat up your entire change-order budget."

Emma stared down at the plans for a long moment. "The reason for removing this wall was to make the floor plan more open. But," she mused, "I get that we need to ensure the structural integrity as well. What if I designed a more open doorway between the pantry and mudroom? It would create a sense of openness without completely removing the wall."

Impressed by the smart suggestion, I nodded. "If you can get Henderson to agree, you're on."

"I'll talk to him." She pointed at me. "But until then, we're still tied."

"Something to look forward to," I said, then walked her out.

Out front in the circular driveway, Ryder's work truck was long gone, leaving just mine and an old green Subaru that looked like it might be on its last breath. It also seemed packed to the gills. "Yours?"

"Yes. I'm still...getting settled." She was busy combing through her messenger bag, presumably for her keys. Finally, with a huff of annoyance, she began pulling things out and setting them on the hood of her car. Three thick architectural books that had to weigh as much as she did. Her laptop. ChapStick. Toothbrush...

"Sleep mask?" I asked at the last item, "Or...kinky blindfold?"

"You wish. *There* you are," she muttered, finding her keys.

"Until next time," I said.

She seemed startled at the thought. Clearly, she'd hoped to never see me again. But on big, complicated jobs like this, there'd be meetings. Many of them.

"I'm curious."

She glanced back.

I slid my hands into my pockets. "You ever going to tell me why you don't like me?"

"I never said I didn't."

"Your face when you first saw me again said it."

She rolled her eyes. "Goodbye, Colburn."

"Until next time, Sumner."

CHAPTER 3

Caleb

THE NEXT MORNING, I lay in bed, eyes closed, taking in the distant bleat of goats, squawks of annoyed chickens, and the faint whir of a tractor. My mind ignored all that to feed me flashes of yesterday's blast from my past.

Emma Sumner had been a whirlwind of creativity and smarts, and the way she lifted her nose ever so slightly when she knew she was right… Damn. Hot as hell.

But appreciating her presence and trusting her were two very different things. She'd long ago proven the lengths she'd go to in order to win. And I wasn't about to let it happen.

I shifted, and my bedmates stirred, lifting their heads. Great, I'd blinked, and now we had to start our day. *We* being me and the two boxers I'd rescued after finding them abandoned on a jobsite a few months ago. They completely owned my heart, but I'd rather they owned it from their cushy, ridiculously expensive dog bed in the corner. Calvin and Klein—named by my sister, not me—were approximately two years old, brothers, and, according to our vet, fully grown. At eighty pounds each, I could only hope so.

"Woo woo woo!"

Translation: *Hey, buddy, it's thirty seconds past breakfast time.*

I sat up, which prompted pandemonium. "Calm," I said.

Calvin immediately settled, panting happily, his eyes warm and attentive—and hopeful. Klein went batshit bonkers, racing around in wild circles over and around me on the mattress. Klein had no calm.

We'd been to training class. Twice. Some things had stuck. Most hadn't. "Klein. Sit."

Klein, whose unfortunate underbite gave him the look of a hooligan, *pretended* to sit, then got the zoomies again.

"Sit."

Klein huffed out a breath but sat, tail going about a hundred miles an hour as Hank padded into my room to join the chaos.

He sat on my bed and said, "Ah."

In the mindfuck of the century, the Colburn sire had suffered two strokes, then a craniotomy, and was now nonverbal. And... different. Different as in he had the temperament of...Klein.

It had been nearly a year now, and I was still waiting for him to become the monster in my closet. Not my goofball dogs though. Nope, they greeted him with exuberant licks to the face until I pushed them off the bed.

Hank just smiled and, since he no longer understood anyone's personal space boundaries, patted me on the head, a question in his eyes.

I managed not to flinch, thanks in no small part to all those years getting beat to hell in hockey. "I've got a doctor's appointment this morning before work," I said, answering his unspoken question. "And since Nell can't take you for another hour, you're coming with." I eyed him. "No shenanigans this time."

Hank gave me an innocent look that I didn't buy for one second.

His medical team had assured us time and time again that it was unlikely he remembered much from before the strokes. That he might never remember. That this personality, this…*puppy*, was here to stay.

I was still working on believing that. My entire goal in life was to survive these next three months with him before passing him off to Tucker for his turn at caretaking.

"I mean it," I said. "Last time you came with me, you flirted with the nurses so they'd feed you goodies and stole a handful of pens, which you stuffed in your pants. Today, none of that is happening, got me?"

"Ah."

Shaking my head, I got up and showered, with Calvin and Klein sitting just outside the shower door wearing forlorn faces because I wouldn't let them join me. By the time I got out, Calvin had fallen asleep on his back, mouth open, legs straight up in the air like roadkill.

Klein was licking the glass door of the shower.

I got myself and my dad dressed with minimal fuss—if I discounted the fact Hank hadn't wanted to wear shoes. I won that battle—bribed him with a cookie—and went to the kitchen to let the dogs out.

My sprinklers were on, and that was my first mistake. Calvin and Klein loved water, and sure enough, they each ran to lie on a sprinkler head, immediately becoming drenched and muddy. "Let's go," I said.

They did not, in fact, go. Instead, they rolled to their backs, wriggling in muddy, wet ecstasy. Assholes. I strode through the wet grass and scooped them up, tucking one under each arm like sacks of flour.

Very heavy sacks of flour.

I felt like my day had been twenty years long by the time I parked in front of my orthopedist's office. I was still damp and smelled like wet dog. I eyed Hank in the passenger seat. "You're going to behave."

"Ah."

Right. *Let the shit show begin.* We walked into the medical office hand in hand. Hank was steady enough on his feet, but making his way through terrain he wasn't used to sometimes tripped him up. He had a cane, but he also wanted to hold my hand.

Something he'd never, ever done before the strokes.

Linda the receptionist, somewhere between Hank's age and a hundred, beamed at the sight of us. "Hank!" Jumping up, she headed straight for him. "I brought you another of those oatmeal raisin cookies you love!"

The old man grinned with a charm I hadn't even realized he had. "Ah," he said, then did something with his face, scrunching both eyes and his mouth up.

"Look at you," Linda said, smiling. "You've almost got the wink down! Have you still been stargazing?" She looked at me. "You're sitting him on the porch at night so he can look for the Legend, right?"

I felt my left eye begin to twitch. My mom had loved the romance of the Legend of Star Falls, but after her death, whimsical things—such as seeing three stars falling in an arc and believing the sight of them would bring you a soulmate—seemed like a load of horseshit.

But then, one night not too long ago, Ryder had seen the three falling stars, and so had Tucker and I—even if we pretended we hadn't. And then Ryder had fallen in love. So now…now I had no idea what to think. "I'm not sure he understands the Legend of Star Falls, so—"

"Ah."

I turned to Hank. "You do?"

"Aw."

My right eye joined in on the twitching action. "And you want to stargaze for the three falling stars so, what, you can find your soulmate?"

"Ah."

I knew the people who lived in Star Falls *loved* the Legend beyond reason. But it never failed to surprise me how many people, in spite of never having seen it themselves, believed unswervingly.

Not me. Except…Ryder had fallen hard for Penny shortly afterward, and something uneasy settled in my gut at the reminder.

But Hank…I was trying to decide whether he had his memories and was just running a long con on me when he made a sound of childlike glee and began pilfering pens from the cup on the counter, slipping them into his pockets.

For fuck's sake. "Sorry," I muttered to Linda, frisking Hank to clear him of stolen goods, including a roll of Scotch tape and three paper clips.

Linda patted Hank's hand. "Don't worry about it, hot stuff. Everyone gets caught at least once in their lifetime."

I led him to a chair in the waiting area. "What are you up to?"

He just sat there with that innocent smile in place. Shaking my head, I texted Ry and Tuck.

ME:

> Dad's a klepto.

> Also, he's looking for his soulmate via the Legend of Star Falls.

BABY BRO:

> It's way too early for you to be drunk.

OLDEST AND UGLIEST BRO:

> Especially when you're supposed to be at work rn.

ME:

> I'm not drunk!

BABY BRO:

> then eat something, you're grumpier than Ry.

OLDEST AND UGLIEST BRO:

> Hey.

I got called to a room, so I shoved my phone away and helped Hank up. Two minutes later, I sat on the patient cot, Hank in the chair in the corner, eating a massive cookie from Linda, crumbs sifting down his front.

I slowly counted to ten in my head, trying to lower my blood pressure.

Nurse Daisy bounced into the room. She was tall, stacked, blond, gorgeous, funny, and wild—all reasons why I'd gone out with her for a whole week in high school. She'd been great. I'd been a thoughtless, reckless asshole.

Daisy eyed the cookie in Hank's hand. "I tried to steal that from Linda this morning. She wasn't having it; she'd brought it for you."

Hank held out the cookie, offering her a bite.

Daisy squeezed his hand. "You're a sweetheart, but you keep it."

Hank did that thing with his face again, which, to be honest, made him look like he was having another stroke.

Without missing a beat, Daisy winked back at him, then came at me to take my vitals, all business now. No less than I deserved.

Over her shoulder, Hank smirked at me.

Helpless old man, my ass. *Knock it off,* I mouthed.

He stopped looking at me. Translation: *Not on your life.*

"You're lucky," Daisy said, wrapping the blood-pressure cuff around my arm. "To still have your dad with you."

No one at school had known what our lives were like back then. We moved around a bit before landing in Star Falls, and we Colburn siblings held our tongues, keeping our eyes on the prize: getting out the second we each turned eighteen.

Which didn't mean that we hadn't gleefully found as much trouble as we could.

"I see a lot of Hank in you," Daisy said.

I was nothing like Hank. He'd been mean and unnecessarily cruel. I'd gone the opposite route. I used charm and charisma to keep everything surface level. That was my comfort zone, and I was good at it, at the casual, fun flirting—

Shit. I stared at Hank. Hank, *the casual, fun flirt.*

Daisy eyed the screen of the blood-pressure cuff and frowned. "Did you run here?"

"No."

"You stressed?"

I laughed mirthlessly. "Me? Of course not."

She snickered and patted my cheek. Hard. Which I probably also deserved. "Then maybe you're just getting old."

I sighed, and she laughed.

"Do you want to know what I think?" she asked, slipping an oxygen monitor on my finger.

"No."

She typed something into my chart, then twirled her stool back to face me, smile gone, voice low now, just for my ears. "I think you're a good man, Caleb. You stepped up at Colburn Restorations for Ryder. You take care of your father, disabilities and all. You—"

"I'm no saint."

Some of her smile came back. "Oh, I know, Mr. Star Falls Athlete of the Year, whom everyone in school wanted to sleep with."

I gave her a long look.

"Yeah, yeah, including me."

We'd had sex under the bleachers.

During a football game.

While her dad had been one of the refs...

"You had zero worries back then," she said.

If only she knew the truth. I'd had *all* the worries...

"It's just good to see you being more than that all-star hockey guy. But take it easy on yourself, okay? You're only human." She rose. "Doctor'll be in any minute." She waved at Hank. "Give him hell."

Two minutes later, Dr. Stranton walked in, cheerful as always. "My favorite hockey star. Miss watching you on TV, kicking ass and taking names. Your alma mater misses you too. They're zero and four this season."

He pulled out a massive needle, and I drew a deep breath.

"You miss it, son? The game?"

If I had a penny for every time someone asked me that, I could quit work, buy a bar on a quiet tropical island somewhere, and chill for the rest of my life. But people wanted to hear only one thing. "Of course."

Doc nodded sympathetically. "How's the leg?"

I nodded. "Good."

"Liar. You lit up your latest scans like a Christmas tree. What's your pain level between one and ready-to-jump-in-front-of-a-hundred-mile-per-hour puck?"

"One."

He gave me a *get real* look.

"Okay, three, tops."

Hank held up both hands, showing all ten fingers.

Dr. Stranton saluted him. "Thank you, kind sir." He eyeballed me, his face stern now, which didn't bode well for me. "You should've come in sooner."

I shrugged. "Work's a bitch."

He shook his head. "You get any migraines lately?"

"No." Yes…

"It's not a weakness; it's a medical condition brought on by your accident on the ice."

"I know." Didn't care. Whenever I got a migraine, either

Tucker or Ryder would give up everything to sit with me through it, and I hated it. Not their company, but the helplessness, the weakness, the lack of control, the need to be babysat.

He shook his head again. "After this steroid injection today, you need to think about scheduling that surgery."

I'd had multiple surgeries in the years since the injury that had ended my hockey career. I had no interest in another. I also had zero interest in having that very long, thick needle shoved into my leg. "Sure."

Knowing I was full of shit, Dr. Stranton leaned over me. "Just a little pinch now."

Pinch, my ass. The shot felt like the aforementioned puck straight to the face.

"Good," Dr. Stranton said, stepping back when he was done torturing me. "You only held your breath until you turned a little blue this time."

I knew I was an intimidating guy. Didn't mean I liked needles. "The joke better not cost extra."

"Not for my favorite hockey star." He patted my shoulder. "No work today; keep the leg up, relax."

"Sure."

Doc almost rolled his eyes, I could tell.

A few minutes later, I got Hank buckled into my work truck and slid my tired ass behind the wheel. Taking a second to lean my head back, I closed my eyes and drew a couple of deep breaths.

"Ah?"

"Need a moment."

Exactly sixty seconds later, Hank once again stirred beside me.

"I'm fine." Proving it, I started the truck and drove him straight to Nell, his absolute saint of a daycare provider, and the grandma to Ryder's fiancée, Penny. In the driveway, I turned to Hank. "Look, we're new at this, and I promised to keep you safe and fed, but we are not friends. We aren't ever going to be friends."

"Ah."

I had no idea what that meant, but I felt like an asshole anyway.

Half an hour later, I walked into Ryder's office at Colburn Restorations. He was on the phone, so I sank into the chair across from his desk, hiding my wince.

Still talking, Ry tossed me a paper bag from his desk, one that smelled like Penny's homemade breakfast burritos. I felt like I'd died and gone to heaven. I was halfway through the burrito when I realized Ry was watching me like a hawk. I hadn't told him about the injection and didn't plan to, or he'd bench me. The fucker was more annoyingly protective than a Rottweiler.

He was two years older and two inches shorter than my six-two frame. His build was lankier than mine, but I knew from experience that he could give me a run for my money in a fight. For a whole bunch of years, he'd played a lot of roles in my life: brother, mom, dad, jailer, defender, and best friend. He, along with Tucker and Kiera, always, *always*, had my back, no questions asked. We were close, even if we often acted like a pack of wild wolves, snapping at one another.

I was making a paper airplane with the wrapping from the burrito when Ryder finally got off the phone. "You're limping."

"You need to get your eyes checked, old man."

Ry didn't back off, just stared at me.

I rolled my eyes. "You don't know."

"I know you need another surgery."

Fucking smart-ass know-it-all. "It can wait."

Ry didn't push me on that. "You need a break from Hank?" he asked. "Penny and I could take him—"

"No." Growing up had been the hardest on Ryder. As the oldest, he'd taken it upon himself to stand between us and Hank. And now he finally had Penny in his life. No way was I going to foist Hank on him. "I'm good."

Tucker strode in and threw himself into the seat next to me. If Ryder was the family badass and I was the wild, restless former hockey player, Tucker was our resident rebel, and by far the most feral and adventurous. He might be the youngest, but he had two inches even on me. Deceptively lanky lean, he could, when he wanted, take me on and win at least half the time. He was also the only one who could go toe-to-toe with Ryder and keep breathing.

"You've got me for..." Tucker eyed the time. "Fifteen minutes."

He was our estimator, and because that was a feast-or-famine type of job, and because he had a hero complex, he'd been working as a volunteer firefighter since high school. But Star Falls had finally gotten funding for their own fire station, and Tucker had been one of the first to be hired on as paid staff. With his schedule of four days on, two days off, he spent his off days working here. Which was good, because everyone knew Tucker was the true heart of our family, and the glue.

He used his iPad to cast on the wall, displaying lists of things we needed to go over. A not-so-subtle hint to hurry the fuck up. Tucker was the best of us on most days, but he hadn't stood in line when patience had been doled out.

"Yeah, yeah," Ryder said. "But first, since we haven't all been in the same room this week…" He looked at me. "Heard you had a date last night."

"You heard wrong." The date had been *two* nights ago, and it had been a favor to a friend of a friend of a friend, so I'd stupidly caved.

"He must've gotten ghosted," Tucker said.

"I didn't get ghosted."

Tucker smiled. "Oh, he *definitely* got ghosted. Don't be embarrassed; you were due."

I rolled my eyes so hard, I saw my own brain. "I'm not embarrassed about something that didn't happen."

"If you say so. *Ghostee*."

"Okay, business it is then," Ryder said quickly, before things dissolved, as they tended to do. He eyed the list on the wall and then looked at me. "How did the architectural meeting go?"

I was pretty sure he didn't want to hear that Emma and I had a mutual dislike/mistrust thing going. Or that I'd had a dirty dream about her last night. And then an even better daydream this morning in the shower. "Handled the change-order list."

"All of it?"

"That's what *handled* means."

He cocked his head. "Emma seems different from Ruth."

If by *different* he meant Emma hadn't yelled, bullied, or called her boss Rosalind Hall when things didn't go her way, then yes. Very different. "Pretty sure we can all agree that's a good thing."

"You and Emma knew each other," Ryder said casually.

"Past tense, yes."

Ryder's eyes narrowed. "What do I need to know?"

Sensing a fight, Tucker stirred. "Is this questioning going somewhere, Ry?"

Ryder didn't take his eyes off me. "In this past tense, did you sleep with her?"

"Jesus, Ry." Tucker shook his head. "Foul on the play. Get to your point."

I was starting to regret getting out of bed this morning.

"I'll rephrase," Ryder said. "You plan to sleep with her during the duration of this job?"

"Out of bounds," Tucker said in reproach.

"No, it's not," Ry said, voice hard. "No sleeping with anyone even remotely connected to one of our jobs."

I opened my mouth to defend myself, but I didn't have a defense, given a past…indiscretion.

Tucker stood. "Great meeting, guys. Thanks for wasting my time." He strode to the door.

"By my watch, I still own five more minutes of your time," Ryder called out.

Tucker rolled his eyes dramatically and crossed his arms over his chest. "I don't have time to break up a fight over one of Caleb's past fuckups—"

I hoisted my paper airplane, and Tucker whipped his head to me.

"Blast me with that thing, and I'll make you regret it."

I promptly sent it flying, and it nailed him in the center of his big, fat forehead. Then I went down laughing as Tucker tackled me. I got to my feet just as Ryder stepped in, hooking an arm around my neck to hold me back. In retaliation, I planted Ry face-first into the wall.

Tucker, every bit as tough as he looked, snorted, then reached for me. Luckily, Ryder kicked his leg out from beneath him, and Tucker hit the floor like a 7.0 earthquake.

From there it was a pileup. My glasses went flying. So did Tucker's iPad and Ryder's phone.

Bill Pierce, our superintendent in charge of all the foremen, appeared in the doorway, his usual scowl firmly in place.

"What the actual fuck are you assholes up to?" he demanded.

"I hope you didn't run here," Ry said from the floor.

Bill had suffered a minor heart attack earlier in the year, freaking us all out. But he liked to say it was so minor, it hadn't even registered, and honestly, he seemed good. Shaped like a spark plug with a fierce persona to match, he never took shit from any of us. Of course, that was because his daughter, Hazel, had been a pseudo-Colburn in our wild teen years, and Bill had been our only positive authority figure growing up. He hadn't gotten the memo that he worked for Ryder now.

Still on the floor, I patted my hands around, looking for my glasses.

Tucker threw them at me and nearly took out an eyeball.

Ryder got to his feet. "Just settling an argument."

"You assholes about finished? Because we need to talk about getting a finish-carpentry subcontractor for the Henderson job."

Awkward silence.

Hazel was a finish carpenter. She ran her own crew, and though she'd left Star Falls after high school and had only recently returned, she had a reputation for being incredibly talented. But Hazel's mom—Bill's deceased wife—had made Ryder promise never to hire both Hazel and Bill at the same time because father and daughter couldn't get along to save their lives.

"I'm just going to say it," Bill said when no one spoke. "Hazel's the best out there, plus she needs the work."

Tucker grimaced. He and Hazel had been close in high school, and even though Bill had made it clear Hazel was completely off-limits to us hooligan Colburns, we all suspected there'd been something between Tucker and Hazel. I'd long ago stopped asking. My baby brother could be a slab of impenetrable steel when he wanted to be.

Ryder blew out a sigh and met Bill's gaze. "Hazel's work is amazing," he said. "And you know how much we all care about her. But—"

"You promised her mom you wouldn't have us both on the same job, yeah, yeah, I know. But Caleb's running the Henderson job, not me. And since, as it turns out, the kid's surprisingly good at his job, I can stay out of it."

"Gee, thanks," I said dryly.

"Come on, son, you know you were a huge question mark when Ryder put you into play, giving you our biggest job to date to oversee. Especially since the last time he gave you more responsibility, you boned the owner's daughter and got us fired."

Ryder rubbed his temples.

Tucker came back to life to smirk.

I hoped he'd choke on it. "Hey, she came on to me at the Cork and Barrel during a darts tournament. I thought it was a one-night thing. I had no idea she'd fall in love in two minutes."

Tucker snorted. "Is that all you gave her? Two minutes?"

I reached out to shove him, but Bill got between us. Brave. Stupid, but brave. "You did your thing and ghosted her," Bill said. "Because you're a serial ghoster."

"I'm not—" I drew a deep breath. Shit.

"Can't even say it with a straight face, can you?" Bill said.

"Enough," Ryder said quietly from behind his desk. "Back off him."

I didn't deserve his defense. Ryder hadn't wanted me to sleep with that client's daughter because it could affect the business, which I ignored because, as usual, I had to prove him wrong. I really, *really* hated it when it turned out I was the fuckup.

"I've already got some feelers out," Ryder said to Bill.

"Is one of them that asshole Ricky Herman?"

Ryder grimaced. "Yes, and—" he said when Bill opened his mouth. "*Yes*, he's an asshole. But he's good, and his price is right. If he doesn't pan out, we'll meet about next steps."

The man nodded, mouth grim. "Fine."

The last half of our meeting was so boring, I drifted off, waking when Ryder kicked my feet off his desk. "Thanks for agreeing so readily," he said almost cheerfully.

I studied him warily. "Agreeing to what?"

"To being the face of Colburn Restorations at the Star Falls gala this weekend."

Oh, hell no. The gala was an annual affair, fancy as shit, and filled with pretentious people and even more pretentious food. "I definitely didn't agree to that."

"You did. I said, 'Who here can't go?' And both Tucker and I raised our hands. You didn't."

I whipped my head to Tucker, who was fighting a grin, the prick. I scrubbed a hand down my face. "Shit."

"Oh, and we're a major sponsor, so you're giving the keynote."

"Shit."

"You already said that."

I pointed at a smirking Tucker. "He should do it. He's prettier."

"Can't," he said. "Have an arson class this weekend."

I was on a sinking ship. "I don't have a speech prepared."

Ry laughed. "Like you'd prepare a speech anyway. We all know you're going to wing it."

True…

"And you did say you wanted more responsibility…"

Damn. I had said that. And I'd meant it. A few years back, Ry had lost his business partner in a skiing accident. Auggie was his best friend, as well as Kiera's—our sister's—husband and the father of her three-year-old twins. His loss devastated all of us. Kiera retreated into herself for two years. Ryder didn't have that luxury; he had to be both himself *and* Auggie at work, and it took a toll on him.

So I'd made it clear that I was all in, willing to do whatever needed to be done in order to back Ryder and the business. But it was also self-serving, because working here with my brothers, renovating historical landmarks, felt like a pretty sweet life.

"The gala was Auggie's thing," Ry said softly. "And you've said you wanted to take on his responsibilities. So…" His voice hardened. "You're doing this."

"I don't have a tux."

"So make sure you've got one by the weekend."

———

Four days later, I stood in my kitchen wearing a stupid tux, handing Hank's backpack over to Tucker. "Everything he needs is in here."

"Thanks, Mom."

"Ha ha, and don't forget, he steals cookies after you think you've put him to bed."

Tucker shrugged. "So?"

"So…sugar keeps him up at night. You'll wake up to him standing over you, his face an inch from yours, wondering why you're screaming like a little girl."

Tucker looked at Hank.

Hank looked back, eyes innocent.

Tucker turned to me, unconvinced. "You seriously telling me he's capable of getting out of bed and to the kitchen to steal cookies?"

"Yes! Don't let that face fool you."

Hank sighed.

Half an hour later, I headed inside Bufford Hotel. I was met by a spectacle of flashy decorations and a sea of black tuxes and fancy sparkling dresses. Drawing a deep breath, I stepped inside, my gaze catching on a stunning woman across the ballroom. Shiny chestnut-brown hair not in a messy ponytail, but falling like silk to her bare shoulders. She was dressed to the nines, wearing an emerald-green dress the exact color of her eyes, not a speck of dust or dirt in sight.

Emma Sumner.

CHAPTER 4

Emma

THE BUFFORD HOTEL'S ELEGANT ballroom was a dazzling marvel. Chandeliers, each a cascade of sparkling crystals, hung from high ceilings, casting a warm glow over the massive room. Tables draped in pristine white linen were laden with colorful floral arrangements, their vibrant hues matching the array of dresses on the women milling around mingling and chatting, their laughter blending with the soft strains of elegant music.

I stood just inside the doorway staring at the black-tie gala, feeling like a fish out of water. A waiter with a tray of champagne flutes filled to the brim stopped and offered me one.

Taking it so I'd have something to do with my hands other than wring them together, I nodded my thanks as I studied the room, electric with energy.

There were only two people here representing Henderson and Hall tonight, and I was one of them, along with co-CEO Rosalind Hall. Gee, no pressure at all. I'd been tasked with meeting and bonding with as many people as I could, told that every connection might be a future client.

And then there was my own agenda—get Rosalind to like me so much, she'd hire me on even after Ruth came back from her leave. I'd gotten lucky enough to maneuver the seating arrangements so I'd be sitting next to her. Okay, so luck had nothing to do with it. When I'd first arrived and given my name to the woman checking us in, I'd feigned horror that I wasn't seated next to my boss as requested, pretended that I was worried I'd be fired for failing at that simple assignment.

Charm wasn't my specialty, but she let me switch my ticket. Now I could only hope I still had some charm left in me to come off as memorable, as someone Henderson and Hall couldn't live without.

I walked the auction aisle and stopped when an item caught my attention. It was the original blueprints of the Cliff House, a famous historical monument in Star Falls, signed by Alden Dorn, the architect whose work I'd studied in college and had admired for as long as I could remember. Even though it was early in the evening, I was still surprised no one had placed a bid.

So I did, going with the minimum reserve—$100. The blueprints would never go for that cheap, not to mention I had no business spending money that was earmarked for living expenses, but I couldn't remember the last time I'd done anything whimsical for myself.

As I straightened and turned to face the room, I caught sight of Rosalind. She was a tall, fit, elegant woman in her early fifties wearing a long, glittery black dress that could probably be seen from space, along with enough bling to singe eyeballs. She too was walking by the silent-auction items, taking it all in.

Everything here tonight was so far out of my budget as to be comical, but I moved closer and feigned interest in an item next to her.

She turned to me and cocked her head. "You look familiar. You washed my hair at the salon the other day, right?"

Well, if that didn't deflate my already-flagging confidence. "No, actually…" This wasn't *at all* humiliating. "I work for you. I'm Emma Sumner, level-one architect, filling in for Ruth, who's—"

"On maternity leave." Rosalind nodded, and if she was embarrassed by not knowing I worked for her, she didn't let on. Henderson and Hall was a massive firm of several hundred employees. My first and only previous architectural firm had employed three people total, including me. The other two had been much older, seasoned male architects, which meant I'd at first spent more time fetching coffee and answering phones. But eventually they'd come to trust me, and I'd learned an incredible amount.

But the Henderson and Hall job was a dream come true—temp or otherwise.

"We love Ruth to the moon and back," Rosaline said. "Can't wait for her return."

I tried not to wilt as I smiled. "I'll do my best to fill her shoes while she's on leave."

"They're big shoes."

"I love a challenge."

"Hmm." Rosalind turned and read the auction item in front of us. "Oh! This is *exactly* what I've been looking for." She pointed at me. "Elain, right?"

I felt my smile congeal. "Emma S—"

"Stay here. Guard my spot. If someone adds their name after mine, put a new bid down for me, going up ten K each time. There are two other items I've got my eye on. I'll handle those myself."

Wait. She didn't mean to up the bid ten *thousand* dollars every single time, did she? "Are you sure—"

But she'd already walked off. I closed my gaping mouth and stared down at the auction item. She'd bid five thousand dollars for a four-day stay at an exclusive five-star resort in Tahoe, an intimate trip for two, including their own sailboat at their beck and call, PGA golf courses, time in a world-class spa, and their own chef and butler.

A woman in a gold sheath, looking like a queen, stopped, hummed appreciatively at the getaway, and…bid eight thousand.

Shit. Shit, shit, shit.

I waited until she'd moved on to pick up the pen. My fingers shook when I put another bid down for Rosalind, upping the amount to eighteen thousand dollars—for a four-day getaway. That much money would change my life.

If I survived this auction.

Pulse racing, I shot daggers at anyone who came too close, when suddenly I felt eyes on me. Turning my head, I locked my gaze on an unbearably familiar and stupidly gorgeous man standing in the doorway of the ballroom.

I knew that build, I knew that face, and I nearly swallowed my tongue as Caleb strode in, wearing a tux that looked made for him. Only, it wasn't those broad shoulders or muscular arms that caught my attention. It wasn't even the dark-rimmed glasses adding a nerd factor that really revved my stupid engines.

Nope, it was the way he crossed the room like he owned it,

his slight limp only adding to the mystique. A confident, charismatic smile graced his mouth, his bright, expressive eyes revealing a hint of mischief and a warmth that seemed to draw people to him like flies to honey as they stopped him to talk.

Good thing I was immune to his charm.

To prove it to myself, I turned away and protectively eyed Rosalind's auction item. Crap, people were milling around. It was getting more crowded, which increased my anxiety by a factor of a trillion. I wasn't sure if I could stomach placing yet another ridiculous bid when someone came up behind me, an overgrown someone who leaned into me and murmured against my ear in a low, husky voice: "Whatcha bidding on?"

I stilled, closing my eyes for a single beat, telling myself that he didn't smell delicious, that I couldn't feel the heat of him through my ridiculously fancy—thrifted—dress that didn't have nearly enough material to keep me warm. He didn't touch me, but I felt him everywhere, his presence overwhelming. His scent surrounded me, something woodsy and dark, with a touch of citrus. Heaven. Hell.

"Nice," he murmured, reading over my shoulder. "Sounds like quite a trip for you and a special plus-one—"

"Yes, so go away." His jaw was so close to mine, a strand of my hair caught on the sexy stubble of his jaw. I turned to face him. A huge mistake, because no one should ever look as effortlessly sexy as he did, and do not get me started on those eyes flashing a promise of trouble—the very best kind of trouble. "Far, far away."

Those hazel orbs took a tour down my body, then made a slow return trip. "You look…"

I squirmed.

"Beautiful." His breath seemed to catch, making his words all the more genuine. "Absolutely beautiful."

His voice went through me, breaking down my hard-built defenses and leaving me momentarily unable to speak. Only momentarily. "Do you still say that to anyone with breasts and legs?"

He gave a small wince. "Granted, I did in college. But you had the power back then; you just never knew it."

"What power?"

I stood between the table and Caleb's big, sexy self, stunned like a deer in the headlights as he leaned in—smelling ridiculously amazing—his mouth at my ear when he whispered, "I had a crush on you the size of the moon."

I felt myself still, then forced a laugh. "Yeah, right."

"Why do you think I kept showing up at the cafeteria where you worked? It sure as hell wasn't because the food was good. Or how I always asked you to help me out on the assignments, pretending I hadn't been paying attention, just to hear you rattle them off with such feistiness. Damn, I loved the way your eyes slayed me whenever I tried to talk to you."

"Are they slaying you now?"

He grinned. "Yep, you still got it. Everyone used to just try and stay out of your way. You remember that one group project where you—"

"We had lots of group projects," I said. "On each of which I did ninety-nine percent of the work, so you'll have to be more specific."

"Yeah." He scrubbed a hand over his jaw. "I think we've established I was a dick back then. But you always managed to knock me down a peg."

"If you're talking about that time we were forced to partner up by our TA because he knew that you needed an A and that I could get it for you—"

"You didn't show up," he said. "I had to pull an all-nighter, and then at the next day's game, I tanked, blundered, and lost us the game. Man, I took a public lashing that week."

"You think that was my fault?" I asked incredulously.

"I think you know how to pick your battles, and you picked with lethal precision."

That was…maybe true, I could admit to myself, not that I'd say it out loud. "You got the grade you needed to stay on top."

"That I did." He glanced at the auction item at my back, and a mischievous look appeared in his eyes that had me immediately wary. "What?"

"I think I should bid on *this* item."

"No!" And damn it, in the past sixty seconds, everyone in the entire ballroom seemed to have made a beeline for the auction items, crowding the aisles, nudging him even closer to me.

In the few seconds I'd grappled to hold my ground, two more bids had been written down.

"Are they glitching?" I whispered to myself.

"Just rich." Caleb lifted a shoulder. "Plus, it's all for a good cause. Every penny will go to the Children's Literacy Initiative."

"Seriously," I said, grabbing the pen from his hand. "Shoo!" All too aware that when it came to my job, I was in the fight of my life, and no one was going to stand in my way, *especially* Caleb Colburn.

The ballroom lights flickered on and off three times, and someone from the stage asked everyone to take their seats. Without another word, I quickly placed one last bid and crossed my fingers that no one else would come along and outbid Rosalind. As I walked away, I pulled my seat ticket from my clutch. The tables each sat twelve. Mine was half-full already. The seat on my left was taken by a man who looked to be in his nineties.

He flashed me a smile and a wink. "You just made my night's wish come true." He patted my chair. "Sit, chickie. I'm Marty Alson."

Even though I knew he was full of it, I smiled at him. A few minutes later, we were discussing the pros and cons of bacon as an ice cream topper when someone sat on my other side. With a ready smile, I turned to talk to Rosalind and froze.

Not Rosalind.

"Guess who," Caleb said, reaching for the pitcher of water, then filling my glass before his.

"No." I snatched the glass out of his hand before he could take a sip. "This isn't your seat."

"It is." He flashed his ticket.

I stared at it in confusion. "No, it was supposed to be the CEO of my company."

"Rosalind Hall? She asked me to switch with her; she wanted to wine and dine someone at my table. As you know, she's a client of ours, so I agreed." He flashed a smile. "I had no idea it would work in my favor."

I glared at him. I had an ongoing mental pros and cons list for this job. The pros were clear, but the cons were really lining up, and every single of one of them was a callback to Caleb. "Go tell her you need to switch back."

He looked across the room to where Rosalind sat, talking animatedly to the woman next to her. "You think she'll be happy about that? 'Cause I don't."

I sagged back in my seat, wishing I'd opted for alcohol

instead of water. "You don't understand. It took me forever to get this temp job, and I need it to turn permanent—which I can't do unless I'm somehow impressive."

His gaze never left mine, the gold in his eyes seeming to glow. "You're already impressive."

I absolutely was *not* going to acknowledge the little tremor low in my belly.

"Hey, stud," Marty said from her other side. "Get your own chickie. I saw this one first. Plus, I'm pretty sure I saw the Legend of Star Falls last month. My nurse said it was just my astigmatism, but I know what I saw. I've been waiting for my soulmate to show up, and she just did, so scram."

"This is Mr. Alson," I told Caleb.

Caleb held out a hand.

Mr. Alson leaned in to shake it but said, "She's still mine."

"Actually, I belong to myself," I said.

"She belongs to herself," Caleb repeated with a firm smile.

"Fine. I gotta go drain the lizard anyway, and with my prostate the size of a postage stamp, it'll take me a while." The old man got to his feet with a groan and pointed at us. "If the food comes and any of mine's gone, I'll know."

After he was gone, Caleb said, "I'm tempted to eat everything on his plate just to see what he'd do."

No, he couldn't cute his way out of this. Was he annoying and untrustworthy? Yes. Was he also clever and gorgeous and viciously funny? Unfortunately, also yes.

And that smile. That damn smile. "Do you have any idea how hard it was to *one*, get invited to represent my company tonight, and then *two*, maneuver the seating arrangements to sit next to Rosalind? And you ruined it in under sixty seconds."

His brows vanished into his casually tousled wavy hair. "Are you, play-it-by-the-book Emma Sumner, admitting you *cheated*?"

"Shh!" My face heated as I looked around. "People will hear."

"First," he cooed in my ear, "they're already looking, because we make a seriously hot couple. And second…no one can hear us."

"Because you're whispering in my ear like we're…"

"Lovers?" He nipped at my earlobe, and I nearly moaned. I certainly shuddered, and a deep sound of satisfaction rumbled from his throat.

Dear God, he was potent.

He pulled back and took in my blush with a rough chuckle. "Who cares what anyone thinks?"

The people pleaser I'd always been wanted to kick him. Instead, I said, "This is all your fault. *You* make me stupid."

He fully turned to face me now, blasting me with a shocking amount of sexiness between that tux, the stubble, the dark ink just barely peeking out from his shirt collar… And don't get me started on the bad-boy thing that had him leaking testosterone and pheromones. He was kryptonite. Sexy kryptonite.

"This isn't funny," I muttered as the food arrived and plates were set before us. Glistening roast chicken, golden-brown potatoes, and a stack of my least favorite food on the planet: steamed green beans.

He studied me intently, and his amusement faded. "You really think you need to sit next to Hall to be in a good position at work?"

"Yes! The competition's fierce, and I'm only temporary." Temp job, temp living situation, temp every damn thing. Hell, my entire life was temporary thanks to a series of unfortunate events, and I was over it. Between college debt and the fire that had claimed everything I owned, this job would be a new start. All I needed were a few weeks of steady paychecks to save up for first and last month's rent and a security deposit. Okay, maybe a month, tops. The thought consumed me; I couldn't wait.

"At our meeting earlier this week, you were incredible." Caleb said this so casually, it took me a moment to process. "You were knowledgeable, asked the right questions, and called me out not once but twice when I tried to get you to agree to something that would have made things easier for us, but weren't exactly as Henderson wanted. You knew your stuff and stood your ground. You've got to be valuable to them."

I rolled my eyes. "Please. I know Ruth's reputation. I bet she's way harder on you."

"She's inflexible, even when she's wrong. Once she's made up her mind, you can't reason with her. You going to eat those potatoes?"

I blocked his already-reaching fork with mine. "Yes, but you can have my green beans. And you meant you can't always get your way."

"Well, yeah." He stabbed his fork on a green bean from my plate and ate it. "Remember how gross the green beans always were in our cafeteria?"

At my involuntary grimace, he nodded. "I swear, I think they made them disgustingly soggy and mushy on purpose. Me and the guys used to chuck them at the ceiling. They'd stick for a bit and then fall on people's heads."

"Mature." I paused. "They weren't that bad if you added a bunch of salt."

"These are perfect," he said, stuffing mine into his mouth. "No salt necessary."

I managed not to shudder. After those lean years, I'd promised myself I'd never have to eat green beans again. "Tell me more about Ruth."

He shrugged. "Sometimes we don't know a design is flawed until the build, and in those situations, the architect needs to be able to adapt. Ruth is good, great even, but unbending. You aren't. You were willing to hear me out and compromise."

I opened my mouth in surprise, but before I could speak, someone showed up onstage, thanking everyone for being here tonight, and especially for bidding. Then he invited up the key speaker. "Tonight, we're lucky to have our own homegrown hero in the house. Please join me in welcoming Caleb Colburn!"

Caleb rose and, catching my shock and surprise, winked at me as he strode to the stage. I was still gaping, stunned, when he stepped up to the microphone and said something that made everyone laugh, but I'd missed it in my stupor.

I craned my head right and left, taking in the large ballroom filled with *hundreds* of people. And Caleb stood in front of them with confidence, like it was no big deal. Talking, conversationally, not seeming bothered in the slightest that everyone's attention was on him.

I'd have died.

"All of us at Colburn Restorations are proud to be a part of this project," he was saying in that sexy gravelly voice. "It's a first for us, and we won't let you down." He smiled, and I realized I smiled back. He had a way of making a person feel like he was talking directly to them, and I was willing to bet that just about everyone in the room felt the same.

"Ryder and I have shared a lot of firsts," he said. "In fact, we shared our very first enemy the day Tucker was born."

Laughter filled the massive room.

He grinned. "Yeah, we took one look at that scrawny, squalling baby and had two questions: What the hell is that thing, and what do we do with it?" He leaned into the crowd, like he was imparting a state secret. "Don't tell anyone, but we used to dangle him down the laundry chute by his feet to see how long he'd last." Once again, the room erupted, and Caleb laughed low in his throat, like he was talking to a small group of friends. "I'm pretty fond of those memories. Oh, and disclaimer: Tucker's fine. No scars. Or at least…" He grinned again. "No physical scars. But if there are any therapists in the room, you might want to check in on him next time you see him."

He then smoothly launched into how Colburn Restorations planned to raise money for the local charities, saying that they were thrilled to have this be their tenth year of doing so, and when he finished talking and walked away from the podium, everyone jumped to their feet, clapping.

Damn. He was amazing, and…I resented the hell out of him for being better than I was at…everything.

Music came on, and a whole bunch of people made their way to the dance floor. Out of the corner of my eye, I caught movement. Caleb was moving through the crowd toward our table. He kept getting stopped, and he gave each person a moment of his time, smiling, even laughing at whatever was said. It tugged at something in me, the way he moved so effortlessly in any circumstance. He could make *anyone* feel comfortable in his presence, could bring a smile to a perfect stranger's face. Even the very air seemed to just be waiting for him to inhale.

Finally, he folded his massive frame into the chair next to me, letting out a barely audible pained breath that told me maybe his leg was bothering him more than he wanted anyone to know.

"I didn't know you had your master's," I heard myself say. The MC had mentioned it while introducing Caleb.

"I went straight to grad school after we graduated." His mouth twisted to one side. "Instead of going pro."

Because of his hockey injury. Was that the reason he limped, all these years later? "I'm sorry about what happened to you."

He shrugged. "It changed the course of my life." He paused. "And you? What did you do after graduation?"

I stared at him. Did he really not realize? All these years I'd managed to hold a grudge against him, and he didn't even know what losing that scholarship and summer internship—to him—had cost me. *Still* costs me. "I took a job at a small firm in Santa Rosa," I said vaguely, not explaining that it had been little more than grunt work, but I'd slowly—painfully slowly—been making my way to actual design, because if he looked at me with the slightest bit of pity, I'd have to dump his drink in his lap.

"Nice," he said quietly, simply. "Congrats."

"You can congratulate me if I get hired on permanently."

He smiled with empathy as Marty returned and held out his hand to me. "Let's do this, chickie."

Did I want to dance? No. Did I want to keep sitting here talking to Caleb and forgetting that he'd ruined my life? Also no. So I rose to my feet. Bonus: Rosalind was out on the dance floor. Maybe I could catch her gaze and exchange a smile. I'd read somewhere that a person had to lay their eyes on something seven times before they bought it. Maybe the theory would apply here.

Luckily, the song wasn't a slow one, but Marty pulled me

into him anyway with a gallantry that had me playing along. He stepped on my toes five times, and I was sliding his hand off my ass for the second time when someone said, "May I cut in?"

"Sure," Marty said, pulling back. "She's not exactly a live wire."

"Hey!" I said, but Marty had walked away.

Caleb smiled. "You're welcome."

"I didn't need saving."

"I know. I was talking to your toes."

I rolled my eyes as a new song came on, a slow one. Caleb cocked his head in question. Since Rosalind was still dancing, I nodded. He offered me a hand, large and warm, a comforting weight against mine. Pulling me into him, he slid an arm around my waist, his free hand now entwined with mine and pressed between us.

My pulse kicked, which I ignored. This was a political move. That was all. I'd be counting each and every second until the song ended. As the music swelled, as we moved with it, the scent of him, some blend of wood and spice, overcame me, and I closed my eyes against the urge to press my nose to the crook of his neck. And maybe take a nibble before working my way down—

"You good?"

I tipped my face up to his. "Yes, why?"

"You just moaned."

I narrowed my eyes, and he laughed. He was yanking my chain. "Keep it up, and I'll step on *your* toes," I promised.

He just grinned, and oh boy, had I made a tactical error. He enjoyed riling me up, and I just kept walking right into his trap. I tried to lose myself in the moment, but it didn't help that Caleb danced totally unselfconsciously, fluid, smooth, and…very, very sexy. I tried not to give myself away with a blush as I wondered if a man who danced with such ease and lack of inhibition might bring that same uninhibited magic to the bedroom. I opened my eyes, my heart pounding in my chest.

He was watching me.

I lifted my chin.

A barely there smile curved his lips. "You're trying to hate dancing with me."

"Well, you *are* terrible at it, so…"

He grinned, the arrogant bastard.

"Don't worry," I said. "I don't think anyone's noticed how bad it is. I mean, it's pretty embarrassing, so—"

He tipped his head back and let out a laugh that rumbled in his chest, the sound as warm and inviting as a crackling fire. "I knew something good would come from being forced to be here tonight," he said.

"Forced?"

"Ryder was supposed to do this, but he decided he'd rather stay home and do unspeakable things to Penny, the love of his life."

"You sound a little envious."

He shrugged, neither denial nor confirmation.

I was an only child, so sibling dynamics had always fascinated me. "Is it hard working for your brother?"

He never missed a beat as he guided us around the dance floor, holding me close, his body warming mine. "Working with family is kinda like Thanksgiving dinner. You get your buttons pushed in ways that only people who've known you since birth can do. But Ryder's a good boss. He's talented, smart, and encourages us all to shine, so it's not like I'm slumming it."

The music slowed, and our bodies closed the gap between

us. His big palm skimmed up my bare back, giving me a shiver. Not wanting him to smirk about that, I spoke before he could. "Is this killing you? Dancing when your leg hurts?"

"It's your dress that's killing me."

He lowered his head so that his mouth was once again near my ear when he laughed softly. "Damn, Emma. You smell so fucking good…"

I ignored my second full-body shiver *and* the butterflies taking flight in my belly.

"And I *really* like the way you move," he murmured.

I bit my tongue before I could admit I liked the way he moved too. "You don't have to do this."

"Do what?"

"Pretend we're friends."

His smile was wry. "You haven't changed, you know. Still like to hand me my balls."

"And you still like to show off. Your speech had them eating out of the palm of your hand. You're comfortable in front of a crowd."

"Playing hockey in front of ten thousand-plus people beats the shy out of you."

"I bet." The song ended, and the lights came up. I blinked like I was coming out of hibernation as I watched Rosalind walk off the dance floor. Chance lost.

Caleb held me for an extra few beats, our bodies swaying gently. I felt like I was in a trance until he sent me one of those charming but oh-so-smug smiles. "Go ahead," he said. "You know you want to."

"Want to what?"

"Grill me about Rosalind."

Ugh. But he was right. I took his hand and led him off the floor to a quiet corner, adding a light push that might have been more of a shove.

He laughed, going willingly until his back was to the wall, but he held on to me, so I ended up making a Caleb sandwich, pinning him between the wall and my body.

"If this is how you grill someone, please continue."

I pointed at him and backed up a step. "Stop playing with me and talk."

"You sound all stern, like Ryder."

"I mean it," I said.

"Oh, I know. He always does too. He forgets that his irritation amuses me."

I stared up at his tall-ass self. "How did you survive without him wanting to kill you on a daily basis?"

He flashed a smile. "I'm quick on my feet."

I drew a purposeful deep breath. "Rosalind."

"Right. I told her that you were going to be the best thing that ever happened to her firm, though your need to be bossy and right all the time was going to be a problem. But possibly, with some psychiatric help, you'd be fine… Oh, and I told her how you cheat when you're on a mission."

I waited for him to laugh. He didn't. "Ohmigod. *Please* tell me you're joking."

"Maybe…though I did say the first part, about you being the best thing to happen to her firm."

His eyes sucked me right in. "I hate that I can't tell if you're being serious. What did she say?"

"Eh." He shrugged. "You know Rosalind."

"I don't! Which was the whole point of attempting to sit next to her!" I drew a breath, which only brushed my chest to his. "Do me a favor and please never mention me again. To anyone. Ever." I turned to walk away, but he caught my hand, then slowly reeled me in.

And then he reversed our positions so that I was the new sandwich. Distracting, since Caleb's body was nearly as hard as the wall, but much warmer. Real. Alive… I felt my body soften and decided it was because it had been too long since I'd been touched.

"Rosalind can be single-minded," he said, eyes on mine, voice low, as if maybe he were also surprised what the physical closeness had made him feel. "But she's shrewd and calculating as hell. She won't get rid of someone who'd benefit the company."

I nodded, then slid out from between him and the wall and walked away, hoping that was all true because suddenly the room felt too crowded, too warm, and I was exhausted. I kept moving, heading out the front of the ballroom and the hotel entrance, right into the blissfully chilly summer night.

Overhead, dark clouds churned, brewing up a summer storm. My nerves jangled. I didn't like storms, hadn't since childhood for a very good reason—but the fear had turned into a full-blown paranoia after the storm-caused fire that had taken out the apartment building where I'd been subleasing a room.

A gust of wind had me shivering, and I quickened my steps to my car, before sliding gratefully behind the wheel. But when I turned the key, nothing happened, just a *click click*. "You've *got* to be kidding me." I blew out a breath, knowing what it meant.

It meant I was screwed.

I got out of the car, sucked in some air against the wind that had goose bumps covering my every inch, and raised the hood to stare into the engine compartment. Like I knew what I was looking for.

Footsteps in the distance had me whirling. The only self-defense move I had was a knee to the balls, but the dark outline of the man coming my way was much bigger and badder and muscular than I was.

He passed under one of the lights, revealing a well-fitted tux, pristine white shirt now open at the collar, then his face, and I blew out a breath of relief. "I nearly unmanned you."

Caleb smiled at the thought, body language relaxed, hands in his pockets, like he was trying to look harmless.

As if.

"Problem?" he asked.

"Nope."

He tilted his head. "Sounds like a dead battery."

I let my shoulders sag. "Fine. I've got a dead battery."

"Roadside service?"

"Nope."

He shrugged and turned to walk away. I stared after him in utter shock. About ten cars from me, he beeped a truck unlocked, climbed in, and…drove off. I was still standing there in complete disbelief when the blast of a horn had me turning around.

Caleb had pulled his truck into the empty spot in the next aisle, nose to nose with my car. He ambled out of his truck, munching on an apple like he hadn't just eaten his share of a four-course meal, along with a good portion of mine.

He popped open his hood, then put the apple in his mouth so he could hook up cables from his battery to mine. Still bent over my engine compartment, his tuxedo pants stretched taut over his unfairly amazing butt, he said around the apple, "When you're done staring at my ass, start the car. Take your time."

Ugh. I slid behind the wheel and turned the key.

And my car started.

Caleb disconnected the cables, shut my hood, and gave me another chin nod through the windshield that I assumed meant I was good to go.

I hadn't shut my car door, so I leaned out. "Thank you." And I really, really meant it. I'd been dreading dipping into my apartment fund to buy a new battery.

"Don't lose me," he said.

I blinked. "What?"

"I'm following you home."

My blood pressure spiked. "No, you most definitely are not."

"It's late. I want to make sure you get there safely."

"*No.*"

He assessed me through my windshield like he was trying to figure out my problem. It was no secret—my problem was him.

"You sure?" he asked with absolutely zero of his usual smugness.

Feeling vulnerable, I nearly caved and told him the truth right then and there, but I'd locked this secret away for too long to let it out needlessly. "Very sure."

He lifted his hands. "Okay. Don't stop anywhere on your way home, and keep the car running for at least fifteen minutes so it can charge."

"Thank you."

He saluted me, and I drove away quickly on the off chance he planned to follow me regardless. Seemed like something the overprotective alpha might do. I repeatedly checked my rearview mirror, but if he was following me, I couldn't catch him at it.

I was stopped at a red light when my phone pinged. I pulled it from my clutch and stared at the unknown number, my stupid and suddenly perky nipples telling me exactly who it was.

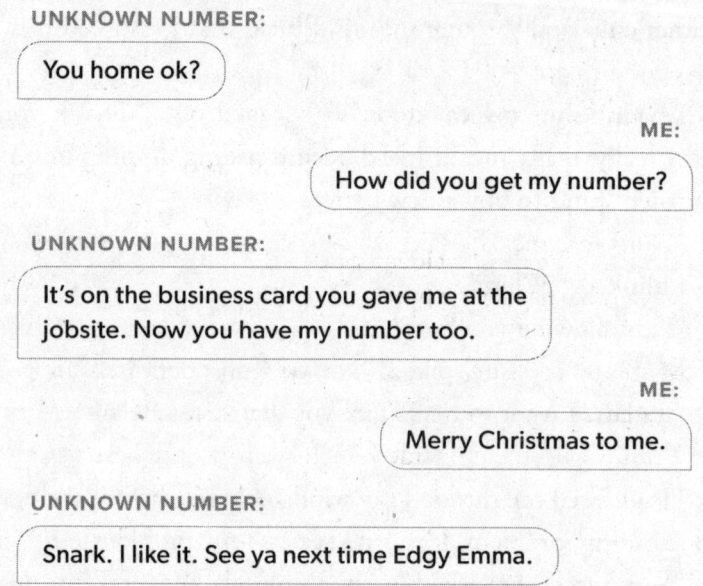

UNKNOWN NUMBER:

You home ok?

ME:

How did you get my number?

UNKNOWN NUMBER:

It's on the business card you gave me at the jobsite. Now you have my number too.

ME:

Merry Christmas to me.

UNKNOWN NUMBER:

Snark. I like it. See ya next time Edgy Emma.

Against my better judgment, I added his number to my contacts, then stared at his name for a long beat, which did something weird and annoying to my pulse. So I changed **Caleb Colburn** to **DON'T EVEN.**

Much better. And when he texted again, which I didn't look at until the next red light, the contact name made me laugh out loud.

DON'T EVEN:

You busy next Friday night?

ME:

Yes.

DON'T EVEN:

Saturday night?

ME:

You're a bad idea.

DON'T EVEN:

Bad ideas are the best ideas. So is leaving the past in the past.

I stared at my screen. What did that mean? I shoved my phone in my purse and decided no answer was the best answer.

CHAPTER 5

Emma

IT WAS PAST MIDNIGHT when I pulled up to the local campground for the night.

I was so late, they'd given my reservation away.

Beating back the panic, I drove the ten minutes to Star Falls's best park. Nestled among towering redwoods, the public space was usually a haven of peace, but tonight, with the winds and creepy sky, it felt too ominous, and I hesitated to park. First thing in the morning, I'd go to the campground before work, reserve a spot, and get a shower.

Exhausted to the bone from surviving my week, I just wanted to sleep, but I took a second, more careful look around, something I'd learned the hard way always to do, no matter what. All I could hear was the wail of the wind through the trees, but I knew enough to follow my instincts. And sure enough, upon a closer look, there, in the far corner…

A cop car sat in my usual spot.

His interior light was on, and I could see him working on a tablet. Probably on a break, but I certainly couldn't stay.

Overnight parking was prohibited. I pulled back onto the road and kept driving, sighing as thick, fat raindrops began plunking onto the roof of the car.

Then harder.

Even as I took this in, it turned to hail, which pelted me, feeling like a thousand tiny ice cubes by a disgruntled sky god. I knew I couldn't just keep driving around all night, wasting gasoline. I needed sleep, needed to be clearheaded for work, which was providing the only thing going to save my ass—paychecks.

I inhaled sharply as anxiety filled my chest. "Just one moment at a time," I whispered to myself. All I had to do right this very second was avoid freezing to death. I pictured a warm campfire. And hot cocoa. And a set of strong, warm, tatted arms coming around me—

Damn it, nope, not going there. Shivering, I stared out into the night, cringing as the hail came down so loudly, I couldn't hear myself think. Pulling over—not turning off the engine—I grabbed my phone to call Suzie. She'd wanted me to stay with her for this first month while I saved up for an apartment, but her house was tiny, her relationship was still new and shiny, and she was hugely pregnant, plus had full custody of her preteen from a previous relationship. So, for the first time in our lives, I'd lied to her. I'd told her I was staying with my aunt back in Santa Rosa—which was just far enough that she wouldn't have the time to stop by unannounced and learn I wasn't there at all.

Or that my aunt had retired and moved to Florida several years ago.

I knew when Suzie found out, she'd be furious, but that was Future Emma's problem. Yet tonight...just tonight, maybe I could borrow her couch. I looked at my phone and realized with a smile that I had a text from her, time-stamped three hours ago.

RIDE OR DIE:

> The flu's hit this house. So much puke and poop, I need an exorcism up in here...

Okay, so now I had a choice: freeze to death, or die by flu. I racked my brain for another option.

The Henderson job. The *empty* Henderson job. The one that didn't have surveillance cameras because Henderson and Hall had privacy concerns, and with good reason—they'd been sued last year when one of their clients had balked at the invasion of privacy after their teenage daughter had gotten caught on film having sex in their garage.

I knew that oftentimes crews worked weekends, which means workers could arrive on-site first thing in the morning, but in the next six hours or so, I could have a hot shower and a big, safe driveway where I could park and sleep in my car.

Indecision bounced around in my gut as I continued to shiver. If I got caught, the consequences would be severe, I knew this. But it was just one night. Who would know? I would slip in just to get ready for bed, then slip out again, leaving everything exactly as I found it.

Before I could talk myself out of it, I drove out to the site and stared at the dark manor for a few minutes.

The good news? There were no other cars in the massive circular driveway and no lights anywhere. The bad? I had access to a key—but that key sat safely inside the Henderson and Hall offices. So I had no way in, except...

When Caleb had given me a tour of the place, I'd noticed a window in the kitchen back door that had been boarded up with cardboard, awaiting replacement. A window that a smallish adult could hopefully squeeze through. I grabbed my backpack—currently holding my most valuable worldly belongings, with the exception of the dainty gold necklace with tiny twin sapphire stones that had been my mom's and now lived around my neck. The stones symbolized her and me, she'd once told me, and all I ever had to do if I missed her was touch the stone that represented her.

I'd rubbed my fingers over that sapphire so often, I was surprised I hadn't worn it down to dust.

Bracing myself, I stepped out into the night, thankful to find it merely lightly raining now. On the back patio, beneath the roof's eaves, I stopped to catch my breath and to bolster my courage.

I used the flashlight app on my phone and nearly wept in relief when I saw the cardboard still covering the back-door window. Problem number one: Would I fit? And problem number two: Was I strong enough to hoist myself through it?

I carefully pulled off the cardboard and leaned it up against the door where I'd be able to reach back for it once inside. Then I removed my backpack and shoved it through the opening.

And then it was my turn. Sucking in a breath, I tried to jump up and into the opening. It took three tries to get myself braced high enough, and I quickly shoved my head and shoulders in.

With the window's edge cutting into my palms, I threw my weight in and unceremoniously tumbled headfirst to the cold, hard subfloor in the kitchen.

But hey, I was inside!

Pushing myself upright, I took stock. Still breathing, so that was good. I reached outside, replaced the cardboard window covering, then grabbed my stuff and tiptoed through the very dark manor, trying to ignore the nerves attacking my stomach. I didn't dare try to find a light. Using just my flashlight app, I climbed the stairs. On the second-floor landing, I froze midstep, one foot still in the air.

Had I heard something? An axe murderer?

Nope. Just my own breathing. Getting a hold of myself, I took the next flight of stairs, climbed the ladder, and entered what I considered the safest room in the place: the attic.

My light flickered over the space, and some of my nerves faded. My shivering did not. I quickly changed into sweats that doubled as pj's and eyed the bed.

I couldn't. Wouldn't. Sleeping inside was a line I wouldn't cross, so I packed everything back into my backpack and took one last look around the room. I'd spent so many years loving architecture and its history that I didn't see the dust and decay. I saw a love story to a previous time and place. I saw a room that had once been a home, a warm, happy one. I could almost feel the memories. I let them seep into me. "Thank you," I whispered, then made my way back out into the cold night and into my car.

I'd just closed my eyes and was taking in the gentle patter of the rain on my car's roof when my phone pinged.

DON'T EVEN:

Tell me you're home safe and sound.

ME:

Safe and sound.

DON'T EVEN:

Still wearing that killer dress?

ME:

Is this a booty call?

DON'T EVEN:

Well, it's a text not a call, so...

ME:

I'm shutting off my phone now.

DON'T EVEN:

Wait. Just wanted to apologize for messing up the seating for you.

ME:

It's okay. Like you said, I cheated.

DON'T EVEN:

For what it's worth, Rosalind caught up to me just as I was leaving, looking for you. She won her auction item and wanted to thank you.

Rosalind had wanted to thank me. And if that weren't crazy enough, the guy I wanted to hate had really had my back tonight, more than once. I hadn't expected either of those things. I picked up my phone again.

ME:

Night, Colburn.

DON'T EVEN:

Night, Enigmatic Emma.

Closing my eyes again, I realized that my frown had finally turned upside down.

CHAPTER 6

Caleb

"CHECK THIS OUT." HAZEL shoulderchecked me, sliding over her phone.

She had Star Falls's Instagram account up, loaded with pictures from last night's gala. "Shit." I tried to hand the phone back, but she wouldn't take it.

"*Look*," she demanded. She was a bossy little thing, probably thanks to growing up with boys. With her slight frame and golden-red hair—and the temperament to go with it—she'd had to work her ass off to prove herself more than just a pretty face. Given her gruff attitude ever since she'd been back, she still believed she had to. But she'd long ago proved herself to me.

Tired of waiting on me, she leaned in and scrolled for me.

I took in the pics with a groan and lowered my head, banging my forehead to my kitchen table a few times.

"Trying to give yourself a migraine?" Hazel asked mildly from across the table, sipping the cup of coffee I'd made her.

It was dawn, and I wanted to still be in bed, especially since

I hadn't been able to fall asleep until a few hours ago. Fantasizing about a woman I'd once wanted to strangle was a mindfuck. "Why are there pictures?"

Hazel looked at me as if I were a very dim bulb. "A hot local celebrity in a tux at a fancy philanthropic gala giving the keynote and making three hundred and fifty people laugh and fork out tens of thousands of dollars for charity? Of course there are pictures."

The two of us had a standing weekly breakfast, which we'd started when she'd come back to Star Falls earlier in the year. We usually had it at my house, because of the two of us, I was the one who made the better coffee and enjoyed cooking breakfast.

Hazel leaned back in her chair and eyed my kitchen. "Love this little place," she said quietly. "It suits you."

I'd bought the house last year, a small but proud beacon of rustic charm, nestled between a bunch of vineyards and ranches. Its gray-and-white exterior that had been softened by time and the elements was contrasted by the vibrant green rolling hills that stretched out in every direction. The wide wraparound porch, where I sometimes sat with a beer in hand after a long day, ran the length of the house. And just beside it sat a weathered windmill, left over from a long-ago owner before he'd sold off the bulk of his land. It stood guard over the house, blades slowly turning in the breeze.

It was my first real home of my own, and I loved it ridiculously. But because it was still dark oh thirty, I couldn't stop yawning. Calvin and Klein, lying at our feet, yawned too, Klein adding a dramatic yowl at the end just to make sure we all knew he was there, under the table, waiting for scraps.

"Stop, all of you." Hazel fought a yawn and lost. "It's contagious."

"I'm exhausted."

"Oh, is dancing all night hard then?"

"I didn't dance all night."

After snatching her phone back, she swiped through the pics, before stopping on one of me on the dance floor.

With Emma.

"Aw, look at you, smitten as a kitten," she teased.

Smitten. That was one way of putting it. Somehow, the more Emma Sumner aggravated me, the more attracted I got.

I'd clearly lost my mind.

"Who is she?" Hazel asked.

"Emma Sumner. Went to college with her. She's the architect liaison for the Henderson project."

"Small world."

I lifted a shoulder.

"You going to fall in love and walk into walls the way Ry does now every time Penny looks his way?"

I choked on my coffee.

Hazel cackled and slid to sit on the floor to hug my ridiculous dogs, who both tried to crawl into her lap. "I'm going to enjoy watching you fall on your face with this Emma."

I shook my head. "You're mean in the mornings."

She shrugged unapologetically. "My coffee hasn't hit yet."

"You ever going to tell me why you're back?"

"You know why. My dad had a heart attack," she said.

"A very minor one, months and months ago, and he's good now." I nudged her. "Admit it—you missed us. That's why you're sticking around."

The tomboy rolled her eyes, then concentrated on stroking my dogs into two puddles of melted pleasure. "I'm…working on some issues," she said softly. She lifted her head to look at me. "You could, too, you know. Work on your issues."

"I don't have any issues."

She laughed. And okay, so did I. Then she nudged my dogs off her lap and went to the counter to add another two heaping spoonfuls of sugar to her coffee. "Okay," she said. "Maybe I'm not all the way ready to deal with my issues."

"You okay?"

"Sure." She shrugged. "Just, you know, living the life."

"Haze."

There was an awkward silence that had never existed between us before. "I'm sorry we didn't hire you for the Henderson job," I said.

She shrugged again. "It's fine. I get it. I burned a lot of bridges with the way I left."

"Not with me, you didn't. You're family, no matter how much time goes by without a word."

She winced, and I quickly said, "I didn't mean that as a diss—"

"I know, and you're family to me too. And I get why you didn't hire me. No hard feelings."

"It wasn't about you. It was—"

"Ry's promise to my mom. My and my dad's inability to get along. I get it." She shrugged. "I'd probably have done the same thing."

"If it were up to me—"

She turned to face me, gratitude in her eyes. "I know. I also heard that you guys hired Ricky Herman yesterday to do the finish carpentry. But seriously? We went to school with that asshole."

"Yeah, and he's still an asshole." We'd used him before, and he was a true master of the craft, but he was also derisive and always spread his bad attitude around. "Unfortunately, we were between a rock and a hard place, and his price was right."

"Welp…" She gave me a bright smile. "Maybe next time then."

"I'll be fighting for you. Maybe you could help the cause and get along with Bill, yeah?"

She shrugged, then smiled, and it was closer to her real smile. She grabbed her purse and lifted her mug. "I'm stealing this."

"Just add it to your collection."

She laughed, because we both knew she had nearly all my mugs by now.

I walked her to the door. "Same time next week?"

"Unless a better offer comes along," she said.

I tugged on her hair like I'd been doing since we were teens, and she did as she'd been doing forever—slugged me in the arm. Since I'd been the one to teach her how to hit, I manfully sucked it up and didn't so much as wince.

Hank appeared in the kitchen doorway, thankfully not in his birthday suit, as he liked to be. I was pretty sure he did it just to wig me out. It was working. Somehow he'd gotten his pants on. His shirt was inside out, but I was still stunned. "Nice."

He seemed mighty proud of himself as he turned and smiled at Hazel.

One of the few people who knew the hell of my childhood, she didn't smile back. "Hello, Hank." She held his gaze for a long beat, then went up on tiptoes to kiss me on the cheek before leaving.

Hank gave me a *tough crowd* look, and I almost laughed. Better than getting mired down in the memories I'd buried deep. "We gotta go. Nell's got some breakfast-for-seniors thing going on at her house, and she wants you there."

Twenty minutes later, I pulled up in front of Nell's house to find her outside, chatting with Ryder and Penny, who were practically glowing like someone had cranked up the sunshine and threw glitter on them. Ry had a dopey, lovestruck grin plastered on his face, the kind you usually see only on a puppy chasing its tail. Penny was all wide-eyed and smiley. They were practically shooting heart-shaped laser beams out of their eyeballs.

Seeing Ryder truly happy for the first time in his life was worth everything. Their connection was easy, comfortable. Real. And deep, deep down, where I usually keep my sarcasm, I wanted what they had—a ride-or-die. I wanted it bad.

CHAPTER 7

Caleb

T HE NEXT DAY I made good time getting Hank and myself
up and ready for a Monday morning. I used to love driving
to work alone; it gave me a few minutes of peace before
the insanity of the workday. But being alone was a thing of the
past. Calvin and Klein lay entangled in the back seat, snoring
so hard that their jowls quivered. Snort, snort, snort…inhale.
Snort, snort, snort…inhale.

Next to me sat Hank. Humming.

Nell didn't work Monday mornings, so he was coming to
work with me for a few hours. He loved jobsites even more than
he liked being naked, so he was beaming.

I was not. I was basically bringing three toddlers to work,
none of whom could speak or follow directions to save their
lives; all of them enjoyed pretending not to hear me and touching stuff they shouldn't.

We went to the Colburn Restorations offices first, as always.
I spent several hours most mornings behind my desk, taking

work from Ryder's plate onto mine, running through various systems to fix problems and put out fires with clients, inventory, contracts, payroll…wherever I was needed.

Grif, Ry's personal admin and also keeper of the gate, met us at the door. He was always impeccably dressed. He sat at the front desk, the sweetest but fiercest bulldog you could ever meet. No one got past Grif unless he wanted them to. He handed Hank an apple—the man's favorite fruit—and me one of his famous green smoothies that were magic, because I could swear I ached less whenever I drank one. "Thank you," I said fervently.

"It's got turmeric and other healing properties in it today, so drink up. And here…" He handed me a stack of files. "Urgent stuff on top; shit that can wait on the bottom."

"'Urgent,' as in *now*?"

"Or yesterday," Grif said sweetly. "And Ricky's meeting you on the Henderson job today. FYI, he's still an asshole." Then he sashayed back to his desk.

Two hours later, my parade and I hit up the Henderson job, which was a little off the beaten path. The rural road had taken a hit from the recent barrage of summer storms. Branches were down, the asphalt guttered and slick as shit. Twenty harrowing minutes later, I pulled into the large circular drive and parked.

I opened the back passenger-side door, and the dogs leaped out. They knew the drill. Barking with joy, they ran around, sniffing every single plant as I turned to Hank, grabbing the backpack I kept for him with his iPad, a few puzzles, and snacks.

He joyfully hefted his to-go bag, the one I'd stopped for when he'd begun yelling, *Ah, ah, ah!* as we passed Al's Diner. Never mind that he'd already eaten.

A faded-green Subaru pulled up and parked behind me, and

a sense of relief hit me that it was running. I had no idea what to expect after the gala, if anything had changed. I'd told myself it hadn't, but that was a big, fat lie. I'd had her sweet, warm body in my arms, and when she'd looked into my eyes that night, I'd no longer seen the past; I'd seen things I hadn't been prepared for.

Luckily, she was on the phone, so no awkward greeting was required. Her driver's door was open, and I got a peek inside. Not that I could see much because the back seat was covered in neatly stacked duffel bags, plus what looked like a few suitcases and boxes. I started to segue closer, wondering if she was moving again, but she caught my gaze, narrowed her eyes, and...shut her door.

Okay then. Message received. I whistled for the dogs to follow me and took Hank's hand to let him up the storm-ravaged yard to the manor.

A large material delivery had been left at the bottom of the porch steps. Looked like the guys had unloaded half of it. I opened the door and gestured the cavalry in. As we walked through the staging area in the front room into the kitchen, I turned to Hank. "It's cold in here. You warm enough?"

He nodded, then smiled over my shoulder, making me turn to look.

Emma had come in behind us. Her dazzling gala dress had been replaced by black pants and a blue silky thing under a blazer, her hair piled on top of her head. Professional. Simple. I'd loved the heart-stopping dress, but I liked this look even better. Especially that glint of *try me, I dare you* attitude gleaming in her eyes.

I was ready to play. "Cute," I said. "You drove all the way out here to tell me you're free this weekend after all."

"Dream on. I'm here to take progress pics for Mr. Henderson, who's in Italy for the next few weeks."

Reasonable, but when you grew up as I had, you got good at reading people. Emma was shifting on her feet, chewing on her bottom lip, and giving me the same smirk that Calvin and Klein would after eating my phone cord. She was nervous, anxious. At seeing me again? No, that didn't make sense. She had no problem telling me exactly how she felt about me. "Everything okay?" I asked.

"Other than the fact I need caffeine more than I need my next breath."

I gestured to the far counter, where we had a coffee pot and all the supplies to go with it. "Help yourself. The roads were a mess. You have any trouble getting here?"

She hesitated oddly. "Nothing I haven't handled before." She busied herself making coffee.

Interesting. Emma Sumner had secrets. "We take progress pics too. You could always just ask me to send them to you."

"It's part of my job," she said.

"Or…you don't want to ask for help."

She put the slightest bit of sugar in her coffee, no cream. "Yeah, well, I'm not great at that."

"A lone wolf."

"Yes. And you're not."

"I've got enough nosy siblings to make the lone-wolf thing impossible. Everyone needs help sometimes; it's just part of being a team. And at the moment, we're on the same team."

She took a sip of caffeine and gave a sigh of pleasure that went straight through me, even though I had to strain to hear it.

"Listen," she said quietly. "I realize that the other night I was all glammed up and probably looked like a delicate little snowflake, but I can assure you, I am not."

The kitten had claws. I lifted my hands in surrender. "Carry on then."

"Thank you for permission to do my job."

Back to adversaries. Noted.

She took another sip of her coffee, then a deep breath. "I wanted to thank you again. For giving me a jump."

"Caffeine hit, huh?" I chuckled when she winced. "And no problem."

She opened her mouth, but from behind us came, "Ah?"

I turned to Hank, who was eyeing Emma curiously.

And vice versa.

I looked at the woman I hadn't stopped thinking about. "Hank, this is Emma, our architect liaison on this project. Emma, this is Hank." I paused. "My father." I didn't even choke on the word as usual.

Emma smiled warmly, and I was man enough to admit I was jealous as fuck since she'd never laid that smile on me, not once.

"Nice to meet you," she said.

"He's nonverbal," I said.

Hank grinned, like he was in on the joke. Only I knew that the joke was on only one person—*me*.

"Hope you both have a good day." Emma slid me a look before leaving the kitchen that said maybe she preferred I didn't have a good day.

I watched her go. She sure had no problem going toe-to-toe with me.

I gestured Hank to a chair and set up the iPad to stream his favorite show: *Jeopardy!*

"You good?"

He held up the bag from the diner. I took it from him, pulled out the breakfast bagel, and fixed the wrapping so he could eat it. He took a bite like he hadn't eaten in a week, then moaned as he chewed, everything A-okay in his world. At least one of us was good. "Stay here, okay? I'll come back every few minutes to check on you. If you need anything, tap on the table a few times."

"Ah."

"I'm serious. You stay right here." Just last week, I'd lost him in the grocery store. He decided he didn't want to go in, but neither did he want to wait in the car. So I left him on a bench in front of the store after making him promise not to move, and when I came back out, he was gone. After I tried to avoid heart failure, someone said he'd gone into the store after me. I ran back in and found him in the ice cream aisle, holding as many containers of mint chocolate chip as he could. Except for the one he'd dropped, melting all over his feet.

"Choose good," I said, then headed to the living room, only to still in surprise at the view out the slider. About twenty-five yards off the back of the house was Emma. She had a remote control in her hands, sunglasses on, legs in a steady stance, head tipped back to the sky, directing a drone. Calvin and Klein sat calmly and politely at her side like her personal security detail.

It was possibly the hottest thing I'd ever seen.

She brought the drone in for a landing with the precision of an F1 fighter pilot. When the drone landed gently without a wobble, Emma dropped to her knees to pack everything up, quickly and efficiently breaking down the equipment. A minute later, she strode inside with her backpack, my dogs trotting after her like lovesick fools.

"I see you've met Calvin and Klein," I said.

She smiled down at the dogs. "They're the sweetest little things, and so well-behaved."

I eyed the boys. Boxers are athletic, with muscular builds, strong legs, square heads. There was nothing "little" about them. Their eyes were expressive and intelligent, capable of conveying a wide range of emotions. They were playful, goofy, ridiculously mischievous, but sweet? *Maybe* if I were holding a treat. "They've got their moments. Nice drone."

"Part of the job." Her phone buzzed. Tension filled her body as she read the preview line of the latest text on her phone screen. My gaze caught on a text preview farther down on the list from a… "Who's Don't Even?"

She blushed and shoved her phone in her pocket.

I watched her for a moment, then grinned. "It's me, isn't it? You had to label me *Don't Even* so you wouldn't be tempted."

"You don't know what you're talking about."

"So that's a yes… It's okay, I get it. I'm pretty tempting."

Those green eyes narrowed. "You do know you're not nearly as hot as you think you are, right?"

"Keep telling yourself that." I gestured to the pocket where she'd put her phone. "Everything okay?"

She shrugged. "Rosalind requested a full presentation of the Henderson job from conception to where it's at now." She paused, and I saw a tangle of emotions cross her face, but couldn't decipher a single one. "I just got a text from one of my coworkers, who warned me it's basically an unspoken audition."

"For what?"

"To see if I'm up for the job if Ruth doesn't return."

The job she wanted more than anything, which I understood more than she could know. "It's better than her *not* asking."

"True. It's just…" She grimaced. "I have to present at a staff meeting, but I'm not great at public speaking." She paused. "And by 'not great,' I mean I really suck at it."

"All it takes is practice."

"Easy for you to say." She jabbed a finger into my chest. "You're one of the few who are good at it."

A compliment…but also, ouch, she had a pointy finger. "I've had to do it a lot. It gets easier every time."

"Says the guy who never runs out of smart and funny things to say."

I raised a brow. "Two compliments in a row. Note to self: *always* offer you caffeine."

She crossed her arms.

I smiled. "Okay, how many people will be listening to this presentation?"

"Everyone. All the satellite offices will Zoom in, and Henderson as well. There could be close to a hundred." She put a hand to her chest, her breath already erratic.

"Breathe."

"I am!"

"You've got this," I said. "Did you get good shit from the drone?"

She nodded.

"Let's see."

She whipped out her phone, sidling up close until my nose brushed her hair as she scrolled through the pictures. Damn, she smelled like sunshine and something else…something that made my brain short-circuit.

"These are great," I said, not surprised. "Really great."

She dropped her armor, her eyes searching mine. "Yeah?"

"Oh yeah. Some of them could be used in the Sonoma Guide—that's how professional they look. You even managed to capture the river in the background, also the cliffs and ocean as well."

Her smile was short-lived. "But when I get to the graphs and diagrams and footnotes of the actual job's progress, I'm going to put them all to sleep."

"Then don't use graphs and diagrams and footnotes."

She stared at me as if I'd suggested she try to explain quantum physics using only sock puppets. "I spent all last night making them."

"Let me see."

She looked startled. "What?"

"Make your presentation to me."

She flushed, looking horrified. "I…can't."

"Sure you can," I said. "Pretend I'm…"

Her brows shot up so far, they vanished into her hair.

I grinned. "What do you think I was about to say?"

She crossed her arms. "Nothing."

"Liar. You thought I was going to say to picture me naked."

"Well, that's what everyone says to do when they give public speaking advice!" she said defensively.

Her face was beet red now, and I laughed but let her off the hook. "I was actually going to say to pretend I'm the Cookie Monster."

She gaped at me.

"Trust me."

"Hard pass on that."

I shrugged and stood. "Good luck with your job interview." I started to walk off. I got five feet.

"Wait."

I shoved my smile deep before I pivoted back to her.

She gestured to the stack of drywall. I sat. Drawing a deep breath, she pulled out her laptop and set it up where I could see it, opening PowerPoint. "Keep in mind," she said, "I haven't edited and loaded the footage from today, but—" She broke off with a frown.

"What?"

She turned her laptop to face me; it had gone black. She tried restarting and got nothing. "No. No, no, no, this isn't happening." She was frantically going through all the tricks to force a reboot.

"How old is it?" I asked.

"Six years. I'm babying it along until I can afford a new one."

"Henderson and Hall didn't give you a work laptop?"

"I've got a desktop at the office. You don't get a laptop as a temp, so I've been using my own." She tried again and then again, muttering to herself. "I should've paid better attention in that manifestation class Suzie made me take. She manifested her computer not dying, and it hasn't."

"What did *you* manifest?"

"More snickerdoodles in my life."

I snorted, and she crossed her arms.

"When things go bad, my go-to fix is to have snickerdoodles," she said.

"And when they go well?"

"Better than anything."

"Nothing's better than sex," I said.

She rolled her eyes. "Snickerdoodles are. Plus, I have a signature-splurge cocktail that goes great with them—sparkling wine, cranberry juice, and a sprig of mint."

I laughed.

She crossed her arms. "I suppose your go-to is something ridiculously manly, like beer."

"Or whiskey. I'm easy to please."

"Shocker."

I ignored this. "Are you backed up to the cloud?" When she nodded, I pushed my laptop toward her. "Use mine."

She signed in and began to rattle off everything she'd done so far, flipping through graphics and diagrams, just as she'd mentioned, her voice so quiet that I had to strain to hear her. Quiet and…flat.

The interesting thing was, she had a beautiful speaking voice, plus charm and charisma in spades—when she chose to use her skills.

When she finished, she looked at me. "You want to yawn, right?"

"Yes, but that's my life and nothing to do with your presentation. You just need to apply some pressure in the right spots and add some pizzazz. May I?"

When she nodded, I stood and came up behind her, reaching around her to go through the presentation again, slowly, making suggestions on how and where to show off the project—rather than spouting dry facts, pointing out the things I thought Rosalind would want to see. "What do you think?"

Emma turned her head from the screen, a move that had our mouths only a few inches apart.

She stared at mine.

I tried not to stare at hers. She was wearing lip balm; I'd seen her put it on, and it was coconut flavored. I wanted to nibble it off. "Tell them how you braved the scary dark basement and actually experienced the spirit of the place, felt the passion of the history. Tell them how it made you feel."

"Why would they care about that?"

"Because Henderson will be on that Zoom." As I spoke, my mouth almost brushed her ear, and she shivered. I stared down at her, unable to tear my eyes away. "He loves the basement, loves the history of this place."

"Damn it." She turned to face me. "I should've thought of that." She paused but didn't shift away. "You know, I never understood why you beat me on every single presentation in school. Every time. But you did it by bringing out the heart and soul of each project. So simple, and yet so few can do it."

"It's about taking info and presenting it with passion."

"Okay." She paused. "Um, how exactly do I bring the passion?"

"You pretend you're talking to the Cookie Monster and selling him on cookies, which he already loves. It makes it feel personal, gives him a stake in you."

"Applying pressure."

"Exactly," I said, trying not to notice how if she so much as took a deep breath, our bodies would be up against each other. And still, she hadn't shifted away.

"What are you doing?" she whispered.

"Helping you."

Her eyes held mine prisoner. "It's more than that. You're… you're sneakily trying to sell me on *you*."

"Am I?"

"You blew into my ear."

"It's called breathing."

"BS." She put a hand to my chest and pushed, and I obligingly stepped back.

"You're applying pressure," she accused.

I smiled. "Did it work?"

"No."

I gave her a look, and she capitulated.

"Fine." She made an *I can't believe I'm saying this* face. "I'd buy whatever you were selling. But you knew that."

I laughed. "You wouldn't. You're immune to my charm."

She muttered something that sounded like, "I wish," but I couldn't press for more information because, of course, everyone chose right then to walk in from out back. Our new master carpenter and his guys, then Ryder, then my crew of Danny, Hawk, Miguel, and even Tucker, who wanted to check over the material drop that had arrived.

Emma said that she had more footage to capture and raced out of there like hellhounds were on her heels. Playing it cool, ignoring Ryder's pointed glance, I resettled Hank out of the way, to a comfortable chair on the back patio with his iPad, deep into an episode of *Golden Girls*.

I met with Ricky and went over how I wanted him to tackle the job. Then the guys and I gathered around the blueprints to discuss today's problems. If I was their fearless leader, Danny was our den mother. He wore his hair in a man bun, had so many piercings I wasn't sure how he managed to stay afloat when he swam, and could cut through bullshit with one word. Hawk—with his namesake mohawk, dark sunglasses, and a ripped T-shirt and jeans like he was a rock star—was the group cutup, and Miguel had the best actual skills. Each of them had been handpicked by me and was sharp as fuck, reliable, and loyal, which made them worth their weight in gold.

"Who was the hot chick?" Danny asked.

I followed his line of sight through the slider to…Emma. "Emma Sumner, architect from Henderson and Hall. She's our liaison."

"Nice," Danny said with a smile. "Think she's single?"

"Ask her, and you're out on your ass."

Danny lifted his hands in surrender and backed off. Our meeting adjourned; the guys scattered. Except for Tucker. My brother slowly took in Emma, then my expression. "Interesting."

"Shut up."

His smile was smug. "You remember months ago, when you and me and Ry were sitting graveside, visiting Auggie?"

Like I could forget. Tuck and I had gone there to find Ryder alone, grieving on what would've been his best friend and business partner's thirty-second birthday. "What about it?"

"Remember seeing three falling stars arcing in unison across the sky?"

Danny, Hawk, and Miguel, who'd only gone to the other side of the room to gather what they needed from their toolboxes, gasped like three little old ladies in church. If they'd been wearing pearls, they'd be clutching them.

"No." I jabbed a finger at Tucker. "*Ryder* saw those stars. I didn't, and you didn't—we had our eyes closed."

"Liar."

Fuck. I glared at my guys, whose heads were swiveling like they were at a tennis match. "Are we paying you to stand there and gawk at our architect, who deserves a safe workspace without feeling ogled?" I asked in my boss voice.

They quickly headed to their work.

"Not to complicate things," he said. "But I know you didn't forget Ryder's decree regarding getting cozy with anyone from work."

I had a long fuse, but both my brothers had a way of cutting it down to the nub and lighting it on fire. Then blowing it up. "All I'm doing is standing here."

"Yeah, and watching her like she's lunch."

Lunch. Dinner. The rest of my life…

Tucker snorted. "You're screwed."

I mean, where was the lie…? "Shut up."

"Sure. But you should swipe that lovesick look off your face before Ry sees it."

"Sees what?" Ry asked from behind us.

Shit. The man needed a bell. I drew a deep breath and turned to face my older brother. But Ry looked to Tucker, brows raised.

I did the same.

Tucker tossed up his hands. "Don't look at me. It was you two who taught me that snitches get stitches." And he walked away.

Out the window, I watched a delivery truck arrive—hopefully with the rest of our order. Nice timing. "Gotta go."

"This isn't over," Ry said to my back.

"No shit, it's never over."

I spent some time making sure Ricky was on point, then checking on my crew, and when I was done, my eyes sought out Emma, who had her knees in the mud, her gaze locked on her screen as she took shots of the high basement window from a side flower planter.

I walked past her. Or I meant to. I really did. But she'd

removed her blazer. Her top was thin and short-sleeved, and I could have counted her goose bumps from here.

"You look cold."

Her head whipped around, flashing that sassy look I liked so much. "I'm not."

"Your lips are turning blue."

"You calling me a liar?"

I smiled. "Right to your face."

"I didn't want to get my blazer dirty."

I tugged off my hoodie and tossed it to her, giving her the choice of catching it or letting it fall.

She caught it.

"Nice save." And since Ry was hollering for me, I saluted her and walked away, but not before catching her lifting my sweatshirt to her nose and taking a deep inhalation, eyes closed.

CHAPTER 8

Emma

M Y PHONE PINGED WITH a text, and I looked up from
my office computer to see a text from Mr. Henderson.

MR. HENDERSON:

> I need pics of the decorative moldings along
> the staircases, which I don't see in the current
> file. I've got a contact here in Rome who's
> got an on-site molding restorer who's an
> expert. Also, I also need a shot of the river
> looking back at the land. Send both asap.

I texted back, reminding him that the molding was already
under contract with Colburn Restorations. This was self-serving.
One, it had been four days since I'd slept in my car at the
Henderson site, and I was still successfully avoiding Caleb, afraid
he'd take one look at me and know I'd played Goldilocks.

My fear of getting caught had nearly manifested itself that

morning. I'd just let myself out the back door when I nearly plowed over Bill from Colburn Restorations. He had a bag from Al's Diner with a delicious scent coming from it that I knew was Al's famous breakfast sandwich.

"Thought *I* was early," he said, head cocked, noting my backpack.

"Early bird gets the worm," I quipped. *Early bird gets the worm?* What, was I, ninety? But sheer panic had taken up all my brain's bandwidth. I flashed what I hoped was a smile. "Just needed to check on some specs for Henderson before heading to the office."

To my surprise, he gave me a gentle smile in return as he took in the way I was shifting nervously on my feet. "Most people your age don't know the meaning of hard work." He opened the bag and handed me a breakfast sandwich.

"Oh no, I can't take your breakfast—"

"You may not have heard," he said, "but I had a minor heart event a few months back. I'm not supposed to be eating these. So you're saving my life by taking it off my hands."

My stomach growled, and his smile faded.

"Do you need anything else?" he asked quietly. "Anything at all?"

"Um, no, thank you." I could scarcely breathe because, somehow, he knew. "I know I should've run this by someone before just letting myself in. I'll probably get in trouble—"

"I don't know what you're talking about," he said, so softly that I got a stupid lump in my throat. "I never saw you."

I think I managed a "thank-you" before I escaped, running all the way to my car, analyzing every look he'd given me. Sweating in the chilly morning air, I drove as fast as I dared, still halfway holding my breath. I'd just turned onto the main road toward town when I caught sight of Ryder in my rearview mirror, turning onto the road that would lead him to the Henderson job.

My poor heart, still revved, kicked hard. Too many close calls. I felt like a criminal. A fact that had not kept me from inhaling the breakfast sandwich.

Now, at the offices, I realized Mr. Henderson hadn't responded to my text. His silence spoke volumes, and I resigned myself to my fate. I grabbed my bag and headed back to the jobsite.

There were several trucks in the circular drive, so I parked at the bottom and walked up the hill. I could hear work going on upstairs, but I didn't see anyone as I took the pics of the molding Henderson had requested. And if I skulked out, it was because if I had to talk to anyone, I knew my guilt would give me away.

Anyone being Caleb. Because his truck was one of the ones in the driveway.

I walked—ran—down the hill to my car and opened the door—then froze.

A new laptop, still in its box, sat on my passenger seat.

"What the…?" I nearly broke my neck craning my head left and right to see if anyone was watching, but there was only one person who'd do such an extravagant, stupid thing.

Laptop under my arm, I stalked back to the manor and through the front door, where this time I found a sea of workers standing around a makeshift table comprised of two large sawhorses and drywall, Ryder being one of them. On top of the drywall, a set of plans was spread out. Caleb—looking his usual burly self in cargos, battered boots, a Colburn Restorations long-sleeved work shirt, and the glasses that somehow magnified the green in his eyes—was talking, face determined, mouth serious as he pointed out something on the plans. It was a give-and-take between him and Ryder, the two of them strategizing on the spot.

As always, Caleb was perfectly at home being in charge, and it was…mesmerizing, watching him. I cleared my throat, and all the heads swiveled to me.

"Morning," Ryder said.

Caleb's easygoing expression didn't change, but I was pretty sure his eyes heated. "Emma."

Not taking my gaze from his, I lifted the laptop box. "Anyone know how this got in my car?"

There was a collective pause.

Ryder eyed his crew. They all shook their heads, except Caleb, who said, "Maybe Santa came early this year."

Ryder turned to look at Caleb with brows up.

Caleb just shrugged and gestured to the plans. "As I was saying about the wainscoting…"

And they all went back to work.

Right. I walked out the front door and straight to Caleb's truck, where I set the laptop on his driver's seat. Santa, my ass…

I was back in my car before I realized I'd forgotten about taking a pic from the river looking back at the property. Shit. I headed back, skirting around the manor this time instead of through.

The path was a little rocky and steep, but beautiful. The sound of the river washing over rocks lowered my blood pressure, but it wasn't the deep-blue water, or the way the coastal live oaks bent over it protectively, or even the musical symphony of the birds in those trees that caught my attention.

It was Hank, standing on the shore about fifteen feet to my

left as if enthralled, so close to the rushing water that the toes of his shoes were wet.

"Hello?" I called softly, moving toward him but not wanting to startle him into falling in and getting washed away. "Hank?"

He turned to look at me, and I put a hand to my chest. "Remember me? I'm Emma."

He smiled, but my heart was thundering with worry that a single breeze might knock him into the rushing water.

"Can I help you back to the manor?"

He offered a hand, and I pulled him up the slight incline, steadying him on the rocky path. I kept a hold of his hand as we went. "It's cold out here, and so muddy. We'll be happier inside, yeah?"

He patted my hand. I was pretty sure he was humoring me, but I didn't mind. He seemed like a perfectly sweet old man. At his pace, it took ten minutes to walk back, and as we got close to the back sliding door off the patio, I could hear Caleb talking.

"We can't reconfigure the windows the way Henderson has now decided he wants, not without going through the historical society's approval process again, which could take months."

"And a lot more money," Ryder said. "He's not going to be happy when you tell him."

"Me?"

"Or talk Emma into doing it. I don't care—just talk him out of it ASAP. This is holding us up, and he's the one harping on about keeping the schedule tight."

"'Talk Emma into doing it'?" Caleb repeated.

"Or do it yourself, *I don't care*." He clapped a hand on Caleb's shoulder. "Either way, you got this, right, Fixer?"

Bill, also huddled around the plans, said, "It's a conflict. Of course he doesn't 'got this.'"

"Too bad you're not asking him to ghost her," another of the guys said. Tucker, if I remembered right. He looked a lot like Ryder and Caleb, so maybe another brother. The guy said, "He's really good at that."

I absorbed that little kernel of knowledge about Caleb to pull out later, like when my mind wandered to the what-ifs. Like, what if he kissed like heaven? What if we gave in to the chemistry I didn't want to acknowledge? What if I made the mistake of falling for him and my greatest fear came true—someone else leaving me? I decided him being bad at conflict and a ghoster to boot was a really good thing to know about him, because it meant there were no what-ifs to worry about.

Caleb put a hand on his look-alike's face and pushed. Everyone laughed and dispersed, while I tried not to stare at Caleb, who'd placed both hands on the table, head bent in concentration, hair falling over his brow as he studied the plans. He'd shoved up the sleeves of his shirt, revealing corded forearms and a hint of ink. I had no idea why my mouth watered. Clearly, I was just hungry.

Still holding Hank's hand, I led him to the slider.

Caleb's head immediately came up, his eyes taking us in, surprise flaring there.

"Look who I ran into outside," I said lightly.

Caleb craned his neck and eyed the chair where Hank had been but was now empty. The tablet was still there, playing a show.

Muttering a soft "shit" beneath his breath, Caleb turned to me, apology and guilt in his churning eyes. "I can't believe I missed seeing him walk off." He took Hank's hand and looked him over. "You okay?"

"Ah."

"He was at the river's edge," I said quietly.

Caleb blinked and looked at his dad. "You got all the way to the river?"

Hank looked mighty proud of himself.

Caleb drew a deep breath, but if he was frustrated or pissed off, it didn't show. He got his dad resituated in the chair. "Just ten more minutes," he told him. "And then I'll take you to Nell's."

Hank didn't answer, already back into his show.

Caleb strode back to me. "Thank you," he murmured. "I owe you big."

Maybe his face was calm, cool, and collected, but I saw the distress in his gaze. Distress and something I'd never seen in him before—vulnerability.

"He's had a stroke," I said.

"Two." He ran a hand through his hair. "He's living with me right now. I've got a caretaker who helps me take care of him, and my sister helps, too, but the man's like a toddler. A sneaky, trouble-loving, determined toddler." He reached out and playfully tugged on a wayward strand of hair that had escaped my ponytail, flashed me a half smile, and walked away.

I stared after him. A week ago, I'd never have taken Caleb for the responsible type. But here he was, going to a gala to raise money for charity, running a crew on a multimillion-dollar job, caring for an elderly parent, helping distressed women in parking lots late at night, *and* handing out laptops.

Who the hell was *this* Caleb Colburn?

I walked to my car, that question bouncing around in my head, when I found the new laptop back on my driver's seat.

CHAPTER 9

Caleb

WHEN I DROVE HIM to Nell's, I was still reeling, furious with myself for letting Hank out of my sight for long enough to get to the fucking river. "No walking off from Nell today."

Hank blinked.

"Don't play innocent. You're going to stay where she can see you. No going off on your own; it's dangerous."

"Ah."

"I hope that's *Ah, of course I'll behave*, and not *Ah, I can't wait to mess up Caleb's life on purpose*."

He gave me a sweet smile that I didn't buy for a minute.

"I mean it."

"Ah."

Fucking great. Twenty minutes later I walked him into Nell's house, and after a brief one-sided argument, I set him up where he wanted to be—at Nell's kitchen table, eating cookies.

I was both impressed by his ability to get what he wanted and feeling a bit like he was yanking my chain.

I left Nell's with just enough time to go by my place for my wingmen—er, wingdogs—and get across town to Henderson and Hall's office building by the end of the day.

My backseat drivers were breathing hot doggy breath on my neck, so I rolled the windows down for them. In two seconds, they had their heads hanging out, air flowing into their jowls, spreading them out like wings.

When I drove into Henderson and Hall's lot, I parked next to the familiar beat-up green Subaru before getting out to lean against the front of my truck and wait.

"Woo, woo, woo," Klein complained sassily.

"Trust me," I said. "I can't believe I'm doing this, either, but you need to zip it."

"Woo, woo, woo."

Calvin put a paw on Klein's face and pushed him to lie down. Klein growled, then curled up and closed his eyes.

Calvin remained sitting up, vigilantly watching my back as always.

It didn't take long. Ten minutes later, Emma came out of the building in the same clothes she'd been in that morning, loose-fitting black trousers and a fitted pale blue blazer. Most would just see a beautiful woman leaving work. And I saw that, but I also zeroed in on the tension in her shoulders, her stride just a little too fast for those heels, suggesting she needed distance between herself and that building. And then there was the grim set of her mouth.

I was getting tired of feeling irritated by her. Truth was, she looked like the best thing I'd seen all day.

I knew the exact second she caught sight of me because she came to a screeching halt right in the middle of the lot, her hand lifted to shield her eyes against the early evening sun. I read her lips as she muttered, "Great." Then she gathered her wits and tilted her chin up so high, she could catch a nosebleed.

She strode the rest of the way to her car. I thought she might ignore me, but she set her bag on the hood and turned to face me.

Silent, waiting for me to speak first.

Smart tactic, which I loved. But what I loved even more was the thrill I got from her challenging me at every turn. "How did it go?" I asked, ignoring Klein, who sat up and barked a greeting for Emma. Calvin, hating to be left out, also had a "woo woo."

"My presentation?" she asked. "*That's* why you're here?" She reached out to pat Klein on his massive head. He rewarded her with a lick to the chin. Next, she stroked Calvin, who politely licked her hand, all the while never taking her eyes off me.

I shrugged. "I feel invested."

She drew a deep breath. Then she let out a smile that rocked my world, altered my brain chemistry, and made my heart thump hard.

"You killed it," I breathed, so fucking proud of her.

She laughed. "I killed it."

"Of course you did." Her laugh had caused most of her tension to drain, and I knew I was grinning widely, but damn, when she smiled like that...

She rolled her head on her shoulders, like maybe she had a neck ache. "The new laptop was invaluable." She met my gaze. "I'll pay you back—"

"Not necessary—"

"I'm *going* to pay you back."

Since she wanted to keep her pride, something I knew quite a bit about, I nodded.

"Seriously, thank you," she said quietly. "I couldn't have done it without you."

I reached behind my back, grabbing a sparkling wine in one hand and a cranberry juice and a sprig of mint in the other, the makings for her signature-splurge cocktail.

She blinked in surprise, and when she spoke, her voice was husky, like she was unbearably moved. "You didn't have to…"

I shrugged. "I was thirsty."

She snorted. "You'd rather die than drink this."

True…

Her head was cocked to the side now. "And if I'd messed it up in there?"

"You weren't going to."

"But if I had…?"

I stood and reached into my passenger-side window, pulling out a box of snickerdoodles.

Emma's mouth fell open. "You remembered—"

"They're not homemade, so don't be too impressed."

"You…*bought* me cookies."

Her disbelief bothered me. Had no one ever done anything nice for her? "It's self-serving," I assured her. "I'm starving and hoping you're sharing."

She grabbed the wine and cookies, then ordered, "Bring the dogs and follow me," as she walked off.

I opened the truck door to let out Calvin and Klein. "You heard the lady. Let's follow."

The Henderson and Hall building backed up to a park, which in turn ended on a slope that gave a heart-stopping view of the rocky bluffs lining the Pacific coast. We crossed the park, nearly losing Klein to a wayward Frisbee, but not Calvin. Calvin had his eyes on the prize: the container of cookies. Calvin was eternally hopeful.

I pulled two doggy chews from my pockets and handed one to each dog, who knew the drill: Lie down, chew on the bone, and chill.

"They're well-behaved," Emma said.

"It's cute that you think so."

She crouched and stroked each dog into nearly a pleasure coma. "Don't listen to him; you're such good boys, and so pretty."

They preened.

And I was fucking jealous of my own dogs.

"Did you bring a cocktail shaker?" she asked, sitting cross-legged on the grass right next to the dogs, slipping out of her blazer, leaving her in a silky cami. I was admiring the view as she kicked off her heels with a long-suffering sigh.

I handed over the shaker and watched as she began making her drink while wriggling her freed toes. "Other than the gala, I've only seen you in work clothes and flats," I said.

She gave me a look that said she was questioning my intelligence when she poured in her ingredients, heavy on the wine. "It was a presentation. I had to kick ass, but also *look* kick-ass."

"You succeeded in both, but how do the heels help exactly?"

"You wouldn't get it," she said, shaking up the drink.

"Why not?"

She handed me the shaker. I'd just taken a sip when she gestured toward my lower body and said, "You've got a penis."

I choked.

She crawled over to me and, on her knees at my side, began

pounding my back with one hand, snatching the shaker from my grasp with the other, and taking a long, deep drink—as she kept smacking me.

I finally managed to lift a hand for mercy, and she stopped trying to kill me.

"Was it the penis thing?" she asked.

I slid her a look.

She laughed at me. "So…whatcha think of the drink?"

I took the shaker back and tried again. It was still horrible. "Great."

"Liar. You can say it: It's a girlie drink."

"I'm not afraid to be girlie."

She let out a startled laugh so warm and genuine that I laughed, too, and that made her laugh harder as she leaned toward me, inadvertently caught her knee on the grass, and…

Spilled her drink down my front.

Sucking in a breath at the cold, I lifted my shirt up and away from my torso.

Emma gasped, eyes glued to my bared stomach. "I'm so sorry!"

"No worries."

She pawed through her bag and came up with a napkin, which she used to dab at my shirt. "I don't want it to stain," she murmured as she wielded the napkin with surgical precision and concentration.

"Emma."

"Hmm?" She still hadn't taken her gaze off my abs.

"You about done?"

"Oh!" She blushed and sat back on her heels. "Just making sure you didn't get cold."

"I'm the opposite of cold."

She groaned and closed her eyes. "I mean, you don't even play hockey anymore, so why do you still have an eight-pack?"

I shrugged. "I like to work out with Tucker at the firehouse."

"It's cruel and unfair."

My grin widened, and she exhaled.

"Look, I'm sorry I ogled you, okay? But seriously. Cruel and unfair."

"Noted." I tossed another doggy biscuit, which Calvin caught midair.

"You didn't even taste that," I chastened.

"Woo woo." Klein, lodging a complaint.

"I didn't forget you." I tossed him a biscuit.

It hit him square between the eyes.

"He's got corneal dystrophy," I said. "Makes it difficult for him to see sometimes."

"Aw." She gave Klein a hug and fussed over him, and I didn't have the heart to tell her that Klein had no idea he was disabled.

"Did you raise them from puppies?" she asked.

"No, I adopted them earlier this year. Actually, they adopted me. Found them abandoned on a jobsite, tied to a tree. I meant only to free them and find them a good home, but it turns out they wanted *my* home. Literally. In the first week, they ate two chairs, three pairs of shoes, and my kitchen table."

Emma laughed. "And yet you still kept them."

"Somehow, after spending a fortune at the vet to get them healthy, and then another fortune replacing everything they ate in my house that first week, we settled in together."

"You love them."

"Go figure." I poured us each another glass, and before I

knew it, we were on our third glass, just as the sun began its descent, casting long, dancing shadows across the rugged coastline. The sky, bright blue only twenty minutes earlier, erupted into a breathtaking canvas of fiery oranges and soft pinks, making me feel not only warm and relaxed, but also something I hadn't allowed in a long time…open.

Emma's cheeks were rosy from success and the wine, and she was smiling in a genuine, carefree way she hadn't shown me before. "You're beautiful," I murmured, the words slipping out before I even realized they were on my tongue.

She waved a hand at me. "It's the spritzer."

"No, it's not." I liked her with her hair piled on top of her head like this, silky strands escaping and falling into her eyes. I liked her with little to no makeup on. I liked her dusty and dirty from the jobsite. I liked her every which way I saw her. "It's you, Emma." Dangerous… She was so fucking dangerous, and still I found myself leaning in.

And then she was leaning toward me. Our noses bumped, and she grinned. I fisted a hand in her hair and tugged until we were better aligned. She sucked in a breath, her lips parting eagerly, her eyes slowly fluttering shut. I couldn't have resisted to save my life, and I nearly groaned in relief as I lowered my head and—

My phone buzzed. "Shit." I patted myself down, searching my pockets.

Emma giggled—*giggled*. I'd never heard such a sound from her before. "Maybe it's my phone." She searched her purse, pulled out her phone, and put it to her ear. "Hello?"

From somewhere, a phone kept buzzing.

"Hello?" she said again into her phone and then pulled it

from her ear to stare at the screen. "Huh. It's not me." She belly laughed then.

And so did I. Suddenly it was the funniest thing in the world, and we were both patting my body down, searching for the offending phone.

"I found it," she said triumphantly.

I stared down at my crotch and Emma's hand on it. "That's not my phone."

"Oh." She gave me a silly smile. "You sure?"

"I don't keep my phone in my pants."

"Sorry." She flushed an even brighter red but didn't let go of my hardening, ever-hopeful dick. She gave a little squeeze that made it even happier. "Found it!"

"Still not my phone."

Her eyes went wide as she yanked her hand back but continued to stare at my crotch.

"Not helping."

She covered her eyes. "I'm sorry."

"I'm not." I finally found my phone in my back pocket and groaned at the name on the screen: **Tucker**. "What?" I said in greeting.

"We're at the bar; you're late."

Me, my brothers, and friends met every few weeks to play darts and pool, and tonight had been the night. "I'm actually a no-show."

"You've never missed a night. Not even when you nearly sawed off your hand at the Rossi job a few years back."

"I'm about to miss one now."

There was a pause. "You getting laid?"

I glanced over at Emma, who was still flushed, now sitting

between my two dogs, an arm around each. Calvin had his head in her lap; Klein's was on her shoulder.

Fuck, that was adorable and sexy at the same time, and my chest tightened. It wasn't the first time I had the sudden urge to run far away from my feelings, but somehow I'd forgotten that I always, without fail, got here. "No," I said to Tucker. I wasn't getting laid. Had I been about to? Maybe. Was I going to? Not now that anxiety was running through my veins instead of blood. I fully blamed Tucker.

To make sure he was as miserable as me, I told him where we were and that I needed him to come get us since we'd been drinking.

Fucking sparkling wine...

Emma looked at me when I slid my phone away. "We're done here?"

I reached for her hands, looking into her eyes, willing her to understand. "It's a bad idea."

She stared at me, then nodded. "No, you're right. So...is this the part where you ghost me? Never mind, don't answer that. It was a rhetorical question." She carefully stood and dusted off her very fine ass, missing some pieces of grass that my hands itched to help with. Instead, I curled them into fists and shoved them into my pockets as I stood too.

She had her back to me now, head tipped to watch the night sky play over the ocean.

Shit. I was such an asshole. "I'm not ghosting you."

She didn't look at me. "Okay."

"Okay."

"Great," she said.

Yeah. Fucking great.

Fifteen minutes later, Tucker showed up. He got out of his truck and studied us. I couldn't be sure because my glasses were so smudged from Emma's fingers that I couldn't see shit, but I thought he was amused.

"You see the irony here, right?" Tucker asked.

I did.

"I don't," Emma said. "X'plain."

"I'm the youngest brother," Tucker said. "Historically, it's always been me who's needed the rescue."

"I didn't need a rescue," I said testily. "Just a ride. You could've sent anyone, but you're a busybody who couldn't help himself."

"That's not nice," Emma told me. "He came all the way out here to drive us home because you scared yourself and got cold feet."

Tucker choked on a laugh.

I tugged off my glasses to properly give him a dirty look.

"She's right," Tucker said, still grinning. "You're not being nice. You can stay here and bum a ride. I'll drive Emma home." He gallantly opened the passenger door for her, then shut it once she was inside.

Tucker came around and eyed me. I opened my mouth, to be an asshole no doubt, but his mouth fell open in surprise as he pointed shakily upward.

I tipped my head back and stilled. "You've gotta be fucking kiddin' me," I said to the three stars falling in a perfect arc across the dark night sky.

"Those stars are clearly talking to you," Tucker said.

"No way," I said. "I'm not seeing anyone."

"The Legend doesn't give a shit if you're seeing someone or not, but are you sure you're not?" Tucker raised a brow as he subtly jerked his head toward Emma.

"Very sure," I said, unsure of which of us I was trying to convince. I let out a breath, suddenly feeling very sober. "And in any case, I think I just accidentally friend zoned myself."

Tucker rocked back on his heels. "Accidentally, or because you always walk away when things get too close?"

"Shut up," I said, then got into the truck. It was a tight fit in the back seat with Klein and Calvin, who'd abandoned me to emotionally adopt Emma.

We dropped Emma off in front of her friend Suzie's house, since Emma said she would take her to her car later, but there'd been something off in her tone. And then there was the fact that she didn't go in the house, instead waiting for us to drive away. "We should've insisted on taking her home to make sure she's safe."

"Only if you want to be known as her stalker," Tucker said.

"I'm serious."

"Pretty sure she's fine. It's you I'm worried about."

"Why?"

Tucker slid me a look. "Because you're googling how to get out of the friend zone."

I ignored him until he pulled up to Kiera's house so I could get Hank. I started to get out, but he put a hand on my arm.

"What?"

He hesitated. Tucker never hesitated.

"Spit it out."

"You going to tell Ryder that you have a thing for her?"

Shit. I drew a deep breath and closed my eyes. What was I doing? "No. Because nothing's going to happen."

"But—"

"*Nothing's* going to happen," I repeated firmly.

Tucker stared at me for a long moment, then nodded. "That's the smart route. Except—"

"Don't. Just…don't—"

But he kept talking. Of course he fucking kept talking. "Are you not freaking out about the stars? Ry saw them, and look at him now. He's turned into a big sap. You've got to be at least a little worried."

"Not even a little." That was the truth. I wasn't a little worried.

I was *massively* worried.

CHAPTER 10

Emma

MY ALARM WENT OFF at 4:00 a.m., and I sat up, confused as to why it had gone off so early. Then my eyes focused in the predawn light, the Henderson Manor looming in the dark.

Around midnight, a fight had broken out in the campground where I'd been fast asleep. Feeling unsafe, I drove here.

I'd set my alarm for an hour earlier than usual to avoid being discovered by Bill again. I made my way inside the manor and got ready for the day. Thirty minutes later, I walked outside, trying not to stagger from exhaustion.

Less than a month now. That was what I told myself. In less than a month, I'd have enough saved up for an apartment.

I stopped short in front of my car. On the roof sat a little brown lunch bag, which held an apple and another breakfast sandwich.

Bill.

I whirled around, looking in every direction, but saw no one.

I knew I should be panicked, but maybe I was too sleep-deprived for that, because all I felt was gratitude. He knew I was here, and if he'd been planning to tell anyone, he not only would have done so by now, he certainly wouldn't be feeding me.

I managed to keep myself too busy to think about anything other than working, keeping track of the apartments up for rent in the area, and maybe also reliving the fun I'd had with Caleb— drinking, eating cookies…the handful I'd accidentally gotten off him.

I got a hot flash every time I thought about it, at least until I remembered he was a kiss avoider.

It's a bad idea.

His words rang in my head in that low, sexy voice of his, making me mad at myself all over again. How had I not seen that coming? Once a player, always a player, and I had no one to blame but myself. I just needed to, in the immortal words of Taylor Swift, shake it off.

So I had. In the past week, I'd buried myself in work. I had three jobs on top of the Henderson project, so it had been easy to keep so busy, my head swam.

It's a bad idea…

"Ugh!" I'd just started packing up to leave when Rosalind texted, asking me to come to her office. Rattled, I hustled up a flight of stairs and down a hallway, before coming to a skidding halt at her open office door.

"Is there a fire?" she asked drolly, sitting behind her desk in a power suit, lipstick perfect, makeup perfect. I bet she'd never felt the need to run to a meeting in her life. How did one get so polished, so sure of themselves, so calm? I needed lessons.

"Sit," she said.

I sat.

Rosalind cocked her head at me. "Your presentation last week was impressive, although anyone with half a brain can make a pretty speech."

Not anyone. I couldn't have, not without Caleb's help.

Rosalind's lips curved in a genuine smile. "Although...not everyone can back it up with the solid work you've been doing."

I blinked from the emotional whiplash. "Thank you."

She clasped her hands on her desk and leaned in slightly. "I think you know we've got three people in-house who want Ruth's job. The competition is fierce."

I nodded even though I hadn't known that.

"So, if I were you, I'd keep up the good work."

"I will. I'm also happy to do extra credit," I quipped.

She eyed me over the top of her glasses. "There's no extra credit."

"I know, I was trying to be funny—Never mind." I bit my tongue to shut myself up.

"I'm handing over two additional projects for you to take care of while I'm in France for the next two weeks."

She wasn't asking, so I swallowed hard and bit back any worry about being able to keep up with the jobs I was already handling. "No problem."

She nodded her approval of my response. "We are very thorough in the hiring process, and as a result, we have little turnover. People come here, and they stay."

I nodded my understanding. "My goal is to stay as well. I love it here."

"And yet you have no family, no ties, and as far as I can tell, no permanent address other than a local PO box."

I smiled past my anxiety, definitely not wanting to discuss any of that. "I'm working on it."

"Good to know." Rosalind stood. "Have a good evening."

Dismissed, I walked calmly—fake calmly—down the hall and out of the building.

Had she just sorta let me know she was rooting for me to keep a job at Henderson and Hall?

Maybe?

I drove through some traffic to the Cork and Barrel, the locals' favorite bar and grill. I was late to Suzie's girls' night—**attendance required**, that's all her earlier text had said, and far be it from me to question the hormonal pregnant chick.

The Cork and Barrel was run by a grumpy but also kinda sweet bartender named Mack, who could remember anyone's order, no matter how big or small. The place was an ode to a bygone era with dark wood-paneled walls adorned with faded sports memorabilia and vintage beer signs. Lights were low; noise was high. Eighties rock blared in tune to the sounds of pool being played, amid lots of talking and laughing. And, if you counted Mack, also some yelling. The place smelled like beer, chicken wings, and relief that the workday was over.

"Finally!" Suzie yelled from a high-top table across the bar, waving madly.

I shoved all my life worries deep and plastered a smile on my face as I headed toward her because her Worry Detector batted a thousand, and she had enough of her own. But my smile threatened to slip when I realized there were two other women with her. I'd come here straight from a very long day and felt like a mess, and…I was tired. Bone-tired. Playing Goldilocks required waiting until late to sneak into the manor to sleep and getting up before the crack of dawn so as not to get caught—washing and repeating daily. It was catching up with me.

Suzie impressively jumped up to greet me with a hug tight enough that I could feel her baby kick. I laughed as she rocked us to and fro. "I'm so glad you came." She pulled back. "I invited everyone I've flaked on recently because I'm busy growing a human." She turned to a redhead in jeans, a tee, and battered work boots and a brunette in a pretty sundress and heels, both sipping something pink and frothy. "You all, this is my BFF, Emma Sumner. And Emma, meet Hazel and Kiera. I met Kiera in hot yoga a few years ago, and Hazel just moved back to town and was dragged to hot yoga by Kiera. Turns out all three of us hate hot yoga with a sweaty passion but love what it does for our asses. Well, not mine right now since I've been benched until I push a watermelon out my hoo-ha, but you know what I mean."

"I know *exactly* what you mean," Kiera said.

"Kiera's got two kiddos, twins," Suzie told me, pouring me a drink from one of the two pitchers on the table. "It's her first girls' night out in a long time."

"Lost my husband, had a breakdown." Kiera waved a hand. "Long story. But I'm back! And an evening away from the dictators—I mean toddlers—is working wonders."

Suzie lifted a hand for the bartender. "We need another pitcher for these two and another mocktail for us two!" she said, gesturing to her and Hazel, rubbing her massive baby bump. "I should probably take some Tums, because at two years pregnant, absolutely nothing agrees with me."

"But you only look eighteen months preggers," Kiera said, and Suzie laughed.

"It's true," Kiera said. "When I was pregnant, my boobs and belly arrived into a room half an hour ahead of me."

"Boobs are Adam's favorite perk of me being pregnant," Suzie said.

"I don't have kids or much in the way of boobs," Hazel told me. "And I'm not sorry about either of those things."

I laughed. "Me neither."

"Don't have a Prince Charming either."

"Same," I said. "If he's out there looking for me, he's clearly riding a turtle…"

Hazel laughed and tapped her mocktail to mine in camaraderie.

"Hazel's a master carpenter," Suzie said. "Her woodwork's amazing." She then turned her attention on me. "And you look cute. Cute dress, cute sandals, cute hair."

"Came right from work," I said. A dress was always my last choice for work, especially since I often ended up on a jobsite, but I needed to do laundry, which required sitting at a laundromat for hours, but I hadn't had time.

"Adam's been working long hours too," Suzie said. "It's making him cranky." She looked at me. "If he keeps it up, I'll need help hiding the body."

Hazel laughed.

Suzie looked at her. "I keep trying to set you up with one of Adam's friends, but you keep dodging." She looked at Kiera. "You too."

Kiera shook her head. "Not ready."

Suzie looked at me.

"No thank you," I said quickly. That night I'd had Tucker and Caleb drop me off at Suzie's house, I hadn't gone inside. I'd ordered an Uber and waited down the street to avoid this very conversation. "I'm dating myself."

Suzie's eyes narrowed. "What was that?"

"What?"

"You only talk that fast when you're lying." She gasped. "Ohmigod. Are you...seeing someone? And you haven't told me?"

"Of course not."

"Which? That you're not seeing anyone, or that you are but haven't told me?"

Suzie should've been an interrogator for the CIA. If I didn't give her something, she'd bug me for the rest of my days. "Okay, so there might've been a near-miss kiss with someone at work, but I'm pretty sure it turned out to be nothing."

Suzie gasped in sheer delight. "Yay!"

"You did hear the 'turned out to be nothing' part, right?"

"You said 'pretty sure,' not *sure sure*."

"I meant *sure sure*."

Suzie sighed in disappointment and turned to Hazel. "You work with hot guys all day long. How is it possible you're in a dry spell?"

Hazel snorted. "Trust me, when you're on a construction site in the thick of things, dirty and sweaty, no one looks sexy."

"What about the Colburns?" Suzie asked. "You're close to those guys, right? They're the definition of *sexy*, and a couple of them are single."

I accidentally inhaled my drink. By the time I'd finished coughing up a lung, everyone was looking at me with interest.

"Went down the wrong pipe," I wheezed. "That's all."

Everyone then swiveled back to Hazel to get her take on the Colburns. "No way am I going to date Tucker—" She sucked her lips into her mouth and grimaced. "I mean, a Colburn." She looked at Kiera. "Um, no offense."

"None taken."

Before I could figure out why Kiera would take offense, Kiera's phone pinged with an incoming text. She checked it and let out a soft smile, turning the phone to show us two adorable kiddos in the bathtub, covered in bubbles, grinning with delight. "I make my babysitters send proof of life," she said. "Since they also sometimes act like three-year-olds—babysitting three-year-olds."

"Her brothers Caleb and Tucker are babysitting," Suzie said. "It takes two of them to keep those twins corralled."

I choked on my drink. Yes, again. "Caleb...*Colburn*?"

"The one and only," Suzie said, patting my back. "Why? You know him?"

"*Everyone* knows him," Kiera said. "He hasn't played hockey since college, but people still stop him to talk about it."

"We sort of work together," I said. "Henderson and Hall hired Colburn Restorations for a big project, and I'm the liaison."

"Wait a minute..." Suzie was watching me carefully. "*Caleb's* your near miss?"

I set down my drink so I didn't almost die again but also kept my mouth shut, not especially wanting to admit that I'd almost kissed Kiera's brother.

"Well, now I'm torn," Suzie said. "Caleb's a great guy, but I wanted you to find a keeper, and the Colburn brothers have never claimed to be keepers." She grimaced at Kiera. "Sorry."

"Again, no offense taken," Kiera said. "Although, for what it's worth, they've pretty much left their wild years behind them."

My cheeks were hot. "I never said it was Caleb!"

"So it was Tucker?"

"No!"

"You're beet red," Kiera pointed out. "Honestly, you could do way worse."

"No," Hazel said flatly. "You can't."

Kiera slid her a look.

Hazel shook her head. "Don't look at me like that; you know what I mean."

"That our upbringing made it hard to trust?" Kiera asked. "Yeah, but I broke the cycle, and now Ryder's doing the same, so I've got hope for Tucker."

A long look was exchanged between the two of them, making me wonder what Hazel's history with Tucker was.

Hazel looked away first. "This is about Emma and Caleb, not me and…your brother."

That she couldn't even say Tucker's name nearly brought me out of my own embarrassment. But then she turned to me. "Look, the Colburn brothers are great guys. Especially Caleb. He's like a brother to me, and I love him. But you seem like a really good person, Emma, one who deserves a keeper, so you should know that Caleb Colburn doesn't do relationships because he'd rather chew glass than break up with a woman. They don't call him *The Ghoster* for nothing."

"Aw, thanks, Haze," said an unbearably familiar male voice. "Really very helpful."

We all turned to find Caleb standing behind us, a to-go order in one hand, a soda in the other.

CHAPTER 11

Caleb

'D ADDRESSED MY STATEMENT to Hazel, but my eyes never left Emma... Emma in that pretty dress, her hair down, intelligent eyes a little wide with surprise at the sight of me.

It had been a week since I'd panicked and said the now-infamous phrase: *It's a bad idea...* Stupid. So stupid. Somehow I'd convinced myself it was for the best, but looking at her now, I knew I'd been fooling myself.

That I was even at the Cork and Barrel was a fluke. After a long day at the office and on the jobsite, during which not much had gone my way, I'd been babysitting the twins with Tucker. I'd lost at rock, paper, scissors, so I was picking up our to-go dinner.

Only to catch sight of Emma smiling, enjoying herself.

I'd seen her worried. Scared. Speculative. Hard at work. And—my favorite—in a lustful stupor over my body. But I'd never seen her letting loose like this, relaxed and having fun.

Drawn like a moth to a flame, I'd moved closer and caught Hazel's comment. I'd responded as expected, mostly because

Hazel's accusation was true, then turned to Emma. "It looks really good on you."

"What?"

"The smile. Haven't seen it since college."

Emma rolled her eyes. "You never saw it then either. You were far too busy with your puck bunnies while I did all our group projects."

"I've apologized for that."

"Have you?"

I put a hand to my chest. "I'm sincerely sorry you were so anal and controlling that you had to manage most of the group projects."

"If it helps, she's slightly less anal and controlling now," the woman next to Emma said and held out her hand. "Suzie," she said sweetly. "Emma's BFF. You're Caleb Colburn? The wild, rough-and-tumble former hockey star."

Kiera grinned. *Traitor.* "Where are my babies?"

"With Tuck."

I was wondering how to kill my sister without going to jail when Suzie said, "Feel free to join us. But fair warning, we've got questions."

I raised my brows. "Such as?"

"Is it true that hockey players don't like to make passes, they just want to…put it in?"

Emma gasped. *"Suzie!"*

"What, it's a valid hockey question. Get your mind out of the gutter." Suzie smiled at me innocently. "Well?"

Emma snatched Suzie's drink and sniffed it.

Suzie grinned and kicked out a stool, patting it in invitation. "Welcome to girls' night out!"

I had no intention of staying, but Emma looked so horrified at the thought, a sick part of me decided to sit for a minute. "So, what have I missed?"

"A lot," Hazel said. "Apparently, Emma had a near-miss kiss with someone at work. Know anything about that?"

Emma choked on her drink.

"*Again?*" Kiera asked, patting her on the back. "We're going to have to toughen you up for this crowd."

"Hello, excuse me." A woman in a teeny-tiny black dress stopped at our table and smiled at me. "You're *the* Caleb Colburn."

"He is," Kiera said. "But he dropped 'the.' He just goes by *Caleb Colburn* now."

I rolled my eyes at my sister while the woman squealed and jumped up and down. By some miracle, the little black dress stayed in place as she waved over two more women from their booth across the bar. "Can we get your autograph?" she asked breathlessly.

"Uh…" I patted myself down. "Don't have a pen."

"Oh, no worries, I do!" The woman produced a Sharpie. "Here you go, and you can just sign right here—" To the delight of both her friends, she started to yank the top of her dress down.

"A napkin'll work." I quickly grabbed one and signed my name, before handing it to her.

If she was disappointed, she didn't say. "Can I get a selfie?"

Before I could answer, she pulled her friends in closer, and they squeezed around me. I gave the obligatory smile, and they all beamed.

"Thank you so much," the woman said. "My name's Gwen. I work at the Core Power Gym. I've seen you working out with your brothers." She grinned. "You've still got it."

"Good to know," I said.

"I think your food just got delivered," Hazel told the women.

With another squeal, they all ran off, and I looked at both Hazel and Kiera. "You two are the opposite of helpful. I'm disowning you both."

"Oh, please," Kiera said. "Like you needed help."

Suzie was still watching me. "So *you're* the near-miss kiss."

Kiera slid me a look. "If that's true, you might want to tread carefully in order to avoid becoming a dead Colburn brother walking."

Hazel snorted. So happy someone was amused.

Emma looked worried. "What does she mean, 'dead brother walking'?"

"Oh, did he forget to tell you?" Kiera asked. "He's not allowed to sleep with anyone from work anymore."

Hazel snorted her drink out her nose. "Damn it," she said, looking down at her now-wet self.

"Thanks," I told my sister. "Very charitable."

Kiera shrugged. "I try."

I turned to Emma. "It's not what it sounds like."

Emma pushed her drink away. "Doesn't matter to me. After all, I'm a bad idea, right?"

"I didn't say *you* were a bad idea. I said—"

My words were cut off by Hazel, who was shaking her head. "Dude. Making it worse."

Suzie glared at me, then put her hand on Emma's arm. "Sweetie, at least it was a near miss and you didn't actually—"

Emma got to her feet, and I didn't know why, but I panicked and caught her arm. "Can we talk—"

"No, you cannot." Suzie got to her feet quickly—impressive

for how pregnant she was. "You're too potent. You might talk her into something that's not a near miss—"

"Oh my God," Emma said. "I love you, but please stop talking!"

Suzie mimed zipping her lips and throwing away the key before sending another glare my way.

Emma said, "I'm going to get us another round," and walked off.

"Don't worry," Kiera said to me. "I'm sure Ry will let you live when he finds out. Probably."

I didn't give a shit that she was just fucking with me. Or that Hazel might choke on her laughter and pass out and fall off her chair. What I cared about was the look on Emma's face, like she hugely, massively regretted having ever met me.

Her eyes had flashed at me with such annoyance and irritation, and fuck, it was sexy as hell. But Kiera was looking at me with a *you're so stupid* look, and I agreed, but not for the reason she thought. I was stupid for letting Emma get under my skin, and not because Ry would kill me. I could take him. Probably. No, I was stupid because Hazel had been right.

I was no keeper.

And Emma deserved better.

CHAPTER 12

Emma

B Y THE TIME I got back to our table armed with a new pitcher, Caleb had left. Good. Great. I wanted him gone.

He's not allowed to sleep with anyone from work anymore…

At least I wasn't a notch on his bedpost.

The girls eyed me with sympathy.

"I'm a hot mess," I admitted.

"But you're my hot mess," Suzie said, slinging an arm around me, hugging me to her. "And even though he's not endgame, you did choose nicely for a near-miss kiss."

Hazel nodded. "I mean, he's not bad on the eyes."

Suzie and Hazel turned to Kiera, silently demanding she also say something nice about Caleb. "He's…uh…*tall?*"

I dropped my forehead to the table. "Ignore me. I'm going home to wrap myself up in a blanket and be paralyzed by my life choices." Even if I didn't exactly have a home to go to…

Hazel nudged me with her arm. "Everyone has their hot-mess moments."

"Yeah?" I lifted my head. "Name one of yours."

Hazel laughed with self-deprecation. "Welp, I made a whole bunch of stupid mistakes and then ran away from them, literally, leaving behind everyone who'd ever cared about me—for a decade."

Kiera leaned across the high top and squeezed her hand. "But you're back now. And we're still right here."

Looking incredibly moved, Hazel swallowed hard, nodding in silent thanks. She looked at me again. "My grandma used to read me this book about caterpillars. There's this whole thing about how they slip into a cocoon, slap on wings, and emerge a beautiful butterfly. My grandma would close the book and say, 'It's not true. Caterpillars have to dissolve into a disgusting pile of goo to become a butterfly. So if you're a mess wrapped up in blankets on the couch, paralyzed by life, keep going, you're on the right track.'"

I thought about that as I snuggled into my sleeping bag an hour later. The night was dark, but I didn't use my lantern or watch a show on my laptop. Instead, I thought about what Hazel had said.

I was smack in the middle of my disgusting-pile-of-goo era. But it was okay. I had a plan, and it was still in play—Caleb Colburn and my asinine crush or no.

CHAPTER 13

Caleb

STOOD IN THE basement with a set of plans and a bad attitude, trying to get a bead on what to do about the wall that wasn't on the plans but was right in front of my face.

I hadn't seen nor talked to Emma since four nights ago at the bar, but she'd emailed that Henderson was willing to do whatever we thought was right as long as it ended up looking how he wanted it to.

No pressure at all.

"We have to move it."

I found Ryder standing behind me, hands on hips, studying the wall, also looking irritated.

Great. I turned to pace the length of the basement, and a flash of fiery pain zapped up my leg.

Ryder's gaze flew directly to my thigh. "You good?"

"Fucking fantastic. And I agree the wall has to go," I said, trying to keep my bad temper from my voice. "But it's gonna hold us up."

"I don't know, Emma seems pretty reasonable," he said.

I laughed shortly. "She's a lot of things. But reasonable isn't always one of them." I knew my mistake the instant his brows went up.

"You've gotten to know her well then?"

"She's our liaison," I pointed out.

"Uh-huh. Tell me nothing's going on."

I stared at him. "Seriously?"

"Seriously."

Nothing *was* going on, all I had to do was say it, but bad temper and pride went hand in hand. "What's your fucking problem today?"

"*My* fucking problem?" Ry asked, voice tinged with disbelief and just loud enough to set me off.

Each of us, after how we'd grown up, had various triggers associated with confrontation. Like how Tucker couldn't handle seeing someone he cared about get hurt. For me, big and intimidating as I knew I could be, a raised masculine voice made me want to throw up. It was embarrassing as hell, so I covered the response by walking away. Always.

Today being no exception, I'd just turned to go—anywhere other than here—when Ryder drew a deep breath and lowered his voice, with clear effort. "My problem," he said much more quietly, "is you. You're the three-date wonder. Hell, you're the one-date wonder. What's going to happen when you get bored with her? The job is at least six more months."

"I'm not going to screw this up," I said, going for calm and failing. "I told you I wanted more responsibility, and I meant it. I'm doing it."

Ryder blew out a breath. "You are, and I'm grateful."

I snorted, and he rolled his eyes. "I am," he insisted. "But I'm going to say this one more time: Think ahead, put the company first. No complicating things. Period."

"Like you did with Penny?"

Ryder stared at his boots for a beat, probably contemplating murdering me with his bare hands. "Fine. Yes, I met Penny at work. But she wasn't an employee and not directly involved in the business in any way."

"Emma isn't your employee either."

"She's *directly* involved," he said.

I stared back, unable to say why I was doing this, pushing the issue when there was nothing going on between me and Emma, thanks to my own big, fat mouth.

"I'm not compromising on this," Ryder said. "Not when the last time cost us a big client. Make your decision."

We stared at each other some more.

"Well?" Ry asked.

Resentment boiled up, hot and fiery. I hated when he pulled the older-brother bullshit, but more than that, when *he'd* started to fall for Penny, it had been me and Tucker to talk him *into* taking that fall. We'd been right there to remind him he deserved love and happiness.

"I'm an adult," I said. "I can think with two body parts at the same time. Stay out of my personal life."

"Then keep your personal life out my business. And for fuck's sake, rest your leg when it gets this bad."

"It's not bad."

"Yeah, and I'm the Easter Bunny." He stalked away, and I flipped him off behind his back.

"I saw that," he said.

"I wanted you to."

The rest of the day kicked my ass. Taking care of Hank and running the jobsite on top of doing my half of the office management as I'd promised Ryder was taking a toll, like it or not. By the time the weekend rolled around, I was completely done in. I needed a few days alone, but that wasn't going to happen. Hank might not be able to talk, but he was still a large presence that required constant supervision. Both Ryder and Tucker had offered to take him as needed, but pride dictated I handle him myself.

Sunday was my one day to sleep in, and since I hadn't been able to fall asleep to save my life, I was trying to make up for it by sleeping past sunrise. At some point just after dawn, I'd finally fallen into a deep sleep when something nudged me awake. I opened my eyes and nearly screamed like a little kid.

Hank stood at my bedside, his face an inch from mine, and thanks to the hall light behind him, he was backlit like a horror-movie villain. All that was missing was his instrument of torture.

"Ah?"

"Jesus." I put a hand to my hammering heart. "The house on fire?"

Hank shook his head.

"You hurt?"

Another shake of Hank's head.

"Then, and I mean this in all sincerity, *what the fuck*?"

Hank lifted his hand, which was holding a coffee mug. An empty coffee mug.

Right. I looked at my phone—10:01 a.m. "Fair," I said.

"Ah." He waved the mug again, and I felt like an asshole.

"Okay, okay, I hear you." I sat up, and shit, flashes of

shimmering spots danced across my vision. Migraine aura. This wasn't my first rodeo or even my hundredth. Ever since my spectacular crash and burn on the ice in the NCAA D1 tournament all those years ago, migraines had been a way of life. They didn't come nearly as often anymore, mostly just when I got too tired or stressed.

Like now.

If I wasn't careful, in an hour or two, I'd be curled in the fetal position on my bathroom floor, puking up my guts, unable to handle so much as a sliver of light or a decibel of sound. I drew a deep breath and got out of bed. I had some time before it hit; I also had meds. I'd be fine. *Fine.* Without turning on a light to make things worse, I passed by Hank, then stopped short.

He was buck-ass naked. "What happened to your pajamas?"

"Ah."

No need to try and interpret that. Hank hated pajamas. Hank hated pants. If I left him alone for any amount of time, he managed to get them off. Last week, I'd put him in the living room recliner to go cook dinner, and when I'd come back five minutes later, he'd been wearing nothing but his reading glasses and socks.

Which was why I now had a blanket spread over his recliner.

We made a pit stop in his bedroom on the way to the kitchen. I opened the top drawer of his dresser, and since I tried to learn from my mistakes, I didn't even bother holding up the first pair of boxers because they were red, and he hated red. I held up the blue.

He shook his head.

I held up green ones, then black, then striped. No to all. With my eyes narrowed, I showed him the only pair left. Red.

"Ah," he said, then smiled his approval.

In that moment, I knew it wouldn't be the migraine to kill me. It would be my father. Death by frustration.

Mornings were a huge production. The days of me rolling out of bed, taking a quick shower, throwing on work clothes, and heading out in less than twenty minutes from when I'd opened my eyes were long over. I had to make Hank coffee, take out the dogs and then feed them, and get both myself and Hank showered and dressed before we could head out. In an impressive downpour, I drove Hank and my dragging ass to Al's Diner for our weekly Sunday "bonding" Colburn sibling meal—Tucker's decree. He said it kept us connected, and he was right. We were connected, for better or worse. We used to do a weekly dinner at the Cork and Barrel, but the alcohol, combined with our competitiveness over darts and pool tournaments, was never a good idea.

So now we did brunch or lunch, sometimes at the diner, sometimes at one of our homes, which only occasionally turned into warfare.

I caught up to everyone as they were just about to pile into a booth. I gave Ry a chin nod, kissed Penny on the cheek, then stopped to wave at Hazel, who'd just walked into the diner.

At the sight of us, she froze.

Kiera waved her over, and Hazel reluctantly headed our way. "Just picking up coffee," she said, awkwardly staring anywhere but at Tucker.

"Stay," Kiera insisted, looking at all of us, especially Tucker. "Right?"

"I've really got to—" Hazel waved a hand toward the door.

Kiera grabbed her hand and held on. "You're staying."

And since no one was stupid enough to talk back to Kiera,

we all crowded into the booth, Hazel going last, perching on the edge of the bench seat as if unsure of her welcome.

Kiera gave me the *do something* eyes, so I nudged Hank in on the other side of the booth next to Ryder, then squished Hazel by practically sitting on her lap until she scooched...right into Tucker, who stiffened.

"Sorry," Hazel said.

"No, that was me," Tucker said, dramatically scooting as far as he could from her, while she did the same, neither making eye contact.

But hey, at least it wasn't my drama, which meant I could sit back and enjoy.

"Ah," Hank said, pointing to his mouth.

Kiera handed him half her breakfast sandwich, and he grinned from ear to ear, then dug in.

Kiera watched him for a moment, her expression unreadable but soft. Even kind.

It had been my biggest shock that of us all, Kiera was the one who seemed able to tolerate him the easiest. I couldn't fathom why. I gave Abi and Alex *gimme* hands, and they squealed in delight and climbed out of Tucker's lap and across Hazel to get to me.

Abi, dressed as a Disney princess—I had no idea which one—complete with a tiara in front of her two tiny space buns, immediately clapped her hands to my cheeks and pressed her forehead to mine, staring into my eyes, breathing through her mouth like a locomotive because she had a cold. "Unca Cal Cal, Alex had an accident in his car seat on the way here, and it smelled bad. Mommy said a bad word."

Alex, wearing *Paw Patrol* sweats and cowboy boots, pushed his face in front of Abi's. "I didn't."

"Mama, Alex telling fibs again."

"I'm not," Alex said. "Unca Cal Cal, guess what?"

"What?"

"Rubble is the one who pooped in my car seat!"

I raised my brows. "Rubble, the yellow *Paw Patrol* pretend dog who drives an excavator even though he's a dog and doesn't have opposable thumbs?"

Alex nodded vigorously.

"Alex, baby," Kiera said across the table. "Remember what you're supposed to do when you're telling tall tales? So that everyone knows you're making something up?"

Alex beamed. "Yes!" He tapped his own nose.

I grinned at him, this tiny human with the Colburn-hazel eyes and strong opinions and stubbornness, whom I loved with all my heart. "Alex, guess what."

"What?"

"I once got to drive Rubble's excavator."

"No way!"

"Way." Then I tapped my nose.

Alex set his head down on my shoulder, smearing the ketchup on his face all over my sweatshirt, but it was worth it for toddler snuggles. I yawned so wide, my jaw cracked, and actually, my head was starting to hurt. I'd forgotten to take the migraine meds. Hugging Alex, I leaned back and closed my eyes for a moment...

Then jerked awake and sat up straight.

The booth was empty, and Kiera was crouched by my side. "Hey, Sleeping Beauty," she said teasingly, but her eyes were serious. "You okay?"

"Wha—" I looked around. "Where did everyone go?"

"Meal's over. They're all loading up in the parking lot. There's a big storm moving in. The news threw around words like *cyclone bomb* and *atmospheric river*. You need to go back to bed."

"Can't." Not only did I have Hank, if the storm was as big as predicted, I needed to go by our ongoing jobs to ensure the guys had tarped all outside equipment and materials, that they'd put out sandbags and netting where they'd been prepping for concrete work, and—

"You're getting a migraine, aren't you?"

"Me? Nah." An easy lie. A self-preservation lie, because if I admitted it, she'd call in the cavalry. The entire family would descend upon my house. Ryder would bully me into taking more meds than I wanted—I hated the wooziness they caused. Tucker would take over the job for me, or whatever I had on my plate. Kiera would cook for an army of thousands and force-feed me. Then they'd sit on me until they deemed me better.

"I'm taking Dad with me for a few days," she said.

I shook my head. "No, you don't have to—"

"Caleb." Even though Kiera barely came to my shoulder, she pulled me upright and out of the booth. "It's happening. Don't worry, you'll pay me back in babysitting."

I couldn't joke about this, not when the look on her face that day I'd left for college, that brave, solemn face, still haunted me. "Ki—"

"I want to know *this* Hank," she said softly. "I know I fell apart when Auggie died, and you guys stupidly dealt with Dad's strokes and the fallout on your own because you—also stupidly—didn't want to burden me. But I'm good now. Or at least I'm getting there." She paused, met my gaze. "I need to feel like I'm a part of this family again."

"Ki, you've *always* been a part of this family. You don't have to do this for me."

"I'm doing it for *me*. And you're going to let me."

I nodded reluctantly, and she nodded back.

"So go home and stay there. The storm's due to hit in an hour. Eighty-mile-per-hour winds, torrential downpours, the whole works, and given how drenched the ground is from the past few weeks of rain, trees are going to come down. Power's going to go out. And there'll be flooding."

Shit. I knew for sure we hadn't prepared the Henderson site for torrential rains.

"Caleb."

"Yeah, I'm going home." *Eventually…*

Half an hour later, I'd gone by every job I felt was in danger except the Henderson project. I was halfway there, happy to have it be my last stop because my head was killing me, when Tucker called.

"What the fuck are you doing?" he demanded.

"Uh…driving?"

"You're heading to the Henderson job. Kiera said you promised to go home."

"How do you know where I'm headed?" I asked. "Because after you stole the Colburn fantasy football trophy from my house a few months ago, I dumped your sorry ass from Find My app."

"Wrong question."

"You hacked my phone."

"You looked like shit at breakfast." Tucker's voice was clipped. His worried tone. He might be the youngest brother, but his hero complex went deep, and he liked to keep track of all of us. Always had. "And I know having Hank at your place is wearing on you—"

"I'm fine."

"I also know Ryder's been on your ass since he gave you the reins on some of the business things, as well as the Henderson job."

"Yeah, well, he's a control freak," I said.

"But you're not the Energizer Bunny. You can't just keep going and going and going in order to avoid shit. You're going to give yourself a migraine. It's already late afternoon, so go the fuck home."

"I'm not avoiding shit. I never avoid shit."

"Yeah, right." He paused. "I already knew this, but you should know a little birdie told me you've got a crush on our architect."

"You seriously going to call Ryder 'a little birdie'?"

"Well, not to his face."

I scrubbed a hand over my face. "Is this going anywhere?"

"Look, if it helps, I've caught Emma staring at you when you weren't looking."

"Because she dreams of strangling me."

Tucker laughed. "Serves you right. All your life, women have fallen at your feet. Welcome to the real world, where the rest of us have to actually put forth some effort."

"Wow."

"So…are you going to put forth effort?" Tucker asked carefully. "With Emma, after what Ryder said—"

"You do realize I heard him the first thousand times, right, Mom?"

"Fuck you. Sideways."

"Right back at ya."

"Turn around, Caleb. Go home." And then he disconnected.

I didn't turn around, even though the drive out to the jobsite got harrowing once I left the main road. Heavy winds battered my truck, knocking it from side to side on the narrow, curvy road. Overhead, gunmetal clouds churned, threatening to let loose. And as I parked in the circular driveway, it did just that— no warning drops, just sheets of rain suddenly coming down hard and heavy.

No surprise. But what was a surprise was the faded-green Subaru I'd parked behind. The wind howled like a banshee as I slid out of my truck, the storm hitting me with the force of a thousand icy fists. The world had shifted into a blur of gray, and I was instantly soaked to the bone. Fighting to stay upright, I peered into Emma's car.

Empty.

I staggered to the front door, but before I could pull out my keys, I was yanked inside.

CHAPTER 14

Emma

WITH MY HEART TAP-DANCING in my throat, I was playing tug-of-war with the wind to close the front door when Caleb stepped up behind me, so close that our bodies brushed together as his hands joined mine, taking over. When the door shut, I hit the bolt, then pressed my forehead to the wood while sucking in air.

Caleb.

Here.

At the jobsite on a Sunday in the early evening. I could feel the heat and easy strength of him, and I closed my eyes as shame and panic bubbled in my throat. I'd had a campsite this week, but the storm warnings of impending mass destruction had sent me scrambling.

I'd planned to go to the library to stay dry and warm, but it wasn't open on a Sunday. Suzie had gone to the ER in the middle of the night, but it had turned out to be false labor. I couldn't bother her, so here I was, along with the one person I needed to avoid like the plague before I was stupid enough to fall for him.

Caleb's hands slid from the doorframe to my arms, his touch sending a jolt of unexpected heat through places that I didn't know needed heating as he turned me to face him. He looked like he'd been swimming in the lake fully clothed, water dripping from his hair and soaking his sweatshirt. His hood was still up, casting his face in shadow, but I could see the tight lines of his mouth, grim and set like a trap. "You're a surprise," he said, his voice rough with something I couldn't name.

"So are you," I said, staring at him. There was something different about him today, but I couldn't place it.

"Anything I should know about?" he asked.

Absolutely not. My childhood fear of high winds had resurrected itself today, but that was my own problem. "Nope."

He started to say something else but then stopped, head tilted. "What's that?"

Gee, only the roaring wind that was going to give me a heart attack. "The storm amplifying."

"No, I hear a truck. Out back, I think." He moved through the living room to the sliding glass door, then stepped out onto the back patio, favoring his leg more than usual today.

By the time I'd crossed the large room, he'd jogged down the steps and into the crazy deluge, glaring at the rear end of a truck speeding away along the river.

That he'd heard that over everything else was a miracle. "One of yours?" I asked.

Shaking his head, Caleb pulled us both back inside and hit a number on his phone. "Anyone on the Henderson job at the moment, besides me?" he barked. "You're sure." He paused to listen. "There was a truck out back, but it sped away after the driver saw me… Yeah," he said, eyes on mine. "I will." He slid his phone away.

"What's going on?"

He shook his head. "Don't know. No one's scheduled to be here. I didn't get the license plate or see the driver." His voice sounded different than usual. Quieter, low and husky, as if everything was too loud for him. "Whatever you need to do here can wait until after the storm," he said. "Go home before the roads get worse. Come on, I'll follow you to make sure you get there safe and sound."

"No need," I said quickly.

Too quickly because he caught my arm before I got past him and stared down at me, eyes tight but worried. "What's wrong?"

"Nothing. Other than this crazy-ass storm, what could be wrong?"

"That's what I'm asking."

I swallowed hard. "I'm not a fan of high winds, is all."

His expression softened, and he opened his mouth, but lightning flashed, illuminating us like Christmas trees. Thunder boomed right on its heels, rattling the windows and my wits enough that my feet shifted closer to Caleb without permission from my brain.

"Yeah, that was a close one." He reached for my hand. "We need to go before we can't. I'll drive you."

God save me from overly protective, obstinate men. "I'll be fine—"

The lights flickered and went out.

"Shit," Caleb said.

Around us, the manor shook. There was still daylight, but

not much, and my beleaguered heart threatened to pound its way out of my chest as dark memories of the fire surfaced without warning. There'd been dry lightning that night, too, and sixty-plus-mile-an-hour winds. Power lines had come down onto a field drier than my dating life. And just like that—poof—my entire apartment building had gone up in flames.

It was amazing how fast your world could burn when it was made of straw. Ten minutes. That's how long it had taken to turn my life into ash.

Sometimes I still smelled smoke in my hair.

Shivering at the memories, I sucked in some air as the sky rumbled like a distant drumbeat, an ominous growl. "It's right over us," I whispered. "And—"

A bright flash of lightning lit us up for a single second before a clap of thunder shook the house to its foundation, followed by a loud, earthshaking thud that I couldn't place while I whimpered and covered my ears.

I heard a rough oath, and then a warm arm slid around my waist and pulled me close. His other hand slid to the base of my neck. "It's okay. I've got you."

"What was that?"

"I'm guessing a tree."

My breath came in panicky little huffs. "I'm not a fan of wind. Or big storms."

"I'm getting that."

I let out an embarrassing little mewl and pressed my face into his chest. "I'm fine," I whispered.

"Think of something else. One of your favorite things."

"Food," I said, then felt the puff of his short laugh against my temple.

"When we get out of here, I'll buy you whatever you want," he promised.

"Burger. Fries. Chocolate shake."

"Done."

He had his moments.

His warm hand at the nape of my neck was shockingly effective at calming me down, but I forced myself to step away from him. "Okay, let's go."

We turned to the front door. Caleb pulled it open and let out a low whistle. "Too late."

There had been a massive coastal oak on either side of the driveway at the bottom, where the asphalt met the street. One had come down, blocking the way out.

"I could off-road us around that," Caleb said, "but even on a normal rainy day, the roads out here wash out regularly. And this…" He gestured to the downpour. "This is no regular heavy rain day. I wouldn't risk it in my truck, much less let you risk it in your car."

"Excuse me," I said. *Let me?*

He ran a hand down his weary face. "I'm just trying to look out for you."

"I don't need you to. I don't need anyone to."

"No shit." He pushed back his hood and unzipped the jacket, before tossing the wet garment aside, leaving him in jeans and a Henley, which he shoved up to his elbows.

There really was something different about him today. I hadn't been able to figure it out before, but his eyes seemed shadowed, his brow furrowed as he rubbed his thumb and index finger over his forehead. "Hey," I said. "You okay?"

"Yeah."

I raised a brow at his clipped tone, giving him a *come on, out with it* gesture.

He rubbed his temples. "I'm getting a stupid migraine." As the rain and wind continued to batter the manor, he dropped to sit on a stack of drywall, head bowed, shoulders slumped, hands still at his temples, eyes closed. When he turned a little green and swallowed hard, I climbed onto the drywall next to him and reached for his hand, pulling it into my lap to pinch the meaty flesh between the base of his thumb and index finger.

Pain. That expression in his eyes was pain, and a great deal of it.

"What are you doing?" His voice was a barely audible growl now.

"It's a trigger point. I've never had a migraine, but my mom used to get them before she passed." I'd always taken care of her, so I knew exactly how bad it could get.

I felt the fingers of his other hand gently squeeze my arm. "I'm sorry."

"It was a long time ago." I squeezed hard and held until my fingers started to cramp before slowly letting off.

He blinked his eyes open.

"Did it help?" I asked.

He let out a long breath, then looked at me. "The urge to puke faded a bit, so yeah, thanks."

"It won't last. Do you have meds?"

"Fuck." He turned back to the door. "I've got an emergency stash in the glove box. I meant to grab a pill before getting out."

I held out my hand. "Keys," I said when he just stared at me, wriggling my fingers.

He pulled them from his pocket with one hand, the other holding his head. "I'll get them—"

I snatched the keys from his palm. Maybe I hadn't been a Division One athlete, but I could really move when I needed to. "Need anything else?"

"A new head. But you're not going out there. No fucking way."

"Oh, but you can?" I opened the door and stepped out into hell, quickly shutting the door behind me. Wind tugged my hood back and whipped at my face as I ran down the steps and… sank into several inches of water already pooled on the bottom step. But if I stopped, the panic would get me, so I kept going, sloshing through the water to Caleb's truck, toes squishing in my beat-up sneakers.

Adrenaline surged as I beeped the passenger door open and scrambled inside like the devil himself was on my heels. Slamming the door shut, I leaned back against the seat, the storm now muted somewhat.

As I reached for the glove box, a six-foot-two hooded shadow appeared in the driver's side window, muscular arms crossed over a broad chest. And his face. Oh boy, his face. He radiated bad temper. Or maybe that was his headache. I hit the fob and unlocked the door for him.

He slid into the seat and slowly turned his head to me.

"Problem?" I asked with faux calm.

"You didn't listen." A lock of wet hair fell into his eyes, and a stupid side of me soaked up the sight of him.

"I always listen," I said. "I just didn't happen to agree." I tossed him the bottle of migraine meds. "I believe the words you're looking for are *thank you*."

He popped a pill without water, which said a lot about how much pain he was in. He hadn't put his jacket back on, and that shirt clung to his torso in ways that should be illegal. "And here I thought *I* was the most stubborn person on the planet," I said dryly.

He shook his head. "I'd like to try to get us out of here, but…"

We both peered through the windshield. The fallen tree lay across the driveway like a monstrous, furry beast. Its root ball, the size of the truck, was a formidable obstacle on one side, while the branch end of the tree was spread wide like a leafy octopus, blocking the other. To top it all off, both ends butted up against the edge of the hill the manor had been built on.

"Shit." Caleb pulled out his phone. "Calling Ryder to see if anyone can help me move the tree."

Move the tree? It was enormous. Lying on its side, it had a circumference far taller than I was. No way could one person, or even two, move this tree. They were going to need an entire crew and equipment.

Ryder's voice came through Caleb's phone, tinny and distant, saying the roads were flooded between here and the highway, that there were dozens of trees down, many across roads. Same for electrical lines, some of which were sparking and dangerous. Complicating everything, the entire county was without power.

"I'll bring a crew with a reach lift the second we can get through," Ryder promised. "Don't worry about Hank or the boys, one of us will keep them."

The boys undoubtedly being Calvin and Klein. Caleb disconnected and turned to me, regret on his face.

And how screwed up was it that I had zero regret? We were stuck here, and regardless of the storm or what Caleb thought, I knew that for tonight at least, I would be sheltered.

CHAPTER 15

Caleb

GRABBED MY EMERGENCY go bag from under the back seat, then took Emma by the hand, hauling her out of the truck and toward the manor.

"Afraid I'll run away?" she asked, trotting to keep up with me.

"Afraid you'll float away." With my head—and leg—throbbing, I struggled to move as fast as I wanted, which really pissed me off.

Maybe you're just getting old…

Daisy's words mocked me. Since when was thirty old? But I had bigger problems. I could hear Emma's teeth chattering, so I pushed us harder.

"Hey," she said breathlessly. "Where's the race? I mean, we're already as wet as we can be."

True, but I was far too close to the lie-in-a-fetal-position-on-the-floor-of-a-dark-bathroom-to-puke-for-hours phase of the migraine. I got us inside, not realizing I'd dropped to my knees until she crouched at my side, a hand on my shoulder.

"I'm fine," I said.

"Of course you are." Her hair was plastered to her head, eyelashes holding drops of rain, her skin pale. "Where do you want to be?"

My mouth curved. "You gonna carry me?"

"I'm stronger than I look."

"Agreed." I drew in a careful breath. The meds must've started to work already; the urge to puke was fading. "Thank you."

"For what?"

"For forcing me to go get the meds. I'd have waited too long," I admitted.

"You *did* wait too long. Guys are ridiculous."

"So I've heard. Listen, we're going to be here awhile. We need to change clothes and find a place to relax and maybe sleep."

Emma stared at me as if I'd suggested she cut off her head. Insulting, but I got it. She was stuck in a storm with a man she didn't trust. I wanted to tell her she *could* trust me, but I knew she shouldn't. I mean, I'd actually thought I could use charm and wit to lull her into being on my side throughout this build.

What a shitty move on my part. Plus, I was in trouble, deep trouble, because I knew something she never would—that this, whatever this was, was no longer just for the job at all, and I had no idea when that had happened. "It'll be okay," I said. "I promise you're safe here with me."

She stared at me for a long beat, then let out a breath and a nod. "I have spare clothes in my car. I'll be right back—"

"No."

She raised a brow. "No?"

"No way are you going back out there. I've got enough to share." I tossed her a spare set of sweats and socks.

She hesitated, then nodded again. "I'm going to change in the bathroom."

While she was gone, I stood and stripped out of everything, then crouched before the duffel bag. I'd been carrying it around ever since a few years ago, when Tucker and I had gotten caught in a surprise snowstorm coming back from a ski weekend at Tahoe. A great weekend, but we'd nearly gotten frostbite waiting out chain control, him in my only spare sweat bottoms and me in only my spare sweatshirt. Ryder still gave us shit about that.

But one thing I didn't have was a towel. Nothing more fun than attempting to stuff my wet, naked ass into dry clothes. I was just reaching for the sweatpants when a beam of light hit me square in the chest, lighting me and said wet, naked ass up like I was on a Broadway stage.

This was accompanied by a sharp gasp—Emma—then the sound of the flashlight hitting the floor and rolling across the room.

CHAPTER 16

Emma

O HMIGOD, I'M SORRY!" I gasped, dropping to my knees for the flashlight, the image of Caleb's nude body burned into the core-memories section of my mind, never to be forgotten. Good, sweet baby Jesus, I'd known he was incredibly fit, but nothing had prepared me for the sight up close and personal.

I mean, fully clothed, he could make a grown woman walk into walls. Naked, he was a walking, talking cardiac arrest, and I was halfway there. He was all powerful shoulders and upper arms with that dark ink I wanted to memorize—with my tongue. Then there were his mouthwatering abs, and let's not forget that vee of muscles that some guys had, which was basically an arrow leading down to his—

"Em?"

I slapped my hands over my eyes. "Huh?"

"You okay?"

I sneaked a peek through my fingers and stopped breathing. "You're naked."

"Good to know that at least one of us doesn't need glasses."

My laugh was pure nerves because my eyes had locked on heavy, knotted scars a few shades lighter than his normal skin tone, running the length of his thigh.

Across the dark room came the rustling of clothes, then a wryly amused "safe to look."

I dropped my hand from my face to find he'd pulled on low-slung black sweatpants and was dropping a long-sleeved T-shirt over his head. I said, "I left my wet clothes in the first downstairs bathroom. Once they dry, I'll get your clothes back to you."

"It's not warm enough in here for them to dry in the next few hours, but please don't worry about the sweats. They look good on you."

I snorted as I watched him spread out his clothes. His clothes were so big on me, I probably looked like a child.

"You okay?" he asked, voice still husky low.

"Do I not look okay?" I asked, twirling in a circle like a princess, gesturing to my wet and wild hair and his oversize sweats.

"You look..." He gave a slow shake of his head. "You going commando in my sweats is my new favorite thing."

I let out a shocked laugh. "How do you know I'm commando? There's almost no light, and these sweats are thick."

"God-given talent."

I opened my mouth to ask if he needed something to drink, but my mouth had other ideas. "Why do you have a tramp stamp of a truck on fire?" I winced at my intimate question, but I really wanted to know. All his other tattoos flowed easily into one another on his arms and shoulders, clearly well-thought-out. The truck at the small of his back didn't fit the theme.

He swiped a hand down his face, covering a rough laugh. "You don't want to know."

"Oh, now I most *definitely* want to know."

He sighed. *Sighed.* "On Tucker's twenty-fifth birthday, the two of us lost a drinking game to Ryder after he drank us under the table. Literally."

I gave him the *go-on* gesture.

"Losers had to either perform an embarrassing public stunt or get a tattoo of Ryder's choosing. Tucker went first, picked the stunt. He had to busk in front of the Bufford Hotel, with a guitar and everything. And trust me when I tell you he can't sing. Or play the guitar."

I snorted. "And you?"

"Well, after that, I sure as hell wasn't going to pick a stunt."

I laughed. "But why a flaming truck?"

"It was in honor of Lucy, a woman I'd dated twice and then…"

"Ghosted?" I asked in amusement.

"Yeah." He blew out a breath. "Lucy was arrested setting my truck on fire."

I laughed so hard, I almost fell over.

He bore it graciously, a sheepish smile tugging at his mouth as he said, "So happy my past pain brings you a little joy."

"More than a little."

He moved toward me, not stopping until his chest nearly brushed mine. Slowly, he lifted a hand and cupped my jaw, rasping his thumb over my skin, eyes locked on mine. "You're taking this unintended adventure well."

I shrugged. I'd taken a lot of unintended adventures. "How's your head?"

"Do you know you always deflect attention away from yourself? It's a tell. You're not okay."

Well, I was a hell of a lot better now with him standing so close, sharing his body heat. His eyes were clearer; his pain had lessened. His mouth was slightly quirked, and I couldn't tear my eyes from it.

"Emma."

"Hmm?" Watching those lips move could become an addiction—

A low, rough laugh escaped him, and I licked my lips, an utterly unconscious movement that had his eyes darkening.

My hands slid up his arms—when had I made that decision?—and his settled on my hips, fingers tightening when I kept staring at that mouth I wanted on me.

"Killing me, Em," he whispered.

"But not a bad way to go, right?"

He made a purely masculine sound, I made a sound of my own, and then I had no idea who moved first, but our mouths connected in a heated, heart-stopping, bone-melting, delicious kiss. With a rough groan, he pulled me hard into him, one hand fisting in my hair, the other stroking up and down my back, farther each time, until he had a palmful of my butt, his fingers squeezing—

His phone beeped.

We broke apart, and I didn't know about him, but my heart was threatening to secede from the United States of Emma, and I couldn't catch my breath.

He ran a hand over his already-tousled hair and let out a long, slow breath, glancing at his text. "Lightning took out a power bank. We're without electricity until tomorrow, at the soonest. I've got to check on some things." He tightened my grip on my flashlight. "Stay inside."

Okay, so we were back to orders. On top of that, we weren't going to discuss the kiss that had rocked me so thoroughly, I was still wearing goose bumps. Noted. Or the fact that I could see either he had a gun in his pants or he was hard as stone. Good. I hoped it was uncomfortable as hell. "You really should rest some more and let the meds continue to do their job."

"They did." He tossed me a sleeping bag. "Pick a room to hole up in. Try to get some sleep," he said over a wind gust that shook the rafters. And me as well, right to my core.

"Caleb."

He turned back to me, distracted, and I drew a deep breath. "Don't leave."

"I wouldn't."

"No, I mean…" I hated admitting weaknesses. "Can we stick together?"

He studied me for a beat, then nodded. "Sure. I can check stuff later. Come on."

"Where are we going?"

"The only bed in this place."

My heart skipped a beat. The attic, where twice now, I'd changed clothes and considered that bed before forcing myself back out to my car rather than do the unethical thing and sleep up there. I knew both times I'd made sure I'd left everything as it was, but I still felt guilty as hell.

Caleb

We climbed into the attic, and I stood there, drawing in some air, my head pounding viciously in rhythm with my heart.

Emma slid the duffel bag off my shoulder, spread it out, and gestured to the bare mattress. "Lie down."

"Bossy Emma," I muttered and let myself fall onto the bed.

"Bossy doesn't start with an *E*," she pointed out.

"Best I've got—" I broke off when those magical healing hands of hers landed on my left thigh, right where it ached like hell. "What—"

"Shh." Her fingers dug in a little, and an involuntary hiss of pain escaped me.

"Too much?"

I shook my head and closed my eyes as she climbed onto the bed with me, making me hum with pleasure, then pain as she worked old and new scar tissue. Her touch was an intoxicating mix of knowing pressure on my aching muscles, while also gently cradling my leg against her body, encouraging me to relax. It felt incredible, so much so that my body decided it was about to get lucky. Even with the residual migraine, my dick refused to take orders from my brain. "Em—"

"Shh," she said again, keeping up the incredible pressure exactly where my leg needed it. "Relax."

I was so relaxed, I was nearly in a coma when she very quietly said, "You like me."

My eyes stayed closed, but I smiled. "How dare you."

She snorted. "You do. You let my icy fingers touch yours."

"Only because you were shaking so hard, it felt like we were having an earthquake."

"So, it was self-serving?"

"Exactly."

"Liar."

"Smart-ass."

We fell silent for maybe ten seconds. Then she spoke quietly, "Can I ask you something?"

"Sure." I hoped I sounded more confident than I felt.

"Are you and your siblings close?"

Not what I'd expected, but I knew she'd heard me and Ryder beefing on the jobsite. "If by 'close,' you mean we care deeply but also aren't opposed to trying to kill one another occasionally, then yes."

She nodded like she understood, but I knew she didn't have siblings. I'd met her at orientation for our freshman year of college. She was smart as hell and often took over group projects so that they'd get done the way she wanted. I was guilty of letting her do it because I never had enough time to study. Instead, I played up my athletic status to get out of the work, while teasing her about her control issues. I was such a dick back then, but there was something about the way she was the only person on campus willing to call me out on my shit, the only one not enthralled by me, that drew me in. I wanted to talk to her, study with her, ask her out, but she had zero interest, remaining aloof.

She'd pushed me, in the best of ways. But looking back, I realized now that the girl with the big green eyes and smart mouth had been grieving and no doubt feeling devastatingly alone.

And what did I do? I thought only of myself those years, finagling my way through college by using every resource available to me, even though it gave me an unfair advantage.

I'd been such an asshole. I buried my face in her hair, pressing my mouth to the back of her neck. "I lost my mom early too. And yeah, my siblings and I are close. We love one another, but we don't always like one another."

"You fight."

"You're talking about Ryder, and yeah. We fight. That wasn't my finest moment, by the way," I admitted. "Sometimes I get triggered by a certain authoritative tone. I have to remove myself from a situation to process my emotions."

She twisted to stare at me in surprise.

"What, you think I don't have emotions?" I teased.

"I think you don't like to admit to them."

I shrugged at the truth of that. "My relationship with Ryder is complicated by him also being my boss, but at the end of the day, we always, and I mean *always*, have each other's back. It's just messy sometimes." I pointed to a scar on my chin. "Got this when Tucker put my head through a wall during a wrestling session, which was not permitted, ever." I tugged the neck of my shirt down to reveal the three scars from when I'd had my shoulder rebuilt. "Got this when Ryder and I borrowed Hank's motorcycle and crashed it into the garage door. Ry was driving, by the way. *I* wouldn't have crashed."

"Sure of yourself much?"

I shrugged. "I know what I can do and what I can't." My biggest *can't* currently had her cold-ass feet tucked against my legs, her sweet body within reach.

"Did you ever get to drive the motorcycle?"

"Sure." I smiled. "After it was fixed and Hank had passed out on the couch."

She snorted. "Our childhoods were very different."

My smile faded. "Be happy for that, Emma."

She searched my gaze for a long moment. "Your childhood wasn't good."

"It was not."

She sat up to look into my face. "I'm sorry."

"Right back at you." And that was about as much as I wanted to say on the matter. Ever.

But, in perhaps one of my favorite things about Emma, she took in my expression and nodded. We lay in silence for a few minutes, and I thought maybe she'd drifted off when her stomach rumbled.

She sighed, and I laughed. "The beast is rivaling the storm."

"Har har." She sighed again. "I listen to a rain track on my calming app sometimes. A light rain, for white noise. It quiets my brain. But right now, since I haven't eaten today, the rain just sounds like chicken frying, and it's making me hungry."

For some reason, I couldn't stand the thought of her being hungry, and I sat up. "Wait here."

CHAPTER 17

Emma

CALEB REAPPEARED A FEW minutes later, arms full. He wore his glasses, long-sleeved T-shirt, and those low-slung sweatpants stuffed into unlaced work boots.

Just looking at him killed a bunch of my brain cells.

"Raided the kitchen and the guys' stash: cheese puffs, Froot Loops, and leftover pizza." He put it all down, along with two waters.

I could've kissed him. But wait…I already had, and we were done with that. Only, as he got back into our makeshift bed, I couldn't remember why. At least, not until he slid back under the open sleeping bag and put his cold feet on mine, making me squeal. "Hey!"

"Payback's a bitch."

I didn't smile. "You know that's several times now."

"What?" he asked.

I busied myself shoving a handful of Froot Loops into my mouth. "That you've told me to 'stay' or 'wait,' like I'm some kind of special snowflake who needs protecting."

"I get it." He opened the cheese puffs. "You're used to being an island of one, but I'm not. We Colburns stick together. Even when we can barely speak civilly to one another."

"Admirable," I said. "Sticking with people you don't always see eye to eye with."

He shrugged. "Family."

"You're lucky to have them."

"Agreed. Who do you have?"

Why did that question make my heart hurt? "I've got an aunt in Santa Rosa." Or at least I used to… "And you've met Suzie." I thought about it. "And the people at my work are nice, but I haven't been there long enough to make close ties." I paused, embarrassed by the small size of my inner circle. "I told you, I'm not good at connecting. Not like you—you can pull out the charm and charisma at the blink of an eye."

"You're better at it than you think," he said cryptically. "And charm and charisma don't earn you respect or love. When I played hockey, people came out of the woodwork, wanting to get close to me. It took getting screwed over a few times before I learned to close myself off to almost everyone except my siblings. With them, I've never had to worry about agenda or motives."

"You know when *else* you don't have to worry about those things?" I asked, munching on more Froot Loops. "When you don't let people in."

"Touché." He was now chewing on a slice of cheese pizza. "I hope you know I've got no agenda or motive here. We're both stuck, so why shouldn't it be a give-and-take?"

"A give-and-take isn't you commanding me to wait."

"That was instinct," he said. "So is sharing the food." He smiled. "Plus, I got to hear you moan over the cereal."

"I did *not* moan."

"Deny it all you want, but the sound now lives rent-free in my head."

I rolled my eyes.

"You also moaned when I kissed you." He smiled. "Which means you like me as much as you like Froot Loops."

"I don't like *anyone* as much as I like Froot Loops."

"Interesting," he said.

"What?"

"You didn't deny that you like me, which I knew because you helped me with the migraine."

I lifted my chin. "I helped you because it was the right thing to do. Has nothing to do with my feelings for you."

"So then maybe you expect a reward." He waggled his brows. "Name it."

"You're insufferable."

"Just admit I'm growing on you."

"I admit nothing other than that you're so full of yourself, I don't know how you fit your head through the doorways when you walk through this place."

He laughed. "Say what you want; the proof was in that kiss."

"Maybe it's just that we're stuck here together."

He cocked his head. "You think so?"

"I want to think so," I muttered, then snagged a piece of pizza. "I'm grateful you're here though, because I wouldn't have eaten anyone's food, so I'd be starving right now."

He snorted. "Good to know I've proven useful."

I wrestled with revealing the truth because he was sure enough of himself already. "I mean it, Caleb. I'm glad I'm not alone, but I'm also glad it's you."

His eyes warmed. "I'm glad it's you as well."

The tiny spark in my chest rekindled. I gestured to the pizza. "This tastes like Happy Pie's, our campus pizza joint, remember? Everyone always went there after games."

"They had the best pizza on the planet."

I took him in, sitting on the bed, hair tousled, eyes heavy-lidded, looking so much like that college kid, it brought me back to that time. "Do you miss hockey?" I asked softly.

He drew a deep breath. "I miss the game, the camaraderie, and the travel. But…" He shrugged, staring at the last piece of pizza. "Hockey was never my endgame."

My mouth fell open in surprise, and I pushed the pizza at him. "No?"

"Mostly, it was a means to an end—a college degree to support myself." He eyed the last slice. "You sure?"

I nodded, and he scooped it up. "I don't really talk about this to anyone. I mean, my family knows, but that's about it."

"Is it a secret?"

He shook his head. "Not really. It's just that most people don't believe me when I tell them I didn't mind not going pro. Either that or they pity me."

I'd been with him on the jobsite, seen firsthand his genuine excitement at the work ahead of him, so I believed every word. "If hockey wasn't your endgame, what was? Coaching? Commentating?"

"This." He gestured around us. "Renovating historical landmarks, working with my brother. Hockey was a way out." He chewed thoughtfully, then gave me a smile that didn't quite meet his eyes as he gestured to himself. "Not just a pretty jock."

I'd been all too guilty of judging him as well. But now,

I'd seen him on the job, in charge, in control, smart, efficient, capable. "Your dad must be so proud of the man you turned out to be."

He opened one of the waters and handed it to me before taking the other for himself. "Doubtful."

"He seems like such a sweet guy," I said carefully.

"He wasn't always like how he is now. Growing up, he was a hard man, exacting and aggressive. Not exactly father-of-the-year material."

"Is that why you call him by his name instead of *Dad*?"

He drank down half his water bottle, then nudged me to drink as well. "He was a staunch military man," he said, "without an ounce of softness, weighed down by four kids when his wife died. We all had a rough go. Ryder put himself on the line to protect us until he left for college, and then I took over. But he's not that same man now. Two years ago, after his strokes and surgery, he changed."

Understanding flooded me. "It must be difficult to adapt to who he is now."

"Difficult," he said on a rough snort. "Yeah, you could say that. A man I hated my entire life suddenly isn't that man anymore." He shook his head. "I haven't quite figured out how to let go of the hate. I know I should leave the past in the past…"

"No one can completely let go of the past. All you can do is learn to accept that the old Hank is gone and, more importantly, the people you love are safe."

He stared at me, then let out a breath.

"What?"

"You've always been so much smarter than I am."

I smiled and ate some cheese puffs. "Not true, but I'm going to keep letting you think that." I looked around. Couldn't see much, but it was easier than meeting Caleb's gaze as I said, "My dad walked out on us. My mom had to work multiple jobs, and it still wasn't always enough to keep a roof over our heads. I never really knew him, and I hated him. For so long I hated him."

"Past tense?"

"Very," I said. "Holding on to it, hugging all that animosity close to my heart like that, gave me anxiety. Stomachaches. Headaches. Stole my sleep. Then one day, in third grade, I blacked out at school. They thought I was sick. I had to go through all sorts of tests that my mom couldn't afford. Weeks and months of trying to figure out what was wrong with me, and we finally got a diagnosis—IBS. But the meds didn't fix anything." I met his gaze. "Because it wasn't IBS. It was stress and anxiety and hate. It was killing me. I had to let it go."

"How did you do it?"

"Ever hear of scream therapy?"

He shook his head.

"My mom took me camping up in the mountains. We sat on a ledge and screamed into the abyss. I was timid and embarrassed at first, but as time went on, I got into it." I smiled at the memory of holding my mom's hand, both of us screaming ourselves hoarse.

He smiled as well. "I can see a young you, bravely sitting on a ledge and screaming your sweet heart out."

Just as I could see a young Caleb having no such outlet for his fears and frustrations...

It took me a moment to realize I'd reached for his hand, not clocking it until his big, warm, calloused one gently squeezed mine in odd but lovely silent solidarity.

I woke with a startled scream and was immediately tugged into a warm, hard body. Caleb cradled me to him, whispering, "You're okay, it was just the wind…"

His voice was low and thick with sleep. Somehow we'd fallen asleep, and I'd woken both of us. "I'm sorry."

"No, it's okay. I've got you."

Despite the fact I could tell he was still more than half-asleep, he did have me. He'd tucked me in close, and I felt wrapped up in care and testosterone—which snapped me all the way awake.

And unfortunately reminded me of an unasked question.

"What did Kiera mean, you're not allowed to sleep with anyone related to the job anymore?"

He stilled for a beat, then sighed against my hair. "Long story."

"Well, we don't have TV, so…"

He ran a hand down his face. "You really want to hear this?"

"I really do." I'd told myself to stay emotionally detached with him, a self-protective measure. But he'd been steadily showing me he wasn't the same Caleb from all those years ago, and in return, I'd shown him more of the real me than I usually showed anyone. Against my better judgment, I wanted him to do the same.

He let out a long exhale. "A few years ago, I went out with the daughter of a very important client. It didn't end well, the client dumped us, I fucked up, the end."

I looked into his eyes, expecting to see wry humor given his calm tone, but regret swam in that golden-green gaze. Regret and…embarrassment. "And so now…what, you're banned from dating anyone related to the job?"

"It's more of a suggestion than a ban. But since I haven't dated anyone in a long time, it's been a nonissue."

An unspoken *until now* hovered in the air between us.

"Let's just say I'm much more discreet now," he said. "I keep my personal life and my business life separate."

I nodded, then shook my head. "Which category am I in?"

He ran a hand up my back, and I stretched like a needy smitten kitten. "I'm no longer sure," he murmured, doing it again.

Thinking was difficult, but I managed. "Is that going to be a problem for you?"

"TBD." He flashed an ironic smile, said, "Rest," and then kept rubbing my back in that slow, lazy way, and whatever I'd been going to say next left me as my eyes closed.

I came awake a bit later, in the deep of the night, alone in the bed. I sat straight up to find the outline of Caleb in a chair he'd dragged over. He was slouched, head back, muscular thighs splayed wide.

"Hey," I said groggily. "What are you doing?"

He lifted his head. "Maybe I got scared of the dark."

Yeah, right. I doubted he was scared of anything. "Or…?"

He rose and came toward me, before squatting; either he was hiding his grimace, or my earlier massage had helped his leg. With his forearm planted on the edge of the mattress, he looked at me. "Or I didn't want you to have another bad dream and wake up alone."

Feeling a little warm and squishy inside at that, I reached out to touch his hand. He was cold. "Come up here, you alpha dumbass."

"Careful with the sweet nothings; I might fall in love with you." He rose to his feet and swayed for a second.

"Caleb—"

"It's the meds. Sometimes they make me a bit woozy for a day or two afterward."

"Get up here before you fall down, you big oaf."

"Thought I was an alpha dumbass."

"You can be two things at the same time."

With a chuckle, he perched on the edge of the bed and looked down at me. "Why are you scared of the wind?"

I let out a slow breath. "There are two reasons. One old and one newer. Which do you want?"

"Both."

I never talked about this, so it took me a second to find the words. "When I was a kid, my mom and I bounced around more than a basketball trying to get steady housing. We were couch surfing at a friend's place on the coast, a little shack right on the beach, when a storm rolled in. The sofa bed we slept on was against a window. I was fast asleep when a tree branch crashed right through the glass in the middle of the night."

"Jesus." He looked horrified. "Were you hurt?"

"Just cuts and bruises, nothing big."

He studied me in the dark, then gently ran a finger over the faded scar just beneath my bottom lip. "That where you got this?"

I nodded.

"The other reason?"

"Before coming to Star Falls, I was still in Santa Rosa, working for a small architectural firm, subletting a room in an apartment downtown. The building was old, but the price was right—until a wild windstorm with sixty-plus-mile-per-hour winds whipped through, took some electrical lines down, and the sparks and subsequent fire lit up the field behind the building like the Fourth of July."

He drew a sharp breath. "Were you in the building?"

"No, I was stuck in traffic, trying to get home from work. By the time I did, there was nothing left."

"Holy shit," he breathed, and…was he closer now? His thigh brushed against mine.

If I shifted a few inches, I could climb right into his lap. "Caleb?"

"Emma…"

My name on his tongue came out husky and a little raspy, tingling along my skin and giving me goose bumps. And hard nipples… "You stayed with me while I slept."

There was a long, loaded pause. "I like to be near you," he finally said.

He could have thrown me across the room and surprised me less. "Mr. This Is a Bad Idea *likes* to be near me?"

He winced at the nickname but nodded. "I do."

I couldn't fathom why. I'd done nothing but be a pain in his ass—not exactly something a guy checks off in the pro column. "Because?"

"You ask a lot of questions."

"*Why*, Caleb?"

The glow from my flashlight highlighted the dark ink of the tats scrawled over his biceps as they flexed when he leaned closer.

"You…calm me," he finally said.

I laughed roughly. "I thought I was a bad idea."

"Not you. Us. We're a bad idea. Or so I keep telling myself."

"Flattering."

"I tell myself that because…" He held my gaze prisoner.

"Deep down I don't believe it. But I have no fucking clue what to do about this. About you."

I knew what I wanted him to do. Me. I wanted him to do me. Which meant my own instinct for self-preservation had left me in the dust.

I should've turned over and gone back to sleep. I should've ignored the chemistry between us, this surprising, undeniable *sexual* chemistry. But I couldn't, not when he'd been slowly showing me sides of himself I hadn't known existed. Compassion. Empathy. Inner strength to match that impressive outer strength… And I didn't want to ignore a thing. "You're trying to tell me something."

"Yes, but I'm better at showing than telling." He pulled me into his lap, wrapped me up tight, and pressed his face into the crook of my neck, inhaling me like I was the last drop of oxygen on Earth.

"God, you always smell so fucking good," he murmured against my skin. "And the way you look at me like I'm full of shit…" I felt him smile against me. "Drives me out of my mind. And then there's your mouth, your smart-ass mouth… I need to taste you again, Emma."

I forgot how to breathe, but not bothered by my impending suffocation, he dragged his teeth along my throat.

I moaned.

"Tell me no, Em."

I opened my mouth to say just that, but my traitorous lips whispered, "*Yes.*"

"Is that *yes, back off* or *yes, kiss me?*"

"It's *yes, if you don't kiss me, I'm going to combust.*"

He lifted his head and met my gaze, his hazel eyes hot and

177

hungry and searching. He must have found what he wanted because he tightened his grip so that our bodies were flush, and I could feel the heat of him radiating into my skin in the chill room, making me sigh with pleasure.

When our mouths collided, I moaned again. He kissed like the world was ending: devouring, demanding, worshipping, giving me such pleasure that it left me utterly defenseless.

Far too quickly, he pulled back and met my gaze, one arm wrapped around my waist, solid as steel, pinning my hips against his. The other hand was in my hair, fingers tangled, using the grip to hold me to him as I struggled with the urge to tear away the clothes between us. "Why did you stop?" I asked breathlessly.

"I felt the need to remind you that you don't like me."

I wanted to both laugh and jump him. "Most people can keep sex and feelings separate. In fact, we should label it a rule."

When he winced, I knew I'd given myself away, that I wasn't *most people*, but I wanted to be. I wanted to be just like everyone else who could take what they wanted and walk away without looking back. "You're not going to ruin this, are you?"

He drew in some air. "Let's just breathe for a sec."

Okay, fine. I let my head fall back, and his lips ghosted across my throat, my jaw. I heard the words he spoke against my ear as much as I felt them inside my body. "Be sure, Em."

I was *so* sure, it was shocking. "Did you want me not to be?"

"No, I want you to be *very* sure."

"I'm not asking for a future, if that's what you think. I know I'm not..." *Easy to fall for.* Nor did I fall easily, at least until recently. After all, I was the girl who'd managed to hold on to a silly grudge simply to ensure I didn't *accidentally* fall for him.

"Not what, Em?" he asked, something in his voice that I couldn't name but made me wary.

"Do you always talk this much?" I threw as much attitude as I could into the question.

He stared at me for a full ten seconds. Which I knew because I'd counted.

"Any other rules?" he finally asked in his low, gravelly voice, the one he never used on the jobsite, only with me, and it made my heart thump wildly in my chest like it was fighting its cage.

It would be so easy to let myself be taken apart by that voice, those hands, the big, hard body I couldn't stop dreaming about. That wasn't the problem. My feelings were the problem. I kept them in that cage alongside my heart, and I was having trouble keeping it locked. "No other rules," I managed to say softly.

Those mesmerizing eyes of his trained on my mouth, his hands angling my face, drawing me to him as he breathed a single word against my lips. "Okay."

"Okay," I whispered back. My heart raced. The bones in my legs were suddenly…unboned. My heart thundered more than the storm around us as we stared at each other, teetering on a precipice.

Then he smiled, all sexy as hell. "I like you like this," he said. "All flushed and discombobulated."

I liked him like this too: bedroom eyes, knowing hands, sexy body… He was beautiful, and I felt like I'd hopped on a Tilt-A-Whirl at the fair. If I could just keep spinning, I could avoid my real fear: falling. Falling into another hopeless relationship. Because when he walked away—and it would happen, as it always did—my heart would be broken beyond repair.

"Kiss me," I said breathlessly, dooming myself.

And then his mouth was on mine again, his fist tightening in my hair, using the grip to angle my face the way he wanted it, and any lingering doubts died in my throat.

This kiss wasn't gentle or soft. It was hungry, and wild, and all-consuming. His arms tightened around me as a rough groan reverberated from his chest and into mine. And every scrap of pent-up desire I'd buried barreled through me like a freight train until I had only one word in my head.

"More."

CHAPTER 18

Caleb

A T THE FIRST TASTE of Emma, I forgot everything as my blood roared in my ears, my heart drumming in tune to the rain. I wanted to believe this was nothing more than two people stuck in a storm, but that was a lie. I wanted this, I wanted *her*, and if I were being honest, I'd wanted her all those years ago too.

But all that faded away when I slanted my lips over hers. The howling rage of the storm around us vanished as the kiss consumed me, dragging me willfully under her spell. I couldn't see shit, hell, I could hardly breathe, but I was surrounded by her scent, her warmth, and the feel of her restlessly squirming against me, letting out the sexiest little whimpers for more, more, more. Her hands were tightly fisted in my hair like she needed me more than air, the sounds she was making heating me up like sunlight on my skin.

I slid my hands just beneath the sweatshirt of mine she wore, teasingly stroking up and down her stomach and ribs to the underside of her breasts, always stopping short until, with a huff of impatience, she grabbed my hands and dragged them where she wanted them.

A rough groan escaped me at the handfuls of soft, warm curves. My thumbs stroked over her peaked nipples, and she let out a choked cry that went straight to my dick. I started to pull back, trying to gain some control, but she held on tight while also tugging until I lay at her side, not letting go until we were plastered together like peanut butter and jelly. She did suck in some air when she felt what she'd done to me, but the woman—on a clear mission now—rocked into my body.

And again.

I was…undone. Wrecked. In the very best of ways. "Emma—"

"Caleb," she said, imitating my low growl with surprising accuracy. Then she smiled at me, her eyes filled with wonder and desire and heat and longing. Her guard was down, revealing the warmth beneath that tough-girl exterior, and it completely unmanned me.

We were the exact same in that regard, impenetrable until we were around each other. I ran a finger along her jaw, down her throat, smiling when she shivered, gently touching the dainty gold necklace with the two blue sapphires she always wore. "Em—"

Rearing up, she kissed me. *Okay, no talking then. Got it.* I rolled her beneath me and took control of the kiss, groaning when she wriggled into me like I was the only thing that mattered on the planet. I was nudging the sweatshirt off her, and she was sliding her hands into the back of my sweats to grip my bare ass when a loud shattering of glass from somewhere below us split through the air.

We jerked apart in shock. My shirt was off, hers was half off, and we were both breathing like we'd forgotten how lungs work.

"What was that?" she whispered, shoving the sweatshirt back into place as I rose to my feet.

I was already on the move, shoving my glasses back on my face, grabbing a flashlight. "Stay."

She grabbed the other flashlight and ran down the stairs right behind me.

"So much for stay," I muttered.

"Because I'm not a dog."

Six rooms loomed ahead, empty and echoing, the fresh drywall still smelling of plaster.

We skidded to a stop at the first door and sucked in a breath. The window was gone, shattered into a million pieces, shards of glass glinting on the floor. Wind and rain howled through the gaping hole, along with the massive gnarled branch that had broken the glass—a wicked-looking reminder of the storm's fury.

Emma backed up a few steps. Her spine hit the wall behind her. "Ohmigod."

"Hey," I said, moving to her. "Hey, it's okay. We're okay."

Her eyes were wide. "Are we? Because last I checked, we're stuck out here, and it could get worse—"

I reached for her, but she pushed me away, turning her back, hugging herself.

"Emma—"

"The plans for this property called for a pruning and trimming of the ten trees around the perimeter of the house," she said tightly.

"Yes," I agreed. "And the tree company's on our schedule; they just haven't gotten to us yet. Look, Emma, I know this is bringing up bad memories, but the manor's huge, so it's easy enough to stay away from windows. We're still safe."

She nodded, then shook her head. "I don't feel safe."

My heart squeezed. "We'll go down to the basement—"

"I didn't mean physically." She met my gaze with her bleak one. "You know how when you start eating M&M's and tell yourself you can only have ten, but deep down you know that's a lie, that you don't intend to stop until they're gone?"

I blinked. "Uh…"

She shook her head. "You were right; this is a bad idea."

I opened my mouth to say that no, we weren't, but that would be me not validating her feelings.

And then there was the other thing. The one I'd conveniently ignored. If we slept together here, then I was basically proving Ryder right, mixing business—his—with pleasure—mine. But something was most definitely different this time. I'd 100 percent connected with Emma on an emotional level. Shockingly easily.

That wasn't the problem. No, the problem was that I had zero idea what to do with these feelings I'd never let myself experience. Feeling left of center, I did what I always did when I had no idea what to do—I defaulted to my manufacturer settings. "If you think we made a mistake," I heard myself say, "then we made a mistake."

She stared at me. Into me. And I could've sworn that, even though she'd started this conversation, she was disappointed.

Well, she could get in line. Disappointing those I loved was my specialty.

Fuck, she was shivering again; I could see her vibrating from head to toe from where I stood, but I couldn't touch her, not with how she stood there hugging herself tight, now no longer looking at me. "Look," I finally said, "there's nothing we can do tonight."

"There's nothing 'we' can do period," she said. "Because there is no we."

Right. I gestured for her to head up the stairs first, still not touching her no matter how badly I wanted to. In silence, we moved to the attic and stared at the bed we'd been sharing only a few minutes before.

"You take it," she said.

"I want you to be warm, Emma."

"Same." She sighed. "We're supposedly grown-ups; we can do this. You can lie one way, and I'll lie the other."

Relieved I wouldn't have to worry about if she was warm enough all night, I moved to where she directed. We settled in, her head at one end, mine at the other.

Outside, the atmospheric river raged on, while inside we lay there in the silence. I was still, not moving, barely breathing. How had we gotten here, to this…this silence? Because if there was one thing Emma and I had never been with each other, it was silent.

She was shifting around, tossing and turning, muttering to herself.

"Problem?"

"No."

But she kept twitching and moving around. "*Emma.*"

"Fine. I'm cold." Her hands brushed against my arm, and I just barely managed not to yelp at the icy touch.

"Come here." I reached out, tugging until she'd turned around, her back against my chest, the backs of her thighs pressed to the fronts of mine, my arms around her, holding tight.

After a beat, she let out a long, slow breath of relief and relaxed into me. "Thank you," she said softly.

CHAPTER 19

Caleb

HAD NO IDEA how much time had gone by or what time it even was when Emma stirred. "Does your go bag have a deck of cards?" she murmured sleepily.

"No, but..." I lifted my now-empty water bottle. "We could play spin the bottle."

She snorted. "There are only two of us."

I grinned. "I like my odds."

She appeared to forget how to use words for a moment. "What about truth or dare?"

Yeah, she was one smart cookie all right. "You want to ask me stuff I don't want to answer."

"Duh."

I chuckled. "On one condition. It's in the cone of silence." I had no idea what I was doing. It was shocking, how badly I wanted her to let me in, if only to prove us both wrong.

Looking intrigued, she bit her lower lip. "Like we're in some sort of time continuum where this doesn't exist outside of right here, right now? Like…whatever happens in a wild and crazy storm *stays* in the wild and crazy storm?"

I grinned. "Exactly."

"You're on," she said. "I like to think it's because I'm incredibly brave, but it may just be that I don't have the back-down gene."

I laughed, because didn't I know it. "So, Em, truth…or dare?"

"Oh boy," she whispered, then drew a deep breath. "Truth. No, wait! Dare."

I smiled. "Chicken."

Her eyes narrowed. "You want me to pick truth so you can finally make me tell you why I didn't like you in college."

"And on the jobsite," I reminded her. "And the gala. And here, until not too many hours ago."

"Why didn't *you* like *me*?" she asked.

This took me aback. "I never didn't like you. Never," I repeated when she gave me a *get real* look. "Okay, maybe for a moment when you ditched me for that project and I lost the game."

"If it helps, I'm not really sorry about that, given how many times you ditched me with a group project."

I snorted. "Touché. And I owe you a most sincere thank-you for all the times you covered my ass." She looked surprised at that, so I leaned in. "I'm truly sorry I was so inconsiderate."

"Wow," she said. "A thank-you and an apology. I'm impressed."

I hated that the bare minimum of manners impressed her, and I promised myself right then and there I'd somehow make up for all the assholes in her past, including me.

Her long, wavy chestnut hair was a tangled mess, half in and half out of a ponytail, the strands framing a face full of intelligence and warmth. She was makeup-free and had a crease across her cheek from the sleeping bag, and…she was the most beautiful woman I'd ever seen. "Don't look back, Em." I flashed a smile. "Remember? What happens in the storm stays in the storm. Ready for your dare?"

"Make it count, Caleb."

I liked the way she said my name. Way too much. "I dare you to…" I smiled. "Do something that proves you're brave."

"Like what? Kiss you again?"

My heart stopped. "Your choice."

She stared at me for a long beat, then crawled across the sleeping bag until she was kneeling at my side. Slowly, she leaned in until I could feel her sweet Froot-Loops breath on my face and drown in those amazing green eyes.

"Say please," she whispered.

Easiest word I'd ever said. "*Please.*"

She gave a soft hum of pleasure, then dragged the very tip of her nose along the underside of my jaw, inhaling like she needed the scent of me more than air. My entire body tightened as she lifted her head, stared down at my mouth—*yeah, babe, go there*—and…kissed me on my cheek.

When she pulled back, she wore a snarky, smug smile. "*What?*"

I nearly laughed. The woman was a witch, and I was here for it. "You know what."

"It wasn't established *where* I should kiss you," she pointed out.

"It was implied."

"You sure?" She tilted her head. "Because I'm uncertain what kind of a kiss you were expecting."

She wanted to play. Playing was my forte. "Shall I show you?"

"Maybe you should."

"Okay," I said. "But just one kiss, no matter how much you beg for more."

She rolled her eyes, and I laughed with sheer joy. Fuck, I was crazy. I wrapped my hand around her messy ponytail and tugged her closer, an arm around her lower back to hold her against me. Her mouth. I couldn't stop staring at it as I lowered my head, starting off with a gentle cradling of lips, slow and sweet, before pulling back.

"That's all you got?" she asked breathlessly.

She had no idea. I soaked up the sight of her, a little ruffled, a lot loved up, and I couldn't tear my gaze away. Then she made grabby hands for me, and I both laughed and fucking melted. Being here with her like this, sequestered from the rest of the world, was everything tonight. Or maybe it was already tomorrow. Whatever day it was, I wanted to kiss her again and again. Slow. Deep. Wet. But I wouldn't. Not yet. I wouldn't take those grabby hands and pin them to the sleeping bag. I wouldn't slide a thigh between hers and plunder her sweet, smart-ass mouth as I slid into her—

"Caleb," she moaned, arching up into me.

I kissed her, just as I'd wanted. I entangled our fingers and drew her hands above her head and pinned her, sliding a thigh between hers.

"More," she demanded.

It took effort to pull back, to lift my head and meet her hungry eyes. "I'm going to give you a truth," I said. "A freebie."

I grazed the pad of my thumb over her lower lip. "You mean something to me, Emma. But you're stuck here with me, and we're all alone. I won't take advantage of you. I'll *never* take advantage of you."

She blinked. "I'm pretty sure I instigated this. And you're just as stuck here with me. Do you feel like I took advantage of you?"

I gave a slow shake of my head.

"You sure?"

I had to smile, because I knew where this was going. Or at least I hoped I knew. "Very."

"Good, because I'm very sure too. Would you like me to sign an NDA?"

"Smart-ass." I nipped at her earlobe. "I'm trying to do the right thing here, which is hard because you've got those big ol' eyes that melt away my common sense and a smile that makes me so fucking stupid, I can't remember my own name half the time."

Emma batted those eyes, and I shook my head. "You're a menace."

She just smiled. "Good to know." She sat up and studied me for a long beat. "Truth or dare, Caleb?"

"It's your turn."

She gave a slow shake of her head. "You gave me a freebie. Doesn't count. Truth or dare?"

Oh shit. If she dared me to touch her, I wouldn't be able to resist, and I needed to. No quickies. No moving too fast and screwing things up. I'd done enough of that in the past, and I liked to think I learned from my mistakes, but if I took her now, it would mean I hadn't learned shit. "Truth."

"Unexpected, but okay…" She stared at me, thinking so hard that I could smell something burning. "What would your dating profile say? Your likes, favorite vices, what you wear to bed, if you have a rebellious side, that sort of thing—and don't hold back," she demanded with a smug smile, so sure I'd balk.

"It would say that I like long walks on the beach and getting caught in the rain."

She rolled her eyes, and I smiled. "It would also say my favorite vice is whiskey, I sleep in my birthday suit, and I admit nothing regarding a rebellious side except this—if it says not to push the button, I'm gonna push the button."

She laughed, and I said, "Your turn."

Emma hesitated. "Dare."

"I dare you to answer a truth."

Her brows scrunched together. "Hey. That's cheating."

"It's not cheating," I said. "Truth, or forfeit."

"Fine!" She tossed up her hands. "Truth."

"Why did *you* hate *me*?"

"I should have seen that one coming," she muttered, then sighed. "And it wasn't that I hated you."

"Felt like it." I had no idea why I was pushing so hard. Tonight had brought us together in a way I hadn't allowed myself to hope for. And normally, this realization was when I'd bail, but for the first time in my life, I didn't want to.

Emma squeezed her eyes shut, and something inside my chest tightened at her obvious pain and reluctance. "It's okay," I said. "Forget it. I don't want to make this hard—"

"It *is* hard," she said quietly. "But not as hard as some of the stuff I was going through at the time. I told you my mom and I…we struggled. So, when she was gone, there was nothing left for me. I was eighteen and had no home, no savings, and no real way to improve my life. I'd gotten into college but hadn't gotten a scholarship or aid. Then I found out about a new scholarship in the architectural-history program. No one could apply until after the first semester, but it was a hundred thousand dollars toward tuition—which would cover two of the four years—*and* a paid summer term in Europe to study the history of architecture there, plus a *guaranteed* internship the summer after graduation."

I realized I'd gone utterly still, was in fact barely breathing.

"The scholarship went to a full-ride hockey player," she said.

"No, it didn't." That summer abroad had changed my life and cemented that it wasn't hockey I needed long-term, but something much more, something that involved history and architecture. "I wasn't a full-ride hockey player. I was a walk-on."

Her mouth fell open. "What?"

"I didn't start playing until my junior year of high school, so I lost out on an entire hockey season and didn't get recruited. When I got to college, I joined an intramural league. The men's hockey coach happened to see me play, told me about open tryouts. I went, he took me on, but there was no money attached. In fact, I didn't get a scholarship until my junior year."

She was staring at me, and then she drew a deep breath. "I...I didn't know that. All this time, I thought..." She blinked, then shook her head, eyes heavy with regret. "I blamed you for the fact that I graduated not only deep in debt, but without that summer worth of experience abroad and no internship."

If the situation had been reversed, I'd have felt the same way. "I understand."

"You shouldn't." She shook her head. "I took all that disap-pointment and fear and anxiety, and I piled it right on your head. I was horrible to you all those years, I—" Her eyes filled. "I'm sorry."

"No, don't apologize. By the time I walked away from hockey, it didn't matter because I had an internship waiting for me." I drew a deep breath. "I'm sorry, so fucking sorry you didn't get it, Emma, but it saved my life. I honestly don't know where I'd be without it."

"You deserved it. I mean it, Caleb. You did. I just didn't know it at the time. I let myself be mired down in resentment."

"You were just trying to survive," I said. "I think a part of me always knew that."

"Is that why you were always nice to me, even when I was hateful?"

I laughed. "You weren't the only one just trying to survive. I needed you pushing me the way you did, challenging me, making me want to try hard for the first time in my life."

Her laugh was a little soggy, but 100 percent contagious. "I don't know how you even saw me. You had girls hanging all over you, even when it was rumored you were in a relationship with…Renee someone or another; she worked in the gym."

My brows rose. "You knew about that?"

"*Everyone* knew. The most likely student to become a pro hockey player with the most likely student to become the world's biggest influencer? Match made in heaven."

"Renee and I didn't go out until my senior year," I said. "And it didn't last. For a bunch of reasons. After I got hurt, everyone was so disappointed. And no one knew how to talk to me or be with me. Renee had thought she was going to be with a version of me who would provide a certain lifestyle. But I was never going to be that guy."

"So you walked before she could," Emma guessed.

"I did. I'm not proud of it, but it was the right thing to do."

Emma studied me for a beat. "I've misjudged you for a long time. I'm sorrier for that than I can say."

"If you did, it's because I wanted you to."

"Then let's be done with that," she said, then crawled into my arms, and the world outside felt very far away.

CHAPTER 20

Emma

MELTED AS CALEB'S sure, knowing hands slowly slid down my arms to my waist, my hips. There was nothing like all those delicious muscles pressed against me, radiating heat into me everywhere we touched, his breath warm on my throat just before he took a nibble, making me shiver and tilt my head, giving him more room.

"I can't stop thinking about you." His voice was sexy gruff as his hands slid back up again, under the sweatshirt this time. "I thought if I kept my distance, I'd get over how badly I want you."

His fingertips were just beneath my aching breasts, and I was already nearly panting. "How's that working?"

His chuckle was low and deep. "There's no getting over you, Emma."

I couldn't breathe. "Sure there is; you just walk away. It's not that hard." Plenty of people had done it...

He tipped my face up to his. "With you, it's hard."

Since I could feel just how *hard* he was, I snorted at the

double entendre, but he didn't smile, just leaned in and kissed my shoulder, my chin, my mouth. "Do you know how much I want you?" he whispered.

What happens in the storm stays in the storm. I repeated the mantra as I ground against him. "I'm starting to get an idea, yes."

He kissed me. And kissed me. He kissed me until I was rocking up into him, desperate for more. When I slid my hands into the back of his sweats and gripped his perfect ass, he groaned into my mouth. I dug my fingers in a little, needing more of that delicious friction, and a thrillingly low rumble escaped him, sounding almost like a purr.

Then suddenly we were both tearing at each other's clothes, no finesse, lots of breathless laughter, trying like hell to get skin to skin. His lips captured mine again, his teeth pulling at my bottom lip. "I've pictured this so many, many times," he growled as he left a trail of bites while he headed south from my throat, past my collarbone, the whole time his hand gliding up and down, up and down, touching…everything, revving me up so that I could hardly draw a breath.

"You make me crazy, Em."

"Right back at you—" A desperate moan escaped me as his mouth latched onto my nipple at the same time his hand slid between my legs. His chuckle reverberated against my chest while I clutched his shoulders, his biceps, his back, anything I could reach, loving the feel of his muscles rippling beneath my fingertips.

Then, suddenly, he was off the bed and on his knees before me. "I need to taste you." His breath curled against my overheated skin.

I raked my fingers through his thick hair, drinking in the

image of his broad shoulders covered in dark ink. I wanted to know what he tasted like, too, what he sounded like when he came apart, how it would feel to share my body with him, and it all made me squirm as the chilly night pebbled goose bumps over my bare skin, puckering my nipples up tight. Only, I knew it wasn't the cold air at all but Caleb and his hot mouth working its way south, past my belly button, his big hands sliding up the inside of my thighs, spreading them.

He gave a ragged groan. "Fucking beautiful," he whispered and rubbed his scruffy jaw gently up one inner thigh, then the other before taking a shockingly slow, *thorough* lick right up my center. Crying out, I arched into his touch, head back, fingers tightening in his hair in case he had thoughts about getting away. *Remember, what happens in the storm stays in the storm—*

Caleb huffed a rough laugh. "I remember."

Well, crap, I'd said it out loud. Mindless, I pressed the back of my head against the mattress, scrunching my eyes closed. "Caleb—"

"No, I get it." He looked up at me from between my legs. "I wouldn't want a Colburn to fall in love with me either."

"It's not that—" I broke off on a full-body shudder as he backed off a little, pressing hot, open-mouthed kisses along the groove of my thigh, a good two inches from where I wanted that talented tongue, so it was a little hard to concentrate on words. "Caleb, it's not—"

"Shh, Em. It's okay." And he certainly made it so, doing wicked things with his knowing mouth and fingers that had me incoherent and rocking up into him for more.

"You make me lose my mind…" he whispered against my damp flesh, in the *exact* right spot, then gave me a soft, sucking kiss that had me crying out.

Caleb groaned, the sound low and dark, matching the rumbling thunder outside. I thought he murmured my name in awe, but I couldn't hear him over the sound of *his* name being ripped from my throat. His mouth was knowing and hungry, and pinned in place as I was by his broad shoulders, by the hands gripping my ass, holding me where he wanted, I came hard, losing my mind and possibly my heart and soul.

When I stopped shuddering and found a scrap of awareness, I sat up and reached for him, pushing him until our positions were reversed and he was sprawled on his back.

He closed his eyes. "Em, you don't have to—"

"I want to." I ran a hand down his carved chest. His abs twitched, and I smiled. "I really, *really* want to." My mouth was watering as I wrapped my fingers around his incredibly impressive—

A honk startled me. And then another, as the sound of trucks, big ones, pulled up outside. Even more startling, night was giving way to dawn, the gunmetal gray of the sky had glimmers of pink and purple to the east.

Swearing, Caleb sat up and looked through the railings to the windows and groaned for an entirely different reason now. "You've gotta be kidding me."

"What is it?"

"My cockblocking brother."

"Hey, princess," Ryder yelled. "Rescue's here."

CHAPTER 21

Caleb

WAS DRAGGING ASS as I walked into the Colburn Restorations building. It wasn't quite yet dawn, that was nothing new, but over the past forty-eight hours, we'd been run ragged repairing the damage the storm had done to our various ongoing jobs.

Since the fire station and search and rescue had called for all hands on deck, we hadn't seen hide nor hair of Tucker. Kiera had kept Hank and the doggos for me, and it was a good thing. I'd been home for a total of maybe four hours over the past two nights.

I slid my glasses off to rub my gritty eyes, trying to wake myself up. All I needed was food, sleep, and a few minutes alone with Emma to make sure she was doing okay. None of that was in the cards for me today.

I could still feel that sweet bod of hers spread out for me, trembling as I took her to the very edge, her arms clutching me tight, fingers fisted in my hair, as if afraid I'd stop. And those sexy little pants she made right before she'd come... She'd imprinted it on my brain, and now all I could see was how she'd looked at me. Like I mattered to her.

She'd left the minute Ryder and the guys had arrived on-site and cleared the tree, and I hadn't seen her since. I'd called, using the excuse that I wanted to make sure she'd gotten home safe and sound, but she hadn't picked up. Nor returned a text.

Message reluctantly received.

Ryder had leveled me a long look when he'd realized Emma had been stranded with me overnight, but he hadn't said a word.

Yet.

As I had been doing for months now, I spent the early morning hours at the Colburn Restorations offices. Ryder might hate the paperwork, the shmoozing of clients, the managing of employees, but I didn't. To me, this part of the job was a puzzle, and putting it all together and keeping it that way was a challenge I thrived on.

Except for maybe today, after too little sleep while trying to face an insurmountable backlog of insurance crap, neglected paperwork, and meetings for each of our ongoing jobs.

Grif slid gracefully into my office and set a smoothie before me.

I drank it down gratefully. "You deserve a raise."

"Wouldn't say no to that."

I met his warm, laughing brown eyes. I knew his story, that seven years ago Ryder had found him as a teen living on the streets, kicked out of his house for being gay. "You're worth it."

Grif winked. "You know I am." And then he dumped more shit to do on my desk.

I swore as he cackled and left me alone. Since sleep wasn't happening, I moved on to my next most pressing need and headed straight into our staff kitchen. The smoothie had been great, but I needed more. By happy coincidence, Penny was there stocking us up.

"You're drooling," she teased when she handed me a plate piled high with fresh food.

I was shoveling it all in as fast as I could chew while she added sourdough toast. "You're marrying the wrong Colburn brother."

Penny snorted. "So you keep saying."

"We both know I'm funnier, not nearly as grumpy, and can take Ry in basketball, football, obviously hockey, and sometimes chess."

"Never in chess," Ryder said from where he leaned casually against the doorjamb, arms crossed.

Penny gave a little squeak of joy and ran over to him. Ryder straightened, arms out, and she jumped right into them, wrapping herself around him like cling wrap.

Since they were blocking the doorway, I did my best to ignore Ryder's hands on Penny's ass, her legs around his waist, and the hungry kissing. But when my plate was empty, I finally said, "Either get a room or break it up, kids. Shit to do, people to see, and all that."

Penny let her legs drop to the floor and backed away, smiling softly at Ryder as she did. "Sorry," she said. "We haven't seen each in two whole days."

Ryder smiled right back at her, his features softening, and any irritation I had with him drained away. At least momentarily. Ryder had saved my life on so many occasions, I'd lost count, starting when we were kids and he'd taken it upon himself to draw Hank's wrath away from the rest of us, and ending when he practically sat on me for a full year after my hockey accident and subsequent surgeries. He always, without fail, single-handedly kept us siblings together through thick and thin, and there'd been a shitload of thin. Never once had he put himself first. He deserved this happiness more than anyone I knew, and I was so incredibly happy for him.

While also being envious as fuck.

I was heading out the door when Ryder said, "Caleb."

Shit. I knew that tone; any softness that seeing Penny had given him was gone. "Let me guess," I said. "Your office."

He nodded.

Penny sent me another smile, this one pure sympathy, then grabbed my brother and kissed him one last time. "Be nice to my backup future husband," she said against his mouth.

"No promises," Ryder said.

Great. We headed to his office in silence, nodding at Grif behind the reception desk and then Bill, who we passed in the hallway. Neither tried to stop us to talk. No one wanted to talk to Ry when he was in a mood.

It was the one thing he'd gotten from the old Hank. Like it or not, all of us had gotten something from him. I had the man's stubbornness. I could dig my toes into the sand and not be budged by a hundred-foot wave. It was my superpower.

And usually my downfall.

In Ryder's office, I went straight to the bank of windows and looked out at the green rolling hills divided by the Russian River meandering along with absolutely zero life worries. I heard my brother come in behind me but remained silent. If he wanted to talk, he could go first.

Two deer bounded playfully along the river. Summer in Star

Falls was usually my favorite season. My brothers and I had a long-standing camping tradition, where we hiked up Mount Saint Helena, slept on the windblown cliffs, played a hybrid—and vicious—Colburn version of touch football until we were bruised and bloody, and then drank until we were stupid. Or at least, stupider than usual.

I wondered if Ryder would want to go this year now that he was with Penny. Or if Tucker would be able to take the time off from the fire station.

Maybe I was the only one who even cared about the trip anymore. I ground my teeth, tired of Ryder's silence, which he used as a strategic argument tool. "Just spit it out," I finally said.

"You should've told me."

Gee, wonder what he's talking about... "You do realize we didn't intend to get stuck there, right?"

"Why were you both even there on a Sunday? Why would you take a date to the jobsite?"

I turned to face him. No one, and I mean no one, could get to me faster than a fellow Colburn, and for a beat, I struggled with the urge to punch his stupid face. "You asked me not to date anyone related to work, and I haven't." Nope, there'd been no dating involved... "Emma was there to get a measurement she'd forgotten." Maybe, because she'd never actually told me what she'd needed there. "And I was checking to make sure nothing had gotten left out that could get damaged in the storm."

Ryder's face was impassive. God forbid he ever be wrong. About anything.

Except.... Fuck. He *wasn't* wrong, and I felt like an asshole. In my defense, I hadn't been this attracted to *anyone* like I was to Emma.

Ry ran a hand over his face, a rare tell. "Just…keep it clean."

Since I hadn't, I went on the defensive. "Like you did?"

Ry inhaled sharply. "What happened between me and Penny had no effect on the job."

I laughed. "You sure about that? Because I was there when you were so stupid in lust, you walked your face into a wall."

Ryder's expression softened, and hell, he even smiled.

I sighed. "She's good for you, man, and I'm happy for you."

"Fuck." He sighed. "I want it for you, too, Caleb. More than anything. But…" He met my gaze, his own serious. "What would you do differently this time? With Emma?"

"Meaning?"

"Meaning, once you've slept with someone, you normally get bored and move on. And now you've already started down the same old path, spending the night together."

"I didn't bring that storm," I said. "And we didn't…*didn't*." That it was only because Ryder himself had shown up was a detail I didn't intend to share. Ever.

"She was wearing your clothes," he pointed out.

"She was cold."

"When I get cold, you tell me to suck it up," Tucker said.

I turned and found my brother propping up the doorway, arms crossed, watching us carefully. If I was The Fixer, he was our arbitrator, because out of us siblings, he alone had a depthless well of patience. I was tapped out, and worse, I was feeling rough and on edge, emotions I tried like hell to always keep at bay.

Tucker casually moved into the office. He slung an arm around Ry's shoulders and then mine—thanks to his stupid six feet four inches of lanky, sneaky strength. Ry and I each turned to glare at him, but he just pinned both our necks in the crooks of his elbows, leaving us nose to nose, cheeks smashed into his chest.

Ry began to struggle, trying to pull his head from Tucker's death grip, but I merely relaxed and snorted.

Ry gave up and did the same, laughing as he threw an elbow that Tucker evaded, still holding us hostage by the neck.

"You've been busy," I said conversationally.

"Storm was a bitch," Tuck agreed casually. "Anyway, here's what's going to happen—Ryder's going to apologize for being a dick when he himself recently fell so stupidly in love in this very building."

Ryder sputtered, but Tucker just tightened his grip, and hell, the guy was stronger than I remembered.

"And," Tucker went on merrily, "Caleb's going to apologize because Ryder's the boss and what he says goes in regard to the business. But Ry gets the right to say he told you so when you get bored or spooked and walk away from Emma, causing trouble on the Henderson job."

My chest tightened, but Ry and I both gave a barely there nod of agreement.

Tucker released us and brushed his hands together like he'd just finished an important task.

I blew out a breath. "He's right," I said to Ryder. "You are the boss, and what you say goes—in regard to the business. But not in my private life."

Tucker nodded his approval and then stared down Ryder, who rolled his eyes and said, "I'm sorry. Not for my orders, but for being...insensitive." His voice softened. "I don't want either of you to ever feel like I'm flaunting my happiness in your face."

"Oh, you are, but we don't hold that against you," I said. "Like I said, you deserve this." As for me and Emma, whatever was between us wasn't up for discussion. What happened in the storm stayed in the storm. We'd both agreed on that, and Emma had silently reinforced it by not returning my calls or texts in the past two days, even when I'd jokingly texted **am I still "Don't Even" in your phone?**

Ryder started to say something, but Ricky, our finish-carpentry subcontractor, burst into the room, looking furious. Grif was right on his heels. "Sorry," Grif said to Ryder. "He refused to take a seat—"

"They're gone," Ricky interrupted, steam coming out of his ears. "All my tools, at least twenty-five K's worth."

"It's okay, Grif, we got this," I said, and when Grif nodded and left, I turned to Ricky. He could've been a linebacker in the NFL. I was a big guy, but he had two inches and probably fifty pounds on me.

And every pound of him got up in my face. "My trailer's gone," he spit out furiously. "Someone stole it from the job, and now every fucking tool I own is gone."

Several times in the past year, we've had materials go missing, along with a few other small weird things like my truck tires being slashed on a jobsite months ago. And then there'd been that mystery truck speeding away from the Henderson job.

Either way, the renovations world was small, and the last thing we needed was for word to get out that we were having troubles. On top of that, as good as Ricky was on the job, he was equally known for his loose scruples. Had his trailer been stolen, or had he seen an opportunity for a payday? "Was the trailer locked?"

A muscle ticked in Ricky's jaw. "What are you saying?"

"I'm not saying anything; I'm asking you a question."

"Yes. Maybe." Ricky hands fisted. "Fuck, I don't know, it doesn't fucking matter. No one but my crew and your people knew I was working here."

I raised a brow, relieved Ry remained quiet, letting me handle this. Ricky was far less likely to try and fight me than my brother. "You think one of our guys stole your tools?" I asked calmly.

"I *know* it." Ricky jabbed a meaty finger in my face. "I also know I was a last-minute hire and that no one wanted me there. So yeah, I think this is an inside job. So here's what's going to happen: You're going to give me money to replace the tools, right here, right now."

Ry and I exchanged a look, the tension between us gone for the moment. It had always been that way. We fought among ourselves but were a united front against the world. "That's not how this works," I told Ricky. "I'll head to the site now to take a look for myself. If your trailer's been stolen, I'll make a police report, and we'll each call our insurance companies and let them do their job."

"*If* my trailer's been stolen?'" Ricky repeated, his voice low and menacing. "You don't believe me?"

"Senior year of high school," Ryder said casually, "you accused a kid of stealing your car. Turned out, you'd gotten drunk with your buddies and forgotten where you parked it."

So much for letting me handle it.

Ricky stared at Ryder for a charged beat. "So what? We were stupid kids."

"True." I shifted, placing myself between my brother and Ricky, since the guy was quick to lead with a fist. "And as I said, if the tools and trailer were stolen, we'll take care of it."

Ricky lunged. I'd faced down my fair share of angry "enforcers" on the ice, but it had been a while. Still, I sidestepped the blow, then grabbed his other fist until he lowered it.

"Get out," I said quietly. "Before we add assault to the situation."

"You gotta be kidding me," Ricky snapped. "Since when does a Colburn back down from and then cry about it?"

"I'll meet you on the jobsite in twenty," I said.

Ricky stared at me, eyes furious and spoiling for a physical altercation. "Fuck you. Fuck all of you." And then he was gone.

Ryder scrubbed a hand down his face. "What are the chances he's telling the truth?"

"Low," Tucker said. "But not zero. Not when you factor in the other incidents."

"Agreed," I said. "The problem with Ricky is that it's always a fight with him. He's already causing chaos on the jobsite, always half-cocked at someone or something, purposely creating rifts. It pisses everyone off."

Ryder looked grim. "Whatever happened, he's gone, even if I have to buy out his contract and do the work myself."

"You don't have time for that," Tucker said. "None of us does. We need another sub, like yesterday."

I nodded. "Agreed. But no more messing around. If we get behind on this project, we're going to accrue some hefty penalty fees." I looked at Ryder. "I know what you promised Hazel's mom, but hell, man, we're desperate. Let me hire Hazel and her crew. I mean, unless you want to accuse me of sleeping with her too."

It was a low blow, and it hit.

"Fuck." Ryder tipped his head back and groaned at the

ceiling. "Fine. Hire Hazel. For this job only," he warned. "We can reevaluate after it's finished. But if she and Bill slow this job down with their personal shit, it's on you."

Oh good. One more thing on me…

The first thing I did when I got to the job was look for Emma's car, but there was no sign of it. She had no reason to be here today, but it didn't stop the pang of disappointment in my gut.

I understood the moment between us was over, she'd made that clear in the past few days, but it didn't change anything for me. I still wanted to know she was okay, and more than that, I wanted to do something to lighten her load. Knowing how hard she was working, I figured I'd send her a meal.

Only, I had no idea where she lived. I texted Kiera, asking if she had Emma's address, and her response was classic Kiera: **Even if I did know, you'd still have to get it from her.**

Fine. Whatever. I texted Hazel that one, I needed to meet with her ASAP, because I was done messing around. I was hiring her for the Henderson job even if I had to sit on her and Bill to get along. And two, ask if she had Emma's address.

My phone buzzed with an incoming call. "I hate texting," Hazel said. "What do you want to meet about? It feels bad. Is it bad?"

"Of course it's not bad. I'm Caleb, not Ryder or Tucker."

She laughed, and I asked, "Are you swamped right now with work?"

"I'm double- and triple-booked."

I paused, surprised. "Really?"

"No." She sighed. "I had a job lined up, but it fell through. I just didn't want to seem like a loser."

"We fired Ricky. The Henderson project is yours if you want it."

Silence.

"Haze?"

"I want twenty percent more than you were paying Ricky."

I smiled. "Done."

"Well, hell, I should've asked for a thirty-percent bump."

"Not in the budget," I said.

"Maybe next time. Get me the plans and specs. I can start tomorrow, I've got a couple of guys who are good, and we'll get the job done, no problem."

That's what I wanted to hear. "And Emma's addy?"

"She told me she was staying with her great-aunt in Santa Rosa, but I don't have details, sorry. I gotta go scream for joy now. See ya."

I slid my phone away, the smile from hiring Hazel fading. Emma living in Santa Rosa didn't compute. Santa Rosa was nearly an hour's drive from here, and Emma had told *me* she lived close to downtown Star Falls.

With concern twisting my gut into knots, I pulled out my phone and brought up our text convo. Nothing.

The ghoster had become the ghostee.

Nothing I could do about that. The ball was in her court, and I wouldn't press. But I *would* still try to feed her. So I quickly ordered an assortment of food to be delivered to her at the Henderson and Hall offices.

That completed, I got out of my truck and looked around. Two mornings ago, this place had looked like a cyclone had swamped it, but today it looked good. Still very damp, but good.

I was walking toward the door when Ricky pulled up, Ryder and Tucker on his heels in separate vehicles. Bill was the caboose, only he hadn't gotten the message to stay calm. He was already red-faced when he got out of his truck and turned on Ricky. "What did I tell you on *day one*? Lock your shit up at night."

"I did."

Bill narrowed his gaze. "You told Caleb you weren't sure."

"Well, I'm sure now."

"I called our insurance rep on the way over here," I said. "And the cops too. Our rep needs a police report."

Ricky shifted nervously. We all knew he was allergic to the cops, and he looked about ready to break out in hives. "Someone better get back to me ASAP on this bullshit," he said, turning away. "And in case you need it spelled out, I quit."

"Where are you going?" I asked.

"You know where I had my trailer parked out back. No need for me to stay."

"The police will want to talk to you."

"Then give them my contact info." And he was gone.

The rest of us walked around the manor to the back of the property, where Ricky had parked his trailer for the job's duration.

The trailer—which had been here during the storm—was indeed gone. We all stared down at the mud where a vehicle—probably a truck by the tire tracks—had come in the back gate, reversed up to the trailer, and then taken off, trailer in tow.

Had it been the truck I'd seen racing out of here the other night? If so, what had he come back to the scene of the crime for?

I snapped some pics, then retraced my steps to the front of the manor.

"What are you doing?" Ryder asked when I crouched in the circular driveway.

"Good news and bad news," I said. "Good news, Ricky's tire tracks match the ones out back. Bad news, so do mine and Bill's, and hell, yours too. We all have the same tires." I looked at Ryder. "I know Henderson and Hall initially didn't want surveillance cameras on the job because of privacy concerns, but at the very least, we need two. One at each entrance."

Ryder nodded. "Do it."

Bill stirred. "I think you all know how I feel about this situation. And I'm trying hard not to say I fucking told you so about Ricky, but I fucking told you so."

"Thanks for your restraint," I said dryly. "And I'm already on it. I talked to Hazel about taking the job."

Bill's eyes lit with relief. "Good."

Tucker, who hadn't said a word, left the property.

Ry looked at me, and I shrugged. We both knew getting Tucker to talk was like bleeding a turnip. He'd tell us what was up his ass when he was good and ready, and not a second before.

CHAPTER 22

Emma

AWOKE WITH A start and sat straight up with a gasp.

I was in a bed.

Oh shit. I was in the Henderson Manor, in the attic bed.

No, wait. I wasn't *in* the bed. I was *on* it, sideways, legs hanging off the mattress. I leaped to my feet in horror, staring at the sunlight streaming through the window.

Heart pounding, I grabbed my stuff and hightailed it to my car like a bat out of hell. Which wasn't as easy as it had used to be. Ever since Ricky's trailer had gone missing, the gates at both entrances of the property had been faithfully locked and covered by surveillance cameras.

But no other cameras had gone up, at least not yet, which meant a person on foot could walk through the woods from the street below, slip through the section of fence that was still down from the storm, and bypass the cameras at the gates.

The second I got to my car, I sped off down the road, pulse at stroke level, brain whirling, religiously checking my rearview mirror as guilt tried to choke the life out of me. It being a Sunday, it was highly unlikely anyone would come by today, but that did not reduce my panic.

How could I have been so stupid?

It had been one week since I'd gotten stuck on-site with Caleb—or, as I was calling it, Stormgate. Yesterday, buoyed by my latest paycheck, I'd driven around town, checking out the available rentals.

I'd done the math. I was so close to having the money I needed, closer than I'd been in a long time. Close enough that I now had a list going with two columns: places I loved but couldn't afford, and places I could almost afford but hated.

I'd been diligent about getting campground reservations, but last night had been stormy as hell, and I'd needed a moment inside. I came here, just to hide for a few minutes. I sat on the bed, remembering being in it with Caleb, the things we'd shared in the dark of the night.

And then I had fallen asleep.

Unbelievable.

I hated myself for it, but I'd never ever planned on sleeping there. That was a line I'd promised myself I wouldn't cross. But now I had. I couldn't imagine what Caleb would think if he ever found out. I still hadn't figured out where we stood. My brain and my heart wanted two very different things.

Who was I kidding? They actually wanted the same thing, but I was shaken by how quickly my feelings had grown for Caleb. Shaken and…scared.

Twenty minutes later, my heart rate had mostly recovered as I parked in front of the apartment building at the top of my list. It was decently priced, but not the greatest neighborhood. Still, it was the best of my options, and according to the manager, they'd have an opening next month.

It was going to be mine, I could feel it, and I couldn't wait to turn the empty space into my own. I'd finally have a place *and* be able to stand, walk, sit, sleep, or eat wherever I wanted without stress.

I was close. So close to having a real life. And yet all I kept thinking about was that stormy night, the long, scary hours passing in the dark, made less scary by Caleb's comforting presence. Whenever I needed calm now, I focused on those memories of rushing heat, Caleb touching me, his mouth at my ear, whispering dirty little nothings before kissing and nibbling his way south, paying such close attention to me and my every reaction that he would stop and linger at all my secret favorite places…

Whew. Maybe *calm* was the wrong word, because all I felt now was revved up.

Shaking it off, I left the lot and headed to the grocery store. I didn't keep much with me, didn't have the room for it, but I'd eaten just about everything. I stocked up, grabbing enough to cover me for the next few days. Back in the car, I thought I'd go into the office for a bit to get through work emails and catch up on some reports I needed to submit. I took a quick glance at myself in the visor mirror to make sure I was presentable enough in case I ran into any coworkers, then stilled.

My necklace…it was gone.

I frantically tore through my bags—nothing. The one thing I had of my mom was gone, and I couldn't accept the loss. With dread deep in my bones, I headed back to the site to search there.

Again, I parked a few streets away and squeezed in through

the hole in the fence, carting the bag of groceries with me because I'd forgotten ice. I'd put everything in the fridge while I searched the manor. Once I found the necklace, I'd be able to think. I moved slowly toward the manor, retracing my steps in case I'd lost the necklace out here.

But I hadn't.

And though I searched the manor top to bottom, I didn't find the necklace anywhere. In the big kitchen, I pulled out my food so I could eat my despair. I had chips, salsa, cut-up veggies and hummus, plus the three ingredients needed for microwave-able mug cakes, which had been proven—by me—to lower anxiety. I'd also splurged on a pack of face masks *guaranteed to rehydrate your skin and take years off your appearance.* In my case, I was hoping it could erase the effects of my teary pity party.

In less than ten minutes, I was wearing a DayGlo-pink face mask and had just made a mug cake in the guys' microwave and was waiting for it to cool off while leaning against the center island, eating some chips, when the back door opened.

I nearly swallowed my tongue as Caleb's team strode in. Danny, Hawk, Miguel, Bill, even Tucker and Ryder, and…of course…Caleb himself—along with Calvin and Klein.

Everyone stopped short and stared at me. Well, everyone but Caleb's dogs, who bounded their way to me before sitting sweetly at my feet.

I stilled, a chip loaded with salsa halfway to my mouth, horror filling me. Caught red-handed. To stall, I crouched low and loved up on the big, goofy boxers, who dropped dramatically to their backs on the floor, exposing their bellies for rubs.

All while everyone else stared at me oddly. Well, everyone except Bill, who gave me a small understanding smile.

Caleb pushed ahead of everyone else, looking like his usual big, tatted up, badass self. I meant to say *Hey* all casual-like, but what came out was a defensive, "What?"

With a smile, he gestured to his face. I automatically put a hand to my own and... Oh, goodie. I was still wearing the DayGlo-pink mask. Before I could rip it off, Tucker picked up the rest of the pack from the counter. "'Takes years off your appearance,'" he read. "You know, I've always wanted to try one of these."

"Help yourselves," I said faintly, then watched, stunned, as these big, alpha, tough guys fought for the box. In seconds, there was a sea of pink faces looking back at me. Even Ryder.

Caleb grinned like some twisted anime character. Tucker gave me a quick hug. "I'm coming off a forty-eight-hour shift and had to skip breakfast because this clown"—he jabbed a thumb at Caleb—"wanted to get the weird electrical gremlins on the top floor beaten into submission today—my only day off." He stared at the food, practically drooling. "And you brought us food. You're incredible, you know that?"

I stared at him for a beat, unable to find words. They didn't know, I assured myself. They had no idea I'd accidentally slept here. I would be okay as long as I kept my cool—admittedly not my strong suit, but...

"*No one* eats her food," Bill said.

Shit, shit, shit. "It's okay," I said cheerfully. "Help yourselves; it's all for you guys."

Bill opened his mouth, but I gave him a beseeching look, and in return he gave me a barely there nod.

My heart was trying to beat its way out of my chest as I pushed the now-perfectly cooled mug cake toward Caleb without meeting his eyes. "Happy Sunday."

He picked up the mug and sniffed. "Smells like I've died and gone to heaven."

I tried to ignore that his hair looked damp and a little wild, like he'd just gotten out of the shower and had done nothing more than run his fingers through it. He smelled so delicious, it should be illegal. I handed him a spoon, laughing as I watched everyone attempting to eat around their face masks.

"You laughing at us?" Caleb asked with mock outrage.

"Wouldn't dream of it." Nope, my dreams were filled with other visions of him, such as the way he'd looked bare-ass naked in the beam of my flashlight. Or how easily he'd taken me apart and put me back together in the sexiest way possible.

"Not that you're not a sight for sore eyes," he said, bringing a spoonful of mug cake to his mouth and carefully taking the bite without messing up his mask. "But what are you doing here? I wasn't alerted to anyone coming or going by the cameras, and I didn't see your car."

Suddenly, once again, my blood rushed through my veins. "Oh, um…I parked down the hill, needed some exercise. I had to check on the doorway between the pantry and mudroom, to make sure the redesign worked out. I've got a meeting with Rosalind on Monday, and I know she's going to ask me about it." I found a broad smile. "It looks amazing, guys. The food is just my way of thanking you all for being so great." *He'll never buy it.*

But he was deep into the mug cake and was moaning sinfully. "I want to marry you and have your mug-cake babies."

Something weird happened to my ability to form words. And my heart rate.

"Didn't you already ask Penny to marry you?" Tucker asked

from behind his mask, stealing the mug and spoon from Caleb and taking a massive bite.

"That was just to piss off Ry." Caleb grabbed the mug back. "Mine." He pointed to me with the spoon. "You're a genius."

"Genius this." Tucker stole the cake again and dodged out of Caleb's way.

Calvin and Klein barked, wanting to join the excitement. Caleb pointed to the blanket in one corner, and they obediently plopped down, resting their faces on their front paws, carefully watching the food, ready for cleanup duty.

The rest of the guys happily dove into the chips and salsa, even the veggies, enjoying the food I'd bought with my last fifty bucks. Well, everyone but Caleb. Having been relieved of the mug, he leaned against the counter directly in front of me, all muscles and tats and those sexy-as-hell glasses, watching me like I was a puzzle missing a few key pieces, but also like he was hungry—only *not* for food.

This set off all sorts of reactions inside my body, most of which should not happen with an audience. I jumped when my phone alarm went off. "That's for the face masks."

We all removed our masks, and the guys marveled at how soft their skin felt. I was eating some chips and salsa before it was all gone, silently mourning the loss of my necklace, when I found Caleb had shifted close, watching me, smile gone.

"What, never seen a girl shove a bunch of chips in her face before?" I asked.

He shifted into my personal space bubble and tilted my chin up to study my face. "What's wrong?"

So much for the mask erasing the ravages of tears. I pushed his hand away and stepped back. "It's a Sunday. What could be wrong?"

"You tell me. Is it what happened last weekend? Between us?"

"Not everything's about you."

His gaze was piercing, filled with concern. I didn't deserve it. "Nothing's wrong." I turned away. The guys were eating, jostling around in good fun, paying us no attention. They'd all known each other forever, inside and out, for better or worse, and I had a feeling they'd each say for better.

That camaraderie, that level of comfort…I envied it. Yes, I had my aunt, but we talked only once a month or so. And, of course, Suzie, but our lives were a million miles apart, and it had put a little distance between us. There were also Kiera and Hazel; we'd all been out several times now and were getting close. But the kind of tight-knit thing the guys had going took years. They were forever ride-or-dies. Caleb would never have to wonder who'd be at his back in any given situation, and jealousy rolled over in my gut.

Caleb's gaze was still on me, trying to read my thoughts. "Emma, we need to talk."

"Maybe later."

He gave a slow shake of his head. "You don't mean that."

He was right. I didn't mean that. I didn't want to talk about what had happened between us last weekend, I didn't want to talk about anything, not with what felt like an elephant sitting on my chest.

Tucker came close and shoved a hummus-dipped carrot into his brother's mouth. "He hasn't eaten," he explained as Caleb chewed, still watching me thoughtfully. "Makes him a hangry bitch."

"I am not hangry," Caleb said.

"*Suuuuure* you're not," Ryder called out from the other side of the island. "You took off Tuck's head on the drive over here for absolutely no reason, but you're not hangry."

"Tuck had it coming." Bill patted Caleb on the head. Not easy since Caleb was a head taller, but he managed.

"It wasn't for no reason," Caleb said. "The asshole ate my breakfast sandwich."

"Because you ate Ry's," Tuck said. "The one Penny made for just him, which you knew because you said there was a private note on there for Ry, implying it was for a…uh, special anniversary. The X-rated kind."

Ryder's eyes narrowed at Caleb.

Caleb held up his hands. "In my defense, I didn't see the note until after I ate it."

"We'll discuss that later."

"Great," Caleb said and slid Tucker a dirty look. "Still no reason for you to eat *my* breakfast."

Tucker smirked.

Ryder popped open a peach tea and handed it to Caleb. "Drink."

"No—"

Ryder tipped up the drink so that his brother had two choices: swallow or drown.

Rolling his eyes, Caleb snatched the drink and downed it in one go.

"Better?" Tucker asked.

"Not yet," Ryder answered for Caleb, then shoved a piece of hummus-laden celery into Caleb's mouth.

"I hate celery; it's like eating string." But he chewed. Swallowed, even if it was more than a little dramatic. "Fine. I was hangry, all right?"

Ryder wrapped a muscled arm around Caleb's neck and gave him a sideways hug. And then he ran his knuckles over the top of Caleb's head. "It's okay. You nearly taking off Tuck's head was the best part of my week."

"Hey," Tuck said.

Caleb just shoved free from Ryder, took another carrot, and flashed me a grin.

These guys really had something here. Something real. Back in college, I'd put Caleb in a box, writing him off as little more than a "bro," believing there'd been nothing genuine about him, but I'd been wrong. He had depth; he had a very full life, certainly more of a life than I'd ever managed. He was like an onion—every time I looked, another layer had peeled away.

Truth was, I *liked* him. I maybe even more than liked him.

Ryder's phone rang. He looked at the screen and let out a breath. "Gotta go." He nodded my way. "Thanks for bringing in supplies. Get Tucker the receipt, and we'll reimburse you." He patted his own face. "And thanks for making my skin soft as a baby's butt." He slid Caleb a look I couldn't interpret, stopped to pet the dogs for a beat, and then was gone.

Caleb turned to Tucker slowly.

Tucker choked on his iced tea, muttered, "Oh shit," and scooted around the island as far as he could get from his brother.

Caleb began to stalk him.

"Is this about me telling Ry you ate his precious breakfast sandwich?" Tucker asked.

"Yep."

"Fuck," Tucker said, then kept moving around the island, tripping over Calvin, who was trying to join the fun. "I don't see what the big deal is. Ry probably won't even kill you." Then he grabbed a strawberry off the tray and chucked it at Caleb.

It hit him in the shoulder and fell to the ground with a faint splat.

Klein gobbled it up, and Calvin gave a mournful "woo woo."

"Hey," Bill protested. "No wasting the goods." He looked to me apologetically. "They were raised by wolves."

Caleb was still moving toward Tucker, who vaulted over the island in one smooth athletic move, before landing on the other side, still rapidly cursing as Caleb continued to come at him.

Bill's eyes darted back and forth between them, like they were in a tennis match.

Calvin and Klein were bounding along after Caleb. "Lie down," he said, eyes still on Tucker.

"Don't lie down," Tucker told them, then pointed at Caleb. "Attack!"

The dogs jumped up on Caleb and licked his face.

"Shouldn't you intervene?" I asked Bill as Caleb made the dogs lie down again and continued to follow Tucker around the kitchen.

"Yes, intervene!" Tucker yelled. "You should definitely intervene!"

"No," Caleb said.

Bill sighed and scrubbed a hand down his face. "You going to kill each other?"

"Yes," Caleb said.

"No," Tucker said.

"Take it out of the kitchen," Bill ordered. "No blood in the kitchen." He caught the look of horror on my face. "Bloodstains are a bitch to get out," he explained.

My mouth fell open.

"Oh, don't worry. They won't maim each other."

"Gee, I feel all better now," I said.

The guys all busted out laughing, like I was hilarious. But I was smiling a little, feeling slightly lighter than when I'd been alone.

CHAPTER 23

Caleb

MOVED ACROSS THE room to where Emma stood watching us boneheads be boneheads. "Hey," I said.

"Hey back." She wore faded Levi's, beat-up sneaks, and a T. Swift T-shirt that showed off the sweet curves I couldn't stop thinking about.

Yet it was those big emerald eyes that drew me right in and made me forget I was a smart guy. I had no idea why, but she'd been crying.

"Do you guys always fight like this?" she asked.

I pleaded the Fifth, but Tucker and his big, fat mouth said, "That wasn't anything close to a fight, but yes."

I knew that our crazy familial dynamics probably seemed foreign to her. "My brothers like to make my life hell."

"I make *your* life hell?" Tucker asked dramatically. "What about the time you and Ry stole Dad's whiskey and made me drink it with you to hide the evidence?"

"You're the one who couldn't stop hiccuping and got us

caught," I said, still holding Emma's gaze. "Thanks to you, we had to dig holes in the backyard for punishment."

"How could I forget?" Tucker asked. "Ryder's drunk ass fell into one, and then we fell in trying to save him and had to spend the night in that muddy hell. I got bitten by a black widow five times and nearly lost my hand."

Emma gasped. "Oh my God."

"He was fine," I said dismissively.

"After a night in the hospital!"

I smiled at Emma. "You can see why we nicknamed him *Drama*."

She made my day by laughing.

"Speaking of drama…" Tucker cocked his head, staring at us. "Do you two know?"

Emma and I looked at each other warily. "Know what?" I asked.

"That the air kinda crackles between you two? It's chemistry," Tucker said, shoving chips into his mouth like it was his job. "Brought on by the Legend of Star Falls."

I groaned, and Emma stared at me. "You've seen the three falling stars?"

"I mean…kinda sorta, but it was an accident."

Bill gasped theatrically.

I slid him a look. "Don't tell me you believe in that shit."

Bill shrugged. "Okay, I won't tell you…"

"It's not the stupid Legend," Hawk said, nabbing the very last chip. "It's animal magnetism." He pointed at me and then Emma. "You two should go out."

"Don't let Ryder hear you say that," Tucker warned.

"Boss man's great, but even he can't control animal

magnetism." Hawk raised his chip like it was a beer. "*Date, date, date*," he chanted, like he was saying, *Chug, chug, chug.*

I turned to Emma.

"We already decided we're not dating," she told the room.

"Chicken?" I asked, and everyone in the room, including my dogs, stared at me in shock. But I already knew my mistake. I'd just issued a challenge, and Emma Sumner never backed down from a challenge.

Sure enough, her eyes narrowed. "I'm no chicken."

"Then…?" I raised a brow, baiting her. It was a cheat, and I was an asshole for using it as a chance to get her to go out with me. But I was tired of fighting my feelings, and Ryder could fuck off; I wasn't nearly as stupid as I'd used to be. Hopefully. "Why not?"

The utter silence in the kitchen—with the exception of Klein, his hind end on the dog bed, his face on the floor, snoring loud enough to rattle the windows—was so delicate and tenuous that I stopped breathing.

"*Why not?*" she finally squeaked. "Because one…" She leaned in to whisper, "One, what happens in the storm stays in the storm, and two, we don't even like each other."

"I like you." I gave her a long look as I thought about the things we'd done that night. When she nibbled on her lower lip, I knew she was thinking about them too.

Miguel made the sound of a chicken. "Brock, brock, brooooooock…"

Everyone laughed, even Tucker, though he shook his head at me, silently asking if I was crazy.

And since the answer was yes, I ignored him.

Emma stared at me. I didn't know what she was searching

for exactly, but I did my best to look like someone she needed in her life. She rolled her eyes. "Fine," she finally said. "But it's not a *date* date. We're going to work." She gestured to her laptop on the counter. "I've got things to go over with you."

"See?" I said to Tucker. "It's work."

"It's your funeral, is what it is," he muttered. "I'll take the boxer boys home with me, but if they eat my remote again, you're buying me that seventy-five-inch screen I want."

"What does them eating the remote have to do with the actual TV?" I asked.

"Nothing, I just want a bigger one." He snapped his fingers, then said, "Come." Calvin and Klein excitedly jumped up and followed him out of the kitchen without a backward glance at me.

Traitors.

"I've got a couple of hours of work I have to do here," I said to Emma. "We could go after that."

She shrugged. "I have stuff to do as well."

She started to walk off, but I managed to catch her hand. "Hey, we don't have to—"

"I want to."

The three words felt like a balm to the soul that I hadn't known I needed. I started to smile at her, and my phone buzzed. "Shit."

"What?"

"It's Kiera FaceTiming me." I always felt a flash of panic because for two years, Kiera had been so mired in her grief of losing her husband that we'd all despaired of getting her back again. I quickly connected the call and saw only a chocolate-smeared mouth. "Hey, Ab."

"Unca Cal Cal!" Abi whispered. "Can I tell you something?"

"Of course."

"Alex won't let me talk."

"Aren't you talking right now?" I asked.

A second chocolate-smeared mouth appeared. Alex. "She's always talking," his mouth said.

"Pop Pop farted really loud, and Mama had to light a candle," Abi said. "She said pop pops do that, and so do her brothers."

Kiera had Hank for me today. To everyone's collective shock, Pop Pop, a.k.a. Hank, had become a twin favorite. Even more shocking, Kiera didn't mind having him around.

"Everyone farts," Alex said.

"No they don't!" Abi cocked her head at me. "Do they?"

"Yeah, baby. Everyone farts."

"But I don't," Abi said.

"Liar!" Alex yelled.

I heard Emma laugh softly. She thought I was cute. Actually, she probably thought the kiddos were cute, but a guy could hope.

The phone wobbled, and then the screen showed me Kiera's living room floor and Kiera's cat eating what might have been a Cheerio.

"I'm gonna tell Mama you dropped her phone again," came Abi's voice.

Alex snatched the phone, and given that the background was now a blur with Alex's face jiggling up and down, he was on the run. "Unca Cal Cal, come over," he whispered breathlessly. His face kept flipping upside down as the camera tried to adjust. "'Member you told me to tell you if Mama cried, and you'd come here?"

My heart sank. "Yes. Is she crying now?"

"No. She's laughing. Can you come anyway?"

I let out a breath of relief. "Yeah, bud, real soon."

"Are you on my phone?" I heard Kiera call out. "Tell me you didn't call nine-one-one again to talk to your Uncle Tucker—" Kiera's face appeared on the screen. "Oh, it's you."

"Aw, nice to see you too."

Kiera sighed. "You know what I meant. And, crap, you're at work, sorry."

"No, I love it when they call," I said. "You look…"

Her eyes narrowed, and I smiled. "What? I was going to say *nice*."

"Liar."

"I mean it." The dark smudges of grief and exhaustion under her eyes were fading. She'd done something to her hair. A cut, and highlights, maybe. Signs of life. I was so relieved, my throat got tight. "I could take the rug rats to the zoo tomorrow. I mean, they belong there anyway, right? Hank too."

She smiled. A real one. "*Yes*." Her attention was diverted. "Hey!" she yelled. "I said no more climbing on the countertops!" She glanced at me. "Gotta go."

I slid my phone back into my pocket and took a deep breath.

"Everything's okay?" Emma asked.

"Yeah, I'm just…" I shook my head, short on words. "She seemed good. She's had a rough few years."

She nodded in understanding, and then one of the guys called my name. Emma gave a *let's do this* shrug. "And so the day begins."

She wasn't kidding. I got the guys going, but someone always needed something clarified, a callout of the plans, or new specs, or vendor info… When I could finally get away for the day, I went in search of Emma.

I found her in the barn, on her knees, inspecting the hinges on the side door, muttering to herself and making notes in her laptop. She had a streak of dirt down the side of her shirt and one on her jaw.

"Hey," I said. "Whatcha doing?"

She swiped her forearm over her forehead. "Well, I really had my heart set on waking up rich today, but since that didn't happen, I'm working."

I smiled. "You need more time before we leave?"

She blinked. "Leave?"

"For our date."

"You mean *work* date."

"Ah, so you *do* remember."

She rolled her eyes, then hesitated. "Just food, right?"

"Unless you want something else…" I knew my smile turned wolflike by the way she bit her lower lip. "You're tempted," I teased.

"I'm also tempted to try skydiving. Doesn't mean I'm adventurous enough to actually do it."

"You think I'm out of your comfort zone."

"You're so far out of my comfort zone, I can't even see my comfort zone." Then she laughed, and damn, it did something deep in my chest—which meant Tucker was right. I was in deep shit. The deepest shit. And suddenly I felt bad for ever mocking Ryder when he'd fallen like a cement block for Penny. I got it now. It was both heavy and amazing. Exhilarating and debilitating.

"Am I still 'Don't Even' in your phone?"

She stood and slid her laptop into her bag. "You'll forever be 'Don't Even.'"

"Another challenge."

"It's not happening."

She sounded certain, but there was a light of amusement and possibly affection in her gaze as she stood and walked past me, chin high, expression dialed to 100 percent sass.

Damn, I was so done for.

CHAPTER 24

Emma

AFTER CALEB HAD MADE a brief—and secret—stop at a store, we were cruising on Highway One, heading north. "So, what's in the bag?" I asked for the tenth time.

He just smiled.

"If it's condoms, I hope you kept the receipt."

He just flashed me a grin. "It's food, but good to know where you're at."

And if that was disappointment flowing in my veins instead of blood, I certainly didn't have to admit it out loud. Nor would I admit that I had a condom buried in the depths of my bag. It had been there since the Ice Age, but no one had to know that either.

The narrow two-lane highway wound along steep, rocky bluffs, each turn revealing a more heart-stopping view of the Pacific Ocean than the previous one. "Where are you taking me?"

He slid me a brief look, eyes behind mirrored sunglasses, wind tousling his mussed-up hair, flashing a smile nearly as amazing as the view. And didn't answer.

"You kidnapping me?"

"I don't have to kidnap you, Enquiring Emma."

Insinuating, of course, that I'd eagerly jumped into his truck because I'm incurably curious. Guilty as charged. He flashed another panty-melting smile, and I turned forward because looking right at him was like looking at the sun.

Dangerous.

Stupid.

Plus, I had goals that didn't involve falling for a man, no matter how funny and hot he was. Especially *this* man, who wouldn't fall for a woman if he tripped over her. "Is where we're going a big secret or something?"

"Or something."

At my huff of annoyance, a smile crossed that mouth I could still feel on my body and dreamed about feeling again. "Maybe I'm worried about whether I'm dressed for where we're going."

"You're perfect as is." He slid me another look. "Maybe you're worried about something else."

That was so close to the truth, I nearly grimaced. I'd—casually as I could—searched again for my necklace, with no luck. I was devastated. "Such as?"

"Such as falling for me." He glanced over at me with a smile. "You falling for me, Em?"

The way he said my name… Gah. "Don't flatter yourself."

"Hasn't anyone ever tried to surprise you with something nice?"

Not that I could remember. "I don't like surprises."

He chuckled. "You don't like storms. You don't like being told what to do. And you don't like surprises. Where's the fun in your life?"

"*No one* likes being told what to do," I said. "Especially you."

"There are…certain places where it can be fun."

I glanced over at him, and he winked at me. I nearly swallowed my tongue. "Do you mean…in bed?" I squeaked.

He didn't answer, just smiled that same very dirty, very naughty smile he'd shot me once before…from in between my legs. Feeling the heat in my face—and other parts—I glued my eyes to the windshield, refusing to look at him.

He pulled off the highway and turned away from the bluffs and ocean, and we began to wind our way through a canopy of emerald green, the Russian River meandering alongside us now. Caleb made a series of turns, taking us deeper into the hills and away from civilization as the road narrowed, twisting and turning through dense forest. The river widened, its current losing momentum, the water spreading out and slowing its pace.

About five miles in, we stopped at a locked gate with a sign that read, NO TRESPASSERS—WE'RE TIRED OF BURYING THE BODIES. I gasped when I realized where we were.

The Cliff House, one of the most famous historical monuments in Star Falls. I'd bid $100 for the blueprints to the place at the auction.

They'd gone for $15,000.

I'd never been here; it hadn't been open to the public in nearly a hundred years. Stunned, I got out of the truck and stood there, soaking it all up: the secluded spot where the river widened into a deep tranquil pool; the towering redwoods reaching to the sky; the sweet scent of pine and the distant hum of insects that filled the air. I felt a peace and solitude I hadn't known I needed, and my foolish heart fluttered.

"How?" I breathed when Caleb came up to my side.

Caleb shrugged. "A friend of a friend of a friend did me a favor."

I turned and gaped at him. "You did this for me?"

He lifted a shoulder. "I knew you were disappointed about not getting the blueprints; plus, I've been lucky enough to be here before. It's incredible. I wanted you to have a chance to see it for yourself. There's no one else here today, so I'm your private tour guide."

I was stunned. Things like this didn't happen to me, ever. The old ranch house stood weathered and forlorn, a relic of a bygone era. Its once-proud facade was now chipped and peeling, the paint faded to a ghostly white. The sprawling porch was overgrown with vines, the windows dark and empty, holding their own secrets from a past long forgotten.

I loved every inch of it.

Caleb pulled a key from his pocket and unlocked the gate and then the door. As we stepped inside and onto the ancient wood floors, the house groaned, its air thick with dust and decay. The staircase, famous for its gravity-defying spiral, was worn and creaky. The shiplap walls were adorned with faded portraits, and a baby grand piano sat silent in a corner, its keys yellowed with age.

All of it was an eternally beautiful testament to the passage of time. We walked around, marveling at every nook and cranny, and when we stepped outside nearly two hours later, fresh air filled our lungs as I turned to him, shaking my head. "Thank you. That was...amazing."

"There's something else I want you to see. Something special."

"Isn't that what every guy thinks about his—"

"Not that, you perv." He walked us back to the truck, where he pulled a backpack from behind his seat, and…a sleeping bag.

"If that's your shag bag, no thank you," I said.

"Noted. But I've never shared this sleeping bag with anyone except you."

Because that was the same sleeping bag we'd used the night we'd gotten stuck in the storm. I looked into his amused but patient eyes, waiting for me to catch up. And damn. His flirty banter was always disarmingly charming, but what was even more charming was when he got past that and was just…real.

Something inside my chest shifted and warmed, but letting Caleb too close could only end in heartbreak, for so many reasons. For one, Ryder was against it, and two, if my employers found out, I'd be done for.

"Come on," Caleb said, then took my hand, leading the way to the river, its crystalline waters gleaming in the late-afternoon light. The banks were canopied by drooping willows, its bed lined with large smooth stones.

Daylight was fading as we headed across a field of wild grass to a drop-off about three feet to the water's edge. The river was wide here and so calm that it looked like a lake, shimmering as the sun began to set.

Not another soul in sight.

Caleb rolled open the sleeping bag, which he unzipped and spread out like a blanket.

I stared at him. "So, you really did bring me here to get lucky?"

Not answering, he unzipped his backpack and rifled through it, before coming up with a knife.

"Or," I said, "you brought me out here to kill me."

He pulled out apples, grapes, cheese, crackers, and a bottle of wine, after which he proceeded to use his knife with quick, expert precision on the apples and cheese. He opened the wine, then muttered, "Shit. I forgot glasses."

"No problem." I took a sip right from the bottle. "You really know how to use that knife. Either you're some kind of secret fancy chef or a serial killer."

"No other options, huh?"

"I guess you could be a competitive knife thrower."

He grinned as he finished cutting everything up. I'd never had a hand kink, but seriously, this man's hands could change my mind. Big, scarred, calloused, and as I knew firsthand they were always warm…

"Or," he said, "I work with a lot of tools, and a knife is one of them."

"Or that." I took an apple slice and a hunk of cheese. "This feels a little…smooth of you."

He rolled his eyes. "You're thinking too hard."

"Yeah?"

"Yeah. Neither of us ate much of the food you had at the jobsite, and I didn't think you'd let me take you to a restaurant, what with how much you enjoy hating on me and all."

"I told you, I'm not…hating on you."

"Then what?" he asked, eyes on mine.

"I don't know exactly," I admitted. "We do have more in common than I thought. We're both…adapters."

He nodded. "Adapting is survival, and we've both had a lot of that." The sun was low in the sky now, the temperature dropping a little with it. The moment felt…romantic. As did the way Caleb's arm brushed against mine. And the way he'd sprawled out, so comfortable in his own skin. And then there was how he looked at me.

"What are we doing here, Caleb?" I asked softly.

"Give it another minute. It's going to happen."

"*What's* going to happen?"

"Patience."

"I don't have any."

"No shit." There was a smile in his voice. "Growing up, we Colburns didn't have a lot, something I never realized until my mom was gone. She had a way of making us feel like we had everything we needed."

He had tipped up his face to study the sky, bursting with color, every color. "Looking back," he said, a soft expression on his face, "I know now how hard holidays were on her. Especially Christmas. She'd bring us kids up here on Christmas Eve. We'd sneak through a broken part of the fence just before the sun went down and sit on a blanket, all wrapped up. Every sunset, downtown Star Falls does this thing that you can't appreciate unless you see it from this spot. It always stunned us into quiet." He chuckled. "My mom used to say it was the one minute a year she could hear herself think."

"What thing?" I asked.

"You'll see."

I almost strangled him, but just then, on the far western horizon, the sun touched down on the rocky bluffs lining the Sonoma coast. At the same time, between the bluffs and us, far below, downtown Star Falls suddenly lit itself up like a postcard, strings of fairy lights on every tree and post and storefront.

Caleb was right. I was stunned into a hushed quiet.

For a long few moments, neither of us spoke, just sat there

while dividing our attention between the twinkling downtown and the sky in sheer wonder. I sat with my legs out in front of me, my hands behind me, propping myself up on the sleeping bag. Caleb was in the exact same pose, his arm and shoulder against mine.

I wasn't quite sure what came over me, but I scooched on my butt closer to the edge of the drop-off, letting my legs hang over. Then I cupped my hands around my mouth and...screamed. I screamed for the frustrating week. I screamed for the long-ago but present pain in my heart over my mom's passing. I screamed for the exasperating and humiliating way my life had gone lately. When I was out of breath, I stopped. I was just about to turn and explain myself when I realized Caleb had scooted to the edge, too, sitting so close that our thighs touched.

And then he let loose a wordless yell. I wasn't sure exactly what he was getting out of his system, but I knew enough. I let my pinkie touch his in solidarity.

When he fell silent, panting a little, I set my head on his shoulder. "Better?"

I felt him look down at me. "Yeah," he said, voice husky and thick.

"Scream therapy always works."

"It's also the company."

I stilled for a beat, then slowly turned my head to find him watching me, a bemused look on his face.

"You're not who I expected," he said quietly.

"Ditto."

His mouth curved very slightly. "Thanks for coming out here with me. I was beginning to think I'd unknowingly had a one-night stand that time in the manor."

I laughed. "We didn't sleep together."

"I beg to differ. We slept. You snored."

My mouth fell open. "I did not."

"Wanna bet?"

"Yes!" I nudged him with my shoulder. "I do *not* snore. I'll bet you right here, right now."

"What does the winner get?"

"I don't know how you're going to prove it, but…" I pointed to the water. "Loser has to go skinny-dipping."

"You sure?" he asked in a low, sure voice that should've given me a clue.

But when backed into a corner or challenged, I always came out swinging. I'd never been able to control myself. "I'm one hundred percent sure that you're about to go skinny-dipping in that very cold water."

He smiled, pulled out his phone, and accessed something before turning the screen so I could see. It was a video. A completely dark video. He tapped the volume button a bunch of times, and then I heard it.

The sound of snoring.

I gaped at him. "That's not me."

"Oh, it's you."

I narrowed my eyes. "Prove it."

He swiped up on the video, where the metadata was listed— date, time, location. In case that wasn't enough, it was also mapped. The video had been taken at 1:00 a.m. the night of the storm, location: the Henderson project.

Damn it.

He gave me a slow smile and gestured to the water.

Damn it.

But I was no squelcher. Bolstered by the wine, I stood up and headed down the hill straight to the river without looking back.

CHAPTER 25

Emma

A T THE WATER, I faltered as moonbeams danced on the river's surface, casting shimmering reflections on the banks. Was I really going to do this? I couldn't believe how much I *wanted* to do this.

Tonight had been the best first date I'd ever been on, and an impromptu one at that. No one had ever done something so romantic and special for me, especially on the fly. I felt... discombobulated.

And attracted to him. So damn attracted. Somehow, when I hadn't been paying attention, the wall I kept between me and my emotions had come down, brick by brick.

Footsteps, steady and even, sounded behind me, and then Caleb's lips ghosted over the sensitive spot just beneath my ear when he whispered, "You know you don't have to."

"I do know." I heard rustling and turned to face him as he pulled off his shirt, baring his well-built tattooed torso, all those muscles shifting while he kicked off his work boots and socks.

When his hands went to the buttons on his Levi's, I squeaked. "But you won."

"You're not going into that water alone." He shoved down his jeans, and my mouth fell open, even though navy-blue boxer briefs covered all his goodies. And he had some seriously ample goodies… When I managed to meet his eyes again, they were smiling.

"Nothing you haven't seen before," he murmured.

He dropped his glasses onto the pile of clothing before losing the boxer briefs too. Then, flashing a world-class ass, he strode right into the river.

For several beats, I imitated a fish out of water as Caleb, the water up to his thighs now, dove the rest of the way in and vanished. He surfaced farther away, only the back of his head visible as he tipped it up to look at the sky.

My heart thundered in my ears as I kicked off my shoes, then captured my hair into a messy bun on top of my head. I stripped and walked into the river, sucking in a breath as it lapped at my shins and then, as I kept moving, my thighs. Caleb turned my way, so I did what he'd done. I dove in and swam toward him, not stopping until I got close enough to touch.

Which I didn't do because I nearly drowned myself when I opened my mouth in a soundless gasp at the sight of his delectable lower body in all its glory. I was still choking when I was suddenly hauled up until my head broke the surface.

"Are you *trying* to drown?"

Sputtering and coughing, I took a moment before I could talk. "I was just thirsty."

A knowing smirk crossed his face. He held me upright, hands on my arms, but respectfully not letting our bodies touch. When

I realized I was pretty much forcing him to keep me above water, I set my feet down and stood on my own, but didn't move back.

Didn't want to.

We stared at each other for a few long beats, him blinking more than usual. He was trying to see me clearly without his glasses, and honestly it was the cutest, sexiest thing. I cupped his face, our noses nearly touching. "This doesn't feel like I lost a bet," I admitted.

His eyes were dark. Hungry. Heated. "What does it feel like?"

Like I'd won the lotto. He'd held back that night in the storm. For me. This time, I didn't want him to hold anything back. "Is this going to be another of those agreements? Like *what happens at the river stays at the river*?"

His lips curved. "Entirely your call."

I bit my lower lip.

"Come here," he breathed, sliding a hand to the nape of my neck, his other arm wrapping tight around my hips, grinding himself against me, letting me feel the proof of his need.

I was starting to understand that when Caleb opened up, he gave himself over to passion without an ounce of insecurity. No barriers, no pretense. Only us.

It evaporated my ability to think as his hands plunged into my wet hair. He used his grip to tug me closer, then closer still as he slowly drew my mouth to his. "Exquisite, Enchanting Emma," he breathed out just before he kissed me.

And, God, the man could kiss. I moaned at the first taste of him, greedily pressing every inch of my chilled body against his, skin to skin. And when even that wasn't enough, I wrapped my legs around his waist, moaning when he gripped my ass tightly, holding us both upright.

Caleb liked to kiss, a lot. Liked taking his time tasting, sucking, gently nibbling, and sometimes doing it not so gently. His thoroughness drove me out of my mind in the very best of ways, but more than anything, I wanted to drive *him* out of his mind. Pulling my mouth free, I flashed him a smile, then kissed my way along his jaw to his ear. Then I sank my teeth into his earlobe, thrilling at his quick intake of breath, then his rough guttural groan when I sucked, soothing the ache with my tongue.

"You're teasing me."

With a smile, I slowly worked my way down along his throat, until Mr. Always Aware of His Surroundings missed a rogue swell that lapped over us.

We came up sputtering, laughing.

But I wasn't done, not even close. I took a deep breath and dropped beneath the surface to wrap my hand around a mouth-wateringly impressive erection. When I guided him into my mouth, we almost drowned a second time.

I was laughing when Caleb scooped me up and over his shoulder in a fireman's hold, then strode to shore, before setting me down on the sleeping bag.

"I'm going to get it all wet!"

"Yes, you are."

I choked out a laugh at the double entendre as he planted a hand next to my head to brace himself and lodged a thigh between mine. "I wasn't done," I complained.

"No, but I would've been in two more seconds," he murmured in a deep, dark voice that nearly gave me an orgasm. "My turn."

I thought we'd be freezing, but as his weight settled against me, his body heat enveloped and caressed my every inch. Slowly, he took in the sight of me from head to toe, then groaned. "I need to taste you again," he breathed. "It's all I've been able to think about." He slid down my body, trailing hot, wet kisses in his wake, lulling me into a trance…

I squealed when he took a nibble at the side of my breast, flashing his white teeth when he said softly, "Payback," and kept going. I was a squirming, overheated, aroused-to-the-point-of-shaking hot mess by the time he rubbed his sexy stubble to first one inner thigh, then the other, all while having an up-front view of my body's reaction.

"Do you know what it's like," he asked in a sex-on-a-stick voice, "to be in a meeting at the office, and all I can think about is *this*…" He kissed me half an inch from where I *desperately* needed him.

"Gah," I managed to say, and he sent me a wicked, dirty smile—then continued to torture me with that stubble, his tongue, his fingers…all while avoiding my good spot. Thinking maybe he'd forgotten where it was, I gripped him by the ears and helpfully guided him.

His huff of laughter danced over my heated wet flesh. "In a hurry?" he asked huskily, his lips caressing me, making me shiver. My hands stilled in his hair, my breathing audible above the lapping of water, and the wind whistling through the trees, and the occasional hoot of an owl.

"No," I said as calmly as I could. "No hurry. Just worried about you getting mosquito bites in…tender areas."

He chuckled against me. "The hell you are. You wouldn't mind if I got my ass all bitten up."

I had to snort. "It would serve you right."

"You want instant gratification."

"Yes, please."

His tongue had me gasping as he skimmed another kiss close but oh so far from where I needed him. I arched up into his mouth, a demand for more. He gave me one singularly glorious, perfect, precise, targeted swipe of his tongue, then gently sucked in a perfect rhythm that had me on the edge in about three seconds. I was shaking, trembling with the force of my impending doomsday orgasm when…

He lifted his head and met my gaze, his own almost wholly glowing gold.

"I hate you."

He smiled. "Trust me?"

"Not my strong suit," I said.

"No shit. But maybe you could try."

I took in the sexy, erotic sight of him and sighed. "Maybe."

"Good girl." One of his big, warm hands stroked up the inside of my thigh to join the torture. I didn't realize I was restlessly shifting my hips to follow his mouth until he gripped them tight, holding me still as he lowered his head and gave me a lick like I was his favorite flavor of lollipop. My legs shifted, opening more for him, a not-so-silent plea. "Caleb, please—"

"Run out of trust already?"

I growled at him, and with a wicked smile, he lowered his head again, flicking his tongue with precision *exactly* where I needed it. Again, and then again. I writhed up into him, barely breathing as he effortlessly held me on the very edge. I glared at him murderously, and he smiled.

Then, saving his own life, he went back to his cause, using that mouth and those diabolical fingers to shove me into a free-falling orgasm. My back arched as I fell apart, murmuring his name over and over.

When my senses finally came back online, Caleb lay on his back, cradling me to his chest, stroking me in gentle, soft lines, even as his own body remained tense.

It took me a moment to regain access to muscle coordination, but I finally managed to lift my head and brush a kiss to his mouth before making my way down his body…

"That smile you're wearing…it's evil," he murmured, a hand in my hair.

"Scared?"

He smiled. "Should I be?"

"Yes, because as you said, *payback*."

I kissed, licked, and nipped my way south, and when I took him into my mouth, he moaned, a low and throaty sound that vibrated through me. I felt the tremor in his muscles and smiled.

He used the grip he had on my hair to raise my head. His expression was a dazed blur, his mouth slightly open as if he needed air. "I'm too close," he said, voice low and raspy.

"Then mission accomplished." I climbed up his body and straddled him.

"Emma." His hands gripped my hips. "Are you—"

I sank down until he filled me so perfectly, I could do nothing but gasp, arching helplessly as he met me with a single sure push of his hips.

With a rough groan and those hands tightening on me, he locked his gaze on mine for a single beat before lowering it to where we were connected. "Emma." He sounded gruff, strained, and it thrilled me.

"I'm sure, Caleb." Truth was, I was more sure about this than anything else in my life.

His hands flexed on my hips, as if trying to hold himself

back, trying to stop this incredible, mind-blowing feeling that threatened to consume him.

"Trust me?" I tried for a teasing tone, but I sounded as desperate as he did.

"With my life," he breathed.

"Good to know." I climbed off him, wrenching a groan of protest from his throat. Then I went to my bag and rifled through it. "Yes!" I whirled back to him, holding up the condom in victory.

I didn't know if I'd ever seen Caleb truly surprised before. His eyes widened as he tugged me down for a hot kiss. "I know you're not supposed to say this when you're naked," he murmured, "but I'm pretty sure I just fell in love with you."

A laugh bubbled out of me as I tossed him the condom and reclaimed my spot on top, sitting on his thighs while he tore the packet open with his teeth. I took the condom from him and rolled it on, enjoying myself so much that I took my sweet-ass time about it too.

Caleb gripped the sleeping bag beneath us in tight fists, swearing the air blue as I tortured him. When he caught my gleeful smile, he growled deep in his throat. "I'm adding up your infractions."

I laughed, but there was a smoldering intensity in his lustful gaze that left me breathless. I slid down, taking him into me again as we both gasped in pleasure.

His hands tightened on my hips as I began to move, and when tremors of pleasure scattered through me everywhere at once and my rhythm faltered, he rolled us, tucking me beneath him, his hands flat on the sleeping bag on either side of my head. He spread my legs with his thighs to make room for himself, his face hovering over mine while I tried to suck in oxygen. By the time his fingers curled under my butt and raised my hips to the perfect angle, I was so stimulated, I started to come the second he surged inside me.

He kept moving, prolonging my pleasure, withdrawing from me almost entirely before plunging back in, until I was crying out, body shuddering as I came undone, taking him with me.

The entire universe seemed to halt as we rocked together, the pleasure seemingly endless. Finally, we both sagged, boneless, clutching each other, panting, sweaty, shaky.

"Caleb," I whispered, the only word in my head.

He pressed a sweet kiss to my damp brow. "Right here."

"That was…"

"I know."

I had no idea how much time passed, the only sound our heavy, stuttered breaths before he pulled back and searched my eyes.

I smiled. No one else. No one else had ever made me feel the way he did, in or out of bed, and I wanted to tell him. I wanted to tell him a lot of things. I was still searching for words when his jeans rang, the pocket lit up by the phone inside.

He ignored it. But when it rang again, he muttered "shit" against my neck and reached for the pants.

"What?" he answered with a bit of a snarl that did something to my insides. Something really, really naughty, but also really, really good.

He listened for a minute, brought his phone down from his ear, and thumbed through his notifications. Then he said "shit" again, with a whole bunch of feeling, before grinding out, "On it."

Then he turned to me.

But I already knew. "You have to go."

He grimaced. "I'm sorry."

A niggle of unease ran through me. I'd gotten caught up in the moment, dropping my guard. We'd had that near miss in the storm, but we hadn't missed tonight, that was for sure. With my body still quivering with tiny little aftershocks, I understood I had a problem.

I liked him way too much, was in far too deep. It left me feeling...exposed, raw.

Vulnerable.

And I didn't like it. I sat up and began pulling my clothes back on. Which, by the way, was a lot harder than taking them off, especially with our bodies damp from the river. What had I been thinking, coming here with this man, the one man who had the power to hurt me?

That was easy—I hadn't been thinking.

But it wasn't too late. I could still play this off. Light. Easy. Casual. No big deal. "Am I about to be ghost girl number one thousand and one?" I asked in a teasing tone. *Look at me, being all mature about accidentally having sex with someone I accidentally feel too much for...*

"That's not what I'm doing." Caleb swiped a hand down his face, then met my gaze. "That was Bill. Both cameras on the Henderson job went down. Could be that the power's out."

"You don't sound like you believe it."

"I want it to be that simple, but since we've had weird, mysterious troubles with inventory and theft, I've gotta go check and make sure. Come on." He pulled me to my feet. "I'll explain on the way."

"About the cameras?"

"No, the ghosting thing." He squeezed my hand. "I'll drive you home, then get your car back to you when I'm done."

His words warmed something inside me that I wasn't ready to face, but they also brought panic. "Unnecessary. Just take me with you to the jobsite, and I'll drive my car home."

"You're cold, and it's late. You told me you live near downtown Star Falls. You'll get home forty minutes sooner if I drop you there."

I'd told him that because it was the location of the apartment I wanted. Which I did not yet have… "Getting to the job's more important," I said quickly. "Just go straight there."

He glanced over at me, something in his tone that I couldn't place, and it was too dark to see his eyes clearly when he said, "You sure?"

Was I sure I didn't want to explain my homeless problem? "Yes."

He got us on the road before taking another look at me, clearly sensing something was wrong.

And there was. I just didn't know how to tell him. I'd waited too long. If I told him now, I'd wreck everything that tonight had been.

And it had been *everything*.

"About my past…" he said quietly.

"You don't have to tell me. I get it."

"I want to make sure." He had his eyes on the road, but I could tell his attention was on me. "You remember what things were like in college for me."

"You mean when you were a hockey phenom and everyone wanted a piece of you, especially those of the female persuasion?"

He grimaced. "Up until then, no one of the 'female

persuasion' ever looked at me twice. I was gawky and awkward, and a bookworm nerd to boot."

I thought of the sheer size of him, the tattoos, the easy strength—inside and out, and I snorted.

"Don't judge the package," he said mildly.

That swiped the smile from my lips, because he was right. I had no right to judge. He'd been through hell growing up, but he'd done his best to leave that in the past, something I'd never quite accomplished.

"When the hockey thing happened," he said, "I didn't know how to handle the sudden attention that came with it. The media was...overwhelming. They created this narrative of me being a player because I never went out with anyone more than once or twice. And it was true, I didn't go out with anyone more than that—because it's hard to make a genuine connection with someone who wants to collect you and then tell the media every sordid detail, which they mostly made up."

He'd been young and thrust into the limelight, and he hadn't had a parent to look out for his best interests. It broke my heart.

"It was never about me as a person," he said quietly. "It was all about the hockey persona. Girls were doggedly determined, and I never could get rid of them unless I just—"

"Ghosted them."

"I thought Renee was different," he said. "I thought we were good together. But after I got hurt and was told I'd never play at the same level again, that I'd be lucky to walk without a limp—" His smile was mirthless. "I saw her disappointment, the fear that I'd become a liability." He shook his head. "In the hospital, in that sterile room I hated with all my being, I couldn't face her

feelings over what had happened to me, so I broke things off."
He slid me a look. "And then there was you."

"Me?"

A knowing smile curved his lips. "The first time I ever
saw you, you were working in the cafeteria with that net over
your hair and a bad attitude all over your face. You didn't want
anything from me. Hell, you wouldn't even give me the time of
day. All you wanted to do was kick my ass in class. I loved it."

I shook my head, mind boggled at how different our perspec-
tives had been back then. I'd been struggling, and although in a
very different way, so had he. "I still want to kick your ass, but
now on the job instead of in class."

He smiled. "And I still love it."

"You're a sick man, Caleb Colburn."

"Guilty as charged."

CHAPTER 26

Caleb

TWENTY MINUTES LATER, WE pulled up to the back gate of the Henderson job and found the gate open and the camera above it dark. After I got out and shimmied up to get a good look, the long fuse on my temper got a lot shorter. "Someone covered the camera with a black trash bag," I told Emma grimly.

Emma's expression tightened, but she didn't say anything as I drove around to the front, before stopping at the bottom of the driveway to check the front camera.

Also covered with a black trash bag.

I called Tucker. "Someone covered the cameras. I need the footage from just before the cameras went down; we had to have caught whoever did this on video."

"I was just about to call you," Tucker said. "I pulled the footage. We heard an engine, possibly a truck, but the only thing the camera registered was a bright light, then nothing but black."

"What the fuck."

"That's what I said. I'm five minutes out. Wait for me to go through the property with you."

Emma waited until I slid my phone back in my pocket. "Last year, there was a break-in on a job I'd helped design. The firm I worked for had cameras placed around the property because there was a lot of expensive equipment on-site and their insurance company insisted on surveillance. A hundred-thousand-dollar reach lift was stolen right under the noses of the cameras. The thieves had discovered that a superpowerful LED flashlight could disable a security camera long enough for them to walk right up to it and spray-paint the lens without being seen."

I stared at her, then pulled her in for a quick, hard smacking kiss on the lips. "Thank you."

She looked dazed. "For...?"

"For being brilliant."

I pulled up the circular drive and parked behind Emma's car, barely catching her hand, stopping her before she could slide out of the truck. I gently tugged until she faced me. An hour ago, she'd pulled a condom from her bag—which had been just about the sexiest thing anyone had ever done for me. Half an hour ago, I'd melted her into a puddle of sated woman.

Somewhere between that riverbank and here, she'd put herself back together far easier than I had, and I had no idea what to make of that. I gently tugged on her hand until she looked at me. Her eyes were a little wide, and filled with...anxiety.

"You okay?" I asked.

"Of course." Pulling free, she hopped out of the truck.

I followed suit, and we stood there under the stars, staring at each other.

"Let me know what you find out," she said softly, making a

show of looking for her keys in her bag.

"I will." I stepped close, dipping my head to hold her gaze. "Em, what's wrong?"

"Nothing."

"It's something." I slid my hands in my pockets rather than reach for her again because everything about her body language said she was uncomfortable—the very last thing I wanted her to be. "You know you can tell me anything, right? Did I—"

"No." She shook her head, adamant. "It's not you."

"You sure? Because if I did something you didn't like, or hurt you—"

"No." She bit her lip, but a hint of a smile curved her mouth. "I think you know just how much I enjoyed myself tonight."

Relief was a balm, and I shifted a little closer. "I'll never be able to go to the river again without getting a hard-on. You riding me on that beach is my new favorite fantasy."

A startled laugh escaped her. "Mine too."

"I'd like to talk about it in graphic detail, slowly and thoroughly, but that'll have to wait. Before you go home and I go investigate, talk to me. What's wrong?"

A sigh shuddered out of her. "I'm not good at this. I don't—" She waved a hand helplessly, and I wrapped my fingers around it and gently squeezed. She stared down at our entwined fingers. "It's been a long time for me, Caleb. I've forgotten how to do the whole awkward 'after' thing."

Everything inside me that had tightened at her clear anxiety loosened again. This—this I understood. "Same."

She rolled her eyes.

"It's true," I said. "And it doesn't have to be awkward. Not between us. No matter what happens."

"Even if…we don't do it again?"

The thought pained me, but it was her call. "Even if. The ball's in your court, Em. Always." I wanted to kiss her to remind her what we'd shared. I didn't want her to walk away and leave it like this between us. So I gestured to the manor. "I've got to call Ry and the police, and check out the property to see if anything's been tampered with—"

"I know, it's okay—"

"Come with me."

"You need an extra set of eyes?"

If that's what would get her to stay… "That would be great."

She nodded, and I leaned in to give her a kiss. Just a sweet, short kiss to seal the deal…just as a Colburn Restorations truck pulled up the drive. Tucker slid out, raising a brow at the sight of us.

Emma

Tucker aimed a charming, charismatic Colburn smile my way, the one that could render a person speechless from a hundred paces. It didn't hurt that he had a tall, lean, athletic build to him and an air of barely leashed Trouble with a capital *T*.

"Sorry to interrupt your evening," he said and turned to Caleb. "Ry's at dinner with Penny in Sonoma. I told him to stay put, that we have it under control."

The two brothers then exchanged a look; Tucker's seemed to be saying, *You're welcome.*

"We need to do a walk-through to see if anything's missing," I said. "We had that expensive tile drop on Friday."

"For all we know, whoever messed with the cameras is still here, hiding out." Tucker eyed the dark manor.

"Or squatting, maybe," Caleb said. "There have been several times I've had the feeling someone had been here overnight."

I sucked in an involuntary breath.

Caleb glanced at me, eyes sharp. "You okay?"

"Fine. Totally fine."

Caleb looked around. "I don't care what Henderson says— we need more cameras, both interior and exterior, and out of reach and hard to access. I don't want any of our employees in danger if they come in early or work late alone."

"Agreed," Tucker said as his phone went off, and when he looked at the screen, he swore and gave Caleb an apologetic look. "Search and rescue call."

"Go," Caleb said. "I've got this." He turned to me when Tucker took off. "Let's go through the manor first."

I nodded, and even though I knew I hadn't left anything behind, that it was all in my car, my nerves bubbled. "Let's go."

Something flared in his eyes—something that should have scared me but didn't.

Caleb

We didn't find anything of interest in the basement or the three floors, including our staging area for tools and material drops.

We stood at the third-floor landing, and I didn't know about Emma, but I was vibrating with tension.

"Should we go back down?"

"One last place to check." I started up the ladder to the attic access.

"Wait—what's up there that you'd be worried about?"

"Nothing, just being thorough." I opened the access door, then ducked to maneuver inside, reaching back for Emma.

She hesitated, then climbed in after me. "Looks okay to me," she said from the door.

I turned to find her wearing her armor-against-the-world smile, her *I'm all good* smile. The only smile I'd ever seen those years in college.

The fake one.

I craned my neck to take in the room. What about this place was unsettling her? I hadn't been up here since the storm. There'd been some dust then, an air of neglect.

But there was no dust now.

I moved to the far side of the room for a different perspective, slowly shining my flashlight over the entire space until it caught on something shiny under the bed, caught between two slats of the wood flooring. I glanced over at Emma, but she'd moved to the window and stood with arms crossed, looking out into the night.

Crouching low, I stared at the familiar gold necklace with two little sapphires, which I'd seen before.

Around Emma's neck.

CHAPTER 27

Caleb

ALONE IN THE KITCHEN of my house, I stood at the window over the sink, just as Emma had in the Henderson attic. A low fog had moved in, blocking the stars. No chance of a *third* sighting of the Star Falls Legend, and I waited for the relief to hit, but it didn't.

I had my hands in my pockets, the fingers of my right hand toying with the necklace I'd found in the manor's attic three nights ago now. After checking over the entire property, where I'd found nothing amiss beyond the covered cameras, I'd walked Emma out to her car and watched her drive off.

I had no idea where she'd gone or if she was safe. I'd texted her, asking her to let me know when she got home.

The minute she'd texted back a perky **safe and sound**, I immediately did a U-turn, heading back to the job.

She hadn't been there.

So was I wrong? Maybe she'd gone up to the attic at some point to…what? Rest? It didn't make sense. Nothing made any fucking sense.

I also had no idea why I hadn't given her back her necklace.

Before she'd gotten into her car, I'd tried to give her a chance to tell me, asking again, "You sure everything's okay?"

She just hummed a vague answer. I hadn't pushed because I wanted her to tell me why her necklace had been under that bed, in a room that had nothing to do with our job.

Even as deep down, I was afraid I knew why.

"I was driving home and saw your light on," Tucker said, letting himself in my kitchen door, hair tousled like he'd been shoving his fingers through it, looking both keyed up and exhausted. "You're up late."

"Not by choice," I said, "and lower your voice. If you wake Hank, he's yours."

Tucker took a deep breath and let it out again. He had his hands braced on the counter, head dropped between his shoulders. It was midnight, but rushing Tucker to speak before he was ready never went well.

Calvin and Klein padded sleepily into the kitchen, looking confused about why we weren't sleeping. Reading the room, they went to Tucker and nudged him for pets. Obligingly, he hunkered down and let them fuss and lick him half to death.

"Rough call?" I asked.

"Ten-year-old drowning victim," he said, face buried in Calvin's neck.

Jesus. I winced, but didn't dare offer sympathy. Tucker hated sympathy, empathy, or any other emotion that he could construe as pity. Instead, I went to the fridge to get him a piece of fruit—he was a weirdo, preferred fruit over comfort food. But when I opened the fruit drawer, I found each apple, orange, and pear had a single bite taken out of it—a toddler-sized bite.

I made a note to throttle the twin heathens later and pulled out a beer. Tucker accepted it gratefully, then proceeded to drink it down in less than ten seconds while I leaned against the opposite counter and waited.

Our version of a hug.

A full minute later, he lifted his head. "Thanks." His stomach growled loudly into the silence.

I went back to the fridge and grabbed all the makings for French toast. Bacon too. I started the French toast while Tucker handled the bacon, the two of us moving in a long-ago-learned dance of synchronicity, not speaking.

In ten minutes, the kitchen smelled so good, my mouth was watering, even as the necklace in my pocket felt heavy enough to weigh me down.

Hank showed up in the kitchen doorway, wearing pink bunny boxers and nothing else. Kiera's idea of funny. I'd told Hank he didn't have to wear them, but he'd hugged them to his chest like they meant something because they'd come from his daughter.

But, hell, maybe that was just me, projecting.

Hank pointed to the French toast and then his mouth. "Ah."

"On it," I said, then grabbed three plates.

We sat at my kitchen table, Hank in his undies, Tucker in his firefighter cargos and button-down, me in soft sleep pants and a long-sleeved Henley. A mismatched group, as always.

"*Ah*," Hank said with feeling after his first bite, then didn't surface again until his stack of French toast and bacon was completely gone.

Tucker watched him but didn't say much. He, like Kiera, didn't seem to harbor as much resentment as me and Ry had managed to hold on to. Maybe because me and Ry had taken the brunt of the abuse.

Hank pushed back from the table.

"You good?" Tucker asked him.

"Ah." He patted Tucker on the head. "Ah?"

Tucker shook this off. "I'm fine. Why don't you come home with me and give Caleb a break."

"Not necessary," I said, taking a longer look at my brother. The old man was right—Tucker was most definitely off. It could be the bad call he'd had tonight, but I got the feeling it was something else.

Tuck looked at Hank. "Get a pair of sweats and a toothbrush?"

Hank vanished down the hall.

"He'll get his toothbrush," I said, "but I wouldn't count on him grabbing clothes."

Tucker shrugged, and I shook my head.

"All right, out with it. What's up?"

"Just living the dream. Now you."

"Same," I said, and we stared at each other. "We're both full of shit."

"You more than me," Tucker said. "Talk."

"I already texted you and Ry a report on what happened the other night." I hadn't included the necklace. "We ordered a better surveillance system and additional cameras. It all came in today, and I'll be putting it in first thing in the morning—"

"Not the job," Tucker said.

"Then what?"

"Whatever the fuck's eating at you. I'm guessing it's Emma and your feelings about her."

"*You* want to talk about *feelings*?"

Insulted, Tucker put his hands on his hips. "Why not?"

"Why not?" I laughed. "Because if there's anyone in this family more closed off from relationships than me, it's you."

"I can still listen," Tucker said, then shrugged. "Or I could beat the shit out of you, if you'd rather."

"You can try, but I'm not taking advice from you. You give bad advice on purpose."

Tucker looked affronted. "When?"

"Remember that time I dated a Lakers cheerleader, and I couldn't figure out how to relate to her? You told me to lead with a compliment, but make it unusual, like 'you have pretty toes.'"

Tucker laughed. "Okay, fine, when we were young and stupid, I did purposely lead you astray once or twice, but in my defense, it was hilarious. I'm sorry."

"You aren't."

"I mean, a little bit, I am, but this time I've got legitimate advice."

I narrowed my eyes in suspicion. "Uh-huh…"

"Tell Emma you like the way her brain smells. Or that her laugh sounds like a symphony of angels farting."

I burst out laughing and shoved him. It was very satisfying when he hit the wall. With his head. "It's a shock you're single."

"I know, right?" Tucker let his smile fade. "Caleb."

"Tucker."

He shook his head, no longer playing. "This is real for you."

Way too real. "I might've lost control of the vehicle," I admitted.

"Ya think? You two put out sparks when you're in the same room."

"Not talking about this."

"Just tell me this." Tucker's voice was low, quiet, utterly serious. "Do you know?"

That I'd fallen for Emma Sumner like a stone from a cliff? I scrubbed a hand down my face. "Yeah. I know."

"I told you, it's the Legend." Tucker grinned from ear to ear. "The stars came for you."

"It's not the Legend." I pointed at him. "And fix your face."

He made an attempt to stop smiling and failed. "Look, I know you're torn between needing to prove something to Ry and how much you want to keep seeing Emma. I'm going to give you my real advice."

"No. You're not—"

"Don't give up a shot at happiness for a job. Even if that job is for Ryder. When he calms down, he'll get it. Just give him time."

Hank showed back up, holding a toothbrush and, unbelievably, sweats. I helped him into them while Tucker got Hank's shoes on. He was at the back door, one hand on Hank's arm steadying him when he threw words back to me: "It was totally the Legend."

"It wasn't!"

But he was already gone.

CHAPTER 28

Emma

MY HEART HAD BEEN in my throat for days now. The night I drove away from the manor was a close call. Too close...

I stayed clear ever since, a task made easier by how much work I had on other jobs at the moment. I'd put in long hours, today being the longest so far. I'd stayed at the campground, but tonight a storm had moved in, an icy one.

I thought about calling Suzie, but it was past midnight. I couldn't do it, couldn't disturb her. So tired, I couldn't stop yawning, I found myself on the street below the Henderson site, staring up the driveway.

I knew now how comfortable that attic bed was, how even though it was so cold tonight, the walls had been insulated, making the manor feel warm and cozy.

Listen to me. I was like a criminal who'd gotten away with her first theft, and now it seemed easier. And less...wrong.

We'd all gotten a team email from Colburn Restorations

notifying us that more sophisticated surveillance equipment had arrived on the Henderson site and would be installed in the morning.

Which meant I could have one more night. Or at least a few hours.

No. No way, I told myself. If I was discovered, I'd be fired on the spot, or worse, accused of being the one messing with this job. I wouldn't sleep there. I'd just go in, take a hot shower to warm up, and get out.

And that was it.

I turned my car around, parked a few streets away to avoid the gate cameras, and began walking in the dark toward the manor. My heart pounded in my chest. I hated that I was in this situation, that I'd chosen warmth and stupidity instead of staying at the campground tonight. The irony was that I was so close to getting an apartment. One more paycheck—two weeks—and I'd have enough to sign a lease.

Hating my own weakness, I let myself inside, took a shower, then sat on the attic bed, pulling on clothes. I yawned so wide, my jaw cracked. God, I was tired, so very tired. I lay back—just for a single minute, I promised myself. With my eyes closed, I reached up to touch my mom's necklace that was no longer around my neck. It had been so long since I'd lost her that I had trouble picturing her face.

Sorrow overcame me, and it was only when I turned my mind to that perfect evening on the riverbank, to when Caleb had been buried deep inside me, that my mind emptied of any thoughts except how I felt when I was with him, and I was able to breathe again.

My eyes flew open, unsure what had woken me. My phone said it was just past three in the morning. All I could hear was a light rain tap-dancing on the roof.

Oh, dear God, I'd done it again. I'd fallen asleep, and this time, I wasn't alone. Terrified, I slid silently from the bed, looking around me for something I could wield as a weapon. My gaze went to the heavy antique brass candlesticks on the dresser.

I grabbed one, and clutching my phone in my other hand so I could call 9-1-1 if I had to, I tiptoed to the door and cracked it open.

Nothing.

With every nerve on high alert, I padded down the stairs. My bare feet landed on the tarp-covered living-room floor just as something creaked. I froze for a long breathless moment but heard nothing. Maybe it had been a dream, but now that I was up, I needed some water. I crossed the big front room and turned toward the kitchen, then froze again.

The kitchen light was on.

I had just enough time to lift the brass candlestick as a big shadow suddenly loomed in front of me. Before I could swing, the candlestick had been confiscated and I was pinned to the wall.

It was instinct to lift a knee, aiming for the family jewels, but the shadow moved faster, shoving my knee aside with a grunt, still pressing me between his big body and the wall.

I knew this body. *Intimately.* I knew his scent, the way his muscles flexed beneath his shirt, the feel of his hands on me, even in the dark, and I instantly relaxed.

So did Caleb. "Jesus, Em."

He hit the hallway lights, and I blinked in the sudden glare.

Caleb stared down at me, expression inscrutable, tension in every hard line of his body. "What are you doing here?"

My stomach plummeted. "I was just about to ask you the same thing."

We both knew he had much more reason to be here than I did, but my brain was a dumpster fire, words and logic escaping me. What would happen now? Would he assume I was the one messing with the cameras and stealing stuff? Would he get me fired? But my biggest worry was…would he ever look at me the same way again?

He spoke into my silence, his stance relaxed, his face calm but serious. "I couldn't sleep. Came here to work, then heard someone on the stairs." Looking at me expectantly, he leaned back against the island, which was covered in blueprints, spread out and held open by a coffee mug, a laptop, reading glasses, and a plate that held nothing but crumbs.

"I, um…" I sucked in a breath as he took in his own—pilfered—sweats covering my body, bare feet, and probably a mop of hair that looked like an explosion in a mattress factory.

"Truth or dare, Emma?" he asked softly.

My heart sank like a stone, all the way to my toes. "Dare," I whispered, *terrified* of truth.

He nodded, eyes warm but serious. "I dare you to tell me you're living here."

"What?" I choked out a laugh, my heart in my throat. "That's ridiculous, I…" My words dried up, and my *everything is great, don't mind me* smile fell from my face.

He held my gaze prisoner. "You're living here," he said so gently that my chest ached.

"No." Meaning, *Please no, this isn't happening…* "It's not what you think—I'm not living here. Yes, tonight I fell asleep upstairs in the attic; it was stupid, and entirely accidental. It's happened once before as well, and I know the consequences, I know I'll be fired, and all I can do is apologize."

He stared at me for a long beat, eyes shuttered behind his glasses, unreadable. Then he pulled something from his pocket, dangling it from his fingers so that it sparkled beneath the lights before setting it to rest on the counter between us.

My necklace.

"Didn't peg you for the jewelry-wearing type," I managed to say.

The very corner of his lip quirked slightly.

"Where did you find it?" I whispered.

"Under the bed in the attic. It was caught in a gap in the wood floor."

I gulped. My heart beat so hard in my chest, I half-expected it to escape my body and fly away. "I wasn't sure where I'd lost it. I…" I was so grateful it hadn't been lost forever that my throat tightened painfully. "It's the only thing I have of my mom."

"Em."

I opened my mouth, but nothing came out. I had no excuses for what had happened tonight, what had happened before as well, nothing but the painful, ugly, humiliating truth. I closed my eyes. "I'm sorry. I know what you must be thinking—"

"What I'm thinking is that even good people have bad things happen to them."

My eyes opened again, yet I couldn't look anywhere but at

my feet. "I have no one to blame but myself." I looked up, met his gaze. "You must be furious."

"No." He shook his head. "I just…" He broke off. "We ate your food."

I blinked. "What?"

"You let all of us eat your fucking food."

"I…well, yes. Ryder made sure I was paid back."

"But you didn't know he would do that when you let us inhale it all."

"I didn't mind sharing."

He pulled off his glasses and pressed his hands to his eyes. "You should've come to me." His hands dropped away. "Did you think I wouldn't help you?"

He wasn't mad? He was…hurt? I couldn't think straight with the panic wreaking havoc in my belly. "Caleb, I didn't steal the tools or mess with the cameras, I swear."

"I know."

I blinked. "You…do?"

"Yes. Is that why you didn't come to me, because you thought you'd be blamed for the vandalism? Fuck, Em." A sharp exhale escaped him, and he ran both hands through his hair, before resting them on the back of his skull as he shook his head. "Whatever's going on, I know you wouldn't put your job in jeopardy if you weren't desperate. And in spite of how expertly you wielded that candlestick a few minutes ago, I also don't believe you could hurt anyone. I've got a gut feeling about you." He paused. "Always have."

"A gut feeling like…I'm a hot mess and you should be running for the hills?" I asked with a weak smile.

"Talk to me, Em. Please."

I sucked in a breath and turned my back, flattening my palms on the cold countertop to center myself. "I'm really not living here. Just sometimes, before the cameras were put in, I parked on the property and slept in my car. Like when I can't get a campsite, or I get a sketchy feeling in the park's lot."

"You don't have a place to live."

"I do. In my car."

He put his glasses back on and studied me intently, in direct opposition to his very quiet, almost-gentle tone. "Did something happen to you?"

That he would ask that instead of the obvious, like how long I had been fooling him, made me close my eyes and lower my head. "Just some bad luck, is all."

He came up behind me and rested his forehead against the back of my neck, his warm breath sending goose bumps down my spine. I'd been braced for anger and then pity, but this wasn't either. It felt like sorrow and regret for what I'd been through. It felt like understanding, an acknowledgment that I wasn't weak for doing what I had, but strong for surviving. It felt like support.

I honestly didn't know what to do with any of that.

"I wish you'd told me." His voice rumbled low and husky in my ear. "I could've helped."

"I didn't want you solving another one of my problems."

Gently, he turned me to him, crooked a finger beneath my chin, and tilted my face up to his. "You can't always be an island of one."

"Lifelong habit."

"And how's it been working out for you?"

A spark of temper flared in my gut. "Not all of us get to have an incredible inner circle, a team at our back at all times."

He let out a rough breath, ragged and tense. "Don't you get it? *Anything* could've happened to you alone all night at a fucking park or campground. Or, hell, *here*. Jesus, Emma, we've got someone messing around on this jobsite, stealing shit, and...I don't even know what else, not yet, and the thought of you here, alone, unprotected—"

"I can handle myself."

"Sure. With a brass candlestick." He drew a deep breath. "What did I do so wrong that you felt you couldn't come to me?"

I let out a mirthless laugh. "Do you think it's easy to admit I'm so bad at adulting that I'm homeless and sleeping on a jobsite? A fact that would get me fired in a heartbeat if anyone found out?"

A furrow appeared between his eyes. "I'd never tell your firm." At whatever he saw in my eyes, he swore softly beneath his breath. "You don't trust me."

When I hesitated, he shoved his fingers in his hair, turning in a slow, agitated circle. "You should know you can trust me by now."

"Because we had sex on the riverbank?"

Frustration flashed in those hazel eyes. "It's so much more than that between us, and you know it."

"Do I?" I tossed up my hands. "And can you really not see how hard it would've been to come clean? I mean, let's look at your life. Everything you've ever tried, you've succeeded in: school, hockey, and now business. You're on top of your world, and I'm..." I felt the prickle of tears and promptly shut up. I swore, if a single one fell, I'd hit *myself* with the candlestick.

"Emma." Pushing off the counter, he came close again, invading my senses with his scent and the inherent warmth and strength of him. Then, so gently that I nearly lost the grip I had on my tears, he cupped my face. "I know you're all too used to being on your own, but you don't have to be. You have people around you who care, who would want to help you. Ask me how I know."

I had to close my eyes, or I'd lose it at the tender, worried look in his. "How do you know?" I whispered.

"Because I'm one of them."

I nodded, then shook my head, my throat so tight that it hurt to speak. "Whatever this has been, I couldn't bet my future by telling you my embarrassing truth."

"Did you think I wouldn't understand?"

"How could you?" I asked, tossing up my hands. "You've never been in this position, and you never would. You have family."

"I do," he agreed. "I'm a lucky son of a bitch, and I know it. I also know you've had too many people leave or walk away from you, and that shit leaves a mark. But, Emma, that isn't me. I'm not going anywhere. I care about you, whether you like it or not."

I turned away and closed my eyes against the pain in his and the matching pain in my chest. "I'm sorry I didn't trust you—"

"Don't you dare apologize, not when you still don't." I heard a rustling and glanced over my shoulder to see him pulling off his sweatshirt, then layering it over the one I already wore.

"You're going to run out of sweatshirts."

"They look better on you anyway." He wrapped me up in it, carefully zipping it to my chin, his fingers as warm as the thick material, making me realize I'd started to shiver.

I didn't tell him it wasn't from the cold but sheer overwhelming dread. "So what now?" I asked softly, hugging his sweatshirt close, letting the heat and scent of him envelop me.

"You're coming home with me."

"What? Caleb, no."

His eyes narrowed. "No?"

I wouldn't move in with him, not like this. "It's kind of you to offer, but—"

"Then tell me you've got a safe place to go."

I paused, and he shook his head. "Em, *everyone* deserves a safe place to sleep. I'm offering you one. What's the problem?"

Gee, I don't know. Pride. Ego. Self-worth... Pick one. "You're already taking care of enough people," I said.

"If you mean Hank, he doesn't count."

"Why not?"

"Because he's a pain in my ass, but you won't be."

"I'm not good with charity."

"It's not charity."

"Of course it is!"

Again, he scrubbed a hand down his tired face. "Look, if it makes you feel better, I watched a scary movie last night and couldn't sleep. Not a fucking wink. You can be my bodyguard. I'll sleep like a baby."

"Caleb."

He shook his head. "You've got a choice. You can either get your stuff or stay here, but if you do, I'll be sleeping in my truck out front tonight to make sure you're safe. That would make two straight nights of no sleep, which'll give me a migraine, and as you know, on this kind of job, that's dangerous. You coming home with me is actually the same thing as saving my life."

I choked out a laugh. "That's a bit of a stretch."

"Your choice," he said again.

I was tired. So tired. The thought of being safe enough to fall deeply asleep without worry was more than I could resist. "If I go with you, you'll want to talk about it."

He gave a very solemn nod. "I will."

My heart skipped a beat. I owed him that much, at the very least. "Okay, but I'm sleeping on the couch."

He raised a brow. "Isn't that a little like closing the barn door after the horse has escaped?"

"Maybe, but this is different. This is a friend helping out a friend. And friends don't sleep together."

"Why not?" For the first time, a light of amusement came into his eyes. "We're so good at it."

No kidding. "Because…" Crap. I forgot why.

His mouth curved, but his eyes remained serious, solemn… intense. "Whatever terms you want, Em. Just say yes."

Everything about his stance told me exactly how important this was to him, that he was not babying or pitying me, but simply wanted me safe. So I took a deep breath. "Yes."

CHAPTER 29

Emma

CALEB LIVED IN A 1920s-era farmhouse-bungalow on the other side of Star Falls. It was quaint and inviting, tucked away on a quiet lane between horse ranches and wineries. The siding was a pale gray with white trim, and the front of the wraparound porch held an old swing and a couple of mismatched Adirondack chairs.

A far cry from the bachelor pad I'd expected.

"Brace yourself. Incoming." He unlocked the front door, and a whirlwind of fur and love barreled at us. Calvin and Klein let out a chorus of barks and happy yips as they showered Caleb with kisses wherever they could reach.

"Down," Caleb said firmly.

The dogs obediently sat, stubby tails swishing back and forth so hard, I was surprised they didn't take flight.

"Good boys." Caleb crouched low, hugging each in turn until they melted to the floor into two piles of happy goo.

I squatted at Caleb's side and rubbed their bellies, which had them writhing for more.

"They like you."

I turned to meet his warm gaze. "They like everyone."

With a laugh, Caleb rose, pulling me up with him. "Go potty."

"Maybe I don't have to go."

He chuckled. "The dogs, smart-ass." He pointed out the door, and the boxers took off like they were at the races, vanishing into the dark yard for about sixty seconds before bouncing back to sit proudly panting at Caleb's feet.

He pulled two treats from his pocket and tossed them.

Calvin caught his midair. Klein's treat hit him squarely between the eyes.

"One day, buddy," Caleb said with sympathy.

I looked around the house. Exposed beams, a reclaimed-wood accent wall, beautiful scarred-wood floors softened with a handful of colorful rugs, and a fireplace that had definitely seen its fair share of marshmallow roasting. Warm. Cozy. Just standing in the living room brought me my first deep breath since Caleb had found me playing Goldilocks. In front of the fireplace sat a massive overstuffed leather couch that looked like it had been the scene of countless naps and whispered secrets, and next to it was a basket overflowing with dog toys. I turned in a slow circle, taking it all in. The walls were adorned with rustic artwork and family photos, books, and plants, giving the space a lived-in, welcoming feel. I didn't know what I'd expected, but it wasn't this very natural domesticity, not when I'd always seen him as a little bit untamed and adventurous.

I didn't realize I was looking around in awe until he said, "Did you expect me to live in a tree house?"

"Well..." I laughed a little. "This place is great."

"Thanks." He looked around as if trying to see through my eyes. "I'm fixing it up a little at a time."

Trying not to think about the reason I was here, I moved closer to the photos. There was one of his entire family at Disneyland. Wait, no, not his entire family, I realized. Hank wasn't there. One of the twins, maybe a year old, sat on Kiera's shoulders, the other on the shoulders of a man I didn't know. Kiera's husband before he'd passed, maybe? Everyone wore Mickey ears and a bright smile, though not a single one of them looked into the camera, instead messing with one another. Caleb had an arm slung around Tucker's neck, Ryder was giving Caleb a knuckle rub across the top of his head, and Kiera was in the middle of elbowing Tucker in the gut.

The next pic was of everyone on paddleboards at what seemed to be Lake Tahoe—except Hank, who stood at the shore smiling.

Caleb appeared at my side. "That was a few months ago, when Kiera came back online after two years of grieving. It was…a family reset, I guess you could say."

I loved it. Abi sat on Caleb's board between his feet. Kiera was using her paddle to splash Tucker in the face. Everyone was smiling or laughing—except for Alex, who was sleeping in Ryder's arms.

A knot grew in my chest and ended up in my throat.

Envy.

I was envious of what this family had—how comfortable they were, whether fighting or laughing, how they stood at one another's backs, always.

Not an easy admission, even to myself. This was his world, his real world.

The kitchen was small but lovely, with open shelving, a

butcher-block island, and a massive fridge. There were a few dishes in the sink, two dog bowls up against the wall. In a corner sat a hockey puck, a baseball bat, and a pair of running shoes. The table had two sets of rolled-up blueprints on it, as well as a plant that could use some water. The whole room felt like the heart of the house. "Do you cook?"

"Yeah, I cook. Started when I was a kid because Ryder burns water. Tucker cooks better than me, but don't tell him I said so. He doesn't need the ego boost." He gestured me down the hall, then stopped at the first bedroom. "This one's Hank's. He's been staying at Kiera's sometimes now; he likes being with the twins. He's at Tucker's tonight though. Hopefully behaving."

The way he could talk so easily about the man who'd made his childhood extremely hard was incredibly admirable. If I'd had the experience he'd had, I'd probably have written the man out of my life and not looked back.

Just like my dad had done to me.

But Caleb… He hadn't forgotten, but somehow he'd forgiven—or at least forgiven enough to be the bigger person and step in when his dad needed help.

I knew without a doubt that if *anyone* in his life needed help, he'd be there, no questions asked.

Would I do the same?

I searched my heart. Past Emma, mired down in grief and anxiety and stress, wouldn't have been able to open herself up enough to help anyone, much less herself.

But I'd like to believe that Present Emma would.

"This bedroom is for the twins." Caleb opened the next door to reveal toddler-sized bunk beds, a dresser, and a massive toy chest, all in bright, fun colors.

"You keep a room here for them?"

"Of course."

Of course. He'd literally given up two-thirds of his house to his family. Amazing. Adorable. Sexy.

"My room's here at the end of the hall," he said, nudging me in. "The bed's all yours."

"I told you I'm not kicking you out of your bed." His bedroom was a study in masculine simplicity. The walls were a deep, soothing shade of gray, the floor the same rich, dark hardwood as the rest of the house. There was a bedside table cluttered with books and a vintage alarm clock, and a large window overlooked what I assumed was the backyard that I couldn't see in the dark. The bed dominated the space, large and inviting, covered in a navy-blue comforter that had two distinct lumps in the center. Calvin and Klein.

I laughed. "Looks like the bed's taken anyway."

Caleb gave his dogs a look, which they missed because they closed their eyes, pretending to sleep. "They're not supposed to get on the bed," he said directly to them, "and they're certainly not supposed to be using my damn pillows."

"Do they know that?" I asked, highly amused.

"Oh, they know. *Down*," Caleb said sternly.

The dogs sighed in unison, then very, *very* slowly got up while continuously glancing at Caleb like he might change his mind.

"Down or no cookie before bed," he said.

They both immediately leaped off the mattress and sat at his feet, staring up at him adoringly, stubby tails swishing the floor.

"Kiss-ups." But he gave them each a quick full-body rub before directing them out of the bedroom.

"You're a big old softy," I said.

"Don't tell anyone."

I smiled. "A cute house, dogs, and even some plants that are alive. I had no idea you were so domestic."

"My biggest secret is that I'm really a pushover at heart."

It was true, and perhaps it was even the most attractive thing about him. That he'd made a real home, something I had not managed.

"Hey." He reached out to run a finger along my hairline, gently tapping my temple. "Where did you go?"

I drew a deep breath. "Your world feels like Mars compared to mine."

He studied me for a beat. "It's just a house, Em."

"No, it's a home. One you share with your tight-knit family and friends and dogs."

"You do know it's not all sweet-faced babies and rainbows and apple pie, right? Hank used to be an abusive asshole. Our mom died. We lost Auggie, and then nearly Kiera to her grief. She retreated, wouldn't talk to us. Ry…floundered, and we thought for a while that we might lose him too. The loss tore us all apart, and we're only now getting back to some semblance of normal. Bad shit happens, Em. Even to good people. Like you." He stepped closer and ran his hands up and down my arms, chasing away my chill. "Stop thinking like you're still on your own. You're not, not anymore."

Again, that lump formed in my throat as I stared up at him, afraid to believe, but desperately wanting to… "You think you see me."

"I *do* see you. And I like what I see. Always have, Em."

I shook my head. "How did I not see you?"

His smile was wry. "I'm good at hiding in plain sight."

I went up on tiptoe to brush my mouth across his. "I see you now, Caleb."

"I see you, too, Em."

I looked into his eyes. "What do you want to know?"

He opened his mouth and—

His phone rang.

Caleb groaned. "I should've tossed it in the freezer when we got here." He eyed the screen. "It's Ry. Sorry, I have to take this."

"Of course." I shifted away, moving down the hall and back to the kitchen to give him some privacy—also to panic because what would happen when they all found out I'd been sleeping on the jobsite?

Caleb's voice carried. I heard him say, "Yeah, I couldn't sleep, was working late. How did you know?" There was a long beat. "Bill shouldn't have bothered you with a text about what time I left the jobsite. Or that Emma was with me." He paused again, and I stopped breathing. "*Coincidence*," he said firmly. "She fell asleep there by accident."

The sick feeling in my gut intensified now that the word was out. I would lose my job. Lose my new friends. Lose...

Caleb.

"If you want me to come kick your ass, keep talking," Caleb said, clearly still on the phone. "Remember when you fell for Penny, Ry? Because I do. You fought it with everything you had, when anyone with eyeballs knew you two were endgame. I did everything I could to support you, even when you were a complete asshole about it. I backed you up no matter what—" He listened for a beat. "I've known Emma for *far* more than a month. I fell for her back in college, and apparently the feelings never went away."

I froze, melting over the sentiment, but also filled with horror that I was causing this fight.

There was a longer silence this time, and when Caleb finally spoke again, he sounded much less frustrated and angry. "Love you, too, dick breath."

Afraid of getting caught eavesdropping, I quickly whirled around for something to do with my hands. Two leashes hung by the back door. Perfect. I leashed up the dogs, which caused a riot of excitement. "Settle," I said, and to my shock, they did as I led the parade out the back door.

The night was chilly, and I shivered when I stepped off the porch and into damp grass. I had no idea where I was going, but I knew it wouldn't be far enough to escape the fallout from getting caught tonight.

Refusing to cry, I kept moving, realizing that Caleb's yard backed up to open land, and none of it was fenced. The night was bright, the moon big and round above, negating the need for a flashlight.

As for the dogs, they were in heaven, sniffing every tree or bush we passed. About a hundred yards from the house, Calvin and Klein stilled in front of me and growled low and shockingly vicious in their throats, hackles standing straight up.

"What is it?" I whispered. "What do you see—Oh. *Oh shit.*"

Glowing eyes about twenty yards ahead, *lots* of them. It could've been aliens or coyotes, but I was going with coyotes. In an unraveling nightmare right in front of my eyes, the dogs tore free, racing across the wild grass, their leashes dragging behind them as they dodged around oak trees and God knew what else. I yelled for them while I ran after them. Then I suddenly hit my hands and knees, but thankfully not my face.

I'd tripped over a low, heavy branch, nearly killing myself in the process. Death by a solo game of red rover… Picking myself up, I took off again, calling for the boxers as the coyotes disappeared over the hill, Calvin and Klein right on their heels.

"*No!*" I skidded to a stop at the top of the hill, out of breath while I squinted into the darkness that suddenly felt all-encompassing. "Calvin! Klein!"

Nothing.

Absolutely zero sounds, not even the hum of a single insect.

"*Calvin! Klein!*" I yelled again and again, whirling back to look at the house on the hopeful chance Caleb had come to find us, and…

There they sat, politely at my feet like two angels. Calvin and Klein looked at me like, *You're cute, but not too bright, are you…?*

I put a hand to my heart and gasped for air. "Are you *kidding* me?"

"*Emma!*"

I caught sight of a flashlight beam bouncing across the terrain to us.

Caleb.

"Here!" I yelled, then snatched up the dogs' leashes, heading toward the bouncing light. I got only a few steps before he was catching me by the arms.

"You okay?" he demanded, carefully looking me over. "I heard the coyotes, then realized you were gone."

And he'd come running. He wasn't breathing as heavy as I was, but he'd clearly moved fast to get to me as soon as he had. "I took the dogs out for a walk to give you privacy on your call," I said. "And we ran into the coyotes—"

"You hurt?"

"No, I'm fine."

He still shined the flashlight over me again, then the dogs, before gently taking their leashes from me. "I'm sorry, they're assholes when they see a coyote."

"There were at least six of them."

He gaped at me. "And you *followed them?*"

Well, when he put it like that…

"Emma, Jesus."

"What?" I tossed up my hands. "You think I was about to come back to the house and explain to you I'd gotten your fur babies eaten?"

He took a deep breath and, with the leashes in one hand, steered me back toward the house.

He waited until we were safely back in his kitchen, leashes off the dogs, dogs banished to bed—theirs, not Caleb's—to take my hand and tug me closer, tipping my face up to his.

"Never," he said, "*never* follow them if they go after a wild animal. They might look stupid, and sometimes act like it, but they're sneaky and crafty as hell. They'll get away safely."

I nodded.

He relaxed marginally. "What was your plan if you caught up to the coyotes?"

I blinked. "Uh, I…didn't really think it through." *Possibly the story of my life…*

Caleb shook his head. "You're cold." He moved to the stove-top. "Tea or hot chocolate?"

"It's the middle of the night. Aren't you exhausted?"

"It's a way of life at this point. I'm having hot cocoa with as many marshmallows as I can fit into the mug." He glanced over his shoulder at me, brows raised.

"Same," I said, glad he wasn't mad that I'd almost gotten his dogs torn apart. "So am I a suspect?"

He set a mug of steaming hot cocoa in front of me, then a massive bag of marshmallows. "No."

I caught his hand with mine over the bag. "You stuck up for me tonight against your own brother."

"Yes."

"Why?"

He turned his hand over and entwined our fingers, giving them a warm, gentle squeeze. "You know why."

He cared about me, a fact that gave me a warm fuzzy feeling I didn't need. "If I were you guys, I'd suspect Goldilocks for sure."

"You wouldn't steal or hurt someone you care about."

The fist that had been squeezed around my chest since he'd caught me earlier in the manor finally loosened. "You seem pretty positive I care about you."

He snorted as he carefully stirred his hot cocoa that had so many marshmallows in it, he had to lower his head and slurp one up with his tongue. "Oh, you do."

"What makes you so sure?"

He took a sip and licked the hot chocolate off his upper lip. "Because I care about you, and when I look into your eyes, I recognize the dismay and disappointment that you feel the same."

I choked out a laugh, and he smiled.

"Caleb?"

"Yeah?"

"I do feel the same. I just...I don't understand why you believe in me so much." *When so few others ever have...*

He hooked a foot around one of my chair legs and dragged

me closer, reaching for my hand. "I realize you don't have a lot of experience with this, a guy standing at your back instead of walking away when things go off the rails, but I promise you—my old public image aside—I am different." He leaned in, holding my gaze prisoner. "So are you. You're strong, inside and out. You've got grit, you've got heart, and you've got a fire burning inside you that won't quit." He shrugged. "It's unbelievably attractive to me."

He said this with simple conviction, and I knew I was in way over my head. Too tired to face any of it, I stood. "I know I owe you a whole bunch of answers, and I promise to give them to you, but we're both exhausted."

"It can wait until morning."

That he would give that to me... I was undone. "You sure?"

"More than answers, I want you comfortable, not stressed out and worried. Do you want to shower before sleep?"

I felt my heart fall over and expose its underbelly that he would give me this. Time. "I want a shower more than I want my next breath," I said fervently. I headed for the living room, not realizing Caleb was right on my heels until I stopped short and he ran into me.

"What—" He got a look over my shoulder. "Oh, fuck me."

Calvin and Klein, usually the picture of canine innocence, were sprawled across what used to be Caleb's perfectly good couch. Now the cushions were shredded, and stuffing had flown everywhere in a fluffy apocalypse.

The dogs stared at us with wide eyes, their stubby tails wagging slowly as if to say, *Oops, our bad*, stuffing clinging to their faces like rogue marshmallows.

"Well, this is new," Caleb said calmly. "I mean, they ate my new work boots last week *and* the contents of my trash the week before, but the furniture destruction is a new low." He pointed at the dogs. "I'm running you a tab. Get down. Go to bed."

Calvin glanced over at the jar of doggy biscuits on the windowsill.

"Dream on."

Calvin sighed and slunk off.

Caleb looked at me. "You're still taking the bed. You want first crack at the shower?"

His shower was big, with the perfect showerhead, and the scent of his soap was woodsy, citrusy, sexy as hell, and pure Caleb. I nearly had an orgasm just sudsing up.

When I was done, I gave the bathroom over to Caleb, and in his bedroom, I pulled on my big, baggy sweats—best birth control out there. It wasn't that I didn't want to sleep with Caleb, because I wanted that more than air, but if I fell for him, I wouldn't be able to get back up, so—

Caleb strode out of his en-suite bathroom in nothing but a towel and a few drops of water making their way south down that amazing body. His hair was wet, and as he walked, he ran his fingers through it, shaking out the excess water.

When he caught me staring, I whirled to the bed. "It's so… big."

He laughed, and I corrected myself. "Your bed. Your *bed* is so big. God, you're such a guy."

"Guilty." He moved to the closet and pulled out a folded blanket and a pillow. "I'll be in a toddler bed down the hall if you need anything."

"You won't fit."

"I've slept on worse."

"Caleb, I can't sleep in this bed if you're not comfortable." I gestured to the massive thing. "It's big enough for ten, just stay."

"Think you can control yourself?"

I hesitated, and he let out a very masculine, very sexy laugh. "You *can't* control yourself."

I sighed. "Shut up."

His grin was smug. "Between one and *jump me* ten, where you at self-control-wise?" he asked.

"Don't flatter yourself. I'm a rock-solid one." Although my stupid voice cracked, giving me away.

He gave a head shake, sending droplets of water across the room, then rubbed a hand over his still-damp and perfect abs. When my eyes followed his every movement, he smirked. "And now?" he asked.

"Two, but only because you're cheating." I spread my arms to give him a good look at me. "And you?"

He took in my sweats, not an inch of my skin revealed between my chin and toes, and his eyes heated. "More than a two."

That low-timbre voice, gah... Was it getting hot in here? And why did the air suddenly crackle like it was electrified? I said, "If I'm making this too hard..."

"You're making *something* hard, all right." He grinned unabashedly. "But the move is yours."

I took in the light in his eyes, which I now knew was not just hunger but affection, and it was a revelation. It lifted the last of the dread in my belly, and I gave him a playful smile. "How much more than a two?"

"Twelve."

My knees did that melt-away thing.

"Not that it matters," he said, "because nothing's happening until you say the word."

"'Until'? Not *if*? Wow, sure of yourself much?"

His mouth curved. Cocky bastard. Then that smile spread as he bit his lower lip at the same time, and just like that, I knew I couldn't control myself, not one little bit.

"The word," I whispered.

"Be sure, Emma."

"I'm irrevocably sure."

His smile went carnal when he came at me with slow, sexy, predatory intent, making my heart race and my breath catch as I backed up a step, *really* hoping he kept coming.

He did.

When my back hit the wall, I leaned against it for support, my pulse skipping a beat as he stopped a foot from me.

"You smell good," I whispered.

He laughed softly, leaning in to bury his face in the crook of my neck. "So do you."

"I used your soap. I smell like you."

"Mm-hmm."

"Caleb?" I whispered.

"Yes?"

I went up on my tiptoes, slid my fingers into his silky, damp hair, and kissed him until we were both breathless. Pulling back only for air, I let my gaze run slowly over his heart-stopping body, let my fingers scrape down his stomach and toy with the edge of his towel. "I'm at a twelve too."

With a wicked smile that promised all sorts of dirty things, he dropped the towel. I was still looking my fill when he settled his big hands on either side of my head and tipped it up so he could kiss me, heated and demanding. My ragged, encouraging moan and his rough breathing were all I could hear as he leaned in, pinning me against the wall.

"You have no idea what you do to me," he said huskily, his lips moving against my neck as his hands slowly, thoroughly, stripped me down to skin. "What you make me want to do to you."

I arched my head back, my knees going weak as he took his mouth on a tour of my body with hungry, aggressive kisses, the intensity of which had me fisting my hands in his hair and tugging his head back so I could stare into his heavy-lidded beautiful eyes. "Take me to bed and show me."

CHAPTER 30

Caleb

RATIONAL THOUGHT LEFT ME. It always did when I had Emma in my arms. I tumbled us down to my bed, then restrained her there while I licked, nibbled, and sucked every inch of her, until she was a panting, gasping, hot, beautiful mess.

And then started over again.

And again.

"Show-off," she managed to say breathlessly when I finally sat back on my heels.

I smiled at how beautiful she looked—tousled, sated, wrecked—until she wriggled out of my clutches and jumped at me, taking me down to the mattress.

"I know you let me do that," she said, straddling me, staring down into my face. "But it's my turn."

That was the only warning I got before she put my hands on my headboard, said, "Don't let go," and then proceeded to use her hands, her lips, her teeth, her every damn thing to torment, torture, and tease me until I was quivering and, *fuck*, begging. She had me deep in her throat when I ripped my hands from the headboard and slid them into her hair, using my grip to pull her off. "If you keep that up," I said hoarsely, "It's going to be over—"

She took my hands out of her hair, put them back on the headboard, and looking gorgeously smug, smiled down at me. The look in her eyes made me want to sign over everything I owned if she'd just stay right here, looking at me like I was the best thing to ever happen to her.

Forever.

It sent my mind spinning even as something inside me unpinched. I didn't deserve her, I truly didn't, but I wanted her more than reason. I was free-falling, my emotions a tangled, agonizing mess as I held her gaze, trying to convince myself that I could have this, her, and not mess it up.

"Tell me you have a condom," she said.

I slapped a hand out to my nightstand drawer and came up with a box.

She smiled. "Unopened."

"I bought it after the river, just in case—" Words escaped me when she tore open a packet and began to roll it down my length. "I—*Fuck*, Em—"

"You bought it after the river just in case what?" she asked sweetly, nudging me to finish my sentence like she didn't have me double-fisted in her hands, stroking me in the exact way I liked.

"In case I—Shit. I…"

Finished rolling the condom on, she bent low and kissed the very tip before sitting up and smiling at me. "In case…"

She was going to be the death of me. "In case I ever got lucky enough to have you in my bed." I'd barely gotten the rest of the sentence out before she lifted up, then sank back down, taking me deep inside her. "Fuck—Em..." Words defied me as she began to move.

I slid my hands to her hips, adding my strength to hers, and when she trembled, I sat up, both of us gasping as it sent me even deeper inside her. I slid my hands to her sweet ass and guided her into a rhythm that had her crying out. "Just like that, Em. God, you're perfect."

Her fingers tangled in my hair, her nails scratching lightly at my skull while we moved in sync. I couldn't take my eyes off her; she was incredible, sexy...*mine*. I kissed her desperately, groaning into her mouth as I held her sweet, warm curves so tight to me, I couldn't have said where I ended and she began.

She was no longer the only one trembling. The angle, the rhythm, it was all so good, so fucking good, I knew I wouldn't last long. I slid a hand between us to stroke her center. Her head fell back, eyes closed, mouth open as she spiraled up and up, sweeter and sweeter, until a press of my thumb had her shattering around me, shoving me off the edge with her, my release hitting hard and bright and hot, convulsing my belly, stopping my breath. I couldn't have spoken to save my life. I didn't know my own name.

Only hers.

Normally, I was awoken before dawn by Calvin and Klein when they jumped on the bed to run circles around and over me until either I got up or one of them fell off the bed and got embarrassed enough to "woo woo" about it.

Their inner clock was set to 5:00 a.m., and if I was even a minute late, they rioted.

But this morning, there were no dogs jumping me. And the light was different. More. Turning my head to eye the time, I blinked in shock—7:12 a.m. I sat straight up, dazed and confused.

The bed was empty of both dogs and Emma.

Where were they? And how long had they been gone? I knew for a fact that Emma had still been in bed a few hours ago when she rolled over in her sleep and snuggled up to me, pressing her icy hands against my stomach. I'd wrapped her up close and shared my body heat, until comfort had turned sensual and we'd had round two before drifting back to sleep together.

I slid out of bed and followed an enticing scent to the kitchen. On the stovetop sat a sourdough grilled-cheese sandwich cooked to perfection. Its twin was in Emma's hand.

Emma sat on the floor in my sweats and the shirt I'd been wearing yesterday—the one we'd left on the floor somewhere—her feet bare, hair adorably wild, eating while chatting to my two goofy hounds like they were all best friends. And why was that the cutest, sexiest thing I'd ever seen?

Calvin and Klein were actually sitting politely for once, heads tilted in perfect unison as she told them the story of the time their "daddy" had come to the cafeteria where she was serving food, acting like a big old jackass jock, so much so that she wouldn't have been surprised if I'd pounded my own chest with my fists.

"Funny," I said.

She smirked up at me, and I wanted to toss her over my shoulder and haul her sweet ass back to bed, where she could smirk at me while I—

"Since you made me breakfast in the middle of the night," she said, "I thought it only fair that I make you lunch this morning." She paused, grimaced. "I hope it's okay that I made myself at home in your fridge. Being in a fully stocked kitchen was a luxury I couldn't pass up."

I thought of how she'd been living, and my heart pinched. "It's very okay. I *want* you to make yourself at home here."

She smiled with a gratitude that made me want to give her the fucking world, not just a place to sleep and access to a damn kitchen.

"I'm a master at grilled cheese, but that's about the extent of my skills," she admitted.

I took a bite of the sandwich she'd left me. She'd combined two different cheeses from the fridge and hadn't been afraid of butter. It was heaven. "Just like last night, one isn't going to be enough," I said around a mouthful.

A blush stained her cheeks, and I wondered what the fuck was wrong with the people who'd been in her life that they hadn't treasured this loving, warm, smart woman with every ounce of their being.

"Thanks for not minding the intrusion," she said softly, hugging Calvin while Klein, almost bigger than her, tried to get into her lap. "It won't be long; in two weeks I'll have enough to sign a lease on an apartment."

I nudged the dogs over—getting dirty looks from each of them—so I could sit on the floor in front of Emma, mimicking her crossed-legs position.

While she feigned interest in the last bite of her sandwich.

"Hey," I said, lowering my head, tilting it to the side so I could see her eyes. "I don't care how long you stay."

"You don't mean that."

"I do." Our gazes locked.

She drew a deep breath. "You have questions."

"I do."

She nodded. "I'm ready. Hit me."

"What happened that you ended up living in your car?"

She broke the last bite of her sandwich in two, spent a few seconds pretending to be engrossed in watching the heated cheese stretch. "I told you about losing the room I was subletting when the building burned down. And because I wasn't on the lease, I hadn't been required to get rental insurance. Not my smartest financial decision."

She could've been killed. I didn't usually allow myself retroactive worry, but it hit me now, just how bad things had been for her. She'd lost everything. "Em. I—"

"Please don't say you're sorry. I don't need your sympathy. And it's not as hard to get by as you might think. I dressed from thrift stores, showered at campgrounds…my car is perfectly comfortable, and it's only temporary."

My chest felt like it had caved in. "Emma."

"It's not that I'm bad with money either. It was just a perfect storm. The fire, school debt, trying to save for a new place…"

And she'd been alone, utterly alone. It was hard for me to even fathom. My whole life, I'd been part of a team. A team of siblings. A hockey team. A work team. Even if I didn't have a penny to my name, I'd never worry about having a roof over my head or where my next meal would come from.

She put a hand over mine, trying to comfort me. *She* was trying to comfort *me*.

"It was my choice," she said quickly. "I had to move fast when I got the temp job at Henderson and Hall, and the housing market here is more expensive than Santa Rosa. But I'm close, just one more paycheck."

"What about Suzie?" I asked. What kind of a best friend doesn't step up to help—

"She doesn't know. She's got a preteen and a baby due any second, plus a brand-new and very worried husband. I couldn't give her one more thing to stress over."

"Emma, she cares about you. She'd *want* to help."

"Exactly why I can't let her. Besides, it wasn't supposed to take me this long to get into a place, but it was hard to find one in my price range, not to mention first and last month's rent, plus a security deposit. But I really am close now, and I even have the exact apartment I want picked out and everything."

I vowed to make sure it happened for her, whatever I had to do.

She lifted her eyes to mine, and I felt sucker punched by the strength in them. "I've got no regrets," she said. "Even losing that scholarship to you. It was hard to see in the moment, or in the many, many hard moments that came after, but I know that things happened the way they had to for me to land here."

I reached for her hand and tugged her into my lap. Cupping her jaw, I tipped her face up and brushed a kiss over her temple, then her mouth, before pulling back just enough to whisper, "Do you have any idea how glad I am that you landed here?" I pressed my forehead to hers. "With me?"

She started to say something that I desperately wanted to hear, but just then my front door flew open, and a ticker-tape parade strolled in.

My entire fucking family.

CHAPTER 31

Emma

WATCHED, A LITTLE awestruck, as the extended Colburn clan strode in like they'd been here a thousand times, boisterous, noisy, talking over one another, laughing but also jostling on purpose as they squeezed into the kitchen.

Hazel was first, carrying a foil-covered platter that smelled like bacon and sausage, grinning and giving me a saucy eyebrow waggle as she caught sight of me standing there in Caleb's shirt and sweats. She set her platter down and hugged me, then Caleb.

"Thanks again," she whispered to him, and I knew she was talking about the finish-carpentry contract for the Henderson job.

"Anything for my favorite sister," he whispered back. "Don't tell Kiera I said that."

Ryder maneuvered his way in next, Abi on his shoulders, a hand on Penny's lower back. Penny was holding a foil-covered platter, wearing a dreamy recently loved-up-on expression as she cheerfully waved at me.

Hank was next, smiling brightly at the sight of me with an "ah," which I interpreted as *Nice to see you again.*

Tucker was right behind him, carrying a massive take-out bag from Al's Diner in one hand and Alex on his shoulders. He nodded at me, then went to set the bag down on the counter next to where Hazel was currently placing her platter. Their arms brushed, and for a single heartbeat, their gazes met before both turned away from each other without a word.

Interesting.

The twins were let loose, and they immediately began running in circles around the island, through the living room, back around the island, and then the living room again.

Followed by the dogs.

"Unca Cal Cal, someone ate your couch!" Alex yelled.

I laughed at the look on Caleb's face. He'd forgotten. He caught Alex on his next loop. "Hey, bud, do you want to adopt Calvin and Klein?"

"NO!" Kiera yelled at her brother, the caboose on the crazy train, shoving everyone aside to get to the stovetop. "My famous crepes, everyone," she said proudly, then shoved a finger in Caleb's face. "And if you give my kids your dogs, I will drop them all off here and go on a year-long cruise. Now we are all going to eat my crepes."

Behind her back, all three brothers grimaced, and Kiera caught it. "Hey!" She pointed at them with a spatula. "I'll beat you all senseless if you make that face where the heathens can see you."

"So violent," Tucker murmured.

"Shh, don't let it hear you," Caleb murmured back. He put his mouth to my ear. "If you value your life, don't eat the crepes."

Kiera whacked him in the chest with the spatula.

Alex and Abi came racing back into the kitchen again, each holding a leash with a dog attached. The four of them knocked into counters, nearly tipped Hank over, and accidentally dumped the trash.

Caleb whistled sharply, and all the chaos stopped on a dime as everyone looked at him. "I'm going to need everyone to at least *pretend* to be human." Then he pointed at his dogs. "Sit."

The dogs sat.

He pointed at the twins. "Sit."

The twins sat.

"Don't even think about telling me to sit," Ryder said.

Caleb rolled his eyes and disconnected the boxers from their leashes before eyeing the twins. "We don't leash the dogs in the house. Do it again, and I'll leash you."

Kiera nodded approvingly. "Should've thought of that." She turned to me, took in my attire and bedhead, and smacked Caleb again, this time on the back of the head.

"Ow," he said, rubbing the spot. "What the hell?"

"You didn't warn her."

"About what, that you crazy lot would shove your way in here and ruin my morning? Slipped my mind."

She smacked him again, then turned to me. "He was raised by wolves."

"So were you," Caleb muttered, and then, to my utter shock, he stepped into me, bracing his hands on the kitchen counter on either side of my body. "*Love* the way you look in my shirt and sweats," he whispered in my ear with a filthy chuckle. "Especially since I know you're not wearing anything beneath." He lowered his head and gave me a big ol' smooch on the mouth, right there in front of his entire family, before turning his attention to the food.

"Oh, please for the love of God, don't let him catch you staring after him like that," Kiera said.

"Like what?"

Hazel was munching on a piece of bacon. "Like he's breakfast, lunch, dinner, *and* dessert."

Kiera grimaced. "Gross."

"Also true," Hazel said.

Caleb was at the stovetop, directing Ry to heat up Kiera's crepes while hanging both twins off his back, one of each of their feet in a big hand over his shoulder like he was a jungle gym.

The kids screamed with glee, laughing the sweetest little belly laughs I'd ever heard.

"Break one of the toddlers," Kiera told him, pulling down plates, "and you have to make me another. I'm out of commission in that department."

My gaze flew to Caleb, sure I'd see him make a face, hating the idea of having kids.

But he only laughed. "All in good time."

No one even blinked at that. Well, except for me. And he caught me at it, too, turning to look at me, that smile still on his face, his happy, joyful smile, the one his family brought out in him.

And me, I realized. He always gave me that smile too.

"Can you grab silverware?" Kiera asked me.

"Sure," I said. Like my world hadn't just been rocked to the core. I was counting out forks when I felt a tug on my shirt. I looked down to find Abi staring up at me with those beautiful hazel eyes.

"Do you wear big-girl panties?"

I blinked. "Uh—"

"'Cause I do. Mommy just got them for me." She yanked down her pants and patted her butt. "These are *Paw Patrol.* What are yours?"

"Um…" I was commando.

Caleb leaned into my other side and whispered in my ear, "I know where they are. They're on my bedroom floor, where they fell after I removed them. With my teeth."

I felt my skin heat.

"Cozy," Tucker said, shoulder bumping Caleb away from me to reach between us and take the silverware in my hands. He winked at me and headed to the table to hand everyone a fork.

"You didn't even give him shit," Kiera complained to Tucker.

"Saving it for later," he assured her.

When the door shut behind his family an hour later, Caleb turned to me and waggled his brows. "Alone at last—" He broke off when he realized I'd picked up my backpack. "You leaving?"

I shifted on my feet. "I was going to head into the office and get some work done."

"Can you work remotely? There's plenty of room here."

I hesitated. "I thought maybe you'd need your own space."

"Not from you."

I wanted to ask how long until he got tired of me and needed me to leave—

"Hey," he said, coming close. "There's no expiration date on my offer. Stay forever if you want."

My heart gave a hard kick, my age-old fear of abandonment rearing its ugly head. I wasn't sure what exactly he meant and was afraid to speculate. All I knew was that I was in way too deep, and if I lost him now, lost his unwavering acceptance and unconditional support, it would level me.

He reached for my hand. "I'm serious, Em. Stay as long as you want."

"I just can't live here for free, and I know how much it costs to rent a room in this area. I couldn't afford it."

"You don't know what I'd charge."

I stared at him, almost afraid to ask. "If you say it's free—"

"Keep me in mug cakes."

"Mug cakes," I repeated.

"Specifically *your* mug cakes."

I narrowed my eyes, but he just smiled sweetly. Innocently. As if he'd ever been innocent a day in his life.

He shrugged. "I'm a simple man."

"You're the most *un*-simple man I've ever met."

"Maybe," he agreed. "But I can promise you, I only say what I mean. Always."

I was getting that. "I appreciate the offer," I said softly. "And I'd like to stay for now. I just…I don't know how to live with someone I'm…"

He raised a brow.

Caleb was going to make me say it. I sighed. "Sleeping with."

He chuckled, then lifted a hand to gently stroke a finger over my heated cheek. "Cute." He brushed his lips to the spot, making me shiver. "I've had my mouth on every inch of you," he murmured. "And, hell, only a little bit ago, you had your mouth around my—"

I put a hand over his mouth.

"You're scared," he said behind my fingers.

"Aren't you?" I whispered.

"*Terrified.*"

That startled a laugh out of me. "Good to know I'm not alone."

"You're not," he said very seriously. "That's my whole point."

I drew a deep breath. "Touché."

"Look, we've got plenty of time to figure this out." He pulled out his phone, then thumbed something into it, and my phone pinged.

"That's the entry code to get into this house. Come and go as you want, just promise me you'll at least sleep here."

I stared down at my phone screen, trying to remember the last time anyone had done something like this for me, much less cared about my well-being as much as he seemed to.

"Emma."

I met his gaze. "Caleb."

His mouth quirked, but he remained serious. "Please, don't use staying here as an excuse to friend-zone me again."

My heart kicked, but I put a smile in my voice. "Pretty sure you friend-zoned yourself the first time. And neither of us is good at this sort of thing. A thousand ghosted women in your wake and all that, remember?"

"I can't change my past. But I also refuse to give up trying."

"Trying for what?"

"The dream," he said. "The house, the kids, the white picket fence." He lowered his voice to a barely audible whisper. "L-O-V-E."

I choked out a laugh. "I think if you have to spell it instead of say it, you're not ready." But I paused. "You want a white picket fence?"

A wry smile curved his lips. "Go figure, right? Just promise me you'll sleep here, or if that really doesn't work for you, that you'll stay with Suzie or with someone where you're safe."

My heart felt like it turned over and showed its underside. "I promise." I waited for the nerves to hit, but none came. "And now I really do have to go to the office, after a shower."

His eyes glazed over, and it seemed like his words left him.

"The thought of work?" I asked.

His voice was sin personified. "The thought of you in my shower again."

CHAPTER 32

Emma

ON MONDAY MORNING, I'D been at work for four hours when Rosalind called me into her office. I didn't know whether to be excited or terrified.

"Take a seat," Rosalind said from behind her desk, gesturing to one of the two chairs in front of it. "How's it going with everything?"

"Good," I said. "I love it here."

Her mouth curved a bit. Not quite enough to call it a smile. "Nice. But I meant on your projects."

Ugh, I had no idea why she always made me feel so stupidly awkward. "My projects are also going well. The Warren job's wrapping up, the Mill job is kicking into gear—I delivered the final set of plans yesterday. The Castaneda job's on hold, as you know, until the engineer gets back to us on the change orders. And the Henderson job is running smoothly."

She shook her head. "There have been problems there. Vandalism, theft... We're concerned."

"The Colburns are on it," I said.

"Good. I'd expect no less for what we're paying."

I had no real reason to take offense at this, but I did. I knew Ryder Colburn was an aboveboard, hardworking, and well-respected businessman who ran a tight ship. He cared about his employees, his subcontractors, and the job. He put his heart and soul into every project. As did Caleb and Tucker. Everyone at Colburn Restorations was talented, dedicated, and incredibly loyal. People didn't leave their jobs there, not employees and not clients—including Henderson and Hall.

"The job's really coming along," I said carefully. "It's beautiful. You should come out and take a look."

"Your reports have been excellent," Rosalind said, then cocked her head. "Are you sleeping with one of them?"

Her words were so conversational, it took a moment for them to sink in, and when they did, my brain went offline. No reception. Zero bars...

Rosalind raised a brow.

"I—I'm currently staying with Caleb Colburn until an apartment is available," I admitted. "We went to college together."

"So you're old friends."

We were old *something*, that was for sure. "Yes."

Rosalind smiled. Her real one this time—which had never before been directed at me. "I had no idea; you should've told me you're so well-connected," she said, voice softer. "Caleb's a good man, and we all consider him a dear friend here. Make sure to tell him how much it means to us that he's taking such good care of one of our employees, won't you?"

"Sure," I said, knowing I wouldn't do any such thing.

"Oh, and while I've got you here..." Rosalind smoothed

down a nonexistent wrinkle on her blazer. "We've just signed onto a new project in old town Star Falls. It was one Ruth was really excited about and campaigned for. Since she's not here, you'll be taking her place on the team."

I had time for another project like I had time for a hole in my head, especially one I felt certain I hadn't earned, but was due to my association to a Colburn. "Thank you, I appreciate your confidence in me."

"Happy to hear that," Rosalind said. "Because connections in this world are everything. And you being connected to the Colburns certainly doesn't hurt things." She paused. "I wasn't going to tell you this yet. I was going to wait until the end of your temporary contract." She paused. "Ruth's let us know she won't be coming back. Her position here will be posted, of course, and formal interviews conducted, so if *you're* still interested…"

"I am," I said quickly. "Very interested."

"Good." She nodded. "Of course, the pay wouldn't be much of a raise from what you're earning now. But you'd get an annual increase, depending, of course, on your performance review."

Much of my excitement instantly drained. What I was earning now would barely get me into that apartment, the one I'd filled out the application for this morning—my way of manifesting. All I had to do was hit the Submit button. Well, and pay seventy-five bucks for said application. "Will there be bonuses?"

Rosalind's mouth quirked. "You mean…like extra credit for doing your actual job that we already pay you for?"

I flushed; I could feel it heat my face. "It's just that I'm hoping to get my own apartment here in Star Falls. With what I'm making now, I'd have to go as far out as Santa Rosa, and the commute would be well over an hour each way."

"That's if you don't hit traffic," Rosalind agreed. "And while I'm sympathetic to your plight, the budget for this job opening is firmly set for now."

The story of my life.

By the time I left the office, I was fried, mentally and physically. I nearly drove out to the campgrounds, until I remembered not *everything* about my life sucked. I wasn't squatting on the jobsite anymore; I was staying with Caleb.

Smart, charismatic, funny, sexy Caleb Colburn. The man was a walking contradiction, all sharp angles and soft smiles, a tornado of charm wrapped in a six-foot-two package.

I was grateful. Beyond grateful.

Turned out, life was pretty great when I wasn't anxious about where I'd be sleeping at night.

And something else shocking? Living with Caleb felt as natural as breathing—which wasn't good. Last night Henderson, forgetting the time difference, had texted me from Italy at three in the morning to remind me he needed new drone shots. Instead of being annoyed at the frustrating wake-up text, Caleb had pinned me to the bed and had his merry way with me.

I was still wearing the smile.

All I had to do was remember that staying in Caleb's house was as temporary as the rest of my life and he wasn't mine to keep.

I made a stop on the way and spent half my week's grocery budget on Thai takeout—Caleb's favorite. A few minutes later, I let myself in the house to find Calvin politely sitting in the foyer, waiting for me, tail stub wagging hard enough to create its own tailwind. Klein, who had zero polite bones in his body, jumped up to give me a full French kiss.

With a laugh, I nudged him aside. I knew Caleb was home, since his truck was in the driveway. And those were his shoes haphazardly left at the doorway, his sweatshirt over the back of the couch, and his backpack on the floor, leaning against the hallway wall.

I set the food down in the kitchen and followed the clues, soon ending up in Caleb's bedroom. The bathroom door was open, steam pouring out from the running shower. Caleb's off-key voice singing "Shake It Off."

I was grinning when I stepped into the bathroom—at least until I caught sight of water and suds sluicing down that incredible body, making my mouth go dry.

Caleb poked his head out of the shower and grinned at me.

"Hi, honey, I'm home," I quipped after I rolled my tongue back into my mouth. "I brought dinner."

"Good, because I'm starving."

"It's Thai."

"Awesome, but that's not what I'm starving for." And then he hauled me into the shower with him.

CHAPTER 33

Caleb

SHUT MY LAPTOP and leaned back in my office chair, my neck and back creaking as I stretched, trying to recover from long hours of schmoozing clients and catching up on the mountain of paperwork Ryder had passed off to me. I didn't mind. Working with his hands was his escape; working with my brain was mine. I'd gotten all the physical escape I'd needed out of hockey. I'd replaced it with weekly basketball, tennis, and football with the guys, depending on my pain level. But these days I needed more than that in my life, and Ryder had provided it. Did he piss me off? On the daily. But in this, I wouldn't fail him.

But maybe I'd been pushing myself too hard because I yawned so wide, I nearly split my head open. Between the long work hours, then spending the nights with Emma, eating, talking, laughing, taking each other apart, then putting us back together again, I was dead on my feet.

After what had to be my twentieth jaw-splitting yawn, I set my head down on my desk, just to rest my eyes for a second...

Then jerked awake to a face an inch from mine.

Ryder. "Remember that renovation job we did for the Royal Co—shit, Caleb, stop screaming—the ones who make luxury toys? They sent us three high-grade squirt guns. We need to break them in."

"I wasn't screaming," I grumbled, rubbing my eyes. "And who's 'we'?"

Tucker's face appeared next to Ryder's. "You're both going down."

"For fuck's sake." I rose and shoved my fingers through my hair. "No one ever knocks."

"We knocked," Tucker said. "You didn't budge. What's the matter with you? You're clearly not sleeping at night. You having nightmares again?"

I hadn't had nightmares since I'd been a kid. "No."

Ryder had been studying me. "My guess is he's making up for lost time."

Tucker stared at me, his expression going from confused to knowing to annoyed. "*Great*. Everyone's getting laid except for me."

Ryder turned to him. "Hazel told me she saw you leaving the bar the other night with a woman."

Tucker stilled. "What?"

"Hazel said—"

"I heard you! When did Hazel see me at the bar?"

Ryder shrugged. "Dunno. A week ago, maybe? Who was the woman?"

"Lena," Tucker said. "She works at the city office. She'd had one too many. I was just giving her a ride." He paused. "Hazel thought we were gonna…?"

"Maybe she wouldn't think it if you spoke with her once in a while," I said. "With words."

Ryder snorted. "Rich coming from you."

I picked up one of the three monstrous squirt guns Ryder had unceremoniously dumped on my desk. He'd already filled them. Nice. I hoisted one, aiming it at my oldest brother, ready to unleash a torrent of watery retribution for the rude awakening.

"Do it, and I'll make you regret it," he warned me cheerfully.

I blasted him. Right in the face. Then I went down snickering as he leaped over my desk and tackled me to the floor.

We tussled and grappled until we were both nailed in the face with water. Gasping, we sat up, swiped at our eyes, and stared at Tucker double-fisting two squirt guns, grinning wildly.

"Get him," Ryder said to me.

We tackled him in unison. The three of us were rolling around, soaked, swearing, and laughing more than fighting, when a voice boomed: "Are you boneheads fuckin' kidding me?"

Bill stood in the doorway, arms folded over his barrel chest, eyes narrowed. "You children or grown-ass men?"

We "children" glanced at one another, silently agreeing, then all aimed our squirt guns and nailed him in unison, drenching him from head to toe.

Ten minutes later, after getting our asses chewed out like we were feral teens once again, we stood in the staff kitchen, raiding the fridge.

Ryder was inhaling a chicken-salad sandwich when he looked at me. "I had this idea…"

"Thanks for the warning."

Ryder lifted his hand and scratched the side of his face. With his middle finger. "It's actually more of a question. You and Emma."

I refused to react and dug into the fridge to see if there was anything I'd missed. "Didn't hear a question."

"You're all in."

Turning to face him, I crossed my arms. "Again, not a question."

Tucker stirred. Probably wondering if the squirt guns were still loaded.

"You and Emma seem to be straddling the fence between long and short term," Ryder clarified.

I stared at him.

He stared back.

Fine. "For me, it's a long-term thing." Weird, but suddenly my heart hammered against my ribs, the drumbeat echoing in my ears. I sank to a chair. "Holy shit," I breathed. "I just said that out loud."

Tucker patted me on the head.

"So," Ryder said. "Back to my question."

"I still haven't heard a fucking question."

Ryder smiled, like me being discombobulated to my very core was so fucking funny. "Colburn Restoration's growing pretty fast. We need more employees."

"No shit," I said. "We still need at least one more office person, plus a bigger dedicated construction crew so we're not relying on subs all the time."

Ryder nodded. "I was thinking about also adding an in-house construction-design management department," he said casually, finishing his sandwich. "With an in-house architect running a CDM division, we'd be a full-service restoration stop."

I froze in the middle of biting into a turkey club. "You playing me?"

"Nope."

I glanced at Tucker, who shrugged. He didn't know shit about this either.

"Think of how much time and money we'd save," Ryder said, "instead of subbing out like we do, paying out the nose for the services."

I was stunned. "Let me get this straight: You didn't want me to go out with Emma because we work together. But now you want to hire her to be here every day, where I also work?"

"Valid question," Tucker said.

"I was wrong."

I choked on a bite. "What?"

Ry scowled. "You heard me."

I whipped my head to Tucker. "Did he just say he was wrong?"

Tucker grinned and pulled out his phone, bringing up his camera. "Maybe we should make him repeat it on video."

"Fuck off," Ryder said, shoving Tucker's phone out of his face. "I'm serious." He looked into my eyes. "I was wrong to hold your past against you. If you'd done that to me, I'd have knocked you on your ass."

"You can try," I said.

"I'm not trying to fight you, dumbass. I want to do the right thing here. For the business. For you. And for Emma, who's really good at the job."

"She's amazing," I agreed.

"And we both know what Henderson and Hall Architects are like. They already work her half to death without paying her what she's worth. They're going to burn her out."

"If you offer her a job with that as your pitch," I said, "she'll kick your ass. She's allergic to pity."

Tucker smiled, presumably at the thought of Emma kicking Ryder's ass. "I'd pay to see that," he said wistfully.

Me too.

"It's not pity," Ryder said. "She's incredibly talented. But I'm not the one who's going to make the offer. You are. That is, if you're good with it."

"You're asking me?"

"You said you wanted to work your way up to a full-fledged partner here."

I stared at him. "I did. I do."

Ryder nodded. "Then yeah, I'm asking you."

I looked at Tucker. "What do you think?"

"I think falling in love is a *terrible* idea."

"Noted," I said dryly. "I'm asking about hiring Emma to work here."

Tucker shrugged. "She's smart, capable, scrappy, and doggedly determined—perfect qualities for the job, so yes to hiring her. As for falling in love? I vote no, again." He hitched a thumb in Ryder's direction. "One of you walking around with a stupid lovestruck look on your face is enough."

"If this is a potential problem for you," Ryder said to me, "we don't go this route."

Something warmed in my chest that I hadn't realized needed warming. But Emma deserved a job as big as her talent, and this would give her that. "There's no one who'll work harder in our new department than Emma."

Ryder nodded. "I asked HR to draw up an offer. I'll leave it up to you to get it to her. Keep me updated."

I watched him walk out, hair and clothes still wet from the squirt guns. "Did that just happen?"

"Yeah." Tucker came up to my side, also watching Ryder go. "And I hope you know what you're doing."

"I absolutely do not."

He clapped a hand on my shoulder. "Gonna be fun then."

CHAPTER 34

Emma

AT THE END OF a long workday, I parked in front of Caleb's house and just breathed. In the past half hour, I'd deposited my paycheck into my bank account, then immediately hit the Submit button for my application on the downtown apartment I'd been eyeing.

I stared at myself in the rearview mirror and smiled through the nerves.

I'd done it.

Before it could really set in, my phone pinged with an incoming email. I'd just submitted the application, so I knew I wouldn't hear back this fast, but it didn't stop my heart from trying to leap right out of my rib cage in hope.

I pawed through my bag for my phone, then frowned. The email was from Henderson and Hall Architects, with…a job offer. For the job that, not long ago, I'd had to compete against four other applicants for.

Until it had become known that I was in with the Colburns.

I read through the terms of the offer, and some of that hope got trampled on. My temp position was hourly, but the offer was for a salaried position. In other words, more time on the job, less money in my pocket. I skimmed through the benefits. Skimpy at best.

Unfavorable at least.

Rosalind had warned me, but I still felt sick because it wasn't going to do much in the way of improving my circumstances. As quickly as it had come, my adrenaline rush vanished, leaving me exhausted while I banged my head on the steering wheel a few times, far too close to tears.

My phone buzzed again, a call this time.

"You okay?" Caleb asked.

"Sure. Why wouldn't I be?"

There was a beat of silence. "Because you've been sitting in your car for ten minutes, talking to yourself. And now you're trying to give yourself a concussion."

"Maybe I'm not done talking to myself."

"Come in and try me; I've got two ears and a brain between them. Your car doesn't have any of that."

"But my car has my emergency stash of chocolate."

"I've got something better than chocolate," he said in his bedroom voice.

Also true…

"Emma, get your sexy ass in here."

Why did that rich, husky voice make me want to do whatever he said? "If I do, you're going to try to solve all my problems—"

My driver's side door opened, and I jumped in surprise as Caleb's big body hunkered down, balancing on the balls of his feet as he studied me. Gently, he took my phone and ended the call, unclicked my seat belt, and offered me a hand. Okay, maybe not *offered*. Maybe it was more like he took my hand captive and used it to tug me out the car.

At his front door, he murmured, "Brace yourself, the boys missed you today," and then he nudged me inside, where I was nearly licked to death by the two cutest, biggest, funniest dogs who'd ever lived.

I dropped to the floor and wrapped my arms around them both, and I had no idea my breath was hitching until suddenly the dogs were gone and Caleb was on his knees in front of me, pulling me into him.

Something about the care with which he gathered me in and the gentle but firm press of his hands holding me to him completely broke me, and I burst into tears.

Without a word, he maneuvered until he was leaning back against the wall with me perched in his lap, my face pressed to the crook of his neck.

"I've got you, Em." His voice was low and gruff. Serious. Then, in perhaps the nicest thing anyone had ever done for me, he let me cry it all out. He rubbed my back, whispered some wordless nonsense in my ear that felt incredibly soothing, rubbed his jaw gently to mine…all without pushing me to talk about it, just quietly giving me the time to get it all out of my system. It was, without a doubt, the most secure I'd ever felt in my entire life.

Finally, I hiccuped a few times, then swiped my eyes on my sleeve and maybe also against his shirt. "I'm okay."

He licked my ear. *Wait, what?*

"Calvin, no," Caleb murmured and nudged his dog away.

I laughed soggily. "He's not nearly as good at that as you are."

"No one is."

I rolled my eyes, but also…he was right. He hadn't pressured me to talk, which was maybe why I did. "I got a job offer from Henderson and Hall," I said. "It's the job I want, but the terms are a little insulting."

He took that in, his hand still moving soothingly up and down my back. "Should I offer a solemn oath of vengeance or… ice cream and cookies?"

I leaned back to look into his face, hoping he was serious.

"Ice cream and cookies it is," he said, cupping my face and using his thumbs to swipe away a few rogue tears.

Two minutes later, I was sitting at his kitchen island with a wooden spoon, eating directly out of a gallon of fudge-brownie ice cream with one hand, the other holding a store-bought chocolate chip cookie that was more delicious than it had a right to be. Right next to me, Caleb, with his own spoon, was doing the exact same.

He waited until the trans fats and sugar hit my system. "So how bad's the offer?"

I sighed. The double fudge was doing a lot for my spirits, but expecting ice cream to solve my life problems seemed like a big ask. "Bad enough that I probably should rescind the apartment application I submitted today."

He looked at me for a long beat.

"What?"

"What if you didn't have to take that job?"

I stared at him. "What?"

"Come work for Colburn Restoration."

"At the risk of repeating myself, *what*?"

"We're expanding too fast and need more staff to support that. We want to add a CDM department."

"Construction-design management?" I asked in surprise, since that was exactly what I did for Henderson and Hall.

"Some of the positions that need filling are construction crew, but we're also looking to hire an engineer, a designer, and an architect. Ideally, that architect would be you."

My stomach slowly slid to my toes. I set down my spoon, then jumped off the counter, heart thudding dully. "A made-up pity job? Really, Caleb?"

"What? No." He set down his spoon as well. "I didn't make up the job; it's a real offer. Ryder and I talked about it, we want an in-house CDM division, and we want you in it. HR has the offer all drawn up."

I shook my head, realizing that the buzzing in my veins was anger. Anger that he would dangle something I wanted so badly, I could taste it in front of me like a carrot. "You've taken handling all my problems to a whole new level, don't you think?" I wouldn't cry, not again. "Or maybe not, since they call you The Fixer. And hell, we both know how much fixing I could use."

He came toward me, his scent, the strength of him washing over me. He could do this, fix my life, and he'd be good at it. But I couldn't let him. "Caleb—"

He didn't stop until we were toe-to-toe, his hands running up my arms, infusing me with his warmth. "Emma, I'm not trying to fix you. I would never do that."

"No? You jump-started my car that night at the gala, you gifted me a new laptop that you tried to tell me was from Santa—"

"I had an extra—"

"And if that weren't enough, you then gave me a place to live, and now a job offer." I shook my head, still far too close to tears. "And in return, what have I done for you? I'll tell you what: nothing."

He cupped my face. "If by 'nothing' you mean making me feel better by looking at me like I mean something to you. Or literally giving me and the guys all your food, helping me through the migraine…being the *one* person in my life who doesn't need anything from me, only wants me for me."

I was already shaking my head in denial. "It's not enough; it's not equal. At some point you'll realize it as well, and once you do, I'll be ghostee number one thousand and one."

He took a step back. "Low blow."

It was a low blow. A really low blow. But, for whatever reason, the panic was a ball in my throat and a weight on my chest, and I couldn't shut myself up. "You telling me you don't have a history of walking away when someone gets a little too close?" *God, listen to me.* I was picking a fight, an excuse to walk out before I got walked out on. Self-sabotage, and no one was better at it than me.

He closed his eyes for a beat, like he was physically pained, then softly said my name. What he did *not* do was deny my statement. My chest ached so unbearably, I had a hand pressed to my heart to keep it in my body.

"I have done that," he admitted.

"Every time."

He nodded. "Every time."

My biggest fear stood right in front of me—falling for someone and then being left behind. I wanted to collapse in a ball. I wanted to eat the rest of the ice cream. I wanted to crawl under the covers and not come out until my world had righted itself, but I had to be alone for that.

I turned to leave the kitchen, and a shattered expression crossed his face. "What are you doing?"

"I think…" I had to swallow hard. "I'm leaving. For once, I'm going to be the one to leave first, since this can't work."

"Emma…" He shook his head, like he didn't know how we'd gotten here. *Join my club…*

"It was working great until about ten seconds ago," he said. "When, if I have this right, you freaked out about how close we've gotten."

Oh, how I hated myself for that look of pain on his face. "I'm just being realistic," I said, with far more calm than I felt. "You have more to give than I do, Caleb. So much more. An unfairly balanced relationship won't last."

"It's not unfairly balanced—" His phone vibrated with an incoming call. "*Fuck.* I really hate my phone." He didn't even look at it. "Listen, you're scared. So am I. Neither of us has a good track record. But that shouldn't stop us from giving this a chance. Listen, I'll sleep on the floor, okay? I don't give a shit, I just…I can't handle the thought of you out there at night—" His phone began to ring again.

I gave him a sad smile. "We both know you need to take that."

"No, I—" He glanced at the screen and grimaced. "Fuck. Yes. I'm sorry."

I waved my hand at him to go ahead. He connected the call with one hand, grabbing one of mine with his other, interlocking our fingers and holding on tight while he listened. "Shit. Yeah, I'll be right there." He met my gaze. "Power went out on the Henderson property. Just before it did, the new security cams caught sight of what might've been someone running from the back gate toward the barn. There've been no known power outages in the area, so it feels suspicious. The police have been called, but I need to be there in person."

My heart rate spiked. I could be there, in that attic right now, in danger. I was so grateful to not still be sleeping there, my legs nearly collapsed.

Still holding my hand, Caleb grabbed his keys from the counter. "Let's go."

"There's no 'let's.'"

A pained expression crossed his face. "You're serious about walking away from me, from this?"

My eyes burned. "Yes."

Something flickered in his gaze, and he swallowed hard. "As always, you're free to do whatever you want." His voice was tight. Frustrated. "Except right now, in this moment, where I have a very bad feeling about that jobsite and exactly who's being targeted, so I'm not letting you out of my sight. You don't have to talk to me, you don't have to like it, but you're coming with me."

"Afraid I'll eat the rest of your ice cream?"

"Afraid you'll pull a me, and I won't see you for another ten years."

"Caleb." I felt tears block my throat. "I'm not sure there's anything else to say."

"Humor me."

It had started raining, and the night was even darker than it had been when I'd left work. Out here on the outskirts of town with no city lights, I could hardly see my hand in front of my face as a silent Caleb drove with intense focus on the problem ahead. He'd found his zone.

In the back seat, Calvin and Klein were in their zones as well, faces pressed to the window, excited about a nighttime drive.

I didn't have a zone.

When Caleb parked in the familiar circular drive, he set a hand on my headrest and craned his neck, looking around. "I don't know how we beat the cops."

I did. He'd driven like a bat out of hell.

From somewhere behind the house came a beam of light, which was gone before I'd even registered it. "Was that a flashlight?"

"Yeah." Caleb turned all his penetrating focus on me, his voice low and dark. Commanding. "New plan. Wait here for the police. I'm leaving you the keys and the boys. Lock the doors when I leave."

"Wait. What?"

"You see anyone who isn't me or a cop, drive away." He started to slide out of the truck, but I grabbed his sleeve before he could slip out. He put his hand over mine and said, "Five minutes, Em, that's all I'm asking. Stay here, please."

Stubborn alphas—not as much fun as they're rumored to be. "You keep saying you want me to stop being an island of one, but you expect me not to worry when *you're* an island of one, going in there alone?"

He gaped at me. "I can handle myself."

No shit. "At least take the dogs to watch your back."

Jaw tight, he shook his head. "Calvin and Klein stay with you." He was half out of the truck, but he twisted to face me when he heard me unclick my seat belt.

"Stay," he ordered as if I were Calvin or Klein. "If I'm not back in five minutes, call nine-one-one again, and then Ryder and Tucker."

And then he was gone.

I'd walked away from him in his kitchen—well, okay, I hadn't gotten the chance, but that had been the plan, and now, only thirty minutes later, he'd done the same to me. *Guess that makes us even.* "I can't believe he did that. He knows how I feel about it…"

Calvin whined.

Klein howled.

I wanted to do both. Instead, still shaking, I let both dogs hop over the console and into the driver's seat even though I knew they weren't allowed up here. Well, Calvin took the driver's seat. Klein took my lap and licked my chin. I hugged him, unsure who was comforting whom. "Trust me, your dad and I are so going to fight about this later. Please feel free to shed all over everything." I kept my eyes on the spot where we'd seen that flickering light. It had probably been someone running with a flashlight. The idea gave me chills.

Caleb was out there, on his own. He'd said we were a team. He'd sworn it, but he hadn't walked the walk or lived his talk. My heart felt cracked in two even if deep, deep down, a part of me knew I was overreacting, but dread made it hard to be logical. Caleb hadn't wanted me walking into danger, and yet he'd run straight for it.

Misguided, protective, stupid, *stupid* man. What if something happened to him while I just sat here? I'd never forgive myself. He was my…well, I'd just broken us up pretty good, so *boyfriend* was out. But he was still my friend, or so I hoped. And a coworker—of sorts. And…and who was I kidding? He was so, so, so much more than any of those things, including a boyfriend. I looked at the dogs. "It's been five minutes by now, right?"

Klein licked my chin. Calvin whined and nudged me with

his cold, wet nose. I didn't know if he agreed with me or just wanted his turn in my lap. I pulled out my phone, my thumb hovering over his contact. I was hesitant to call Caleb and have his phone make a noise if he was closing in on whoever that flashlight belonged to. The last thing I wanted to do was put him in more danger.

The dogs barked, and I heard stress and worry in their tones. Well, okay, so that might have been me projecting, but still. I called 9-1-1 and was told police were en route. I called Ryder next, but he didn't answer his phone, so I left a voicemail giving him the gist and added one last word—*hurry*. I tried Tucker next; no answer there either. I left him the same half-hysterical message I'd left for Ryder.

Then I stared out the windshield, desperately hoping to see Caleb coming toward me so I could kill him for scaring me. Only, I saw nothing except a very dark night. Sucking in a breath, I slid out of the truck, flanked by a dog on either side. I had a tight grip on their leashes this time.

Where was Caleb? Was he hurt?

Or worse?

It was a chilly night, but the backs of my knees were sweating. Fear crawled along my skin, and it pissed me off. I'd lived here for weeks. I was comfortable here, and no one was going to take that away from me.

And no one was going to take Caleb, either, even though I was so mad at him, I could scarcely breathe. First chance I got, I was going to eat the rest of his ice cream and put the empty container back into his freezer.

Caleb had gone around the side of the manor, so the doggos and I did the same, huddling close to the building, wanting a better vantage point to see the back of the property. I didn't dare use the flashlight app and broadcast my presence, but just as I got to the back corner, I heard something. Footsteps. Relief flooded me, and I opened my mouth to call out to Caleb, but twin low growls from either side of me had me going still.

Not Caleb.

I tightened my grip on the leashes, but then they stopped growling. I had enough time to relax for a beat before I was shoved from behind, sending me flying. I heard someone scream, then lights out.

———————

"Wha…" Confused, I blinked rapidly to clear my vision, but it remained cobwebby. What was going on? I was on the ground. Why was I on the ground? I shifted, and pain slashed through my skull. "*Ouch.*"

The dogs were nudging me with their noses, whining for me to get up. "Okay, okay…" I tried harder to sit, but hot, oily nausea washed over me. Swallowing hard to keep my stomach out of my throat, I put my hand to my head.

It came away sticky and wet. "That can't be good," I said weakly, closing my eyes and lying back down. "Someone please stop the merry-go-round."

"Omigod, omigod… *Emma?*"

I blinked, but my vision wouldn't clear.

Then Hazel's face appeared above me. She was gasping for breath with…*a baseball bat in her hand*?

When she saw my gaze go to it, she dropped the bat and crouched at my side. "Oh my God! Are you okay?"

"Did you…hit me with a baseball bat?"

"No!" Hazel's face paled. "You don't remember what happened?"

I shook my head, moaned, then closed my eyes again, dizzy, nauseous.

"No, open your eyes! Please, Emma." I could feel her huddled over me protectively, uneasy and scared. "I didn't hit you," she whispered. "I swear."

I believed her. Mostly because if she had, I'd probably be dead. I was pretty sure after I'd been shoved from behind, I'd hit the stucco corner of the manor. But then why did I hear a roaring in my head, like…waves? "Are we at the ocean?"

"We're at the Henderson job." She touched the side of my face. I winced and jerked back. She was staring at her fingers. "Okay, that's a lot of blood," she said shakily, running her hands over me, checking for other injuries. "Can you hear me okay? No, keep your eyes open! *Emma!*" She shook me gently. "Stay awake!"

"Don't—" Something was weird with my tongue. And if she shook me again, I was going to throw up all over both of us.

She didn't shake me, but I threw up anyway, retching and gasping for air. Hazel rolled me to my side, holding me there as I lost my cookies. Literally.

"Shit, Emma." Hazel was trying to hold my hair back while fumbling with her phone. "I'm calling nine-one-one."

I swiped my mouth with my sleeve. Disgusting. "Already did," I said. Or at least, that's what I meant to say, but it came out all weird. I closed my eyes and lay back. "I don't like merry-go-rounds—"

"Damn it, don't you dare die. Caleb will kill me." Hazel

yanked off her sweatshirt, balled it up, and pressed it to the side of my head. "Hold this. With pressure."

I lifted my hand and pressed down on the sweatshirt against my face and decided to take a nap.

CHAPTER 35

Caleb

'D RUN A QUICK perimeter check around the manor, and the only thing I had was a really bad feeling. The hair on the back of my neck was still standing straight up, and everything in my gut told me that I wasn't the only one out here.

I moved quickly across the property out back and found the gate to the river wide open, near fresh truck tracks.

I ran to the barn. Two windows smashed in, and the barn doors were open wide. I'd have to explore that later because my five minutes had been up five minutes ago, and *everything* in me was urging me to get back to the truck.

To Emma.

I turned and moved as quickly as I could in the dark on the rough terrain. I'd waited my whole life to meet my match, and Emma was certainly that. She questioned me, she pushed me, she never backed down, and I loved all that about her.

And right about now, she was probably planning my murder.

Hell, maybe she'd taken my truck and driven off. She'd tried to leave me back at my house. Something had spooked her. We'd gotten too close, and old fears had gripped her. I got it. I really did. But I believed in how close we'd come, and how we seemed drawn to each other like jelly on peanut butter, believed I'd have time to soothe her worries, to make her promises. To let her know she made me whole and real and worthy and…*everything*. She made me feel everything.

And what had I done? I'd promised her she wasn't alone, that we were a team, and when the call had come, my first chance to prove I meant what I'd said, I'd left her behind.

The kicker was, I couldn't, didn't, regret it. I would always, *always*, err on the side of caution when it came to keeping her safe.

And now I knew what it would cost me.

I was almost back to my truck when I plowed into someone who swore viciously in a voice I knew as well as my own. "Shit, Tucker."

My brother lifted his hands in surrender. "You okay?"

"No." I kept moving. "Where did you come from? You see anyone?"

"I parked at the back gate, which was open. Saw the fresh tracks. Then I saw someone moving quickly toward the front and came running."

"Me."

"You," he agreed. "I didn't get a chance to check out the barn."

I would've told him what I'd seen, but we were at my truck. My empty truck. I yanked open the passenger door and stilled. "*Fuck.*"

"What?"

"It's empty."

"Uh, yeah, because you're not in it," Tucker said.

"I left Emma here."

"You left her alone in your truck?"

"She had the dogs."

"You mean the most passive boxers in the entire world, who'd sell you for a bite of anything even halfway edible?"

"Not helping." I craned my neck and took in the dark all around us. "Where would she have—"

A scream cut through the night, and my heart stopped. Emma.

Tucker and I flat-out hauled ass, following the echo of her scream.

"Did it come from the east or south?" Tucker asked as we passed the front porch of the manor.

"I don't fucking know." It had reverberated off my brain, sending a chilled horror through my bones. "You take the south; I'll go east." I didn't slow to see if he agreed with the plan, just kept running. "Emma!" I yelled. I could hear Tucker calling for her as well. I took the corner of the manor at full speed, then nearly tripped over someone hovering over a body on the ground.

Hazel.

And that was Emma on the ground, Calvin and Klein standing guard over them both. With my heart thundering in my chest, I dropped to my knees. "Emma." I pushed the hair from her face, and my hand came away wet with her blood. Fuck. "Emma, open your eyes."

"Okay," she slurred.

But she didn't open her eyes.

"She keeps going in and out," Hazel said, voice thick with tears.

"You hurt?" I asked her.

She shook her head and swiped at her wet eyes.

Calvin whined and nudged my hand. "It's okay, buddy." But it wasn't. I felt out of control, ruled by senses I hadn't even known I had, on edge and ready to tear out anyone's throat if they got too close. Never taking my eyes off Emma, I yanked out my phone and called 9-1-1. I was informed police officers were already en route, though they'd been delayed by a train stuck on the tracks, and they'd dispatch EMS as well. I dropped my phone and ran my hands over Emma carefully, looking for any other injuries. "Emma. Can you hear me?"

One eye slitted open, but she moaned and immediately shut it again.

"Caleb," Hazel said softly, her eyes filled with regret and guilt. "I pushed her. I thought she was the trespasser."

I realized there was a baseball bat on the ground next to her. Catching the path of my gaze, Hazel paled. "I didn't hit her with the bat, I swear—" On a sob, she rose to her feet and backed up a step, right into—

"What the fuck?" Tucker asked, panting for breath, hands coming up to steady Hazel.

"Emma's hurt," I said.

Tucker immediately dropped to his knees at Emma's other side. "Hey, Em," he said softly. "How you doing?"

"She's not hurt anywhere else. I already checked," Hazel said as Tucker checked Emma over. "I saw the barn, the broken glass, and knew something bad was happening. I was trying to get out of here when I heard running footsteps in front of me. But when I called out, they didn't stop, and then they slowed in front of me. I thought it was whoever'd broken into the barn, so I shoved them." A sob broke loose, and she covered her mouth. "Only, it was Emma, and she hit the corner of the stucco wall. I didn't mean to hurt her—" She lifted her wet gaze to me. "Caleb, you know I wouldn't."

"I do."

Hazel looked at Tucker. He didn't say anything, and more tears fell down Hazel's face.

Sirens sounded in the distance as I turned to my brother. "Does she need a C-collar, or can I carry her to the front to meet EMS?"

"C-collar to be safe. Stay with her; I'll go get them."

"Hurry."

"My middle name," Tucker said, then took a beat to squeeze Emma's hand. "We've got you, just a few minutes longer." And then he was gone.

Hazel watched him go, a grim tightness to her mouth.

"You sure you're okay?" I asked her.

She drew a shaky breath and, hugging herself, nodded.

Emma was shivering now, and since I couldn't scoop her into my arms like I wanted, couldn't bury my face in her hair or neck and beg for forgiveness for hurting her feelings when all I'd wanted was to keep her protected, I lowered myself to the dirt and lay as close as I could get, sharing my body heat, my arm across her middle while I ran my hand up and down her chilled arm.

"No," she moaned, trying to roll away. "I'll throw up on you."

"It's okay. Slow breaths, Em. With me. In…"

Shakily, she inhaled. "I'm fine."

"I know. Out…"

She mirrored my breathing, her eyes tightly shut, a pained grimace on her face.

"It's going to be okay."

In answer, she threw up.

"Second time," Hazel murmured to me quietly, crouched low, holding back Emma's hair while I kept her propped on her side so she didn't aspirate.

Things got a little crazy after that.

The EMS team knew and respected Tucker, so he took over, getting Emma stable before leading the way around the manor to the front and into the waiting ambulance.

They blocked me from climbing in as well. I opened my mouth to argue, but the police arrived, lighting the place up with their red and blue lights. We were told in no certain terms to back the fuck up. I opened my mouth to argue, but Tucker dragged me clear.

I twisted to get a view of Emma in the ambulance. She was talking. That had to be a good sign. "Let me go."

"Take a minute," Tucker said. "Heads bleed a lot. You know this from personal experience."

What I knew was I'd earned a gold medal in making bad choices tonight. "She dumped me."

Tucker turned his head to mine, disbelief in his gaze. "No way. That girl's crazy about you, man. None of us can figure out why, but she is."

"I think she was afraid I'd walk first, something that's happened too many times in her life."

"Were you going to?"

"No, but my track record's there. Everyone knows it."

Tucker shook his head. "The past is the past. You can fix this."

"How?"

"Hell, you think I know? Tell her…" He searched for words. "Tell her it only takes one. One person in your whole life to make you stay. And she's that person for you. All those others, none of them made it into your heart. Nothing compares to what you feel for her."

I stared at him. "You get that from a book? A movie? Google?"

"Fuck you." He gave me a shove. "Fight for her like you used to fight for the puck. Like you used to fight Ryder for being a know-it-all dick. Like you fought Dad that one time you thought he was going to kill me. Fight like this is the biggest fight of your life."

I turned to the ambulance, but two officers stepped between us and the rig, looking apologetic but firm. "We need to speak to you both. Separately."

We were questioned about the events of the evening, while I champed at the bit to get back to Emma.

Tucker and a cop were talking a few feet away. They clearly knew each other, my brother's body language relaxed and calm— at least on the surface, which told me he was cleared too. Beneath that demeanor, though, I could tell he was seriously pissed off.

"Going to the hospital," I said.

Tucker had his gaze locked on Hazel, who was sitting on the sidewalk, looking up at the two cops questioning her.

"They want her to go to the station for questioning," Tucker said.

"What? *No*."

"That's what I said." He moved closer to Hazel and the cops. "She isn't the one who broke in."

Hazel's mouth fell open in shock.

"It's policy," the male cop said.

"It's fine." Hazel rose. "I've got nothing to hide." She looked at me, not Tucker. "It's just a formality. There's a surveillance tape of me running from the barn."

"Were you here working?" I asked.

"I was…" She seemed to struggle oddly, tripping over her words. "I was looking for my dad."

I turned to the cop. "If she needs a lawyer, we'll send ours. But she didn't do this."

Hazel's eyes shimmered with gratitude, and I squeezed her hand. "Did they take Emma to General?"

The cop nodded, and I looked at Tucker.

"I'll keep the dogs and secure the scene after everyone's gone," he assured me. "Ryder's on his way. He's got Hank. Go. We'll meet you at the hospital."

I ran to my truck, kicking my own ass as I did.

The thought of Emma being hurt made it feel like ice was flowing through my veins instead of blood.

I got to the ER at the same time as Ryder, Hank in tow.

"How is she?" Ryder asked.

"Don't know yet." Which was killing me slowly.

Hank…fucking Hank of all people, put a steadying hand on my shoulder, making me realize I was a mess. Emma's blood was all over me. But he looked right into my eyes and managed to say "ah" in a tone that expressed something I'd never heard directed my way before from him.

Worry. Empathy.

Obviously, the man couldn't speak, and who the hell knew what he'd say if he even could. I couldn't control that any more than I could control keeping Emma safe.

I will keep you safe and fed, but we are not friends, you get me?

My long-ago harsh words to him rang in my ears as we stared at each other. A few months ago, I'd have flung his hand off me or, worse, flinched at his touch. But that was due to the memory of a man who no longer existed. The person I was looking at would never be that guy again. And I couldn't live with the age-old anger. Life was too fucking short. I couldn't live letting it all fester in my gut. Shutting down my heart to keep it safe had never worked. To be the man I wanted to be—for Emma, for my family, for me—I had to tear down the brick wall around my heart.

So I put one of my hands on top of Hank's and nodded my understanding. Something flickered in his eyes—simple joy maybe? I managed a smile and moved to the nurse's station to ask about Emma.

"You family?" a nurse asked.

I lied so easily that I scared myself. "Husband."

She eyed me, then Ryder behind me, then Hank.

"Ah," Hank said.

The nurse turned back to me. "She didn't say anything about a husband, much less that husband being a famous hockey star named Caleb Colburn."

"Former hockey star." I smiled grimly. "And she's mad at me."

She remained unimpressed. "You the one who clocked her?"

"No, ma'am, that was a stucco wall, and I wasn't there."

She stared at me.

I stared back, then softened my posture. "Please," I said quietly. "I need to see her."

Tucker came through the double doors and flashed a smile at the nurse. "Hey, Shel. My brother giving you a hard time?"

"As a Colburn does."

Tucker grinned. "I beat you *one* time at family poker night at the station."

"And you won't beat me again." She pointed at him. "Lenny said I had his permission to wipe the rug with you next time. Now, let me guess—you're calling in a favor for your brother, who tried to lie his way in here."

"Is it a lie, or is he just manifesting?" Tucker asked.

I took in the words and blinked. Oh shit. He was right. I wanted it to be true. Knees shaky, I dropped into one of those stupid metal waiting chairs that guaranteed a numb ass in two minutes or less. Emma was it for me. The end. Period. She understood me like no one else, and she made me want to be a better person. "Fuck. I *love* her."

Shel smiled. "You should see the look on your face right now."

Tucker crossed his arms over his chest, not an ounce of surprise in them. "And?" he asked me.

I let out a mirthless laugh and dropped my head back, knocking it against the wall. "I think she loves me too. At least, I think she did before tonight."

Tucker turned back to Shel and lowered his voice. "Listen, obviously, he's a hot mess. I'd consider it a personal favor if you let him go back there."

"Is he good enough for her?" Shel said. "'Cause all that girl's done since arriving here tonight is worry about all of you. She's special."

"She is," Tucker agreed.

Shel gave me a long look.

"She's the best thing to ever happen to me," I said.

She studied me for a long beat. Looked around, and when no one was paying any mind, she held up eight fingers.

"Bay eight," Tucker murmured to me under his breath. "Let's go."

We left Ryder in the waiting room with Hank, and five minutes and a long, windy walk down several corridors later, Tucker pulled back a curtain to reveal…an empty bed.

My heart stopped.

"She's getting a CT scan," a harried-looking nurse said. "She'll be back soon."

I let out a slow breath. We sat, me in the lone chair in the room, Tucker on the doctor's stool.

"Hazel?" I asked.

"Bill showed up at the site and went with her to the station."

"She isn't our bad guy," I said.

Tucker's eyes were tight. "Never thought she was."

"No, I mean we have actual proof it's not her. Ryder texted me the surveillance footage from tonight. It was a male, taller and beefier than her."

Tucker nodded. "The cops said they wouldn't keep her, that she wasn't being charged, just questioned on what she saw and how Emma got hurt."

"You ever going to tell me why you two aren't speaking?"

"No."

I opened my mouth to prod for more, but Kiera strode in, kicked my feet until I stood up, then plopped in my chair. "Sitrep."

She wasn't the daughter of a military man for nothing.

"Well, for one thing, Caleb's one bad decision away from needing a life coach," Tucker said.

Kiera snorted. "My name's Kiera Colburn, and I approve this message."

I glared at her. "How did you get back here?"

"Shel."

"And the kids?"

"Sitting with Penny, Ryder, and Hank."

Tucker's head swiveled to her. "And Hazel?"

Kiera's brow rose at the question, but she nodded. "She was released. I don't know where she is now. Also, I don't have much time. Like a rookie, Ryder fed the twins sugar from the vending machine, so they're probably bouncing off the walls."

"Why's everyone here?" I asked.

"Because even though you're stupid, we love you."

She pulled a soda from her bag and had just taken a sip when a different nurse poked her head in and looked at me. "You're the husband, right?"

Kiera choked on the soda while I nodded so quickly, my head spun. "Yes."

Kiera choked some more, and Tucker patted her on the back, but given the sound Kiera made, it was more of a pounding than a pat.

"The radiologist said she's got a mild cerebral contusion," the nurse said. "Grade-one concussion. She needs stitches but then will most likely be released if she's got someone to watch over her."

"She does," I said firmly.

Then Emma was rolled into the cubicle. She'd been changed into a hospital gown, and there was still blood in her hair and on her face. Her eyes were closed, her face pale, and my heart rolled over in my chest.

"I'm fine," she whispered without opening her eyes.

Leaning over her, I brushed her hair back from her face and pressed a kiss to her uninjured temple. She still didn't look at me, but she squeezed my fingers and held on tight, the helpless weight of regret and my own fears sitting like an elephant on my chest.

"I want a toothbrush," Emma said so softly, I barely heard. She cracked open one eye. "I have throw-up breath."

I didn't dare smile but turned to my family. Kiera stood up, nodded at me, then left.

"Toothbrush coming right up," I said.

I didn't know how she did it. I'd long ago given up questioning Kiera's unflagging determination, but no more than four minutes later, she was back with a small plastic-wrapped toothbrush and tiny sample toothpaste.

Eyes barely slitted open and full of pain, Emma brushed her teeth, and as I turned in a circle, looking for something for her to spit in, she swallowed the tiny dab of toothpaste I'd given her and lay back again, pasty white and still.

"I can hear you thinking too hard from here," she whispered. "What's wrong?"

"He's freaking out that you got hurt," Tucker said.

"Yes," I said. "Join me, won't you?"

"Sit." Tucker kicked the stool Kiera had abandoned over to me. "Calm down."

"I'm not a Taylor Swift song. And *you* calm down. I've never been calmer in my life." Okay, so I wasn't handling this well. Taking the stool, I stroked the hair back from Emma's face again just for the excuse to touch her. "You're going to be okay."

"I know."

"You've got a mild concussion and need a few stitches."

"All I need's a Band-Aid. I can't imagine what they charge for even just a Band-Aid."

She was most definitely not paying the bill.

I reached for her hand, and her eyes finally opened. "What are you doing?" she asked.

"Oh, he's visiting his wife," Tucker said jauntily. "And blaming himself for what happened to you tonight."

I gave Tucker a look that promised I'd be kicking his ass as soon as possible. "I am at fault," I said.

"I left the truck of my own volition."

I looked at my siblings, silently ordering them out of the room. Nobody moved. Assholes. Leaning in, I brought our entwined hands to my chest and met her half-mast gaze, hating the pain I saw in those beautiful green eyes. I spoke as softly as I could, for her ears only. "Why did you leave the truck after I'd asked you to stay?"

"You didn't ask. You ordered."

"Yeah, he's pretty bossy," Kiera said helpfully.

I slid her a look, and she must've felt bad because she sighed. "He doesn't mean to be an ass though. He's just used to being a bossy know-it-all protector. He was trying to keep you safe."

"I was," I said. "But I was wrong—"

The doctor strode in, followed by the nurse, who eyed the group. "Everyone out," she said.

I held on to Emma's hand. I wasn't going anywhere.

"They can stay," Emma said.

They. Not a good sign that she lumped me in with everyone else, but I'd take it.

The nurse looked annoyed, but the doctor smiled at the bunch of us. "Love to see a good support system."

And then he got to work, first carefully cleaning Emma's wound, then pulling out his equipment. I leaned in and held Emma's gaze so she wouldn't look at the big-ass needle the doctor wielded. As he numbed her up, he moved the needle around, making her hiss through her teeth and me have to work at not ripping that needle out of her head.

"You must've hit just right for maximum damage," the doctor murmured, making little sounds of sympathy every time Emma sucked in a pain-filled gulp of air. She had a grip on my hand so tight, I'd be lucky to have any fingers left. I didn't care; she could have them.

When he finished stitching her up, he smiled. "Scar should be minimal. My nurse will give you instructions on how to care for the wound."

And then he was gone.

I took a shuddering breath, feeling all the energy drain out of me, replaced by a sick dread in the pit of my stomach, knowing what would come next. Me getting kicked out on my ass. I turned to Emma. "About earlier tonight. I—" Shit. I'd forgotten what I was saying when the doctor had come in earlier.

"You were saying you were wrong," Kiera said helpfully.

I bared my teeth at her, then drew a breath.

"It's okay," Emma said. Her voice was soft and careful, like every word hurt. That, along with the blood drying in her hair, made me feel murderous.

"It's not," I said. "Kiera's right, I *was* wrong."

"You mean when you told me we were a team, but at the first opportunity, you benched me?"

"Nice sports analogy," Tucker said.

Emma gave him a weak curve of her lips.

I drew a deep breath. "I did that, and I'm sorry. I care about you and your safety, but if I could redo it, I'd *ask* you to wait, and when you refused, because let's face it, you would"—I paused when she snorted—"I'd then take you with me because I'd know it would be the safest place for you."

"Because you *care* about me."

"Yes," I said in an unequivocal tone, leaving no room for doubt. "Deeply, Emma. So much, it makes me feel overprotective. I'll work on that."

"Wow," Tucker murmured. "Never heard that come out his mouth before."

"Hell must've frozen over," Kiera said.

Over Emma's head I flipped them both off.

The nurse stuck her head back in and caught me at it. "Do I need to eject every single one of you?"

"No, ma'am," I said.

Tucker and Kiera mimed zipping their lips.

Nurse Hatchet glared at me.

I mimed zipping my lips, too, and I was pretty sure Emma's mouth quirked slightly with amusement. I nearly collapsed with relief to see it.

I slid my hand back in hers, silently vowing to make her smile for the rest of her life.

CHAPTER 36

Emma

MY HEAD WAS POUNDING, and I was pretty sure I still smelled like vomit. My eyelids drooped, but I couldn't tear my gaze away from Caleb, who loomed over me like a protective grizzly. His big form towered over the bed, his eyes filled with concern, that five-o'clock shadow of his giving him a rugged, almost-feral look that, even in my groggy state, sent a shiver down my spine. "I was wrong too," I whispered.

"About not waiting?"

"No, I'm actually not sorry about that."

"Ohmigod, I love her," Kiera whispered to Tucker.

I started to smile, but it hurt, so I sucked in a breath instead. "Earlier, back at your house, when I said we were done. That was me running scared."

Caleb shifted closer, his broad shoulders blocking out the harsh hospital lights. His hazel eyes, more green than golden brown today, held mine. "You ghosted me."

Regret was a lead ball in my gut. "I mean, I told you I was leaving, which technically is different from ghosting."

He tilted his head, eyes wry. "*Technically*, you wanted to walk out on me before I could walk out on you. Because that's what you believed would happen eventually. You didn't think I could stick around."

"I didn't think you could stick with *me*," I corrected. "It was about me and my failings, Caleb, not yours."

He gently squeezed my hand, then brushed a kiss over my palm. "You don't think you're worthy of me staying. But, Emma, I've never been with anyone more worthy of love. I fell for you in spite of myself, hopelessly and fully."

I blinked. "Either the meds are messing with me, or you just told me you...like me a lot."

Tucker and Kiera both chortled with wicked glee, and when Caleb swiveled his head to glare at them, Tucker managed to wipe the amusement off his face. "I mean, wow, this is brand-new information."

"Never could've guessed," Kiera said innocently.

"Get out." Caleb turned back to me, and because we were chronic dumbasses, we just stared at each other.

Finally, I gave him a tight smile. "We haven't exactly said this to each other before. The whole L-word thing."

He let out a long breath. "We...haven't."

"I mean, we could pretend you didn't say it, or..." I was certain the entire emergency department could hear my heart pounding. "Or I could tell you I feel the same."

His smile was brilliant, and in those eyes of his, I saw my past, present, and future as he drank me in like I was all he needed.

"Cute," Tucker said. "They're both terrified of the…" He lowered his voice into a dramatic whisper. "L-word."

"Shh," Kiera said, swatting him. "He might still blow this, and I don't want to miss it."

Caleb's head dropped to my shoulder as he took in a few gulps of air. "*I'm begging you both to get the fuck out*," he said against my skin.

"You know what's even cuter?" Kiera asked Tucker. "He actually thinks we'll leave just when it's getting good."

Tucker snorted.

Caleb continued to inhale me, like I was his oxygen. I slid my fingers into his silky hair so he couldn't leave. He simply tightened his grip on me, like he'd *never* leave, not unless I wanted him to.

"What happened tonight?" I asked.

Caleb lifted his head to meet my gaze. "You don't remember?"

"Some. I remember walking along the side of the manor and hearing running steps. And then being shoved." I looked into Caleb's eyes. "I heard you calling for me, and then you appeared." He'd dropped to his knees at my side, panting for breath like he'd been running.

The way he'd looked at me, the comforting scrape of his calluses when he'd rested his palm on my cheek, the feel of his fingers as they'd slid into my hair, how he'd stared into my eyes with intensity and relief while begging me to keep my eyes open.

Tucker rose from his perch and came closer, looking down at his phone.

Ryder was on FaceTime from the waiting room. He had Hank on one side of him, Penny on the other. Alex was on Ryder's lap, eating his way through a bag of chips—Cheetos, by the looks of his orange fingers and the equally orange finger-prints all over Ryder. Ali was sitting on his shoulders, holding onto his hair like he was her personal steed. She had an orange mustache.

"Seriously, Ry?" Kiera asked.

"Hey, you told me to keep the heathens busy; I'm keeping the heathens busy." Ry looked at me. "Emma, how you feeling?"

"Like I had a fight with a stucco wall and lost."

His eyes softened. "I'm so sorry you got hurt."

"I'm fine."

Ryder let out a mirthless chuckle in Caleb's direction. "She's as bullheaded as you."

Caleb squeezed my hand. "Tell me something I don't know. You go through the rest of the surveillance footage?"

Ryder nodded. "Saw a white truck racing away from the site through the back gate. Probably the same one you saw." His expression was grim. "The motion sensor didn't trigger the lights, so we didn't get a plate or a look at the driver. But there's something else—Ricky's missing trailer filled with tools? It's parked in the far back of the barn."

Tucker and Caleb stared at him, astonished. I figured I was already wearing the same expression from the events of the night.

"It's fucking back," Ry said. "Right where it vanished from, like it was never gone."

Tucker shook his head in disbelief. "What does that even mean?"

Ry shook his head. "I don't know. *Yet.*" He looked at Caleb again. "Hoping our fixer figures it out."

Caleb nodded, and I knew that look. Come hell or high water, he'd get to the bottom of it.

Ryder's gaze turned to me. "From what I hear, you're going to be released, but you'll have to take it easy for a few days. Is there anything I can do for you?"

"Can you let Rosalind know I won't be in tomorrow?"

Ry looked at his watch. "It's already tomorrow, and yes, I'll let her know." He paused. "I understand you got an offer from them. And us."

I glanced at Caleb and found him watching me. "I did." Several things had become clear to me tonight. I wasn't going to let myself be afraid of losing good things in my life. Not ever again. "I'm…taking the job."

"Which one?" Ryder asked.

Caleb had stilled. I wasn't sure he was even breathing.

"Yours," I whispered.

The little bay we were all crowded in seemed to take a collective breath of relief. Caleb squeezed my hand, a slow, warm smile on his face.

"We're lucky to have you," Ryder said.

My eyes stayed locked on Caleb. "I'm also taking your brother."

Ryder shrugged. "Everyone's got their weak spots."

Caleb disconnected and leaned over me. "Thank you," he whispered, then dropped a very gentle kiss to my mouth.

"For accepting the job?" I asked.

"For accepting me."

"Holy shit," Kiera said. "This is real. Caleb landed someone we actually all love."

"Shh," Tucker said. "He still has to tell her it's because he saw the Legend of Star Falls."

Kiera gasped. "He saw it? For real? Like Ryder did right before he fell in love with Penny?"

Caleb dropped his head to my shoulder, mumbling about nosy-ass siblings who never mind their own business.

The nurse came into the bay with release papers. "We're cutting you loose, but only if you have people at home to keep an eye on you."

Everyone in the room raised their hand.

The nurse smiled at me. "Seems you're a lucky girl; you've got a lot of people who care about you."

I took them all in and realized just how true that was. It had happened so slowly, I hadn't even realized I truly was no longer alone. Caleb caught my gaze and clearly read my thoughts, because he gave me a warm, just-for-me smile.

"So," the nurse said, "who's in charge of her for the next twenty-four hours?"

"Me," Caleb said firmly. "I've got her."

Two days later, I sat up and gave a sigh of relief. No headache. No lingering exhaustion. No pain where my stitches were. My legs were numb, but that was the deadweight of the two boxers lying across my thighs.

Calvin and Klein lifted their sleepy, ridiculously cute heads, and I swore they smiled at me.

"Where's your dad?" I asked, because Caleb's side of the bed was empty.

And cold. He'd been gone awhile then. I eyed the clock, and my jaw dropped.

Ten in the morning!

I tossed the covers aside and stood just as Caleb appeared in the doorway, wearing only his glasses and low-slung cotton sleep pants that clung to his incredible bod, showing off tattoos and muscles and generally just making my mouth water. But that might have been because he was carrying a tray full of food.

"Sleeping Beauty awakens."

I rolled my eyes, and hey, even that didn't hurt. Flashing a smile, I sniffed appreciatively. Yes, the man smelled amazing, but the food… "You made me breakfast in bed?"

"Don't tell anyone."

I laughed, then laughed again when he ordered the dogs to get down and neither moved. He pulled out his alpha male voice. "Down, *now*."

With a sigh, both dogs jumped off the bed but didn't go far, plopping to the floor, their noses twitching at the delicious breakfast scents.

I gave Caleb the *gimme* hands, and he set the tray in my lap. A stack of pancakes, crispy bacon, and a bowl of strawberries… I was in heaven.

"If I could get you alone for five minutes, I'd get you to look at me like that."

I couldn't respond because my mouth was already full, but I grinned at him with my eyes. He wasn't kidding—we hadn't been alone. His house had been Grand Central Station, but after being on my own for so long, I thrived on the company.

We had the dogs, plus Hank was usually here, and there was a new quiet peace between him and Caleb. On top of that, someone else was always stopping by. Kiera with the twins. Tucker, to watch a ball game or play basketball in the driveway with Caleb, which was more like a game of survival, the way the two of them went at each other one-on-one. Ryder had been here a lot, sometimes with Penny, who always brought the most amazing food. Suzie had been by, and there'd been a tough few moments when she'd cried about me not confiding in her about my circumstances. She'd made me pinkie promise to never ever keep anything from her again.

Hazel had been around too. At first, I thought it was because she and Caleb were so close or that she felt bad about what had happened. Turned out it was both, and more. We had a lot in common. We'd both lost our moms too soon, had difficult relationships with our dad, and had spent years trying to find our place in this world. Our new friendship meant a lot to me.

Rosalind had also come to see me, to ask me to reconsider their offer. I'd thanked her for everything, but I was going to stick with Colburn Restorations, and for the first time in my life, I felt happy and secure and safe, all at the very same time.

And now, finally, it was just me and Caleb—and the dogs. I patted the spot beside me. He slid his sexy ass next to mine, wrapped one arm around me, and, with his free hand, grabbed some bacon.

"Soooo…" Nerves had my pulse kicking. "There's something I've been wanting to talk about."

"Yeah?" He chewed. Swallowed. Kissed me. He waggled his brows suggestively. "That's a euphemism for all the sex we haven't had over the past few days, right?"

"Wrong!" I laughed, pressing up against his body, and had second thoughts. "Well, okay, yes, but first, a question."

He looked deeply into my eyes. "Anything."

He meant it, and I snuggled into him, my hand running up and down his torso, north and south and north and south again…and his reaction—a rough groan and an obvious erection—encouraged me to stay south for the winter, even if it was summer.

On a rough chuckle, he caught my hand from sliding into his sleep pants. "Your question."

Right. "The Legend. You saw it for real?" I'd never met anyone who'd actually seen the three falling stars firsthand, other than Ryder and Penny.

"Yeah," he said, muffled against my throat. "I saw the Legend." He chuckled. "Scared?"

I wasn't sure... If I believed in the Legend, then I was accepting predestination, not choice. I didn't like that, but I also believed that we made our *own* fate, Legend or otherwise.

My silence must've gone on too long because he lifted his head. "You gave me your heart, and there're no takebacks, Emma. I'm keeping it. But I promise you"—his eyes were serious now—"it's the most precious thing I own. I'll take care of it and protect it forever."

I sucked in a breath. "Forever?"

"Or as long as you'll have me."

I blinked, considering him.

He didn't waver. Behind him, out the window, the day had begun without us, the sky a pure azure, not a cloud in sight. But all I could see was Caleb watching me, patiently waiting for me to put words to my thoughts.

He'd seen me at my worst and still loved me. It was... the most amazing thing to ever have happened to me, and I knew my life would never be the same. I took in his face, that beautiful, expressive face, the one I wanted to see grow old, and knew life would continue after this moment, a series of befores and afters that would become our story. And I knew

I'd choose this, him, every single time. I had no doubt of that, or his love for me.

Or mine for him.

His eyes were bright with an emotion I now knew the name of, and I smiled. "It might be a really long time."

"Counting on it."

EPILOGUE

Caleb

THE JEWELRY SHOP OWNER smiled sweetly as she handed me a small bag with little handles on it.

"Thanks," I said, chest full to bursting as I left the store and stepped onto the bustling wintery streets of Star Falls. It had been months since that terrifying night in the hospital when Emma had gotten hurt. We were deep into fall and heading straight into winter.

Emma had taken to Colburn Restorations like she'd been born for the job. She'd gotten the apartment she'd dreamed of, and we'd been trading off sleeping at each other's places but had discussed moving in together.

As a couple this time.

The minute her lease was up, she was going to move into my house in the same way she'd moved into my heart, and I couldn't wait.

I still hadn't found out how or why Ricky's trailer had reappeared, but there had been no further incidents on any jobs, thanks in no small part to a massively increased surveillance presence for every single project we took on.

It had rained last night, leaving the streets clean and the trees lining those streets glistening in the weak sun. I slowed my steps. My plan had been to wait until I got back to my truck parked on the next street over, but I couldn't. So I ducked into an alley and stood between two time-weathered brick walls to pull the small box from the bag—

"Gotta be more aware of your surroundings, man."

My head snapped up to find Ry and Tuck standing at the entrance to the alleyway.

Fuck. I dropped the box back into the bag as if I'd been burned, then held it behind my back when I approached my meddling, interfering brothers. "Do I even want to know why you're tailing me?" I asked, maneuvering around them and stepping back out onto the main street. I knew better than to remain in the tight alley, where I could get pinned between them while they tried to wring information from me.

But their footsteps followed, flanking me.

"Everyone knows you're the best gifter of all us Colburns," Tucker said casually.

How much had they witnessed? Had they seen what I'd purchased? Did they think this was about Christmas? "So you what, caught sight of me by sheer good luck and decided to tail me?"

"Yep," Ry said.

Bullshit. I rolled my eyes as we weaved and bobbed around the shoppers on the streets.

"Did you buy Emma a necklace or something?" Tucker asked.

Or something…

"He always gets quiet when he's up to no good," Ryder said to Tucker.

"Fuck off," I said.

"*And* he clearly skipped breakfast," Tucker said on a laugh.

In fact, I'd had breakfast. Twice—first a breakfast with Emma, and then a breakfast *of* Emma.

So, no, hunger was not the cause of my irritation. It was that I was trying to plan quite possibly the biggest surprise of my entire existence, and the two worst secret keepers on the planet might be on to me. I eyed Ryder. "You need help finding something for Penny, just say so—"

Taking advantage of my distraction, Tucker snatched the bag out of my hand. I whirled, reaching for it, but Ry gripped my arm, towing me toward one of the benches that lined the street along with massive redwoods, all lit for the holidays.

I gritted my teeth as Tucker plucked the small box out of the bag.

"Tuck, I swear to—"

He sat on the bench. "Wonder what we've got here—" He opened the box and stared in surprise.

I pulled free of Ryder's hold, seized the box, and snapped it shut, before shoving it into my jacket pocket and glowering at my fuckwit brothers.

Ryder leaned past me, trying to get a better look at Tucker's stunned expression. "What was it?"

Tucker didn't take his eyes off me. "I'm sorry. I didn't think—"

"*What was it?*" Ryder repeated, sounding like Alex when he missed out on something.

"It looks like..." Tucker began hesitantly. "Like maybe Caleb's planning to propose to Emma."

It was strange to hear someone else say it. To say out loud

what I'd known I wanted for a long time now—that I wanted a lifetime with Emma.

Tucker sank against the back of the bench, emotion swimming in his eyes as he looked at me. I hadn't seen him feel much of anything in a long time, I realized.

"What, surprised I found someone to love me?" I said, trying to lighten things up.

"No." Tucker refused to let me laugh this off. "Surprised that you let yourself be loved. You too," he said to Ry. "Hell, even Kiera let herself do the same with Auggie. It's…hope personified." He rubbed over his chest like it ached. "After all we've been through, it's a miracle."

"I honestly didn't believe I could let myself fall," I admitted.

"You hit the lotto with Emma," Ryder said, nudging my gut with his elbow. Hard. "Don't fuck it up."

"Don't intend to. I can't even remember what my life was like without her."

Ryder clapped me on the shoulder. "Then there's only one thing left for you to do."

"Right. Ask her if she'll shackle herself to me for the rest of her life." Not terrifying at all…

Tucker shrugged. "If it helps, I'm about seventy-five percent sure she'll say yes." He paused. "Okay, sixty percent."

"Thanks."

We all turned at the sounds of heels clicking down the street past us.

Emma herself.

She stopped short in surprise, smiling so sweetly and joyfully at the sight of me, it drained all lingering annoyance at my brothers.

"Emma," Ryder said smoothly. "What's up?"

"I'm meeting this guy"—she nudged her chin in my direction—"for coffee at Penny's café."

"You're early," I blurted out.

"Ignore him," Ryder said. "He was dropped on his head as a baby."

Emma laughed, but her eyes narrowed in on me. "Whatcha got?"

I must've had panic all over my face because Tucker quickly said, "Just a little something I got someone for Christmas. I needed opinions."

"I always have opinions," Emma said, then looked at us expectantly.

I couldn't do it; I couldn't lie to her. "Actually, it's something *I* got. For someone. Not for Christmas."

Tucker shrugged. He'd tried to save me. Unfortunately all he'd done was make Emma more curious.

"Why do I feel like I'm missing something?" she asked.

The sun had slid into the alley, casting a golden glow over the brick walls on either side of us. A gentle breeze carried the scent of burgers frying on our right and sweet flowers from the flower shop on our left. *It could be worse*, I decided.

"Emma…" Shit. I was ready for this, more than ready, but was she? "Em—"

"She knows her name, man," Tucker said.

I looked forward to killing him. Later. For now, my heart had begun to pound as I pulled the little black box from the pocket and…

Fumbled it.

Dropping to my knees, I grabbed the box.

"I've never seen him fumble anything in his entire life," Ryder said conversationally to Tucker.

I flipped him off, then looked up at Emma. "This isn't exactly as I planned."

Her eyes were wide, and it felt like there was a meat grinder in my gut.

"Are you…?" She swallowed. "Are you about to…?"

"I love you, Emma. More than anything. I love you in the mornings pre-caffeinated and not sure what year it is. I love watching you at work, all creative and badass. I love being with you in the evenings, swearing at your laptop." I drew a deep breath. "I didn't know I could feel this way, like my world is whole because you're in it. And I don't know what your schedule looks like for, say, the next fifty or sixty years, but if you're free, I'd love to grow old with you."

"That was good," Ryder whispered.

"Who knew he had it in him?" Tucker whispered back.

Emma's pupils were blown as she dropped to her knees in front of me, right there on the sidewalk, like maybe they were too weak to hold her upright. "You…you really want this? You want to marry *me*?"

"Desperately."

She smiled through suspiciously shiny eyes. "Me too."

I slid my fingers into that beautiful, silky-soft chestnut hair. "Just how desperate are we talking?"

She cupped my face. "Desperate enough to wish that we were completely alone so I could show you just how much."

I groaned and dropped my forehead to hers as my brothers finally took a hint and vanished.

"And you?" Emma asked softly. "Just how desperate are you to have me in your life until the end of time?"

I smiled. "Somewhere between *completely* and *utterly*."

READ ON FOR MORE
SWOONY ROMANCE FROM
JILL SHALVIS IN

He Falls First

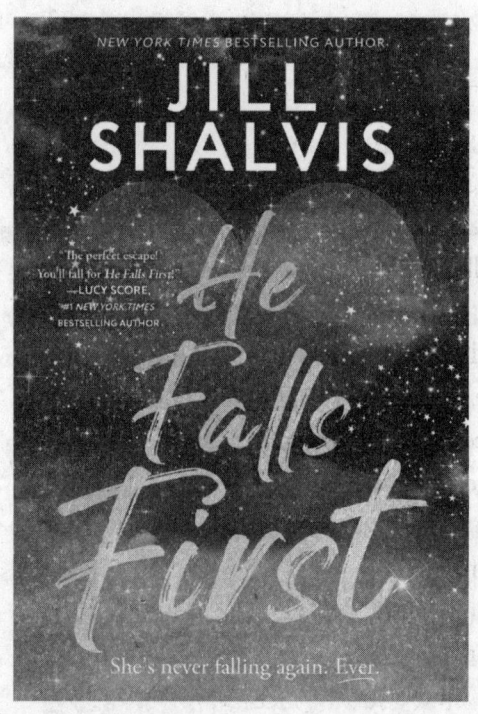

PROLOGUE

Ryder

F ASTER! *DON'T LOOK BACK!*" I yelled to Caleb and Tucker as we scrambled across the rocky bluffs and windswept cliffs high above the river, breath heaving, terror in our veins.

The Colburn siblings lived by one rule: If you poke the bear, run like hell. At twelve, I was the oldest and fastest, so I should've had a huge lead. After all, if we got caught, I'd be the one he'd go after first.

But since my baby sister Kiera had been the one to crash her bike into good old dad's precious truck, leaving both a dent and a chip in the paint, I had her by the hand, ruthlessly dragging her along with me to keep her safe.

The going was tough thanks to the uneven, choppy terrain that made up the rugged Sonoma, California, coastline. Dirt, sand, and jagged rocks shifted dangerously beneath our feet as we scrambled through wild grass that came up to our navels, and it didn't help that the night was pitch black thanks to a sky churning with an incoming late spring storm.

Hopefully it made us hard to see.

Except…nope. Over the distant roar of the crashing waves that met the end of the river, I heard pounding footsteps behind us.

"Captain Asshole's gaining ground!" my brother Caleb warned, right on my heels. "*Shit, how is the old man still so fast?*"

I knew exactly how. Hank Colburn, aka Captain Asshole, aka Dad, was military born and raised, and tough as nails to boot, not to mention mean as a snake. My heart pounded in my ears from dread and panic. To our left, the land stretched out to a sharp ledge that pointed over the sea. Straight ahead were the hidden caves we'd found years ago, where we stood a chance of losing him, since for all his physical agility, Hank suffered from claustrophobia as a part of his post-traumatic stress. We flat-out hauled ass toward those caves, the horizon rising and falling away, an illusion thanks to the hills all around us.

But then Kiera slipped, her hand yanked from mine as she hit her knees. "Ry!" she cried, and in that split second, I knew.

We weren't getting away.

But I also knew exactly how furious my dad was. He loved his truck, certainly more than us, more than *anything*. Twisting, I scooped up my now sobbing sister, tossed her to Caleb and Tucker, and then shoved all of them ahead of me…

Just as a heavy, sweaty hand snatched the back of my shirt with a grip of iron. I didn't fight. But, heart thundering in my chest, I also didn't turn to face Hank, not until I watched my brothers and sister slide past the massive moss-lined boulders designating the caves' entrance and vanish from sight.

CHAPTER 1

Penny

Present day

THE GROUND RATTLED THE bones of grandma's 1928 red brick Queen Anne Victorian house, and I jerked awake with a gasp. My bed was still rocking and rolling as I threw myself out of it and into the hallway, yelling a warning.

"*Earthquake!*"

Grandma Nell appeared at the bottom of the stairs in a candy apple-red silk nighty—wielding a hammer. "Sorry, sweetheart, it's just me. But good news, I got the old generator right where I want her."

At seventy-four, her confidence was impressive. She'd survived a lot in her lifetime. Two mild heart attacks and the same number of bad husbands. It was the curse all the Rose women bore; when it came to love, we *always* chose poorly, and I was no exception.

"Why are you working on the generator at..." I padded barefoot down the squeaky stairs past five-decades-old flowery wallpaper and squinted at the antique grandfather clock against the far living room wall. "Three forty-five in the morning?"

"Well, when you're old like me, you sleep like crap. I needed something to do." Grandma fondly patted the pink-and-white wainscoting closest to her. "Luckily, our old house is always happy to provide me with work."

No lie. The hard oak floors were scarred, the walls and dramatic high-vaulted ceilings and intricate crown moldings needed attention, the furniture was hopelessly outdated, but to me, this was home. The place meant everything to us—cranky pipes, rickety stairs, leaky roof, and all.

"You couldn't have picked something quieter to do? Like, I don't know, demo our hopelessly outdated kitchen?"

Grandma chortled. She liked my sarcasm. I'm pretty sure she was the only one who did.

"And didn't we talk about you not pushing yourself too hard?" I asked. "Not to mention, wearing actual clothes in the common area so we don't scar my little brother?"

"*You* talked." But Grandma grabbed her thick, terry cloth robe from the back of a chair. The robe was the same pink as the wainscoting and possibly as old. "And no need to worry about Wyatt. We both know a twelve-year-old boy will sleep until we drag him out of bed. And even then, he wouldn't take his gaze off that gaming console of his, earthquake or zombie apocalypse."

Fact. "You actually got the generator running?" I asked. The thing was nearly as old as Grandma, but since we couldn't afford a new one anytime soon, I had my fingers crossed on a light winter in Star Falls this year. Sonoma County was famous for its lush coastline and wineries, but in recent years we'd had extreme weather with wildfires and more rain than Noah's Ark had ever seen, which meant rolling blackouts. And it'd actually *snowed* two winters running.

"I sure did get the generator running," Grandma said proudly. "For ten whole seconds."

I drew a deep breath, then nearly leapt out of my skin when someone screeched out in a sing-song voice, "*Goooooooooood mornin'!*"

I flicked on a lamp and eyed Pika-boo, grandma's green and yellow parrot. The budgie blinked sleepily at me, the tuft of feathers on top of his head sticking straight up like he was coming off a three-day bender.

Spreading his wings to show off, he said, "I'm so pretty. Did you poop?"

That was the thing about budgies. They had an extensive vocabulary and were usually far too smart for their own good. But Grandma just cackled, amused by Pika-boo's propensity to repeat back whatever phrases he'd heard that would get him the biggest reaction.

"You're *very* pretty," I said to the preening bird, who was doing a little morning gig routine. "But maybe we could cut down on asking people if they've pooped."

"Hi," he said in an exact replica of my voice. "How are you?" He paused. "Did you poop?"

Smart-ass. Not that I dared say it out loud and teach him yet another new word. I yawned so wide, my jaw cracked. "It's too early for this. I've got a few minutes left before my alarm goes off. I'm going back to bed." I pointed at Pika-boo. "Be a good boy."

He bobbed his little head. "Be a good boy."

In the warm glow of the lamp, Grandma tenderly cupped my face with both of her weathered palms. "Sorry I woke you." One of her thumbs gently skimmed over the bandage at the curve of my jaw. Her eyes filled with sorrow and grief. Unable to face the reason for that, I shook my head and gently stepped back.

She simply gave me a warm, loving smile. "You need to drink more water, honey. You look pale. And eat more. I'm going to get dressed for work." She headed up the stairs in that red nightie and pink robe.

You had to admire a woman who didn't care what anyone thought. I'd always cared too much, which was probably why my life was currently circling the drain. I needed to be more like grandma—formidable and fearless.

I touched the bandage at my jaw. I'd been back home for six months now. Before that, I'd been sharing a rental house with a few roommates in Seattle and running my own ready-made meals business while navigating a bad relationship. (Was there any other kind?) Mitch had presented himself as one of the good ones, and I'd bought it hook, line, and sinker. I hadn't seen the red flags in time to get out unscathed by the sneaky emotional and mental abuse, but the important thing was that I had gotten out.

Leaving him had coincided with my half brother Wyatt calling me in a panic. Mom had taken a job as a lounge singer on a cruise line in the Bahamas, abandoning him and grandma.

So I'd come home, gotten a job at a local catering company. It hadn't been easy. I'd had to remind Mitch several times that we were never ever getting back together—a message he hadn't fully accepted until a week ago, when I'd made a quick trip back to Seattle for some more of my things.

The bandage under my fingers hid the reason Mitch now had a restraining order against him. It was temporary, but I couldn't see Mitch further risking his career for more trouble. Or so I told myself on the nights I couldn't sleep.

I climbed the stairs and crawled back into bed, whimpering at the soft, warm bedding, needing these last few moments of peace more than I needed anything in my life. I eyed last night's half-eaten bag of cheese puffs calling my name from my nightstand and remembered Grandma telling me to eat more. No problem. I popped a few in my mouth before lying back, sighing with bliss as the trans fats hit my system. *Ahhhh—*

Beep, beep, beep…

Damn. I slid out of bed—again—grabbed my water bottle, and headed down the hall to get a quick shower before work, taking a long swig from the bottle as I…

Bumped into a brick wall that didn't belong to the house.

I sucked in a breath and choked on the water as it went down the wrong pipe because…*not a brick wall.*

But a man.

A tall, built, shadowy man.

Still coughing up a lung from accidentally waterboarding myself, I went into a *hi-ya, I'll-kick-your-ass* stance. I didn't know karate from a waltz, but I knew it was all in the attitude—which I had in spades.

"*Easy,*" the shadow said in a low, husky voice as a disembodied hand patted me on my heaving back.

Eyes streaming, throat burning, I jerked back. "I'm going to 'easy' my foot right up your—"

The hall light flicked on. Blinking rapidly to adjust my vision, I caught sight of an imposingly built man who was… *not* a stranger. Nope, it was Ryder Colburn, a client of Hungry Bee, the catering service where I worked. All I knew about him was that he had brooding eyes, an athletic way of moving that drew my attention, and a gruff voice, though he always nodded politely at me on the rare times our paths crossed—which was a good thing since I'd given up men, especially the hot ones. Well, at least my brain and heart had. My body was still in dispute on the subject.

His eyes lit with an annoying smirk, and I realized I still held my karate chop pose. Awesome, because why humiliate myself once, when I could do it twice? Dropping my hands to my sides, I straightened, and a cheese puff fell out of my shirt.

We both stared at it. "Well, that's not embarrassing at all," I muttered.

Ryder snorted. I tried not to stare, but my eyes had a mind of their own. His wavy, sun-kissed brown hair was tousled, like he hadn't bothered to do more than run his fingers through it. The ends curled around his ears and the collar of his perfectly tailored suit that probably cost more than my car. He was sans tie today, with the top two buttons on his shirt undone, revealing an alluring hint of dark ink. He had some nerve looking so good this early in the morning.

He hadn't said anything since his soft but commanding "easy." As usual, his expression gave little away. I'd been delivering food to his building for six months now, and I still didn't know much about him other than he'd turned being enigmatic into an art form.

"What are you doing up here?" I asked.

"Dropping off Hank."

Right. Grandma was Hank's daytime caregiver, and Hank was Ryder's father. I had no idea why Ryder always used his dad's given name in a tone that suggested aggravation instead of calling him "Dad." Personally, I thought Hank was a sweetheart, and he kept Grandma busy. She loved taking care of people, so the job was a natural fit, and her paycheck went into an account for Wyatt's future education.

Assuming, of course, that we got the kid through middle and high school first. "It's early," I said. Usually the drop-off happened long after I was at work.

"Yes."

That was all he said. Apparently, he didn't like to waste words, which was frustrating for someone like me who had the opposite problem. But I knew he was quiet. Not shy, not even close. I'd seen him direct a large, rowdy crew with ease, speak to a conference room full of suits, and once I'd watched him wade into a vicious traffic fight in front of his building, breaking it up with only a few words.

"This might be hard for you to believe," I said, "but I'm going to need more than 'yes.'"

Ryder almost smiled, I could tell, but then his gaze caught on the bandage just under my jaw. Lifting my hand to cover it was utterly involuntary.

He met my eyes, quiet for a beat, during which I silently requested that he not ask. Finally, he said, "I have an early meeting in Petaluma. Nell said she didn't mind, but if Hank's any sort of problem, please let me know."

Wow. That added up to more words than he'd spoken to me in the whole time I'd known him. "So you *can* speak in full sentences."

The corner of his mouth twitched. Maybe amusement, maybe annoyance.

"And Hank's never a problem," I added.

Something came and went in his eyes. Doubt maybe? I had no idea. All he said was, "Let me know if that changes."

I nodded, then shivered from the water I'd spit down the front of myself. I wanted to hop into the shower, but the thought of doing so while Ryder was only two feet from the bathroom door made me feel uncomfortably vulnerable. This was a relatively new anxiety for me. I no longer seemed able to like someone, much less *trust* them, until I'd seen them lose their temper. And I was willing to bet no one ever saw gruff, imperturbable, stoic Ryder Colburn be anything except perfectly composed.

Which meant I could never like him.

Not that it mattered, since there was that whole gave-up-men thing...

His gaze slid down my body, and his almost smile reappeared, making me realize I'd somehow forgotten I stood there in my pj's, which consisted of my baggiest, oldest pair of sweatpants and a long-sleeve tee with Wonder Woman swinging her golden lasso over her head.

Correction: a very wet tee, now plastered to my skin. Great. "I'm feeling self-conscious."

"That's not what I'm feeling."

I met his hazel eyes, and it wasn't humor I caught, but a surprising heat, which both unnerved me and caused an answering thrum low in my belly.

Stupid belly.

I reminded it that I didn't want to feel *anything*, but apparently Ryder, who embodied an island-of-one stance with a side of fuck-that, could make a dead woman come back to life.

Along with my nipples.

It was ironic, really, because my choice in sleepwear should've been...well, a walking/talking advertisement for abstinence. Personally, I loved Wonder Woman, who was everything I only wished I could be—strong, fierce, brave. *Yes, hi, my name is Penny Rose, and I'm twenty-seven years old and want to be Wonder Woman when I grow up.*

A corner of Ryder's mouth twitched, so I did what I do—went on the defensive. "You have a problem with Wonder Woman?"

He gave a leisurely shake of his head. "Nope." Then he gestured with his chin toward my chest. "She goes with your attitude."

"I don't have an attitude."

"*I don't have an attitude!*" Pika-boo yelled, imitating me from the living room below. "Did you poop yet?"

Ryder's lips twitched.

I grimaced. "Last month, he ate something he wasn't supposed to and plugged himself up. So for a week or so we were constantly asking him if he pooped yet, and now he likes the reaction he gets when *he's* the one asking that question."

Another lip twitch and I tossed up my hands. "*What?*"

"Cute." His gaze slid to my shirt once more before murmuring, "And fighting doesn't make you a hero."

I blinked. "Did you just..." *Quote my absolute favorite Wonder Woman saying to my face?*

But he was already walking away, jogging down the stairs and out the front door, without another word.

ABOUT THE AUTHOR

New York Times and *USA Today* bestselling author Jill Shalvis writes contemporary romance and romantic comedies filled with madcap adventures and shenanigans and sexy times. She's sold twenty million-plus copies worldwide to date and lives with her family in a small mountain town near Lake Tahoe full of quirky characters. (Any resemblance to the quirky characters in her books is mostly coincidental.)

Website: jillshalvis.com
Facebook: JillShalvis
Instagram/TikTok: @jillshalvis